THE WORLD'S CLASSICS

The Oxford Sherlock Holmes

A STUDY IN SCARLET

SIR ARTHUR CONAN DOYLE was born in Edinburgh in 1859 to Irish Catholic parents. A Jesuit pupil at Stonyhurst, he graduated in medicine from Edinburgh (1881), and won his doctorate (1885). He practised medicine at Southsea in the 1880s as well as in a Greenland whaler, a West African trader and (after 20 years' retirement) a Boer War hospital. His literary career began in *Chambers's Edinburgh Journal* before he was 20, and he invented Sherlock Holmes when 26. After moving to London he transferred Holmes and Watson to short stories in the newly launched *Strand* magazine (1891) where he remained the lead author. A master of the short story, Conan Doyle's other great series revolved around Brigadier Gerard and Napoleon, while of his longer stories the same mix of comedy with adventure characterized his historical and scientific fiction, with unforgettable heroes such as the minute bellicose Sir Nigel, the Puritan crook Decimus Saxon, and the Shavian egomaniac Professor Challenger. His influence on the detective story was omnipresent, but his own literary stature as classic is only now receiving its scholarly due. He died in 1930.

OWEN DUDLEY EDWARDS is the editor of this volume and the General Editor of the Oxford Sherlock Holmes. Reader in History at the University of Edinburgh, he is the author of the *The Quest for Sherlock Holmes: A Biographical Study of Sir Arthur Conan Doyle*.

THE OXFORD SHERLOCK HOLMES

GENERAL EDITOR: OWEN DUDLEY EDWARDS

'Here it is at last, the definitive edition.'
Julian Symons, *Sunday Times*

'This outstanding edition of the five collections of stories and the four novels does Conan Doyle's great creation full justice . . . maintaining the right mixture of scholarly precision and infectious enthusiasm. These volumes, a delight to handle, are a bargain.'   Sean French, *Observer*

'The riches of the textual apparatus . . . will be a source of endless joy to veteran Sherlockians . . .'
John Bayley, *Times Literary Supplement*

'The hawk-faced maestro of Baker Street has been well served.'   Brian Fallon, *Irish Times*

'The definitive and most desirable edition of these milestones in crime fiction.'   F. E. Pardoe, *Brimingham Post*

'The Oxford is the edition to curl up with on a winter's night.'   John McAleer, *Chicago Tribune*

CONTENTS

A STUDY IN SCARLET

PART 1: *Being a reprint from the reminiscences of John H. Watson MD, late of the Army Medical Department*

PART 2: *The Country of the Saints*

CONTENTS

A STUDY IN SCARLET

Being a Reprint from the Reminiscences of John H. Watson, late of the Army Medical Department

THE WORLD'S CLASSICS

ARTHUR CONAN DOYLE

A Study in Scarlet

Edited with an Introduction by
OWEN DUDLEY EDWARDS

Oxford   New York
OXFORD UNIVERSITY PRESS
1994

Oxford University Press, Walton Street, Oxford OX2 6DP

Oxford New York
Athens Auckland Bangkok Bombay
Calcutta Cape Town Dar es Salaam Delhi
Florence Hong Kong Istanbul Karachi
Kuala Lumpur Madras Madrid Melbourne
Mexico City Nairobi Paris Singapore
Taipei Tokyo Toronto

and associated companies in
Berlin Ibadan

Oxford is a trade mark of Oxford University Press

General Editor's Preface, Introduction, Select Bibliography, Chronology,
and Notes © Owen Dudley Edwards 1993

First published in the Oxford Sherlock Holmes 1993
First published as a World's Classics paperback 1994

British Library Cataloguing in Publication Data
Data available

Library of Congress Cataloging in Publication Data
Doyle, Arthur Conan, Sir, 1859-1930.
A study in scarlet / Arthur Conan Doyle ; edited with an
introduction by Owen Dudley Edwards.
p. cm.—(The World's classics)
Includes bibliographical references (p.).
1. Holmes, Sherlock (Fictitious character)—Fiction. 2. Private
investigators—England—Fiction. I. Edwards, Owen Dudley.
PR4622.S76 1994 823'.8—dc20 94-5820
ISBN 0-19-282380-9

1 3 5 7 9 10 8 6 4 2

Printed in Great Britain by
BPC Paperbacks Ltd
Aylesbury, Bucks

ACKNOWLEDGEMENTS

A STUDY IN SCARLET, as the first volume, carries the acknowledgements for the series as a whole.

Our first and greatest thanks must go to Sir Arthur Conan Doyle, without whose inspiration our work would be valueless. Two great institutions lie at the heart of this enterprise: Oxford University Press, and the National Library of Scotland in Edinburgh, Conan Doyle's native city. The name of Michael Cox, our commissioning editor at OUP, should be on our title-pages and have equal shares in any honours; Angus Phillips has been a joy to work with; Enid Barker and her team have saved much that would otherwise have been amiss. At the NLS, the whole place has united to enable the fullest resources build this monument to Conan Doyle, from the personal enthusiasm and support of the Librarian, Ian McGowan, who follows so admirably in the work of his great predecessor Dennis Roberts, to every member of his staff, on almost all of whom we seem to have drawn. It in no way slights the help of so great a number to single out Margaret Deas, Superintendent of Reference Services, Roger Duce of Music, I. C. Cunningham, Stanley Simpson, Iain Gordon Brown and Julian Russell in Manuscripts; and also Ron Hoggan, T. A. F. Cherry, Pauline Thomson, Sally Harrower, Fiona Aitken, W. A. Kelly, Alison Harvey Wood, and—for services beyond all powers of acknowledgement—Dougie Mathieson.

Our deep thanks are also due to the University of Edinburgh and its Librarian Brenda Moon, her Deputy Peter Freshwater, D. P. Ferro of Readers Services and its staff, J. V. Howard of Manuscripts and its services (and his predecessor John Hall, now of the Cambridge University Library), and the staff of the Erskine Medical Library. In the University itself, the series owes its gratitude to Professors Emeritus K. J. Fielding, Rosalind Mitchison, Denys Hay, and above all George Shepperson. Tom Barron of the

International Office, Ray Footman in Information, Kenneth Fielden, Rosemary Gentleman, and Gloria Ketchin in the Department of History, and Pat Storey in Archaeology, have been towers of strength.

The series owes much to June Lancelyn Green, the late Roger Lancelyn Green, Barbara Roden, Sue Roden, Anne Robson, Hugh Robson, Bonnie, Leila, Sara, and Michael Dudley Edwards, Elizabeth Lee, the late Howard Stavers Lee, the Very Revd Anthony Ross OP, the New Spode Family Week, Elizabeth Wall, Mary Dudley Edwards, Ruth Dudley Edwards, the late Robin and Sheila Dudley Edwards, and Conan Rafferty.

Finally, the editors owe the most profound thanks to each other.

The nine volumes of The Oxford Sherlock Holmes have been lightly revised for inclusion in The World's Classics, very occasionally for the inclusion of information newly come to hand, usually for correction of typographical and other errors. Thanks are due to our more industrious reviewers and to several correspondents in drawing our attention to errors and omissions, among them Georgina Doyle, Michael Homer, Roger Johnson, David Cairns, Rev. Charles R. Heriot, Rev. Thomas Kearns OP, Peter E. Blau, J. S. F. Parker, Squadron Leader Philip Weller, Wayne B. Smith, and the National Horse Racing Museum, Newmarket, England. Roger Savage, Allan Boyd, and Sister Sara Rose Dudley Edwards OP played major parts in the improvement of the present edition, as did Susie Casement for the publishers. Richard Lancelyn Green and Christopher Roden went to great trouble to further the work of revision. To our deepest sorrow W. W. Robson, our colleague and fount of critical inspiration, never saw The Oxford Sherlock Holmes, whose advance copies were ready for their editors a week after he died on 31 July 1993. His profound insights as a scholar were matched by his humanity as a teacher and generosity as a friend.

O. D. E.

21 January 1994

GENERAL EDITOR'S PREFACE
TO THE SERIES

ARTHUR CONAN DOYLE told his *Strand* editor, Herbert Greenhough Smith (1855–1935), that 'A story always comes to me as an organic thing and I never can recast it without the Life going out of it.'[1]

On the whole, this certainly seems to describe Conan Doyle's method with the Sherlock Holmes stories, long and short. Such manuscript evidence as survives (approximately half the stories) generally bears this out: there is remarkably little revision. Sketches or scenarios are another matter. Conan Doyle was no more bound by these at the end of his literary life than at the beginning, whence scraps of paper survive to tell us of 221B Upper Baker Street where lived Ormond Sacker and J. Sherrinford Holmes. But very little such evidence is currently available for analysis.

Conan Doyle's relationship with his most famous creation was far from the silly label 'The Man Who Hated Sherlock Holmes': equally, there was no indulgence in it. Though the somewhat too liberal Puritan Micah Clarke was perhaps dearer to him than Holmes, Micah proved unable to sustain a sequel to the eponymous novel of 1889. By contrast, 'Sherlock' (as his creator irreverently alluded to him when not creating him) proved his capacity for renewal 59 times (which Conan Doyle called 'a striking example of the patience and loyalty of the British public'). He dropped Holmes in 1893, apparently into the Reichenbach Falls, as a matter of literary integrity: he did not intend to be written off as 'the Holmes man'. But public clamour turned Holmes into an economic asset that could not be ignored. Even so, Conan Doyle could not have continued to write about

[1] Undated letter, quoted by Cameron Hollyer, 'Author to Editor', *ACD— The Journal of the Arthur Conan Doyle Society*, 3 (1992), 19–20. Conan Doyle's remark was probably *à propos* 'The Red Circle' (*His Last Bow*).

Holmes without taking some pleasure in the activity, or indeed without becoming quietly proud of him.

Such Sherlock Holmes manuscripts as survive are frequently in private keeping, and very few have remained in Britain. In this series we have made the most of two recent facsimiles, of 'The Dying Detective' and 'The Lion's Mane'. In general, manuscript evidence shows Conan Doyle consistently underpunctuating, and to show the implications of this 'The Dying Detective' (*His Last Bow*) has been printed from the manuscript. 'The Lion's Mane', however, offers the one case known to us of drastic alterations in the surviving manuscript, from which it is clear from deletions that the story was entirely altered, and Holmes's role transformed, in the process of its creation.

Given Conan Doyle's general lack of close supervision of the Holmes texts, it is not always easy to determine his final wishes. In one case, it is clear that 'His Last Bow', as a deliberate contribution to war propaganda, underwent a ruthless revision at proof stage—although (as we note for the first time) this was carried out on the magazine text and lost when published in book form. But nothing comparable exists elsewhere.

In general, American texts of the stories are closer to the magazine texts than British book texts. Textual discrepancies, in many instances, may simply result from the conflicts of sub-editors. Undoubtedly, Conan Doyle did some re-reading, especially when returning to Holmes after an absence; but on the whole he showed little interest in the constitution of his texts. In his correspondence with editors he seldom alluded to proofs, discouraged ideas for revision, and raised few—if any—objections to editorial changes. For instance, we know that the *Strand*'s preference for 'Halloa' was not Conan Doyle's original usage, and in this case we have restored the original orthography. On the other hand, we also know that the *Strand* texts consistently eliminated anything (mostly expletives) of an apparently blasphemous character, but in the absence of manuscript confirmation we have normally been unable to restore what were probably stronger original versions. (In any case, it is perfectly possible that Conan Doyle, the consummate professional, may have come to exercise self-censorship in the certain knowledge that editorial changes would be imposed.)

Throughout the series we have corrected any obvious errors, though these are comparatively few: the instances are at all times noted. (For a medical man, Conan Doyle's handwriting was commendably legible, though his 'o' could look like an 'a'.) Regarding the order of individual stories, internal evidence makes it clear that 'A Case of Identity' (*Adventures*) was written before 'The Red-Headed League' and was intended to be so printed; but the 'League' was the stronger story and the *Strand*, in its own infancy, may have wanted the series of Holmes stories established as quickly as possible (at this point the future of both the Holmes series and the magazine was uncertain). Surviving letters show that the composition of 'The Solitary Cyclist' (*Return*) preceded that of 'The Dancing Men' (with the exception of the former's first paragraph, which was rewritten later); consequently, the order of these stories has been reversed. Similarly, the stories in *His Last Bow* and *The Case-Book of Sherlock Holmes* have been rearranged in their original order of publication, which—as far as is known—reflects the order of composition. The intention has been to allow readers to follow the fictional evolution of Sherlock Holmes over the forty years of his existence.

The one exception to this principle will be found in *His Last Bow*, where the final and eponymous story was actually written and published after *The Valley of Fear*, which takes its place in the Holmes canon directly after the magazine publication of the other stories in *His Last Bow*; but the removal of the title story to the beginning of the *Case-Book* would have been too radically pedantic and would have made *His Last Bow* ludicrously short. Readers will note that we have already reduced the extent of *His Last Bow* by returning 'The Cardboard Box' to its original location in the *Memoirs of Sherlock Holmes* (after 'Silver Blaze' and before 'The Yellow Face'). The removal of 'The Cardboard Box' from the original sequence led to the inclusion of its introductory passage in 'The Resident Patient': this, too, has been returned to its original position and the proper opening of 'The Resident Patient' restored. Generally, texts have been derived from first book publication collated with magazine texts and, where possible, manuscripts; in the case of 'The Cardboard Box' and 'The Resident Patient', however, we have employed the *Strand* texts, partly because of the restoration of the latter's opening, partly to give readers a flavour of the magazine in which the Holmes stories made their first, vital conquests.

In all textual decisions the overriding desire has been to meet the author's wishes, so far as these can be legitimately ascertained from documentary evidence or application of the rule of reason.

One final plea. If you come to these stories for the first time, proceed now to the texts themselves, putting the introductions and explanatory notes temporarily aside. Our introductions are not meant to introduce: Dr Watson will perform that duty, and no one could do it better. Then, when you have mastered the stories, and they have mastered you, come back to us.

OWEN DUDLEY EDWARDS

University of Edinburgh

INTRODUCTION

I

First begin
Taking in.
Cargo stored,
All aboard,
Think about
Giving out.
Empty ship,
Useless trip!

(Conan Doyle, 'Advice to a Young Author',
Songs of the Road, 1911)

A STUDY IN SCARLET was Arthur Conan Doyle's first published book, appearing in *Beeton's Christmas Annual* for 1887 and subsequently republished as a single volume by the annual's publishers, Ward, Lock & Co., in July 1888. But it had been completed over eighteen months earlier, a rejection from James Payn (1830–98), editor of the *Cornhill* magazine, being dated 7 May 1886 and admitting 'I have kept your story an unconscionably long time'.

So Sherlock Holmes and Dr Watson, two of the most famous fictional characters of all time, came into being while their creator was still twenty-five. With them came their Baker Street flat and its London milieu, based in reality on an enlargement of Conan Doyle's Edinburgh. For the young doctor of Southsea knew very little of London, where he did not settle until January 1891, in the year that the first Holmes short stories began appearing in the *Strand* magazine. Few who looked back from *The Adventures of Sherlock Holmes* to *A Study in Scarlet* would have noted the presence of Edinburgh, or of Birmingham, Plymouth, or Southsea—all to be found beneath the palimpsest of *A Study in Scarlet*'s London. Yet like his older fellow-emigrant from Edinburgh, Robert Louis Stevenson (1850–94), Conan

xiii

Doyle composed his metropolis from elements of places from which so many of its immigrants came. Holmes, Watson, even Lestrade, no less than Dr Jekyll, were in reality Edinburgh immigrants to London specifically because Conan Doyle had not yet completed his own migration to the capital. Familiarity might not have eventually bred contempt, but it might perhaps have deprived Conan Doyle's sense of London of its freshness and vitality. Initially, Sherlock Holmes knew his London because Arthur Conan Doyle did not.

But *A Study in Scarlet* also contained Conan Doyle's first published piece of historical fiction, in its background setting amongst the Mormons from 1847 to 1860. Here was more of a false start. The sensual Puritan cant of its villains reflects Conan Doyle's seventeenth-century researches, but *Micah Clarke: His Statement* (1889) has the perspective 'The Country of the Saints' lacks. More particularly, the one major portrait of a real person, the Mormon prophet Brigham Young, differs startlingly from almost all of Conan Doyle's later fictionalized historical portraits in its apparent indifference to considerations of fidelity. By contrast, his portrayals of Monmouth, Judge Jeffreys, Nelson, Napoleon, Bertrand du Guesclin, or Louis XIV were often historically faithful but frozen.

Conan Doyle's Brigham Young is akin to the sententious Bible-spouting stage Mormon of *The Danites in the Sierras* (1881) by Joaquin [Cincinnatus Hiner] Miller (1839–1913). Whether or not he knew Miller's novel, *First Families of the Sierras*, on which the play was based, Conan Doyle was aware of its conventions. We may imagine how eagerly the young Southsea doctor, already sharpening his pen for the picture of Judge Jeffreys in the final scenes of *Micah Clarke*, might have relished the language of the real Brigham Young: 'You manifest a choice to leave an incensed public in incense still . . . when the spirit of persecution manifests itself in the flippancy of rhetoric for female insult and desecration, it is time that I forbear to hold my peace, lest the thundering anathemas of nations born and unborn, should rest upon my head, when the marrow of my bones shall be illy prepared to sustained the threatened blow.' Yet the Brigham Young he produced, while owing more to the English Jesuits and Scots Calvinists of his own past, carried one quality of its historical original: his force. As a portrait of a Moses in irony, admonition, and wrath, it is terrific. For all its weaknesses, in its concentration and economy it was a worthy first sketch for the finest of all Conan Doyle's historical evocations—Napoleon in the Brigadier Gerard stories.

Brigham Young has no precursors in Conan Doyle's writing. But Holmes and Watson do. It is possible to discern them both in primitive form seven years before the completion of *A Study in Scarlet*. This may have played a part in Conan Doyle's consistent undervaluations of the two characters and of the stories in which they appeared. He thought of them secretly as having been born of childish things, and as work too easily created. Yet they had been born of powerful, if invisible, struggles, and their germination derived from eminently distinguished literary antecedents and real-life originals (such as his Stonyhurst companionship with James Paul Emile Ryan (1860–1920), whose devotion is reflected in Watson's relationship with Holmes).

It was at Stonyhurst, or perhaps Feldkirch, that Conan Doyle seems to have discovered Sir Walter Scott and Edgar Allan Poe, and probably also began his lifelong devotion to Boswell's *Life of Johnson*. Scott gave him Watson; Poe gave him Holmes; Boswell provided the outline of their relationship. There were many other influences, some of which may never be known; but Holmes and Watson immediately took on a life of their own and, as they progressed from story to story, exhibited qualities that went far beyond their original designs—and did so almost despite their author's conscious will. But as shown by his poem 'The Inner Room' (see the introduction to *The Memoirs of Sherlock Holmes* in the present series), Conan Doyle was aware of his own self-contradictions: what he might remark of Holmes and Watson in public could be far from what he intended as he privately fashioned and refashioned them over their sixty manifestations. Holmes begins in *A Study in Scarlet* by being presented as the 'calculating-machine'; he ends as the confessor of 'The Veiled Lodger' (*Case-Book*). The supposedly humourless Watson sardonically estimates the probabilities of his own and Holmes's arrest in *The Sign of the Four*, calculates the likelihood of a litigious crank suing an archaeologist for opening a neolithic barrow without consent of the next of kin in *The Hound of the Baskervilles*, and mischievously traps Holmes in a net of his own vanity in *The Valley of Fear*. There are inconsistencies from the start. No sooner is Holmes established as the calculating-machine than he is carolling like a lark in anticipation of Norman-Neruda's violin playing or speculating on a point of seventeenth-century bibliography.

Scott's great contribution to the making of Watson lies in that central focus which Georg Lukács identified as the great vantage point for Scott's historical observation: the marginal Edward Waverley, or Guy Mannering, or Frank Osbaldistone (in *Rob Roy*), or Henry Morton (in *Old Mortality*), who are all swept into critical and incomplete sympathy with the main protagonist. Each is confronted by a world that is new to him, but which is old and dying: in *Waverley* it is that of the Highland Jacobites; in *Old Mortality*, the authoritarian Royalist Claverhouse is confronted by the Covenanter zealots. *A Study in Scarlet* was written while Conan Doyle was systematizing his ideas about creating a historical novel (*Micah Clarke*) on the model of Scott, and it shows. Watson is variously repelled and attracted by Holmes's arrogance and professionalism (as Morton is by Claverhouse), or captivated by his undreamed-of skills (as Osbaldistone is by Di Vernon, or Edward Waverley by Flora and Fergus MacIvor). In the process Watson too becomes the secondary witness of a dying world: the pioneer West, symbolized by the stoical fortitude and guardianship of John Ferrier (a product of Conan Doyle's reading of Scott's disciple, James Fenimore Cooper); by the pious zeal and self-sacrifice of the Mormon migrants, polluted by the degraded servitude of Stangerson and the drunken lechery of Drebber; and by the romance between Jefferson Hope and Lucy Ferrier, reduced to a vengeful and demented quest. Scott, said Lukács, 'sees the endless field of ruin, wrecked existences, wrecked or wasted heroic, human endeavour, broken social formations, etc., which are the necessary preconditions of end-result'.[1] *A Study in Scarlet* is only the first of the fields of ruin Holmes is to plough and Watson to chronicle.

There was another aspect to Scott's influence. 'To the Scottish-born man', wrote Conan Doyle in *Through the Magic Door*, 'those novels which deal with Scottish life and character have a quality of raciness which gives them a place apart. There is a rich humour of the soil in such books as *Old Mortality*, *The Antiquary*, and *Rob Roy*, which puts them in a different class from the others. His old Scottish women are, next to his soldiers, the best series of types that he has drawn.' *A Study in Scarlet* has its old woman, too, who vanquishes Sherlock Holmes, and does so with such brio and humour that it draws laughter from him and so proves his humanity—the joke being that the 'old woman' is an actor in drag. Like Scott, Conan Doyle perceived how vital comedy is to the effective working-out of tragedy.

Poe provided inspiration of a different sort: as a master of the short story. Conan Doyle's consideration of Poe's genius in *Through the Magic Door* is worth quoting at some length.

Poe is the master of all . . . Poe is, to my mind, the supreme original short story writer of all time. His brain was like a seed-pod full of seeds which flew carelessly around, and from which have sprung nearly all our modern types of story . . . To him must be ascribed the monstrous progeny of writers on the detection of crime—'*quorum pars parva fui!*'[2] Each may find some little development of his own, but his main art must trace back to those admirable stories of Monsieur Dupin, so wonderful in their masterful force, their reticence, their quick dramatic point. After all, mental acuteness is the one quality which can be ascribed to the ideal detective, and when that has once been admirably done, succeeding writers must necessarily be content for all time to follow in the same main track. But not only is Poe the originator of the detective story; all treasure-hunting, cryptogram-solving

[1] George Lukács, *The Historical Novel* (1935–7; English translation, 1962), 52.
[2] 'of which I was a little part'; a parody of Aeneas on the Trojan war, 'of which I was a great [*magna*] part': Virgil, *Aeneid*, II. vi.

yarns trace back to his 'Gold Bug', just as all pseudo-scientific Verne-and-Wells stories have their prototypes in the 'Voyage to the Moon' [i.e. 'The Unparalleled Adventure of one Hans Pfaall'] and '[The Facts in] the Case of Monsieur Valdemar' . . . [As to] the 'Gold Bug' [or] the 'Murder[s] in the Rue Morgue', I do not see how either of those could be bettered. But I would not admit *perfect* excellence to any other of his stories. These two have a proportion and a perspective which are lacking in the others, the horror or weirdness of the idea intensified by the coolness of the narrator and of the principal actor . . . I am sure if I had to name the few books which have really influenced my own life I should have to put [Poe's tales] second only to Macaulay's Essays. I read it young when my mind was plastic. It stimulated my imagination and set before me a supreme example of dignity and force in the methods of telling a story (108–10, 114).

Conan Doyle went on to wonder where Poe got his style: 'There is a sombre majesty about his best work, as if it were carved from polished jet, which is peculiarly his own.' But this was the Poe that Conan Doyle regarded as being beyond him. The Poe who urged him forward offered voids to be filled: 'The mere suspicion of scientific thought or scientific methods has a great charm in any branch of literature, however far it may be removed from actual research. Poe's tales, for example, owe much to this effect, though in his case it was pure illusion' (233). Thus Sherlock Holmes arose out of Conan Doyle's attempts to put the methods of Dupin on a scientific footing.

Conan Doyle was well in advance of his time in his admiration for Poe, so far as the English-speaking world went. True, Stevenson had drawn on 'William Wilson' for both Dr Jekyll and Mr Hyde; Swinburne, the Rossettis, and William Allingham took poetic inspiration from him; and Professor John Nichol (1833–94), of the University of Glasgow, asserted that Poe, 'standing on the border-land between romance and reality, seems to prove himself the potential prince of all detectives'.[3] But such enthusiasm was still rare in Britain.

---

[3] *American Literature 1620–1880* (1882), 163.

With Boswell's *Johnson*, Conan Doyle was on popular ground; but his perspective was unusual, and we may get a sense of what Holmes owes to Watson from *The Magic Door*:

That book interests me—fascinates me—and yet I wish I could join heartily in that chorus of praise which the kind-hearted old bully has enjoyed . . . If Boswell had not lived I wonder how much we should hear now of his huge friend? With Scotch persistance he has succeeded in inoculating the whole world with his hero worship. It was most natural that he should himself admire him. The relations between the two men were delightful and reflect all credit upon each. But they are not a safe basis from which any third person could argue . . . [W]here he excels as a biographer is in telling you just those little things that you want to know. How often you read the life of a man and are left without the remotest idea of his personality. It is not so here. The man lives again . . . (47–50).

This is the clearest light Conan Doyle ever threw on why Holmes can be truly said to live, whereas Dupin is merely *device du Poe*. As Holmes justly says in the first short story ('A Scandal in Bohemia', *Adventures*), he is 'lost without my Boswell'. The man lives again—so much so that there are many people who cannot reconcile themselves to the fact that he never lived at all.

But Conan Doyle's first known attempt to create a Holmes–Watson pairing embodied other factors besides his love of Scott, Poe, and Boswell. MS 4791 in the National Library of Scotland arrived there with the Blackwood MSS—unknown to the publishing house in whose custody it had remained for close on a century. Entitled 'The Haunted Grange of Goresthorpe', it bears no date nor (to judge by the many that survive) any covering letter from its author, whose signature is on every page. We may deduce that in his youthful eagerness Conan Doyle took the MS to the publishers in person and that any note Blackwood's staff may have taken of its origin has been lost. It can be confidently dated before his first published work, 'The Mystery of Sasassa Valley', published in another Edinburgh magazine, *Chambers's Journal* (6 September 1879).

'Goresthorpe' means 'village of blood', a thought that Conan Doyle kept in mind when writing his satire on ghost fiction, 'Selecting a Ghost', a few years later (*Uncollected Stories*). But no jokes are intended here. The young writer has a horror to unfold. There is no foretaste of the rhythms of nomenclature which so characterized almost every person in the Holmes saga from the bestial Drebber, the formidable Stangerson and the dedicated Jefferson Hope, to the latter-day Buck Sir Robert Norberton of Shoscombe Old Place (*Case-Book*). The ghost is Godfrey Marsden, whose appearance so terrorizes Job Garston and is duly investigated by Tom Hulton and his friend, the narrator Jack. Jack has an estate, although he troubles us little with squirearchical impedimenta; he has also been a doctor. Tom is a dedicated ghost-hunter in pursuit of the 'idea of a creditable ghost'; Jack is sceptical and his house-guest remonstrates:

Tom, when he argued was wont to produce a certain large briar root pipe of his, and by this time he was surrounded by a dense wreath of smoke, from the midst of which his voice issued like the Oracle of Delphi, while his stalwart figure loomed through the haze.

'... Of course, Jack, I know that you are one of these "*credo-quod-tango*" medicals, who walk in the narrow path of certain fact, and quite right too in such a profession as yours ... It's not such an easy matter, you see, to explain it to another, even though I can define it in my own mind well enough ...'

'It's very easy to laugh at the matter', answered Tom, 'but there are few facts in this world which have not been laughed at, sometime or another.'

Tom resolves to spend a night in the local haunted house:

'For heaven's sake, don't think of doing such a foolhardy thing', I exclaimed 'why only one man has slept at Goresthorpe Grange during a hundred years, and he went mad to my certain knowledge'.

'Ha! That sounds promising, very promising' cried Tom in high delight. 'Now just observe the thickheadedness of the British public, yourself included, Jack ...

'... Now suppose there was said to be white crows or some other natural curiosity in Yorkshire, and someone assured you that there is not, because he had been all through Wales without seeing one, you would naturally consider the man an idiot . . .'

. . . it certainly looked more comfortable than I had ever dared to expect.

Tom seemed unutterably disgusted and discontented by the result: 'Call this a haunted house' he said 'why we might as well sit up in a hotel and expect to see a ghost! This isn't by any means the sort of thing I have been looking forward to.'

Eventually they find their ghost, that of a murderer fleeing in terror from the ghost of the wife he murdered (an idea ultimately used by Conan Doyle forty years later with respect to the ghost of a brutal pugilist who, after almost laying out a living opponent, flees from the ghost of a little dog he had murdered horribly in his lifetime ('The Bully of Brocas Court', in *Tales of the Ring and the Camp*)). Tom's lines of argument, his dependence on smoke-laden surroundings, his greater confidence in assertion than explanation, his enthusiasm for the quest, his anger at the apparent destruction of suggestive atmosphere, all prefigure Holmes at various characteristic moments. Even his 'Ha!' is early Holmes (it was apparently a trick of the Doyle family's lodger-benefactor, Bryan Charles Waller; Waller, as an estate-owning doctor, is also a link with Jack). The most suggestive point is that Tom uses rational argument to assert the existence of ghosts and insists on their visiting a haunted house, at which prospect Jack, who does not believe in ghosts, is terrified. Tom is a Don Quixote figure; Jack is a Sancho Panza who has a little of the final laugh when Tom flees as rapidly as himself from the object of his quest. But when Holmes and Watson really appear in *A Study in Scarlet*, Watson is the romantic, Holmes the realist; Watson the spiritual and Holmes the scientific figure; Watson is heart and Holmes is head. Tom survives in Holmes's unrealistic drug addiction, Jack in Watson's hostility and ultimate victory against it. Singularly enough, the drug *motif* is proposed only to be dismissed in *A Study in Scarlet*, although it opens *The Sign of the Four*; similarly, Holmes's subsequent eagerness for the chase, joyfully and heartlessly proclaimed as some wretched client unveils his or her tragedy, contrasts with the indifference with which he enters on his *Study in Scarlet*. The Tom-and-Jack roots of Holmes-and-Watson were lasting, but unobtrusive. On the other hand, Goresthorpe Grange lent a few ugly details to Number 3, Lauriston Gardens, Brixton.

Holmes had no other predecessor in Conan Doyle's fiction after Tom other than the guru Ram Singh in *The Mystery of Cloomber* (1888, but drafted in 1883: see my article 'The Mystery of *The Mystery of Cloomber*', *ACD*, 2/2 (Autumn 1991), 101–33). Ram brings a foretaste of scientific wit to his prophesies that prove as disconcerting as Holmes's personal deductions. The medical student Hugh Lawrence of Baker Street, with his friend John H. Thurston ('Uncle Jeremy's Household', *Uncollected Stories*), is but the innocent narrator, simply chancing on the events, and Thurston a friend whose inheritance is endangered. The story—completed but not yet accepted for publication when Conan Doyle was writing *A Study in Scarlet*—supplied the latter with a local habitation (Baker Street) and its narrator with a first name (John); but if anything its weaknesses caused its most instructive effect, for it reminded its author that the narrator should not be the main protagonist. The line of development from 'The Haunted Grange of Goresthorpe' was one of solid, careful exercise in the art of first-person narration. Conan Doyle experimented with a variety of narrator types, from poltroon ('That Little Square Box'), marriageable girl ('Our Derby Sweepstakes'), and gullible *nouveau riche* ('Selecting a Ghost') to an English fortune-hunter in Ireland ('The Heiress of Glenmahowley'), misanthrope ('The Man from Archangel'), and, importantly, a doctor (in his greatest achievements to date, 'J. Habakuk Jephson's Statement' and 'The Captain of the "Pole-Star" ', as well as in the minor stories 'My Friend the Murderer' and 'Crabbe's Practice'). He had also used the technique of narrative within narrative in 'The Cabman's Story'. By early 1886 Conan Doyle had refined his idea of the perfect narrator, the instrument of Sherlock Holmes's immortality: John H. Watson.

II

Never strain
Weary brain.
Hardly fit,
Wait a bit!
After rest
Comes the best.
Sitting still,
Let it fill;
Never press;
Nerve stress
Always shows.
Nature knows.

('Advice to a Young Author')

A Study in Scarlet is a pantomime title for a pantomime book. Sherlock Holmes might have lived and died in the one novel, had not its author enjoyed himself so much. The enjoyment shows in the send-up of the London press; in making Holmes a blatant imitation of various Edinburgh medical characters; in having Holmes dismiss the fictional detectives he so obviously caricatures and profess ignorance of Carlyle whilst quoting him and being himself constructed according to Carlyle's heroic prescription; in delivering Watson perfectly tricked out with the biographical details (only slightly adjusted) of a very real namesake; and in calling the book by a punning translation of the first novel by the most popular of contemporary detective novelists, *L'Affaire Lerouge* (1866) by Émile Gaboriau (1832–73).

Other French influences are strong, but they greatly antedate Gaboriau. Like in a tragedy by Racine, the protagonists make their appearance in Part 2 already doomed, and like a Molière comedy there is a ruthless movement from slapstick to high satire against religious hypocrisy. There is the wonderful magician—Holmes: scientific, logical, and self-sustaining. But the whole effect is theatrical. He practically calls the reader on stage to be deduced in person (the Marine Sergeant's entrance is the same effect); and the stage magician must have his assistant, his *confidant*, his straight man. Thus the pantomime or music-hall principle of duet is established: Holmes and Watson, but also Lestrade and Gregson, their joke rivals, and the two villains Drebber and Stangerson, drunk and sober, rich and poor, foolish and cunning. And in a glorious cameo, enter the pantomime dame in a flurry of bobs and bows: 'she' hoodwinks the magician and, at the end, receives applause from the magician himself. And we have a hero, Jefferson Hope, at first invisible, known only by his footprints and long nails and by a word in blood on a wall, then disguised as a drunk, and finally at bay, his disguise plucked off. A stage battle ensues: our hero seems certain to escape, but then when he is caught comes general reconciliation (in true pantomimic fashion), even with death: 'On the very night after his capture the aneurism burst, and he was found in the morning stretched upon the floor of the cell, with a placid smile upon his face, as though he had been able in his dying moments to look back upon a useful life, and on work well done.'

With a change of scene and a second curtain rise the heroine, Lucy, is disclosed, seen first as a little girl with her guardian against the backdrop of a pitiless desert. To Lucy's protector, John Ferrier, enters the terrible ogre, a Bluebeard seeking a wife, not to add to his own harem, but for those who would be like him: ' "We Elders have many heifers, but our children must also be provided." ' The machinations of the young Bluebeards, Drebber and Stangerson, are temporarily foiled by the return of the hero; but then, in an evil moment, they triumph: old John Ferrier is killed, Lucy is abducted, raped, and eventually dies.

In *A Study in Scarlet*, tragedy is plucked from the heart of comedy, like in the medieval miracle plays on which Holmes discourses in *The Sign of the Four*. The use of lengthy explanatory flashback to elucidate the tragedy is often assumed to have been the result of Conan Doyle's uncritical reading of Gaboriau, who made extensive use of the same device; but this does justice to neither writer. In many respects, detection plays surprisingly little part in Gaboriau's novels: it simply happens at a brilliant and intense level when it does. Gaboriau's main thrust is against the exploitative privileges of the French aristocracy and clergy. Police procedure is worked out intricately and ably, but the presentation of the detectives Lecoq and Tabaret is wildly inconsistent across the novels—Lecoq especially. Both he and Tabaret were devices to Gaboriau's purpose, as was Dupin to Poe's. Holmes and Watson might occasionally be put to social purposes, but they were—essentially and overwhelmingly—conceived for their own sake.

Conan Doyle also differed from Gaboriau in the economy of his narrative (in this his mentor was Maupassant). Events are telescoped and inferred rather than laboriously described. The contrast is between the professional writer wearing himself out producing wordage by the page, and the doctor writing in his spare time—writing, too, in the manner of his caricaturist grandfather in clear vignettes, each one graphically pushing the story on and unadorned by needless exposition. Holmes requires the provision of every relevant detail, but Conan Doyle is very careful to ensure that we get nothing beyond the purpose.

A possible childhood source for the pantomimic elements in *A Study in Scarlet* is *The Rose and the Ring* (1855) by W. M. Thackeray (1811–63), a Doyle family friend, who subtitled the book a 'Fireside Pantomime for Great and Small Children'. Fairy Blackstick supplies fresh identities from a bag, like Holmes flourishing new identities from his clues; and the murderer produced out of a cabman seems an appropriate heir to the husband discovered in a door-knocker, whilst the ring that changes hands and meaning echoes Thackeray's ring, which transforms its wearer. But neither Thackeray nor Conan Doyle wrote their pantomimes for the public stage: they simply made their private stage, its drapes, extras, and scenery, rise before their readers.

For the American scenery in Part 2 of *A Study in Scarlet*, inspiration came to Conan Doyle from another very early source. 'My tastes were boylike enough', he remarked of himself at the age of nine in *Memories and Adventures*, 'for [Captain Thomas] Mayne Reid was my favourite author, and his *Scalp Hunters* my favourite book.'⁴ Reid (1818–83) may have commended himself to Conan Doyle's parents by his Irish birth and to his youthful reader by his American experiences (which included an admiring friendship with Poe). He knew the American South-West well and distinguished its contrasting landscapes in the first chapter of *The Scalp Hunters* (1852): one concludes that the excessive size of the desert in the first chapter of *A Study in Scarlet*, while warranted by common myth, was known by Conan Doyle to be an exaggeration. Its awesome extent, as well as its proximity to the Mormon trail, were evidently within Conan Doyle's Law of the Line:

Was it not [Oliver] Wendell Holmes who described the prosaic man, who enters a drawing-room with a couple of facts, like ill-conditioned bull-dogs at his heels, ready to let them loose on any play of fancy? The great writer can never go wrong. If Shakespeare gives a sea-coast to Bohemia, or if Victor Hugo calls an English prize-fighter Mr Jim-John-Jack—well, it *was* so, and that's an end of it. 'There is no second line of rails at that point' said an editor to a minor author [almost certainly himself]. 'I make a second line', said the author; and he was within his rights, if he can carry his readers' conviction with him (*Through the Magic Door*, 26–7).

But the form of the desert's introduction is Mayne Reid's: 'Approach, and examine them!' comes from *The Scalp Hunters*' second paragraph: 'You are looking upon a land whose features are unfurrowed by human hands, still bearing the marks of the Almighty mould, as upon the morning of creation'. The boy had pictured the landscapes at Mayne Reid's call: the man prepared his scenery on the same principle.

Mayne Reid also supplied Conan Doyle with other apparatus, from the mustang which brought Lucy under the arm of Hope, to the vengeance-dream as vocation with

⁴ Coincidentally, a long appreciation of 'Captain Mayne Reid: Soldier and Novelist', by Maltus Questell Holyoake, appeared in the same issue of the *Strand Magazine* as the first Holmes short story, 'A Scandal in Bohemia'.

which he fulfilled his love of her. But dreams of vengeance were literary staples, whether conveyed by the Comte de Monte Christo of Alexandre Dumas *père* (1802–70) or his disciple Gaboriau, whose romances were devoured by Conan Doyle in the mid-1880s. Another pupil of Dumas, Robert Louis Stevenson, augmented the pantomime spirit with his *New Arabian Nights* (1882) and its sequel (1885): but where Prince Florizel of Bohemia might be sufficiently mythical to close his 'Suicide Club' vengeance quest with a duel, science countered romance in Conan Doyle so closely that Vengeance in *A Study in Scarlet* must fight its duel with pills as weapons. For this pantomime is played with a cast drawn from a houseful of doctors and deliberately introduces Holmes as a solitary student of medicine. Stevenson and his wife Fanny Vandegrift Stevenson (1840–1914) created a new inversion of the incredible in *More New Arabian Nights: the Dynamiter*, in which Mormon vigilance causes fugitives to retreat on seeing 'on the face of the rock, drawn very rudely with charred wood, the great Open Eye which is the emblem of the Mormon faith'. Conan Doyle gave the vigilance a more terrifying, because human and secret, form. The contrast in the stories was that the Stevensons were using pantomime to invite, not to suspend, disbelief, whereas Conan Doyle sought to capture his readers by commanding their grief at the fate of the Ferriers.

The composition of *A Study in Scarlet* is directly known to us only from two fragments, both presumably dating from after November 1885, when he sent his long novel *The Firm of Girdlestone* on its travels to unsympathetic editors and publishers. An entry in Southsea notebook no. 1 '1885', reproduced in John Dickson Carr's *Life*, shows a title 'A Tangled Skein' (inspired by the opening of Lewis Carroll's *Through the Looking-Glass*?), deleted (possibly on later re-reading) in favour of 'A Study in scarlet'. The note reads: 'The terrified woman rushing up to the cabman. The two going in search of a policeman. John Reeves had been 7 years in the force, John Reeves went back with them.' Any deductions here must be extremely speculative. The woman may have been a cab-fare who found a dead body in the cab, such as is discovered by a cabbie and a flunkey in Conan Doyle's 'The Cabman's Story—The Mysteries of a London "Growler" ' (*Cassell's Saturday Journal*, 17 May 1884). (The Jefferson Hope cab is evidently a 'growler' also.) John Reeves became John Rance. But is the cabman the murderer? And is the policeman the detective? (The latter, on the basis of this note, seems more likely than the former.)

One source to whom Conan Doyle owed more than he ever expressed was William Wilkie Collins (1824–89), whose *The Moonstone* (1868) had profoundly influenced Conan Doyle's first (but, in 1886, still unpublished) novel *The Mystery of Cloomber* and 'The Rajah's Diamond' in Stevenson's *New Arabian Nights*. Sergeant Richard Cuff would prefigure Holmes in his deductions, in his industry, in his use of juvenile assistance, and in his gnomic announcements. If Reeves really was the first doodle for a detective, he suffered a cruel decline into John Rance, a portrait reflecting the naturalism of George Ohnet (1848–1918), whom Conan Doyle was reading at the time. Conan Doyle's recollection of starting work on the book is not wholly incompatible with a police-detective as protagonist, although he was quickly transposed into private consulting detective:

Gaboriau had rather attracted me by the neat dove-tailing of his plots, and Poe's masterful detective, M. Dupin, had from boyhood been one of my heroes. But could I bring an addition of my own? I thought of my old teacher Joe Bell, of his eagle face, of his curious ways, of his eerie trick of spotting details. If he were a detective he would surely reduce this fascinating but unorganized business to something nearer an exact science. I would try if I could get this effect. It was surely possible in real life, so why should I not make it possible in fiction? It is all very well to say that a man is clever, but the reader wants to see examples of it—such examples as Bell gave us every day in the wards. The idea amused me. What should I call the fellow? I still possess the leaf of a notebook with various alternative names. One rebelled against the elementary art which gives some inkling of character in the name, and creates a Mr Sharps or Mr Ferrets. First it was Sherringford Holmes; then it was Sherlock Holmes. He could not tell his own exploits, so he must have a commonplace comrade as a foil—an educated man of action who could both join his exploits and narrate them. A drab, quiet name for this unostentatious man. Watson would do. And so I had my puppets and wrote my *Study in Scarlet* (*Memories and Adventures*, 90).

Conan Doyle's first thoughts can be seen in a draft from the closed family papers reproduced by Pierre Nordon:[5]

A Study in Scarlet

Ormond Sacker— ~~from Soudan~~ from Afghanistan
      Lived at 221 B Upper Baker Street
  with
      J Sherrinford Holmes—
          The Laws of Evidence
      Reserved—
  Sleepy eyed young man—philosopher—Collector of rare Violins.
An Amati—   Chemical laboratory
          I have four hundred a year—
  I am a Consulting detective—

What rot this is' I cried—throwing the volume
: petulantly aside 'I must say that I have no
patience with people who build up fine theories in their
own armchairs which can never be reduced to
practice—
               Lecoq was a bungler—
  Dupin was better. Dupin was decidedly smart—
His trick of following a train of thought was more
   sensational than clever   but still he had analytical genius.

Conan Doyle visited his mother's Catholic Foley relatives in Ireland in 1881 and 1885. They had land at Lismore, Co. Waterford, on the east Blackwater River, a few miles north of its mouth at Youghal, Co. Cork. Inspector Youghal ('The Mazarin Stone', *Case-Book*), the Earl of Blackwater ('The Priory School', *Return*), Lord Backwater ('The Noble Bachelor', *Adventures*, and 'Silver Blaze', *Memoirs*) are derivatives. The

---

[5] Pierre Nordon, *Conan Doyle* (1966), facing p. 212.

name Foley, or Ó Foghladha, derives from *foghlaidhe*, a plunderer, and Ormond, *ur-Mhumhan* (east Munster), is Foley country: hence 'Ormond Sacker' simply means Foley. Conan Doyle would use Foley, uncoded, as an officer's name in 'The Green Flag' (1893), his story (in the eponymous collection) about the mutiny of Irish agrarian rebels in the British Army quartered in the Sudan (cf. Conan Doyle's first thought for Ormond Sacker's service career). It was a very striking personal identification: whatever he would allege subsequently, Watson lay profoundly at the heart of his own identity. Doyle country was to the east, in Wexford, whose River Slaney supplied the Chicago gangster in love with Mrs Elsie Cubitt in 'The Dancing Men' (*Return*). Between the two lay the River Suir, whose town Carrick-on-Suir means the rock in the Suir: an alternative method of crossing would be a ford, hence presumably Sherrinford (a name otherwise inexplicable). Holmes is a local name, anglicized from Mac Thomáis ('Th' is pronounced 'H' in Irish): Killmacthomas (i.e. 'Holmeschurch') was a town in the next barony to the Foleys. Sherlock, when Conan Doyle got round to it, was also another Waterford name, this time recusant Catholic of English origin, unlike the Gaelic Holmes. Patrick Sherlock had been a fellow-pupil of Conan Doyle's at Stonyhurst. The Jesuits, as was their custom, would no doubt have re-called that his namesake, the Revd Paul Sherlock, SJ (1595–1646), had been driven from Waterford to Rome, where he became Superior of the Irish College. Thomas Sherlock brought out a popular life of the Home Rule leader Charles Stewart Parnell (1846–91) in 1882, and Conan Doyle probably saw it on railway bookstalls in 1885 (when, on the eve of his conversion to Unionism, Parnell was greatly exercising his mind).

The name Holmes projected other Holmeses, of whom at least one, Oliver Wendell, played a critical part in Sherlock's composition, most notably in self-definition. In *The Sign of the Four* Sherlock Holmes turns in his own review of *A Study in Scarlet*, a piece of internal deconstructionism well in advance of our own century:

He shook his head sadly.

'I glanced over it', said he. 'Honestly, I cannot congratulate you on it. Detection is, or ought to be, an exact science, and should be treated in the same cold and unemotional manner. You have attempted to tinge it with romanticism, which produces much the same effect as if you worked a love story or an elopement into the fifth proposition of Euclid.'

'But the romance was there', I remonstrated. 'I could not tamper with the facts.'

'Some facts should be suppressed, or, at least, a just sense of proportion should be observed in treating them. The only point in the case which deserved mention was the curious analytical reasoning from effects to causes, by which I succeeded in unravelling it.'

'Holmes is as inhuman as a Babbage's Calculating Machine', Conan Doyle wrote to Joseph Bell on 16 June 1892.[6] In so writing, he was thinking of his beloved Oliver Wendell Holmes in *The Autocrat of the Breakfast-Table* (section I):

Given certain factors, and a sound brain should always evolve the same fixed product with the certainty of Babbage's calculating machine.

—What a satire, by the way, is that machine on the mere mathematician! A Frankenstein-monster, a thing without brains and without heart, too stupid to make a blunder; that turns out results like a corn-sheller, and never grows any wiser or better, though it grind a thousand bushels of them!

Conan Doyle would sometimes see Sherlock Holmes as his own inescapable Frankenstein-monster; but it was the use of Oliver Wendell Holmes among other influences which kept his namesake human. As Conan Doyle put it, 'Wendell Holmes is for ever touching some note which awakens an answering vibration within my own mind' (*Through the Magic Door*, 236). Thus it was Oliver Wendell Holmes who said 'Insanity is often the logic of an accurate mind overtasked', but is very much Sherlock Holmes in his best manner, with rhythms familiar from other contexts.

Oliver Wendell Holmes studied anatomy at Edinburgh almost half a century before Conan Doyle, but it was much

---

[6] Quoted in Ely Liebow, *Dr Joe Bell: Model for Sherlock Holmes* (1982), 173.

more the home-grown variety of Edinburgh medic who actually started *A Study in Scarlet* moving. Bell was only one of a number of figures who went into the making of Sherlock Holmes, before his own chemistry took over. But it was useful for Conan Doyle to keep attention focused on Bell when models began to be sought in the early 1890s.

It was the idea of Bell's deductive capability that Conan Doyle had in mind for his creature's most distinguishing trait. That would naturally have lead to a re-reading of Bell's few writings, notably his *Manual of the Operations of Surgery*, then (1883) in its fifth edition. There he would have found mention of Timothy Holmes (1825–1907), the hard-bitten editor of the four-volume *A System of Surgery*. 'Excision of the hip-joint (Mr Holmes)' was promptly followed by 'Excision of the knee-joint (Dr Watson)' (pp. 132–35). Timothy Holmes, a Cambridge and London surgeon, was probably personally unknown to Conan Doyle; but he would have known Dr (afterwards Sir) Patrick Heron Watson (1832–1907), surgeon at the Royal Infirmary at Edinburgh in his time and held in near-universal affection (in contrast to the austere Bell). Moreover, the story of his life undoubtedly suggested the fictional biography of John H. Watson, MD.

In the year 1853 Patrick Watson took his degree of Doctor of Medicine at the University of Edinburgh, and proceeded to Woolwich to go through the course prescribed for surgeons in the army. Having completed his studies there, he was duly attached to the Royal Artillery as Assistant Surgeon. The regiment was stationed in the Crimea at the time, and before he could join it the Crimean war had broken out. On landing at Balaclava, he learned that his corps was deep in the enemy's country. He followed, however, with many other officers who were in the same situation as himself, succeeded in finding his regiment, and at once entered upon his new duties.

The campaign brought honours and promotion to many, but to him it had nothing but misfortune and disaster (and the Crimean, Turkish, and Sardinian medals). He was struck down by enteric fever, that curse of the Crimean hospitals.

For months his life was despaired of, and when at last he came to himself and became convalescent, he was so weak and emaciated that a medical board determined that not a day should be lost in sending him back to Scotland. He was despatched, accordingly, in a troopship; or, to abandon the beginning of *A Study in Scarlet* for Watson's obituary in the *British Medical Journal* (4 January 1908), 'At the time it seemed as if he were returning home only to die, but his vigorous constitution finally triumphed.' It triumphed so well, indeed, that five years later, in 1861, he published his monograph on *The Modern Pathology and Treatment of Venereal Disease*, a work of outstanding significance for Conan Doyle's doctoral research in 1885. For the rest, his refusal to specialize cost him a university professorship but he was worshipped by his patients—his obituaries enthusiastically quoted the aphorism by a professional colleague from his prime: 'Nobody in Scotland is willing to die till they have seen Watson.'

So *A Study in Scarlet* was begun, not by the pen of Dr J. H. Watson, but by the life of Dr P. H. Watson. Allusions in the Southsea Notebook no. 1 to the First Afghan War (already being used by Conan Doyle for his as yet unpublished first novel *The Mystery of Cloomber*) show that Conan Doyle had been thinking of the ride of the half-dead Dr William Bryden (1811–73), sole survivor of the retreat from Kabul in 1842: hence J. H. Watson's escape from Maiwand. Having appropriated Watson's name, war fever, and invalid status, Conan Doyle wrote on enthusiastically and worried himself not a jot about the rashness of modelling so close to reality. In any case, P. H. Watson was far too good natured and sensible to make a protest. The existing scenario moved the Watson campaign from the Crimea to the Second Afghan War (ironically new to Conan Doyle, who had been on the Greenland whaler *Hope* when the newspapers reported its progress).

The great partnership was in its author's sights: he had, as the *British Medical Journal* would put it in his obituary (12 July 1930), 'hit on the idea of an amateur detective who should apply the methods of Joseph Bell to the unravelling of mysteries, with a sort of medical Boswell as foil and showman'. Or, to give the considered judgement of Agatha Christie (1890–1976) through the mouth of Hercule Poirot in *The Clocks* (1963):

'*The Adventures of Sherlock Holmes*', he murmured lovingly, and even uttered reverently the one word '*Maître*!'

'Sherlock Holmes?' I asked.

'Ah, *non, non*, not Sherlock Holmes! It is the author, Sir Arthur Conan Doyle, that I salute. These tales of Sherlock Holmes are in reality far-fetched, full of fallacies and most artificially contrived. But the art of writing—ah, that is entirely different. The pleasure of the language, the creation above all of that magnificent character, Dr Watson. Ah, that was indeed a triumph.'

Not everyone might agree with Conan Doyle that Holmes and his rivals were merely walkers in the footsteps of Dupin, or with Poirot (implicitly) that others could approach Holmes; but the Holmes *type* became and remains open for continual appropriation. Few of the imitations can be conceded as masterpieces—E. W. Hornung's Raffles, G. K. Chesterton's Father Brown, Bernard Shaw's Professor Higgins, P. G. Wodehouse's Jeeves, F. Scott Fitzgerald's Gatsby, Umberto Eco's Brother William of Baskerville—but Watsons of this calibre are far rarer: of the counterparts to the above group, only Bertie Wooster and Nick Carroway are candidates. There may have been other originals after P. H. Watson; but Conan Doyle had worked so long and so hard with the first-person narrator that what he wanted with Watson was less a model than a key, in the musical sense of the word. He found it, and never lost it, and the result was a just successor of the Greek tragic chorus, Plato, St John the Evangelist, Sancho Panza, Boswell, and the juvenile heroes of Sir Walter Scott. We naturally think of Watson and these precursors as secondary personalities, there to interpret great but unfathomable heroes to us, or bring them within our reach, if not our grasp. But Watson is also in another tradition, that of Everyman, of Bunyan's pilgrim Christian, of the poet Langland as his own creation in *Piers Plowman*: in the century that gave birth to Watson his most notable forebear would seem to be Pierre in one of Conan Doyle's favourite novels, Tolstoy's *War and Peace*. In Watson, the eternal seeker is crossed with the eternal disciple.

As for Holmes, the delicious irony of his birth lies in its juxtaposition with his creator's paper delivered to the Portsmouth Literary and Scientific Society on 19 January 1886, 'Thomas Carlyle and his Works' (Edinburgh University Library MS). The work is a celebration of Carlyle (1795–1881), in the intoxication of whose writings Conan Doyle at that moment rejoiced. In Holmes he created, not Frankensteinmonster, but Carlylean hero. For all of Conan Doyle's championship of Carlyle, he demonstrated his sense of humour by creating a Carlylean hero ignorant of Carlyle. And yet so much of Carlyle went into the making of Holmes and his ethos:

'Hero-worship', if you will,—yes, friends; but, first of all, by being ourselves of heroic mind. A whole world of Heroes; a world not of Flunkeys, where no Hero-King *can* reign: that is what we aim at! . . . For now we shall know quacks when we see them; cant, when we hear it, shall be horrible to us! . . . 'Arrestment of the knaves and dastards:' ah, we know what a work that is; how long it will be before *they* are all or mostly got 'arrested:'—but here is one; arrest him, in God's name; it is one fewer! . . . Infallibly: for light spreads; all human souls, never so bedarkened, love light: light once kindled spreads, till all is luminous . . . Courage! even that is a whole world of heroes to end with, or what we poor Two can do in furtherance thereof! (*Past and Present*, Ch. 6)

There was a deal of irony to be added, and a deal of modification to be supplied: but what Carlyle meant was that it was the false prophets, the Lestrades and Gregsons, who had to be 'arrested'.

The satirical element was present from the first in Conan Doyle's writing, above all in the Holmes saga; and though the family tragedies and personal privations of his youth gave him just cause for bitterness, his satire is normally exuberant. His warm and affectionate nature deplored the emotional repression of many of his teachers at Stonyhurst and Edinburgh, and the Holmes cycle in its totality can be seen as the story of how the warm-hearted Watson made a human being of the cold-blooded Holmes. Certainly, his ironies could become savage when cruelty or hypocrisy came under the narrative view; yet he learned from the detachment of his masters at school and university to allow the accumulation of data become in itself the most devastating form of indictment, and he made the scientific structure of the medical case-report the basis for his art.

It is what Wilde would call a triumph of the critic as artist that the supreme exhibition of that structure should have been made in satirical form: Ronald Knox's 'Studies in the Literature of Sherlock Holmes', published in 1912 and subsequently collected in his *Essays in Satire* (1928). Knox saw *A Study in Scarlet* as laying out the quintessential eleven parts of the Holmes story:

The order of them may in some cases be changed about, and more or less of them may appear as the story is closer to or further from the ideal type. Only the *Study in Scarlet* exhibits all the eleven; the *Sign of the Four* and 'Silver Blaze' have ten, the 'Boscombe Valley Mystery' and 'The Beryl Coronet' nine, the *Hound of the Baskervilles*, the 'Speckled Band', the 'Reigate Squire', and the 'Naval Treaty' eight, and so on till we reach the 'Five Orange Pips', the 'Crooked Man', and the 'Final Problem' with five, and the 'Gloria Scott' with only four.

The first part is the Prooimion, a homely Baker Street scene, with invaluable personal touches, and sometimes a demonstration by the detective. Then follows the first explanation, or Exegesis kata ton diokonta, that is, the client's statement of the case, followed by the Ichneusis, or personal investigation, often including the famous floor-walk on hands and knees. No. 1 is invariable, nos. 2 and 3 almost always present. Nos. 4, 5 and 6 are less necessary: they include the Anaskeue, or refutation on its own merits of the official theory of Scotland Yard, the first Promenusis (exoterike) which gives a few stray hints to the police, which they never adopt, and the second Promenusis (esoterike), which adumbrates the true course of the investigation to Watson alone. This is sometimes wrong, as in the 'Yellow Face'. No. 7 is the Exetasis, or further following up of the trail, including the cross-questioning of relatives, dependants, etc. of the corpse (if there is one), visits to the Record Office, and various investigations in an assumed character. No. 8 is the Anagnorisis, in which the criminal is caught or exposed, No. 9 the second Exegesis (kata ton pheugonta), that is to say the criminal's confession, No. 10 the Metamenusis, in which Holmes describes what his clues were and how he followed them, and No. 11 the Epilogos, sometimes comprised in a single sentence. This conclusion is, like the Prooimion, invariable and often contains a gnome or quotation from some standard author.[7]

Knox's paper was originally written for the Gryphon Club in his own college, Trinity, Oxford. If anything, Oxford was late in the field, Cambridge having produced a number of parodists and pseudo-critics some ten years earlier, of whom the most significant, Bertram Fletcher Robinson, made valuable constructive suggestions for the Holmes saga (see the introductions to *The Hound of the Baskervilles* and *The Return of Sherlock Holmes* in the present series). Universities are given to accentuating their own significance, but the interplay of intellects and the deflation of pretensions—however pretentiously done—appropriately provided the background both for Knox's analysis and Fletcher Robinson's stimulus; for the Holmes cycle derived in itself from gentle and appreciative mockery of certain embattled protagonists at Edinburgh University and its medical school. This is easier to see when Conan Doyle wheels the professors on stage in *The Lost World*, or when we allow ourselves to ask why Holmes's arch-enemy and apparent destroyer was a professor. Eighteenth-century Edinburgh produced the Scottish Enlightenment; nineteenth-century Edinburgh produced *The Heart of Midlothian* and the *Edinburgh Review*, Dr Jekyll and Mr Holmes.

In *A Study in Scarlet* Holmes comes into being virtually fully formed. He was subsequently refined, honed, and angled so as to become one of the giants in the literary landscape of the 1890s. University culture had a crucial part to play in the creation of Holmes, but other forces were also at work. The joy of lone intellectual discovery, on one's own terms,

---

[7] Whilst remaining extremely courteous to his classical student, Conan Doyle seems to have enjoyed breaking away from the system after 1912.

for its own sake, and in the privacy of individual effort, is another essential aspect of Conan Doyle's work—the equally vital innocence to complement defensive sophistication. It was, after all, in medicine that he had worked at university: he taught himself literature.

> Critics kind,
> Never mind!
> Critics flatter,
> No matter!
> Critics curse,
> None the worse!
> Critics blame,
> All the same!
> *Do your best.*
> Hang the rest!

('Advice to a Young Author')

OWEN DUDLEY EDWARDS

NOTE ON THE TEXT

Conan Doyle was paid £25 by Ward, Lock & Co. for all the British rights in *A Study in Scarlet* ('the Copyright and all my interest in the book written by me entitled A STUDY IN SCARLET', as the contract of 20 November 1886 phrased it). He therefore refused to revise the text thereafter, and no variant readings appeared in the 'Author's Edition' (1903), the *Complete Sherlock Holmes Long Stories* (1929), or in any American or other edition. There is no surviving MS. The text of this edition is therefore that of *Beeton's Christmas Annual* for 1887, in which the work first appeared; but the second, third, 'Author's', and omnibus (both British and American) editions have also been examined. Apart from punctuation vagaries, two corrupt readings which passed into the first book edition have been rectified here: the name of Lucy's mustang in Pt. 2, Ch. 2, and the quotation from Horace at the end of the book.

SELECT BIBLIOGRAPHY

1. A. CONAN DOYLE: PRINCIPAL WORKS

(a) *Fiction*

A Study in Scarlet (Ward, Lock, & Co., 1888)
The Mystery of Cloomber (Ward & Downey, 1888)
Micah Clarke (Longmans, Green, & Co., 1889)
The Captain of the Pole-Star and Other Tales (Longmans, Green, & Co., 1890)
The Sign of the Four (Spencer Blackett, 1890)
The Firm of Girdlestone (Chatto & Windus, 1890)
The White Company (Smith, Elder, & Co., 1891)
The Adventures of Sherlock Holmes (George Newnes, 1892)
The Great Shadow (Arrowsmith, 1892)
The Refugees (Longmans, Green, & Co., 1893)
The Memoirs of Sherlock Holmes (George Newnes, 1893)
Round the Red Lamp (Methuen & Co., 1894)
The Stark Munro Letters (Longmans, Green, & Co., 1895)
The Exploits of Brigadier Gerard (George Newnes, 1896)
Rodney Stone (Smith, Elder, & Co., 1896)
Uncle Bernac (Smith, Elder, & Co., 1897)
The Tragedy of the Korosko (Smith, Elder, & Co., 1898)
A Duet With an Occasional Chorus (Grant Richards, 1899)
The Green Flag and Other Stories of War and Sport (Smith, Elder, & Co., 1900)
The Hound of the Baskervilles (George Newnes, 1902)
Adventures of Gerard (George Newnes, 1903)
The Return of Sherlock Holmes (George Newnes, 1905)
Sir Nigel (Smith, Elder, & Co., 1906)
Round the Fire Stories (Smith, Elder, & Co., 1908)
The Last Galley (Smith, Elder, & Co., 1911)
The Lost World (Hodder & Stoughton, 1912)
The Poison Belt (Hodder & Stoughton, 1913)
The Valley of Fear (Smith, Elder, & Co., 1915)
His Last Bow (John Murray, 1917)
Danger! and Other Stories (John Murray, 1918)
The Land of Mist (Hutchinson & Co., 1926)
The Case-Book of Sherlock Holmes (John Murray, 1927)
The Maracot Deep and Other Stories (John Murray, 1929)

The Complete Sherlock Holmes Short Stories (John Murray, 1928)
The Conan Doyle Stories (John Murray, 1929)
The Complete Sherlock Holmes Long Stories (John Murray, 1929)

(b) *Non-fiction*

The Great Boer War (Smith, Elder, & Co., 1900)
The Story of Mr George Edalji (T. Harrison Roberts, 1907)
Through the Magic Door (Smith, Elder, & Co., 1907)
The Crime of the Congo (Hutchinson & Co., 1909)
The Case of Oscar Slater (Hodder & Stoughton, 1912)
The German War (Hodder & Stoughton, 1914)
The British Campaign in France and Flanders (Hodder & Stoughton, 6 vols., 1916–20)
The Poems of Arthur Conan Doyle (John Murray, 1922)
Memories and Adventures (Hodder & Stoughton, 1924; revised edn., 1930)
The History of Spiritualism (Cassell & Co., 1926)

2. MISCELLANEOUS

A Bibliography of A. Conan Doyle (Soho Bibliographies 23: Oxford, 1983) by Richard Lancelyn Green and John Michael Gibson, with a foreword by Graham Greene, is the standard—and indispensable—source of bibliographical information, and of much else besides. Green and Gibson have also assembled and introduced *The Unknown Conan Doyle*, comprising *Uncollected Stories* (those never previously published in book form); *Essays on Photography* (documenting a little-known enthusiasm of Conan Doyle's during his time as a student and young doctor), both published in 1982; and *Letters to the Press* (1986). Alone, Richard Lancelyn Green has compiled (1) *The Uncollected Sherlock Holmes* (1983), an impressive assemblage of Holmesiana, containing almost all Conan Doyle's writing about his creation (other than the stories themselves) together with related material by Joseph Bell, J. M. Barrie, and Beverley Nichols; (2) *The Further Adventures of Sherlock Holmes* (1985), a selection of eleven apocryphal Holmes adventures by various authors, all diplomatically introduced; (3) *The Sherlock Holmes Letters* (1986), a collection of noteworthy public correspondence on Holmes and Holmesiana and far more valuable than its title suggests; and (4) *Letters to Sherlock Holmes* (1984), a powerful testimony to the power of the Holmes stories.

Though much of Conan Doyle's work is now readily available there are still gaps. Some of his very earliest fiction now only survives in rare piracies (apart, that is, from the magazines in which they were first published), including items of intrinsic genre interest such as 'The Gully of Bluemansdyke' (1881) and its sequel 'My Friend the Murderer' (1882), which both turn on the theme of the murderer-informer (handled very differently—and far better—in the Holmes story of 'The Resident Patient' (*Memoirs*)): both of these were used as book-titles for the same pirate collection first issued as *Mysteries and Adventures* (1889). Other stories achieved book publication only after severe pruning—for example, 'The Surgeon of Gaster Fell', reprinted in *Danger!* many years after magazine publication (1890). Some items given initial book publication were not included in the collected edition of *The Conan Doyle Stories*. Particularly deplorable losses were 'John Barrington Cowles' (1884: included subsequently in *Edinburgh Stories of Arthur Conan Doyle* (1981)), 'A Foreign Office Romance' (1894), 'The Club-Footed Grocer' (1898), 'A Shadow Before' (1898), and 'Danger!' (1914). Three of these may have been post-war casualties, as seeming to deal too lightheartedly with the outbreak of other wars; 'John Barrington Cowles' may have been dismissed as juvenile work; but why Conan Doyle discarded a story as good as 'The Club-Footed Grocer' would baffle even Holmes.

At the other end of his life, Conan Doyle's tidying impaired the survival of his most recent work, some of which well merited lasting recognition. *The Maracot Deep and Other Stories* appeared in 1929, a little over a month after *The Conan Doyle Stories*; 'Maracot' itself found a separate paperback life as a short novel; the two Professor Challenger stories, 'The Disintegration Machine' and 'When the World Screamed', were naturally included in John Murray's *The Professor Challenger Stories* (1952); but the fourth item, 'The Story of Spedegue's Dropper', passed beyond the ken of most of Conan Doyle's readers. These three stories show the author, in his seventieth year, still at the height of his powers.

In 1980 Gaslight Publications, of Bloomington, Ind., reprinted *The Mystery of Cloomber*, *The Firm of Girdlestone*, *The Doings of Raffles Haw* (1892), *Beyond the City* (1893), *The Parasite* (1894; also reprinted in *Edinburgh Stories of Arthur Conan Doyle*), *The Stark Munro Letters*, *The Tragedy of the Korosko*, and *A Duet*. *Memories and Adventures*, Conan Doyle's enthralling but impressionistic recollections, are best read in the revised (1930) edition. *Through the Magic Door* remains the best introduction to the literary mind of Conan Doyle, whilst some of his volumes on Spiritualism have autobiographical material of literary significance.

ACD: The Journal of the Arthur Conan Doyle Society (ed. Christopher Roden, David Stuart Davies [to 1991], and Barbara Roden [from 1992]), together with its newsletter, *The Parish Magazine*, is a useful source of critical and biographical material on Conan Doyle. The enormous body of 'Sherlockiana' is best pursued in *The Baker Street Journal*, published by Fordham University Press, or in the *Sherlock Holmes Journal* (Sherlock Holmes Society of London), itemized up to 1974 in the colossal *World Bibliography of Sherlock Holmes and Doctor Watson* (1974) by Ronald Burt De Waal (see also De Waal, *The International Sherlock Holmes* (1980)) and digested in *The Annotated Sherlock Holmes* (2 vols., 1968) by William S. Baring-Gould, whose industry has been invaluable for the Oxford Sherlock Holmes editors. Jack Tracy, *The Encyclopaedia Sherlockiana* (1979) is a very helpful compilation of relevant data. Those who can nerve themselves to consult it despite its title will benefit greatly from Christopher Redmond, *In Bed With Sherlock Holmes* (1984). The classic 'Sherlockian' work is Ronald A. Knox, 'Studies in the Literature of Sherlock Holmes', first published in *The Blue Book* (July 1912) and reprinted in his *Essays in Satire* (1928).

The serious student of Conan Doyle may perhaps deplore the vast extent of 'Sherlockian' literature, even though the size of this output is testimony in itself to the scale and nature of Conan Doyle's achievement. But there is undoubtedly some wheat amongst the chaff. At the head stands Dorothy L. Sayers, *Unpopular Opinions* (1946); also of some interest are T. S. Blakeney, *Sherlock Holmes: Fact or Fiction* (1932), H. W. Bell, *Sherlock Holmes and Dr Watson* (1932), Vincent Starrett, *The Private Life of Sherlock Holmes* (1934), Gavin Brend, *My Dear Holmes* (1951), S. C. Roberts, *Holmes and Watson* (1953) and Roberts's introduction to *Sherlock Holmes: Selected Stories* (Oxford: The World's Classics, 1951), James E. Holroyd, *Baker Street Byways* (1959), Ian McQueen, *Sherlock Holmes Detected* (1974), and Trevor H. Hall, *Sherlock Holmes and his Creator* (1978). One Sherlockian item certainly falls into the category of the genuinely essential: D. Martin Dakin, *A Sherlock Holmes Commentary* (1972), to which all the editors of the present series are indebted.

Michael Pointer, *The Public Life of Sherlock Holmes* (1975) contains invaluable information concerning dramatizations of the Sherlock Holmes stories for radio, stage, and the cinema; of complementary interest are Chris Steinbrunner and Norman Michaels, *The Films of Sherlock Holmes* (1978) and David Stuart Davies, *Holmes of the Movies* (1976), whilst Philip Weller with Christopher Roden, *The Life and Times of Sherlock Holmes* (1992) summarizes a great deal of useful information concerning Conan Doyle's life and Holmes's cases, and in addition is delightfully illustrated. The more concrete products of the Holmes industry are dealt with in Charles Hall, *The Sherlock Holmes Collection* (1987). For a useful retrospective view, Allen Eyles, *Sherlock Holmes: A Centenary Celebration* (1986) rises to the occasion. Both useful and engaging are Peter Haining, *The Sherlock Holmes Scrapbook* (1973) and Charles Viney, *Sherlock Holmes in London* (1989).

Of the many anthologies of Holmesiana, P. A. Shreffler (ed.), *The Baker Street Reader* (1984) is exceptionally useful. D. A. Redmond, *Sherlock Holmes: A Study in Sources* (1982) is similarly indispensable. Michael Hardwick, *The Complete Guide to Sherlock Holmes* (1986) is both reliable and entertaining; Michael Harrison, *In the Footsteps of Sherlock Holmes* (1958) is occasionally helpful.

For more general studies of the detective story, the standard history is Julian Symons, *Bloody Murder* (1972, 1985, 1992). Necessary but a great deal less satisfactory is Howard Haycraft, *Murder for Pleasure* (1942); of more value is Haycraft's critical anthology *The Art of the Mystery Story* (1946), which contains many choice period items. Both R. F. Stewart, *. . . And Always a Detective* (1980) and Colin Watson, *Snobbery with Violence* (1971) are occasionally useful. Dorothy Sayers's pioneering introduction to *Great Short Stories of* → *Detection, Mystery and Horror* (First Series, 1928), despite some inspired howlers, is essential reading; Raymond Chandler's riposte, 'The Simple Art of Murder' (1944), is reprinted in Haycraft, *The Art of the Mystery Story* (see above). Less well known than Sayers's essay but with an equal claim to pioneer status is E. M. Wrong's introduction to *Crime and Detection*, First Series (Oxford: The World's Classics, 1926). See also Michael Cox (ed.), *Victorian Tales of Mystery and Detection: An Oxford Anthology* (1992).

Amongst biographical studies of Conan Doyle one of the most distinguished is Jon L. Lellenberg's survey, *The Quest for Sir Arthur Conan Doyle* (1987), with a Foreword by Dame Jean Conan Doyle (much the best piece of writing on ACD by any member of his family). The four earliest biographers—the Revd John Lamond (1931), Hesketh Pearson (1943), John Dickson Carr (1949), and Pierre Nordon (1964)—all had access to the family archives, subsequently closed to researchers following a lawsuit; hence all four biographies contain valuable documentary material, though Nordon handles the evidence best (the French text is fuller than the English version, published in 1966). Of the others, Lamond seems only to have made little use of the material available to him;

Pearson is irreverent and wildly careless with dates; Dickson Carr has a strong fictionalizing element. Both he and Nordon paid a price for their access to the Conan Doyle papers by deferring to the far from impartial editorial demands of Adrian Conan Doyle; Nordon nevertheless remains the best available biography. The best short sketch is Julian Symons, *Conan Doyle* (1979) (and for the late Victorian milieu of the Holmes cycle some of Symons's own fiction, such as *The Blackheath Poisonings* and *The Detling Secret*, can be thoroughly recommended). Harold Orel (ed.), *Critical Essays on Sir Arthur Conan Doyle* (1992) is a good and varied collection, whilst Robin Winks, *The Historian as Detective* (1969) contains many insights and examples applicable to the Holmes corpus; Winks's *Detective Fiction: A Collection of Critical Essays* (1980) is an admirable working handbook, with a useful critical bibliography. Edmund Wilson's famous essay 'Mr Holmes, they were the footprints of a gigantic hound' (1944) may be found in his *Classics and Commercials: A Literary Chronicle of the Forties* (1950).

Specialized biographical areas are covered in Owen Dudley Edwards, *The Quest for Sherlock Holmes: A Biographical Study of Arthur Conan Doyle* (1983) and in Geoffrey Stavert, *A Study in Southsea: The Unrevealed Life of Dr Arthur Conan Doyle* (1987), which respectively assess the significance of the years up to 1882, and from 1882 to 1890. Alvin E. Rodin and Jack D. Key provide a thorough study of Conan Doyle's medical career and its literary implications in *Medical Casebook of Dr Arthur Conan Doyle* (1984). Peter Costello, in *The Real World of Sherlock Holmes: The True Crimes Investigated by Arthur Conan Doyle* (1991) claims too much, but it is useful to be reminded of events that came within Conan Doyle's orbit, even if they are sometimes tangential or even irrelevant. Christopher Redmond, *Welcome to America, Mr Sherlock Holmes* (1987) is a thorough account of Conan Doyle's tour of North America in 1894.

Other than Baring-Gould (see above), the only serious attempt to annotate the nine volumes of the Holmes cycle has been in the Longman Heritage of Literature series (1979–80), to which the present editors are also indebted. Of introductions to individual texts, H. R. F. Keating's to the *Adventures* and *The Hound of the Baskervilles* (published in one volume under the dubious title *The Best of Sherlock Holmes* (1992)) is worthy of particular mention.

A CHRONOLOGY OF
ARTHUR CONAN DOYLE

1855   Charles Altamont Doyle, youngest son of the political cartoonist John Doyle ('HB'), and Mary Foley, his Irish landlady's daughter, marry in Edinburgh on 31 July.

1859   Arthur Ignatius Conan Doyle, third child and elder son of ten siblings, born at 11 Picardy Place, Edinburgh, on 22 May and baptized into the Roman Catholic religion of his parents.

1868–75   ACD commences two years' education under the Jesuits at Hodder, followed by five years at its senior sister college, Stonyhurst, both in the Ribble Valley, Lancashire; becomes a popular storyteller amongst his fellow pupils, writes verses, edits a school paper, and makes one close friend, James Ryan of Glasgow and Ceylon. Doyle family resides at 3 Sciennes Hill Place, Edinburgh.

1875–6   ACD passes London Matriculation Examination at Stonyhurst and studies for a year in the Jesuit college at Feldkirch, Austria.

1876–7   ACD becomes a student of medicine at Edinburgh University on the advice of Bryan Charles Waller, now lodging with the Doyle family at 2 Argyle Park Terrace.

1877–80   Waller leases 23 George Square, Edinburgh as a 'consulting pathologist', with all the Doyles as residents. ACD continues medical studies, becoming surgeon's clerk to Joseph Bell at Edinburgh; also takes temporary medical assistantships at Sheffield, Ruyton (Salop), and Birmingham, the last leading to a close friendship with his employer's family, the Hoares. First story published, 'The Mystery of Sasassa Valley', in *Chambers's Journal* (6 Sept. 1879); first non-fiction published—'Gelseminum as a Poison', *British Medical Journal* (20 Sept. 1879). Sometime previously ACD sends 'The Haunted Grange of Goresthorpe' to *Blackwood's Edinburgh Magazine*, but it is filed and forgotten.

1880   (Feb.–Sept.) ACD serves as surgeon on the Greenland whaler *Hope* of Peterhead.

1881   ACD graduates MB, CM (Edin.); Waller and the Doyles living at 15 Lonsdale Terrace, Edinburgh.

1881–2   (Oct.–Jan.) ACD serves as surgeon on the steamer *Mayumba* to West Africa, spending three days with US Minister to Liberia, Henry Highland Garnet, black abolitionist leader, then dying. (July–Aug.) Visits Foley relatives in Lismore, Co. Waterford.

1882   Ill-fated partnership with George Turnavine Budd in Plymouth. ACD moves to Southsea, Portsmouth, in June. ACD published in *London Society, All the Year Round, Lancet,* and *British Journal of Photography.* Over the next eight years ACD becomes an increasingly successful general practitioner at Southsea.

1882–3   Breakup of the Doyle family in Edinburgh. Charles Altamont Doyle henceforth confined because of alcoholism and epilepsy. Mary Foley Doyle resident in Masongill Cottage on the Waller estate at Masongill, Yorkshire. Innes Doyle (b. 1873) resident with ACD as schoolboy and surgery page from Sept. 1882.

1883   'The Captain of the *Pole-Star*' published (*Temple Bar,* Jan.), as well as a steady stream of minor pieces. Works on *The Mystery of Cloomber.*

1884   ACD publishes 'J. Habakuk Jephson's Statement' (*Cornhill Magazine,* Jan.), 'The Heiress of Glenmahowley' (*Temple Bar,* Jan.), 'The Cabman's Story' (*Cassell's Saturday Journal,* May); working on *The Firm of Girdlestone.*

1885   Publishes 'The Man from Archangel' (*London Society,* Jan.). John Hawkins, briefly a resident patient with ACD, dies of cerebral meningitis. Louisa Hawkins, his sister, marries ACD. (Aug.) Travels in Ireland for honeymoon. Awarded Edinburgh MD.

1886   Writing *A Study in Scarlet.*

1887   *A Study in Scarlet* published in *Beeton's Christmas Annual.*

1888   (July) First book edition of *A Study in Scarlet* published by Ward, Lock; (Dec.) *The Mystery of Cloomber* published.

1889   (Feb.) *Micah Clarke* (ACD's novel of the Monmouth Rebellion of 1685) published. Mary Louise Conan

Doyle, ACD's eldest child, born. Unauthorized publication of *Mysteries and Adventures* (published later as *The Gully of Bluemansdyke* and *My Friend the Murderer*). *The Sign of the Four* and Oscar Wilde's *The Picture of Dorian Gray* commissioned by Lippincott's.

1890 (Jan.) 'Mr [R. L.] Stevenson's Methods in Fiction' published in the *National Review*. (Feb.) *The Sign of the Four* published in *Lippincott's Monthly Magazine*; (Mar.) First authorized short-story collection, *The Captain of the Pole-Star and Other Tales*, published; (Apr.) *The Firm of Girdlestone* published; (Oct.) First book edition of the *Sign* published by Spencer Blackett.

1891 ACD sets up as an eye specialist in 2 Upper Wimpole Street, off Harley Street, while living at Montague Place. Moves to South Norwood. (July–Dec.) The first six 'Adventures of Sherlock Holmes' published in George Newnes's *Strand Magazine*. (Oct.) *The White Company* published; *Beyond the City* first published in *Good Cheer*, the special Christmas number of *Good Words*.

1892 (Jan.–June) Six more Holmes stories published in the *Strand*, with another in Dec. (Mar.) *The Doings of Raffles Haw* published (first serialized in Alfred Harmsworth's penny paper *Answers*, Dec. 1891–Feb. 1892). (14 Oct.) *The Adventures of Sherlock Holmes* published by Newnes. (31 Oct.) Waterloo story *The Great Shadow* published. Alleyne Kingsley Conan Doyle born. Newnes republishes the *Sign*.

1893 'Adventures of Sherlock Holmes' (second series) continues in the *Strand*, to be published by Newnes as *The Memoirs of Sherlock Holmes* (Dec.), minus 'The Cardboard Box'. Holmes apparently killed in 'The Final Problem' (Dec.) to free ACD for 'more serious literary work'. (May) *The Refugees* published. *Jane Annie; or, the Good Conduct Prize* (musical comedy co-written with J. M. Barrie) fails at the Savoy Theatre. (10 Oct.) Charles Altamont Doyle dies.

1894 (Oct.) *Round the Red Lamp*, a collection of medical short stories, published, several for the first time. *The Stark Munro Letters*, a fictionalized autobiography, begun, to be concluded the following year. ACD on US lecture tour with Innes Doyle. (Dec.) *The Parasite* published; 'The Medal of Brigadier Gerard' published in the *Strand*.

1895   'The Exploits of Brigadier Gerard' published in the *Strand*.

1896   (Feb.) *The Exploits of Brigadier Gerard* published by Newnes. ACD settles at Hindhead, Surrey, to minimize effects of his wife's tuberculosis. (Nov.) *Rodney Stone*, a pre-Regency mystery, published. Self-pastiche, 'The Field Bazaar', appears in the Edinburgh University *Student* (20 Nov.).

1897   (May) Napoleonic novel *Uncle Bernac* published; three 'Captain Sharkey' pirate stories published in *Pearson's Magazine* (Jan., Mar., May). Home at Undershaw, Hindhead.

1898   (Feb.) *The Tragedy of the Korosko* published. (June) Publishes *Songs of Action*, a verse collection. (June–Dec.) Begins to publish 'Round the Fire Stories' in the *Strand*—'The Beetle Hunter', 'The Man with the Watches', 'The Lost Special', 'The Sealed Room', 'The Black Doctor', 'The Club-Footed Grocer', and 'The Brazilian Cat'. Ernest William Hornung (ACD's brother-in-law) creates A. J. Raffles and in 1899 dedicates the first stories to ACD.

1899   (Jan.–May) Concludes 'Round the Fire' series in the *Strand* with 'The Japanned Box', 'The Jew's Breast-Plate', 'B. 24', 'The Latin Tutor', and 'The Brown Hand'. (Mar.) Publishes *A Duet with an Occasional Chorus*, a version of his own romance. (Oct.–Dec.) 'The Croxley Master', a boxing story, published in the *Strand*. William Gillette begins 33 years starring in *Sherlock Holmes*, a play by Gillette and ACD.

1900   Accompanies volunteer-staffed Langman hospital as unofficial supervisor to support British forces in the Boer War. (Mar.) Publishes short-story collection, *The Green Flag and Other Stories of War and Sport*. (Oct.) *The Great Boer War* published. Unsuccessful Liberal Unionist parliamentary candidate for Edinburgh Central.

1901   (Aug.) 'The Hound of the Baskervilles' begins serialization in the *Strand*, subtitled 'Another Adventure of Sherlock Holmes'.

1902   (Jan.) *The War in South Africa: Its Cause and Conduct* published. 'Sherlockian' higher criticism begun by Frank

Sidgwick in the *Cambridge Review* (23 Jan.). (Mar.) *The Hound of the Baskervilles* published by Newnes. ACD accepts knighthood with reluctance.

1903   (Sept.) *Adventures of Gerard* published by Newnes (previously serialized in the *Strand*). (Oct.) 'The Return of Sherlock Holmes' begins in the *Strand*. Author's Edition of ACD's major works published in twelve volumes by Smith, Elder and thirteen by D. Appleton & Co. of New York, with prefaces by ACD; many titles omitted.

1904   'Return of Sherlock Holmes' continues in the *Strand*; series designed to conclude with 'The Abbey Grange' (Sept.), but ACD develops earlier allusions and produces 'The Second Stain' (Dec.).

1905   (Mar.) *The Return of Sherlock Holmes* published by Newnes. (Dec.) Serialization of 'Sir Nigel' begun in the *Strand* (concluded Dec. 1906).

1906   (Nov.) Book publication of *Sir Nigel*. ACD defeated as Unionist candidate for Hawick District in general election. (4 July) Death of Louisa ('Touie'), Lady Conan Doyle. ACD deeply affected.

1907   ACD clears the name of George Edalji (convicted in 1903 of cattle-maiming). (18 Sept.) Marries Jean Leckie. (Nov.) Publishes *Through the Magic Door*, a celebration of his literary mentors (earlier version serialized in *Great Thoughts*, 1894).

1908   Moves to Windlesham, Crowborough, Sussex. (Jan.) Death of Sidney Paget. (Sept.) *Round the Fire Stories* published, including some not in earlier *Strand* series. (Sept.–Oct.) 'The Singular Experience of Mr John Scott Eccles' (later retitled as 'The Adventure of Wisteria Lodge') begins occasional series of Holmes stories in the *Strand*.

1909   ACD becomes President of the Divorce Law Reform Union (until 1919). Denis Percy Stewart Conan Doyle born. Takes up agitation against Belgian oppression in the Congo.

1910   (Sept.) 'The Marriage of the Brigadier', the last Gerard story, published in the *Strand*, and (Dec.) the Holmes story of 'The Devil's Foot'. ACD takes six-month lease on Adelphi Theatre; the play *The Speckled Band* opens there, eventually running to 346 performances. Adrian Malcolm Conan Doyle born.

1911   (Apr.) *The Last Galley* (short stories, mostly historical) published. Two more Holmes stories appear in the *Strand*: 'The Red Circle' (Mar., Apr.) and 'The Disappearance of Lady Frances Carfax' (Dec.). ACD declares for Irish Home Rule, under the influence of Sir Roger Casement.

1912   (Apr.–Nov.) The first Professor Challenger story, *The Lost World*, published in the *Strand*, book publication in Oct. Jean Lena Annette Conan Doyle (afterwards Air Commandant Dame Jean Conan Doyle, Lady Bromet) born.

1913   (Feb.) Writes 'Great Britain and the Next War' (*Fortnightly Review*). (Aug.) Second Challenger story, *The Poison Belt*, published. (Dec.) 'The Dying Detective' published in the *Strand*. ACD campaigns for a channel tunnel.

1914   (July) 'Danger!', warning of the dangers of a war-time blockade of Britain, published in the *Strand*. (4 Aug.) Britain declares war on Germany; ACD forms local volunteer force.

1914–15   (Sept.) *The Valley of Fear* begins serialization in the *Strand* (concluding May 1915).

1915   (27 Feb.) *The Valley of Fear* published by George H. Doran in New York. (June) *The Valley of Fear* published in London by Smith, Elder (transferred with rest of ACD stock to John Murray when the firm is sold on the death of Reginald Smith). Five Holmes films released in Germany (ten more during the war).

1916   (Apr., May) First instalments of *The British Campaign in France and Flanders 1914* appear in the *Strand*. (Aug.) *A Visit to Three Fronts* published. Sir Roger Casement convicted of high treason after Dublin Easter Week Rising and executed despite appeals for clemency by ACD and others.

1917   War censor interdicts ACD's history of the 1916 campaigns in the *Strand*. (Sept.) 'His Last Bow' published in the *Strand*. (Oct.) *His Last Bow* published by John Murray (includes 'The Cardboard Box').

1918   (Apr.) ACD publishes *The New Revelation*, proclaiming himself a Spiritualist. (Dec.) *Danger! and Other Stories* published. Permitted to resume accounts of 1916 and 1917 campaigns in the *Strand*, but that for 1918 never serialized. Death of eldest son, Captain Kingsley Conan Doyle, from influenza aggravated by war wounds.

1919   Death of Brigadier-General Innes Doyle, from post-war pneumonia.

1920–30   ACD engaged in world-wide crusade for Spiritualism.

1921–2   ACD's one-act play, *The Crown Diamond*, tours with Dennis Neilson-Terry as Holmes.

1921   (Oct.) 'The Mazarin Stone' (apparently based on *The Crown Diamond*) published in the *Strand*. Death of mother, Mary Foley Doyle.

1922   (Feb.–Mar.) 'The Problem of Thor Bridge' in the *Strand*. (July) John Murray publishes a collected edition of the non-Holmes short stories in six volumes: *Tales of the Ring and the Camp*, *Tales of Pirates and Blue Water*, *Tales of Terror and Mystery*, *Tales of Twilight and the Unseen*, *Tales of Adventure and Medical Life*, and (Nov.) *Tales of Long Ago*. (Sept.) Collected edition of ACD's *Poems* published by Murray.

1923   (Mar.) 'The Creeping Man' published in the *Strand*.

1924   (Jan.) 'The Sussex Vampire' appears in the *Strand*. (June) 'How Watson Learned the Trick', ACD's own Holmes pastiche, appears in *The Book of the Queen's Dolls' House Library*. (Sept.) *Memories and Adventures* published (reprinted with additions and deletions 1930).

1925   (Jan.) 'The Three Garridebs' and (Feb.–Mar.) 'The Illustrious Client' published in the *Strand*. (July) *The Land of Mist*, a Spiritualist novel featuring Challenger, begins serialization in the *Strand*.

1926   (Mar.) *The Land of Mist* published. *Strand* publishes 'The Three Gables' (Oct.), 'The Blanched Soldier' (Nov.), and 'The Lion's Mane' (Dec.).

1927   *Strand* publishes 'The Retired Colourman' (Jan.), 'The Veiled Lodger' (Feb.), and 'Shoscombe Old Place' (Apr.). (June) Murray publishes *The Case-Book of Sherlock Holmes*.

1928   (Oct.) *The Complete Sherlock Holmes Short Stories* published by Murray.

1929   (June) *The Conan Doyle Stories* (containing the six separate volumes issued by Murray in 1922) published. (July) *The Maracot Deep and Other Stories*, ACD's last collection of his fictional work.

1930   (7 July, 8.30 a.m.) Death of Arthur Conan Doyle. 'Education never ends, Watson. It is a series of lessons with the greatest for the last' ('The Red Circle').

A Study in Scarlet

PART 1

*Being a reprint from
the reminiscences of John H. Watson MD,
late* of the Army Medical Department*

· CHAPTER 1 ·

Mr Sherlock Holmes

IN the year 1878* I took my degree of Doctor of Medicine of the University of London,* and proceeded to
Netley* to go through the course prescribed for surgeons in
the army. Having completed my studies there, I was duly
attached to the Fifth Northumberland Fusiliers* as Assistant
Surgeon. The regiment was stationed in India at the time,
and before I could join it, the second Afghan war* had
broken out. On landing at Bombay,* I learned that my
corps* had advanced through the passes, and was already
deep in the enemy's country. I followed, however, with
many other officers who were in the same situation as
myself, and succeeded in reaching Candahar* in safety,
where I found my regiment, and at once entered upon my
new duties.

The campaign brought honours and promotion to many,*
but for me it had nothing but misfortune and disaster. I was
removed from my brigade and attached to the Berkshires,*
with whom I served at the fatal battle of Maiwand.* There
I was struck on the shoulder* by a Jezail bullet,* which
shattered the bone and grazed the subclavian artery.* I
should have fallen into the hands of the murderous Ghazis*
had it not been for the devotion and courage shown by
Murray,* my orderly,* who threw me across a pack-horse,*
and succeeded in bringing me safely to the British lines.

Worn with pain, and weak from the prolonged hardships
which I had undergone, I was removed, with a great train*
of wounded sufferers, to the base hospital at Peshawur.*
Here I rallied, and had already improved so far as to be able
to walk about the wards, and even to bask a little upon the
verandah, when I was struck down by enteric fever,* that
curse of our Indian possessions.* For months my life was

despaired of, and when at last I came to myself and became convalescent, I was so weak and emaciated that a medical board determined that not a day should be lost in sending me back to England. I was dispatched, accordingly, in the troopship *Orontes*,* and landed a month later on Portsmouth jetty,* with my health irretrievably ruined,* but with permission from a paternal government to spend the next nine months* in attempting to improve it.

I had neither kith nor kin in England, and was therefore as free as air—or as free as an income of eleven shillings and sixpence a day* will permit a man to be. Under such circumstances I naturally gravitated to London, that great cesspool into which all the loungers and idlers of the Empire are irresistibly drained.* There I stayed for some time at a private hotel in the Strand, leading a comfortless, meaningless existence,* and spending such money as I had, considerably more freely than I ought. So alarming did the state of my finances become that I soon realized that I must either leave the metropolis and rusticate* somewhere in the country, or that I must make a complete alteration in my style of living. Choosing the latter alternative, I began by making up my mind to leave the hotel, and to take up my quarters in some less pretentious and less expensive domicile.

On the very day that I had come to this conclusion, I was standing at the Criterion Bar,* when someone tapped me on the shoulder, and turning round I recognized young Stamford,* who had been a dresser* under me at Barts.* The sight of a friendly face in the great wilderness of London is a pleasant thing indeed to a lonely man. In old days Stamford had never been a particular crony of mine, but now I hailed him with enthusiasm, and he, in his turn, appeared to be delighted to see me. In the exuberance of my joy, I asked him to lunch with me at the Holborn,* and we started off together in a hansom.*

'Whatever have you been doing with yourself, Watson?' he asked in undisguised wonder, as we rattled through the crowded London streets. 'You are as thin as a lath and as brown as a nut.'

I gave him a short sketch of my adventures, and had hardly concluded it by the time that we reached our destination.

'Poor devil!' he said, commiseratingly, after he had listened to my misfortunes. 'What are you up to now?'

'Looking for lodgings,' I answered. 'Trying to solve the problem as to whether it is possible to get comfortable rooms at a reasonable price.'

'That's a strange thing,' remarked my companion, 'you are the second man to-day that has used that expression to me.'

'And who was the first?' I asked.

'A fellow who is working at the chemical laboratory up at the hospital. He was bemoaning himself this morning because he could not get someone to go halves with him in some nice rooms which he had found, and which were too much for his purse.'*

'By Jove!' I cried; 'if he really wants some one to share the rooms and the expense, I am the very man for him. I should prefer having a partner to being alone.'

Young Stamford looked rather strangely at me over his wine-glass. 'You don't know Sherlock Holmes yet,' he said; 'perhaps you would not care for him as a constant companion.'

'Why, what is there against him?'

'Oh, I didn't say there was anything against him. He is a little queer in his ideas—an enthusiast in some branches of science. As far as I know he is a decent fellow enough.'

'A medical student, I suppose?' said I.

'No—I have no idea what he intends to go in for. I believe he is well up in anatomy, and he is a first-class chemist; but, as far as I know, he has never taken out any systematic medical classes.* His studies are very desultory and eccentric, but he has amassed a lot of out-of-the-way knowledge which would astonish his professors.'*

'Did you never ask him what he was going in for?' I asked.

'No; he is not a man that it is easy to draw out, though he can be communicative enough when the fancy seizes him.'

7

'I should like to meet him,' I said. 'If I am to lodge with anyone, I should prefer a man of studious and quiet habits. I am not strong enough yet to stand much noise or excitement. I had enough of both in Afghanistan to last me for the remainder of my natural existence. How could I meet this friend of yours?'

'He is sure to be at the laboratory,'* returned my companion. 'He either avoids the place for weeks, or else he works there from morning till night. If you like, we will drive round together after luncheon.'

'Certainly,' I answered, and the conversation drifted away into other channels.

As we made our way to the hospital after leaving the Holborn, Stamford gave me a few more particulars about the gentleman whom I proposed to take as a fellow-lodger.

'You mustn't blame me if you don't get on with him,' he said; 'I know nothing more of him than I have learned from meeting him occasionally in the laboratory. You proposed this arrangement, so you must not hold me responsible.'

'If we don't get on it will be easy to part company,' I answered. 'It seems to me, Stamford,' I added, looking hard at my companion, 'that you have some reason for washing your hands of the matter.* Is this fellow's temper so formidable, or what is it? Don't be mealy-mouthed* about it.'

'It is not easy to express the inexpressible,' he answered with a laugh. 'Holmes is a little too scientific for my tastes—it approaches to cold-bloodedness. I could imagine his giving a friend a little pinch of the latest vegetable alkaloid,* not out of malevolence, you understand, but simply out of a spirit of inquiry in order to have an accurate idea of the effects. To do him justice, I think that he would take it himself with the same readiness.* He appears to have a passion for definite and exact knowledge.'

'Very right too.'

'Yes, but it may be pushed to excess. When it comes to beating the subjects in the dissecting-rooms with a stick,* it is certainly taking rather a bizarre shape.'

'Beating the subjects!'

8

'Yes, to verify how far bruises may be produced after death. I saw him at it with my own eyes.'

'And yet you say he is not a medical student?'

'No. Heaven knows what the objects of his studies are. But here we are, and you must form your own impressions about him.' As he spoke, we turned down a narrow lane and passed through a small side-door which opened into a wing of the great hospital. It was familiar ground to me, and I needed no guiding as we ascended the bleak stone staircase and made our way down the long corridor with its vista of whitewashed wall and dun-coloured doors. Near the farther end a low arched passage branched away from it and led to the chemical laboratory.

This was a lofty chamber, lined and littered with countless bottles. Broad, low tables were scattered about, which bristled with retorts,* test-tubes,* and little Bunsen lamps* with their blue flickering flames. There was only one student in the room, who was bending over a distant table absorbed in his work. At the sound of our steps he glanced round and sprang to his feet with a cry of pleasure. 'I've found it! I've found it,' he shouted to my companion, running towards us with a test-tube in his hand. 'I have found a re-agent which is precipitated by haemoglobin,* and by nothing else.' Had he discovered a gold mine, greater delight could not have shone upon his features.

'Dr Watson, Mr Sherlock Holmes,' said Stamford, introducing us.

'How are you?' he said cordially, gripping my hand with a strength for which I should hardly have given him credit. 'You have been in Afghanistan, I perceive.'*

'How on earth did you know that?' I asked in astonishment.

'Never mind,' said he, chuckling to himself. 'The question now is about haemoglobin. No doubt you see the significance of this discovery of mine?'

'It is interesting, chemically, no doubt,' I answered, 'but practically—'

'Why, man, it is the most practical medico-legal discovery for years. Don't you see* that it gives us an infallible test for

9

blood stains. Come over here now!' He seized me by the coat-sleeve in his eagerness, and drew me over to the table at which he had been working. 'Let us have some fresh blood,' he said, digging a long bodkin* into his finger, and drawing off the resulting drop of blood in a chemical pipette.* 'Now, I add this small quantity of blood to a litre of water. You perceive that the resulting mixture has the appearance of pure water. The proportion of blood cannot be more than one in a million. I have no doubt, however, that we shall be able to obtain the characteristic reaction.' As he spoke, he threw into the vessel a few white crystals, and then added some drops of a transparent fluid. In an instant the contents assumed a dull mahogany* colour, and a brownish dust was precipitated to the bottom of the glass jar.

'Ha! ha!' he cried, clapping his hands, and looking as delighted as a child with a new toy. 'What do you think of that?'

'It seems to be a very delicate test,' I remarked.

'Beautiful! beautiful! The old guaiacum test* was very clumsy and uncertain. So is the microscopic examination for blood corpuscles.* The latter is valueless if the stains are a few hours old. Now, this appears to act as well whether the blood is old or new. Had this test been invented, there are hundreds of men now walking the earth who would long ago have paid the penalty of their crimes.'

'Indeed!' I murmured.

'Criminal cases are continually hinging upon that one point. A man is suspected of a crime months perhaps after it has been committed. His linen or clothes are examined and brownish stains discovered upon them. Are they blood stains, or mud stains, or rust stains, or fruit stains, or what are they? That is a question which has puzzled many an expert, and why? Because there was no reliable test. Now we have the Sherlock Holmes test,* and there will no longer be any difficulty.'

His eyes fairly glittered as he spoke, and he put his hand over his heart and bowed as if to some applauding crowd conjured up by his imagination.

'You are to be congratulated,' I remarked, considerably surprised at his enthusiasm.

'There was the case of Von Bischoff at Frankfort* last year. He would certainly have been hung had this test been in existence. Then there was Mason of Bradford,* and the notorious Muller,* and Lefevre of Montpellier,* and Samson of New Orleans.* I could name a score of cases in which it would have been decisive.'

'You seem to be a walking calendar of crime,' said Stamford with a laugh. 'You might start a paper on those lines. Call it the "Police News of the Past".'

'Very interesting reading it might be made, too,' remarked Sherlock Holmes, sticking a small piece of plaster over the prick on his finger. 'I have to be careful,' he continued, turning to me with a smile, 'for I dabble with poisons a good deal.' He held out his hand as he spoke, and I noticed that it was all mottled over with similar pieces of plaster, and discoloured with strong acids.

'We came here on business,' said Stamford, sitting down on a high three-legged stool, and pushing another one in my direction with his foot. 'My friend here wants to take diggings;* and as you were complaining that you could get no one to go halves with you, I thought that I had better bring you together.'

Sherlock Holmes seemed delighted at the idea of sharing his rooms with me. 'I have my eye on a suite in Baker Street,' he said, 'which would suit us down to the ground. You don't mind the smell of strong tobacco, I hope?'

'I always smoke "ship's"* myself,' I answered.

'That's good enough. I generally have chemicals about, and occasionally do experiments. Would that annoy you?'

'By no means.'

'Let me see—what are my other shortcomings. I get in the dumps* at times, and don't open my mouth for days on end. You must not think I am sulky when I do that. Just let me alone, and I'll soon be right. What have you to confess now? It's just as well for two fellows* to know the worst of one another before they begin to live together.'

I laughed at this cross-examination. 'I keep a bull pup,'* I said, 'and I object to rows because my nerves are shaken, and I get up at all sorts of ungodly hours,* and I am extremely lazy. I have another set of vices* when I'm well, but those are the principal ones at present.'

'Do you include violin playing* in your category of rows?' he asked, anxiously.

'It depends on the player,' I answered. 'A well-played violin is a treat for the gods—a badly-played one—'

'Oh, that's all right,' he cried, with a merry laugh. 'I think we may consider the thing as settled—that is, if the rooms are agreeable to you.'

'When shall we see them?'

'Call for me here at noon to-morrow, and we'll go together and settle everything,' he answered.

'All right—noon exactly,' said I, shaking his hand.

We left him working among his chemicals, and we walked together towards my hotel.

'By the way,' I asked suddenly, stopping and turning upon Stamford, 'how the deuce* did he know that I had come from Afghanistan?'

My companion smiled an enigmatical smile. 'That's just his little peculiarity,' he said. 'A good many people have wanted to know how he finds things out.'

'Oh! a mystery is it?' I cried, rubbing my hands. 'This is very piquant.* I am much obliged to you for bringing us together. "The proper study of mankind is man,"* you know.'

'You must study* him, then,' Stamford said, as he bade me good-bye. 'You'll find him a knotty problem, though. I'll wager he learns more about you than you about him.* Good-bye.'

'Good-bye,'* I answered, and strolled on to my hotel, considerably interested in my new acquaintance.

· CHAPTER 2 ·

The Science of Deduction

W E met next day as he had arranged, and inspected the rooms at No. 221B, Baker Street,* of which he had spoken at our meeting. They consisted of a couple of comfortable bedrooms* and a single large airy sitting-room, cheerfully furnished, and illuminated by two broad windows.* So desirable in every way were the apartments, and so moderate did the terms seem when divided between us,* that the bargain was concluded upon the spot, and we at once entered into possession. That very evening I moved my things round from the hotel, and on the following morning Sherlock Holmes followed me with several boxes and portmanteaus. For a day or two we were busily employed in unpacking and laying out our property to the best advantage. That done, we gradually began to settle down and to accommodate ourselves to our new surroundings.

Holmes was certainly not a difficult man to live with. He was quiet in his ways, and his habits were regular. It was rare for him to be up after ten at night, and he had invariably breakfasted and gone out before I rose in the morning. Sometimes he spent his day at the chemical laboratory, sometimes in the dissecting-rooms, and occasionally in long walks, which appeared to take him into the lowest portions of the city.* Nothing could exceed his energy when the working fit was upon him; but now and again a reaction would seize him, and for days on end he would lie upon the sofa in the sitting-room, hardly uttering a word or moving a muscle from morning to night. On these occasions I have noticed such a dreamy, vacant expression in his eyes, that I might have suspected him of being addicted to the use of some narcotic, had not the temperance and cleanliness of his whole life forbidden such a notion.*

13

As the weeks went by, my interest in him and my curiosity as to his aims in life gradually deepened and increased. His very person and appearance were such as to strike the attention of the most casual observer. In height he was rather over six feet, and so excessively lean that he seemed to be considerably taller. His eyes were sharp and piercing, save during those intervals of torpor to which I have alluded; and his thin, hawk-like nose gave his whole expression an air of alertness and decision. His chin, too, had the prominence and squareness which mark the man of determination.* His hands were invariably blotted with ink and stained with chemicals,* yet he was possessed of extraordinary delicacy of touch,* as I frequently had occasion to observe when I watched him manipulating his fragile philosophical* instruments.

The reader may set me down as a hopeless busybody, when I confess how much this man stimulated my curiosity, and how often I endeavoured to break through the reticence which he showed on all that concerned himself. Before pronouncing judgement, however, be it remembered how objectless was my life,* and how little there was to engage my attention. My health forbade me from venturing out unless the weather was exceptionally genial,* and I had no friends* who would call upon me and break the monotony of my daily existence. Under these circumstances I eagerly hailed the little mystery which hung around my companion, and spent much of my time in endeavouring to unravel it.

He was not studying medicine. He had himself, in reply to a question, confirmed Stamford's opinion in that point. Neither did he appear to have pursued any course of reading which might fit him for a degree in science or any other recognized portal which would give him an entrance into the learned world. Yet his zeal for certain studies was remarkable, and within eccentric limits his knowledge was so extraordinarily ample and minute that his observations have fairly astounded me. Surely no man would work so hard or attain such precise information unless he had some definite end in view. Desultory readers are seldom remarkable for the exactness of their learning. No man burdens his mind with small matters unless he has some very good reason for doing so.*

His ignorance was as remarkable as his knowledge. Of contemporary literature, philosophy and politics he appeared to know next to nothing. Upon my quoting Thomas Carlyle, he inquired in the naïvest way who he might be and what he had done.* My surprise reached a climax, however, when I found incidentally that he was ignorant of the Copernican Theory and of the composition of the Solar System.* That any civilized human being in this nineteenth century should not be aware that the earth travelled round the sun appeared to be to me such an extraordinary fact that I could hardly realize it.

'You appear to be astonished,' he said, smiling at my expression of surprise. 'Now that I do know it I shall do my best to forget it.'

'To forget it!'

'You see,' he explained, 'I consider that a man's brain originally is like a little empty attic, and you have to stock it with such furniture as you choose. A fool takes in all the lumber* of every sort that he comes across, so that the knowledge which might be useful to him gets crowded out, or at best is jumbled up with a lot of other things, so that he has a difficulty in laying his hands upon it. Now the skilful workman is very careful indeed as to what he takes into his brain-attic. He will have nothing but the tools which may help him in doing his work, but of these he has a large assortment, and all in the most perfect order. It is a mistake to think that that little room has elastic walls and can distend to any extent. Depend upon it there comes a time when for every addition of knowledge you forget something that you knew before. It is of the highest importance, therefore, not to have useless facts elbowing out the useful ones.'*

'But the Solar System!' I protested.

'What the deuce is it to me?' he interrupted impatiently: 'you say that we go round the sun. If we went round the moon it would not make a penny-worth of difference to me or to my work.'*

I was on the point of asking him what that work might be, but something in his manner showed me that the question would be an unwelcome one. I pondered over our short conversation, however, and endeavoured to draw my deductions from it. He said that he would acquire no knowledge which did not bear upon his object. Therefore all the knowledge which he possessed was such as would be useful to him. I enumerated in my own mind all the various points upon which he had shown me that he was exceptionally well-informed. I even took a pencil and jotted them down. I could not help smiling at the document when I had completed it. It ran in this way:

SHERLOCK HOLMES—*his limits*

1 Knowledge of Literature.—Nil.
2 Knowledge of Philosophy.—Nil.
3 Knowledge of Astronomy.—Nil.
4 Knowledge of Politics.—Feeble.
5 Knowledge of Botany.—Variable. Well up in belladonna,* opium,* and poisons generally. Knows nothing of practical gardening.
6 Knowledge of Geology: Practical, but limited. Tells at a glance different soils from each other. After walks has shown me splashes upon his trousers, and told me by their colour and consistence in what part of London he had received them.
7 Knowledge of Chemistry.—Profound.
8 Knowledge of Anatomy.—Accurate, but unsystematic.
9 Knowledge of Sensational Literature.—Immense. He appears to know every detail of every horror perpetrated in the century.*
10 Plays the violin well.
11 Is an expert singlestick* player, boxer, and swordsman.
12 Has a good practical knowledge of British law.

When I had got so far in my list I threw it into the fire in despair. 'If I can only find what the fellow is driving at by reconciling all these accomplishments, and discovering a calling which needs them all,' I said to myself, 'I may as well give up the attempt at once.'

I see that I have alluded above to his powers upon the violin. These were very remarkable, but as eccentric as all his other accomplishments. That he could play pieces, and difficult pieces, I knew well, because at my request he has played me some of Mendelssohn's Lieder,* and other favourites. When left to himself, however, he would seldom produce any music or attempt any recognized air. Leaning back in his arm-chair of an evening, he would close his eyes and scrape carelessly at the fiddle which was thrown across his knee. Sometimes the chords were sonorous and melancholy. Occasionally they were fantastic and cheerful. Clearly they reflected the thoughts which possessed him, but whether the music aided those thoughts, or whether the playing was simply the result of a whim or fancy, was more than I could determine. I might have rebelled against these exasperating solos had it not been that he usually terminated them by playing in quick succession a whole series of my favourite airs as a slight compensation for the trial upon my patience.

During the first week or so we had no callers, and I had begun to think that my companion was as friendless a man as I was myself. Presently, however, I found that he had many acquaintances, and those in the most different classes of society. There was one little sallow, rat-faced, dark-eyed fellow, who was introduced to me as Mr Lestrade,* and who came three or four times in a single week. One morning a young girl called, fashionably dressed, and stayed for half an hour or more. The same afternoon brought a grey-headed, seedy visitor, looking like a Jew pedlar,* who appeared to me to be much excited, and who was closely followed by a slip-shod elderly woman. On another occasion an old white-haired gentleman had an interview with my companion; and on another, a railway porter in his velveteen* uniform. When any of these nondescript individuals put in an appearance, Sherlock Holmes used to beg for the use of the sitting-room,* and I would retire to my bed-room. He always apologized to me for putting me to this inconvenience. 'I have to use this room as a place of business,' he said, 'and these people are my clients.' Again I had an opportunity of asking him a point-blank question, and again my delicacy prevented me from forcing another man to confide in me. I imagined at the time that he had some strong reason for not alluding to it, but he soon dispelled the idea by coming round to the subject of his own accord.

It was upon the 4th of March, as I have good reason to remember, that I rose somewhat earlier than usual, and found that Sherlock Holmes had not yet finished his breakfast. The landlady* had become so accustomed to my late habits that my place had not been laid nor my coffee prepared. With the unreasonable petulance of mankind* I rang the bell and gave a curt intimation that I was ready. Then I picked up a magazine from the table and attempted to while away the time with it, while my companion munched silently at his toast. One of the articles had a pencil mark at the heading, and I naturally began to run my eye through it.

Its somewhat ambitious title was 'The Book of Life',* and it attempted to show how much an observant man might learn by an accurate and systematic examination of all that came in his way. It struck me as being a remarkable mixture of shrewdness and of absurdity. The reasoning was close and intense, but the deductions appeared to me to be far-fetched and exaggerated. The writer claimed by a momentary expression, a twitch of a muscle or a glance of an eye, to fathom a man's inmost thoughts. Deceit, according to him, was an impossibility in the case of one trained to observation and analysis. His conclusions were as infallible as so many propositions of Euclid.* So startling would his results appear to the uninitiated that until they learned the processes by which he had arrived at them they might well consider him as a necromancer.*

'From a drop of water,' said the writer,

a logician could infer the possibility of an Atlantic or a Niagara without having seen or heard of one or the other. So all life is a great chain, the nature of which is known whenever we are shown

18

a single link of it. Like all other arts, the Science of Deduction and Analysis is one which can only be acquired by long and patient study, nor is life long enough to allow any mortal to attain the highest possible perfection in it. Before turning to these moral and mental aspects of the matter which present the greatest difficulties, let the inquirer begin by mastering more elementary problems. Let him on meeting a fellow-mortal,* learn at a glance to distinguish the history of the man, and the trade or profession* to which he belongs. Puerile as such an exercise may seem, it sharpens the faculties of observation, and teaches one where to look and what to look for. By a man's finger-nails, by his coat-sleeve, by his boot, by his trouser-knees, by the callosities* of his forefinger and thumb, by his expression, by his shirt-cuffs—by each of these things a man's calling is plainly revealed. That all united should fail to enlighten the competent inquirer in any case is almost inconceivable.

'What ineffable twaddle!'* I cried, slapping the magazine down on the table; 'I never read such rubbish in my life.'

'What is it?' asked Sherlock Holmes.

'Why, this article,' I said, pointing at it with my egg-spoon as I sat down to my breakfast. 'I see that you have read it since you have marked it. I don't deny that it is smartly written. It irritates me, though. It is evidently the theory of some arm-chair lounger who evolves all these neat little paradoxes* in the seclusion of his own study. It is not practical. I should like to see him clapped down in a third-class carriage on the Underground,* and asked to give the trades of all his fellow-travellers. I would lay a thousand to one against him.'

'You would lose your money,' Holmes remarked calmly. 'As for the article, I wrote it myself.'

'You!'

'Yes; I have a turn both for observation and for deduction. The theories which I have expressed there, and which appear to you to be so chimerical,* are really extremely practical—so practical that I depend upon them for my bread and cheese.'

'And how?' I asked involuntarily.

'Well, I have a trade of my own. I suppose I am the only one in the world. I'm a consulting detective,* if you can understand what that is. Here in London we have lots of Government detectives and lots of private ones. When these fellows are at fault, they come to me, and I manage to put them on the right scent. They lay all the evidence before me, and I am generally able, by the help of my knowledge of the history of crime,* to set them straight. There is a strong family resemblance about misdeeds, and if you have all the details of a thousand at your finger ends, it is odd if you can't unravel the thousand and first. Lestrade is a well-known detective. He got himself into a fog recently over a forgery case, and that was what brought him here.'

'And these other people?'

'They are mostly sent on by private inquiry agencies. They are all people who are in trouble about something and want a little enlightening.* I listen to their story, they listen to my comments, and then I pocket my fee.'

'But do you mean to say,' I said, 'that without leaving your room you can unravel some knot which other men can make nothing of, although they have seen every detail for themselves?'

'Quite so. I have a kind of intuition that way. Now and again a case turns up which is a little more complex. Then I have to bustle about and see things with my own eyes. You see I have a lot of special knowledge which I apply to the problem, and which facilitates matters wonderfully. Those rules of deduction laid down in that article which aroused your scorn are invaluable to me in practical work. Observation with me is second nature. You appeared to be surprised when I told you, on our first meeting, that you had come from Afghanistan.'

'You were told, no doubt.'

'Nothing of the sort. I *knew* you came from Afghanistan. From long habit the train of thoughts ran so swiftly through my mind that I arrived at the conclusion without being conscious of intermediate steps. There were such steps, however. The train of reasoning ran: "Here is a gentleman of a medical type, but with the air of a military man. Clearly an army doctor then. He has just come from the tropics, for his face is dark, and that is not the natural tint of his skin, for his wrists are fair. He has undergone hardship and sickness, as his haggard face says clearly. His left arm has been injured. He holds it in a stiff and unnatural manner. Where in the tropics could an English army doctor have seen much hardship and got his arm wounded? Clearly in Afghanistan." The whole train of thought did not occupy a second. I then remarked that you came from Afghanistan, and you were astonished.'

'It is simple enough as you explain it,' I said, smiling. 'You remind me of Edgar Allan Poe's Dupin.* I had no idea that such individuals did exist outside of stories.'

Sherlock Holmes rose and lit his pipe. 'No doubt you think that you are complimenting me in comparing me to Dupin,' he observed. 'Now, in my opinion, Dupin was a very inferior fellow. That trick of his* of breaking in on his friends' thoughts with an apropos remark after a quarter of an hour's silence is really very showy and superficial. He had some analytical genius, no doubt; but he was by no means such a phenomenon as Poe appeared to imagine.'

'Have you read Gaboriau's works?'* I asked. 'Does Lecoq come up to your idea of a detective?'

Sherlock Holmes sniffed sardonically. 'Lecoq was a miserable bungler,' he said, in an angry voice; 'he had only one thing to recommend him, and that was his energy. That book made me positively ill. The question was how to identify an unknown prisoner. I could have done it in twenty-four hours. Lecoq took six months or so. It might be made a text-book for detectives to teach them what to avoid.'

I felt rather indignant at having two characters whom I had admired* treated in this cavalier style. I walked over to the window, and stood looking out into the busy street. 'This fellow may be very clever,' I said to myself, 'but he is certainly very conceited.'

'There are no crimes and no criminals in these days,' he said, querulously. 'What is the use of having brains in our profession?* I know well that I have it in me to make my name famous. No man lives or has ever lived who has brought the same amount of study and of natural talent to the detection of crime which I have done. And what is the result? There is no crime to detect, or, at most, some bungling villainy with a motive so transparent that even a Scotland Yard official* can see through it.'

I was still annoyed at his bumptious style of conversation. I thought it best to change the topic.

'I wonder what that fellow is looking for?' I asked, pointing to a stalwart, plainly-dressed individual who was walking slowly down the other side of the street, looking anxiously at the numbers. He had a large blue envelope in his hand, and was evidently the bearer of a message.

'You mean the retired sergeant of Marines,' said Sherlock Holmes.

'Brag and bounce!' thought I to myself. 'He knows that I cannot verify his guess.'

The thought had hardly passed through my mind when the man whom we were watching caught sight of the number on our door, and ran rapidly across the roadway. We heard a loud knock, a deep voice below, and heavy steps ascending the stair.

'For Mr Sherlock Holmes,' he said, stepping into the room and handing my friend the letter.

Here was an opportunity of taking the conceit out of him. He little thought of this when he made that random shot. 'May I ask, my lad,' I said, in the blandest voice, 'what your trade may be?'

'Commissionaire, sir,' he said, gruffly. 'Uniform away for repairs.'

'And you were?' I asked, with a slightly malicious glance at my companion.

'A sergeant, sir, Royal Marine Light Infantry,* sir. No answer? Right, sir.'

He clicked his heels together, raised his hand in a salute, and was gone.

· CHAPTER 3 ·

The Lauriston Gardens Mystery

I CONFESS that I was considerably startled by this fresh proof of the practical nature of my companion's theories. My respect for his powers of analysis increased wondrously.* There still remained some lurking suspicion in my mind, however, that the whole thing was a prearranged episode, intended to dazzle me, though what earthly object he could have in taking me in was past my comprehension. When I looked at him, he had finished reading the note, and his eyes had assumed the vacant, lack-lustre expression which showed mental abstraction.

'How in the world did you deduce that?' I asked.

'Deduce what?' said he, petulantly.

'Why, that he was a retired sergeant of Marines.'

'I have no time for trifles,' he answered brusquely; then with a smile: 'Excuse my rudeness. You broke the thread of my thoughts; but perhaps it is as well. So you actually were not able to see that that man was a sergeant of Marines?'

'No, indeed.'

'It was easier to know it than to explain why I know it.* If you were asked to prove that two and two made four, you might find some difficulty, and yet you are quite sure of the fact. Even across the street I could see a great blue anchor tattooed on the back of the fellow's hand. That smacked of the sea. He had a military carriage, however, and regulation side whiskers. There we have the marine. He was a man with some amount of self-importance and a certain air of command. You must have observed the way in which he held his head and swung his cane. A steady, respectable, middle-aged man, too, on the face of him—all facts which led me to believe that he had been a sergeant.'

'Wonderful!' I ejaculated.

23

'Commonplace,'* said Holmes, though I thought from his expression that he was pleased at my evident surprise and admiration. 'I said just now that there were no criminals. It appears that I am wrong—look at this!' He threw me over the note which the commissionaire had brought.

'Why,' I cried, as I cast my eye over it, 'this is terrible!'

'It does seem to be a little out of the common,' he remarked, calmly. 'Would you mind reading it to me aloud?'

This is the letter which I read to him:

' "My dear Mr Sherlock Holmes, There has been a bad business during the night at 3, Lauriston Gardens,* off the Brixton Road. Our man on the beat saw a light there about two in the morning, and as the house was an empty one, suspected that something was amiss. He found the door open, and in the front room, which is bare of furniture, discovered the body of a gentleman, well dressed, and having cards in his pocket bearing the name of 'Enoch J. Drebber,* Cleveland, Ohio, U.S.A.' There had been no robbery, nor is there any evidence as to how the man met his death. There are marks of blood in the room, but there is no wound upon his person. We are at a loss as to how he came into the empty house; indeed, the whole affair is a puzzler. If you can come round to the house any time before twelve, you will find me there. I have left everything *in statu quo** until I hear from you. If you are unable to come, I shall give you fuller details, and would esteem it a great kindness if you would favour me with your opinion. Yours faithfully, TOBIAS GREGSON." '*

'Gregson is the smartest of the Scotland Yarders,' my friend remarked; 'he and Lestrade are the pick of a bad lot. They are both quick and energetic, but conventional—shockingly so. They have their knives into one another, too. They are as jealous as a pair of professional beauties. There will be some fun over this case if they are both put upon the scent.'

I was amazed at the calm way in which he rippled on. 'Surely there is not a moment to be lost,' I cried; 'shall I go and order you a cab?'

'I'm not sure about whether I shall go. I am the most incurably lazy devil* that ever stood in shoe leather—that is, when the fit is on me, for I can be spry enough at times.'

'Why, it is just such a chance as you have been longing for.'

'My dear fellow, what does it matter to me? Supposing I unravel the whole matter, you may be sure that Gregson, Lestrade, and Co. will pocket all the credit. That comes of being an unofficial personage.'*

'But he begs you to help him.'

'Yes. He knows that I am his superior, and acknowledges it to me; but he would cut his tongue out before he would own it to any third person. However, we may as well go and have a look. I shall work it out on my own hook. I may have a laugh at them, if I have nothing else. Come on!'

He hustled on his overcoat, and bustled about in a way that showed that an energetic fit had superseded the apathetic one.

'Get your hat,' he said.

'You wish me to come?'

'Yes, if you have nothing better to do.' A minute later we were both in a hansom, driving furiously for the Brixton Road.

It was a foggy, cloudy morning, and a dun-coloured veil hung over the house-tops, looking like the reflection of the mud-coloured streets beneath. My companion was in the best of spirits, and prattled away about Cremona fiddles, and the difference between a Stradivarius and an Amati.* As for myself, I was silent, for the dull weather and the melancholy business upon which we were engaged, depressed my spirits.

'You don't seem to give much thought to the matter in hand,' I said at last, interrupting Holmes's musical disquisition.

'No data yet,' he answered. 'It is a capital mistake to theorize before you have all the evidence. It biases the judgement.'*

'You will have your data soon,' I remarked, pointing with my finger; 'this is the Brixton Road, and that is the house, if I am not very much mistaken.'

'So it is. Stop, driver, stop!' We were still a hundred yards or so from it, but he insisted upon our alighting, and we finished our journey upon foot.

Number 3, Lauriston Gardens, wore an ill-omened and minatory look. It was one of four which stood back some little way from the street, two being occupied and two empty. The latter looked out with three tiers of vacant melancholy windows, which were blank and dreary, save that here and there a 'To Let' card had developed like a cataract* upon the bleared panes. A small garden sprinkled over with a scattered eruption* of sickly plants separated each of these houses from the street, and was traversed by a narrow pathway, yellowish in colour, and consisting apparently of a mixture of clay and of gravel. The whole place was very sloppy from the rain which had fallen through the night. The garden was bounded by a three-foot brick wall with a fringe of wood rails upon the top, and against this wall was leaning a stalwart police constable, surrounded by a small knot of loafers,* who craned their necks and strained their eyes in the vain hope of catching some glimpse of the proceedings within.

I had imagined that Sherlock Holmes would at once have hurried into the house and plunged into a study of the mystery. Nothing appeared to be further from his intention. With an air of nonchalance which, under the circumstances, seemed to me to border upon affectation, he lounged up and down the pavement, and gazed vacantly at the ground, the sky, the opposite houses and the line of railings. Having finished his scrutiny, he proceeded slowly down the path, or rather down the fringe of grass which flanked the path, keeping his eyes riveted upon the ground. Twice he stopped, and once I saw him smile, and heard him utter an exclamation of satisfaction. There were many marks of footsteps upon the wet clayey soil; but since the police had been coming and going over it, I was unable to see how my companion could hope to learn anything from it. Still, I had had such extraordinary evidence of the quickness of his perceptive faculties, that I had no doubt that he could see a great deal which was hidden from me.

At the door of the house we were met by a tall, white-faced, flaxen-haired man, with a notebook in his hand, who rushed forward and wrung my companion's hand with effusion. 'It is indeed kind of you to come,' he said, 'I have had everything left untouched.'

'Except that!' my friend answered, pointing at the pathway. 'If a herd of buffaloes had passed along there could not be a greater mess.* No doubt, however, you had drawn your own conclusions, Gregson, before you permitted this.'

'I have had so much to do inside the house,' the detective said evasively. 'My colleague, Mr Lestrade, is here. I had relied upon him to look after this.'

Holmes glanced at me and raised his eyebrows sardonically. 'With two such men as yourself and Lestrade upon the ground, there will not be much for a third party to find out,' he said.

Gregson rubbed his hands in a self-satisfied way. 'I think we have done all that can be done,' he answered; 'it's a queer case though, and I knew your taste for such things.'

'You did not come here in a cab?'* asked Sherlock Holmes.

'No, sir.'

'Nor Lestrade?'

'No, sir.'

'Then let us go and look at the room.' With which inconsequent remark he strode on into the house,* followed by Gregson, whose features expressed his astonishment.

A short passage, bare-planked and dusty, led to the kitchen and offices.* Two doors opened out of it to the left and to the right. One of these had obviously been closed for many weeks. The other belonged to the dining-room, which was the apartment in which the mysterious affair had occurred. Holmes walked in, and I followed him with that subdued feeling at my heart which the presence of death inspires.

It was a large square room, looking all the larger from the absence of all furniture. A vulgar flaring paper adorned the walls, but it was blotched in places with mildew, and here

and there great strips had become detached and hung
down,* exposing the yellow plaster beneath. Opposite the
door was a showy fireplace, surmounted by a mantel-piece
of imitation white marble. On one corner of this was stuck
the stump of a red wax candle. The solitary window was so
dirty that the light was hazy and uncertain, giving a dull
grey tinge to everything, which was intensified by the thick
layer of dust which coated the whole apartment.

All these details I observed afterwards. At present my
attention was centred upon the single, grim, motionless
figure which lay stretched upon the boards, with vacant,
sightless eyes staring up at the discoloured ceiling. It was
that of a man about forty-three or forty-four years of age,
middle-sized, broad-shouldered, with crisp curling black hair,
and a short, stubbly beard. He was dressed in a heavy broadcloth frock coat* and waistcoat, with light-coloured trousers,
and immaculate collar and cuffs. A top hat, well brushed
and trim, was placed upon the floor beside him. His hands
were clenched and his arms thrown abroad, while his lower
limbs were interlocked, as though his death struggle had been
a grievous one. On his rigid face there stood an expression
of horror, and, as it seemed to me, of hatred, such as I have
never seen upon human features. This malignant and terrible contortion, combined with the low forehead, blunt
nose, and prognathous jaw, gave the dead man a singularly
simious and ape-like appearance,* which was increased by
his writhing, unnatural posture. I have seen death in many
forms, but never has it appeared to me in a more fearsome
aspect than in that dark, grimy apartment, which looked out
upon one of the main arteries of suburban London.

Lestrade, lean and ferret-like* as ever, was standing by the
doorway, and greeted my companion and myself.

'This case will make a stir, sir,' he remarked. 'It beats
anything I have seen, and I am no chicken.'

'There is no clue!'* said Gregson.

'None at all,' chimed in Lestrade.

Sherlock Holmes approached the body, and, kneeling
down, examined it intently. 'You are sure that there is no

wound?' he asked, pointing to numerous gouts and splashes of blood which lay all round.

'Positive!' cried both detectives.

'Then, of course, this blood belongs to a second individual—presumably the murderer, if murder has been committed. It reminds me of the circumstances attendant on the death of Van Jansen, in Utrecht,* in the year '34. Do you remember the case, Gregson?'

'No, sir.'

'Read it up—you really should. There is nothing new under the sun.* It has all been done before.'

As he spoke, his nimble fingers were flying here, there, and everywhere, feeling, pressing, unbuttoning, examining, while his eyes wore the same faraway expression which I have already remarked upon. So swiftly was the examination made, that one would hardly have guessed the minuteness with which it was conducted. Finally, he sniffed the dead man's lips, and then glanced at the soles of his patent leather boots.

'He has not been moved at all?' he asked.

'No more than was necessary for the purposes of our examination.'

'You can take him to the mortuary now,' he said. 'There is nothing more to be learned.'

Gregson had a stretcher and four men at hand. At his call they entered the room, and the stranger was lifted and carried out. As they raised him, a ring tinkled down and rolled across the floor. Lestrade grabbed it up and stared at it with mystified eyes.

'There's been a woman here,' he cried. 'It's a woman's wedding-ring.'

He held it out, as he spoke, upon the palm of his hand. We all gathered round him and gazed at it. There could be no doubt that that circlet of plain gold had once adorned the finger of a bride.

'This complicates matters,' said Gregson. 'Heaven knows, they were complicated enough before.'

'You're sure it doesn't simplify them?' observed Holmes. 'There's nothing to be learned by staring at it. What did you find in his pockets?'

'We have it all here,' said Gregson, pointing to a litter of objects upon one of the bottom steps of the stairs. 'A gold watch, No. 97163, by Barraud, of London.* Gold Albert chain,* very heavy and solid. Gold ring, with masonic device.* Gold pin—bull-dog's head, with rubies as eyes. Russian leather card-case with cards of Enoch J. Drebber of Cleveland, corresponding with the E. J. D. upon the linen. No purse, but loose money to the extent of seven pounds thirteen. Pocket edition of Boccaccio's *Decameron*,* with name of Joseph Stangerson* upon the fly-leaf. Two letters—one addressed to E. J. Drebber and one to Joseph Stangerson.'*

'At what address?'

'American Exchange, Strand*—to be left till called for. They are both from the Guion Steamship Company,* and refer to the sailing of their boats from Liverpool. It is clear that this unfortunate man was about to return to New York.'

'Have you made any inquiries as to this man Stangerson?'

'I did it at once, sir,' said Gregson. 'I have had advertisements sent to all the newspapers, and one of my men has gone to the American Exchange, but he has not returned yet.'

'Have you sent to Cleveland?'

'We telegraphed this morning.'

'How did you word your inquiries?'

'We simply detailed the circumstances, and said that we should be glad of any information which could help us.'

'You did not ask for particulars on any point which appeared to you to be crucial?'

'I asked about Stangerson.'

'Nothing else? Is there no circumstance on which this whole case appears to hinge? Will you not telegraph again?'

'I have said all I have to say,' said Gregson, in an offended voice.

Sherlock Holmes chuckled to himself, and appeared to be about to make some remark, when Lestrade, who had been in the front room while we were holding this conversation in the hall, reappeared upon the scene, rubbing his hands* in a pompous and self-satisfied manner.

'Mr Gregson,' he said, 'I have just made a discovery of the highest importance, and one which would have been overlooked had I not made a careful examination of the walls.'

The little man's eyes sparkled as he spoke, and he was evidently in a state of suppressed exultation at having scored a point against his colleague.

'Come here,' he said, bustling back into the room, the atmosphere of which felt clearer since the removal of its ghastly inmate. 'Now, stand there!'

He struck a match on his boot and held it up against the wall.

'Look at that!' he said, triumphantly.

I have remarked that the paper had fallen away in parts. In this particular corner of the room a large piece had peeled off, leaving a yellow square of coarse plastering. Across this bare space there was scrawled in blood-red letters a single word*—

RACHE

'What do you think of that?' cried the detective, with the air of a showman exhibiting his show. 'This was overlooked because it was in the darkest corner of the room, and no one thought of looking there. The murderer has written it with his or her own blood. See this smear where it has trickled down the wall! That disposes of the idea of suicide anyhow. Why was that corner chosen to write it on? I will tell you. See that candle on the mantelpiece. It was lit at the time, and if it was lit this corner would be the brightest instead of the darkest portion of the wall.'

'And what does it mean now that you *have* found it?' asked Gregson in a deprecatory voice.

'Mean? Why, it means that the writer was going to put the female name Rachel,* but was disturbed before he or she had time to finish. You mark my words, when this case comes to be cleared up you will find that a woman named Rachel has something to do with it. It's all very well for you to laugh, Mr Sherlock Holmes. You may be very smart and clever, but the old hound is the best, when all is said and done.'

'I really beg your pardon!' said my companion, who had ruffled the little man's temper by bursting into an explosion of laughter. 'You certainly have the credit of being the first of us to find this out and, as you say, it bears every mark of having been written by the other participant in last night's mystery. I have not had time to examine this room yet, but with your permission I shall do so now.'

As he spoke, he whipped a tape measure and a large round magnifying glass from his pocket. With these two implements he trotted noiselessly about the room, sometimes stopping, occasionally kneeling, and once lying flat upon his face. So engrossed was he with his occupation that he appeared to have forgotten our presence, for he chattered away to himself under his breath the whole time, keeping up a running fire of exclamations, groans, whistles, and little cries suggestive of encouragement and of hope. As I watched him I was irresistibly reminded of a pure-blooded, well-trained foxhound as it dashes backwards and forwards through the covert,* whining in its eagerness, until it comes across the lost scent. For twenty minutes or more he continued his researches, measuring with the most exact care the distance between marks which were entirely invisible to me, and occasionally applying his tape to the walls in an equally incomprehensible manner. In one place he gathered up very carefully a little pile of grey dust from the floor, and packed it away in an envelope. Finally he examined with his glass the word upon the wall, going over every letter of it with the most minute exactness. This done, he appeared to be satisfied, for he replaced his tape and his glass in his pocket.

'They say that genius is an infinite capacity for taking pains,'* he remarked with a smile. 'It's a very bad definition, but it does apply to detective work.'

Gregson and Lestrade had watched the manoeuvres of their amateur companion with considerable curiosity and some contempt. They evidently failed to appreciate the fact, which I had begun to realize, that Sherlock Holmes's smallest actions were all directed towards some definite and practical end.

'What do you think of it, sir?'* they both asked.

'It would be robbing you of the credit of the case if I was to presume to help you,' remarked my friend. 'You are doing so well now that it would be a pity for anyone to interfere.' There was a world of sarcasm in his voice as he spoke. 'If you will let me know how your investigations go,' he continued, 'I shall be happy to give you any help I can. In the meantime I should like to speak to the constable who found the body. Can you give me his name and address?'

Lestrade glanced at his note-book. 'John Rance,' he said. 'He is off duty now. You will find him at 46, Audley Court,* Kennington Park Gate.'

Holmes took a note of the address.

'Come along, Doctor,' he said; 'we shall go and look him up. I'll tell you one thing which may help you in the case,' he continued, turning to the two detectives. 'There has been murder done, and the murderer was a man. He was more than six feet high, was in the prime of life, had small feet for his height, wore coarse, square-toed boots and smoked a Trichinopoly cigar.* He came here with his victim in a four-wheeled cab, which was drawn by a horse with three old shoes and one new one on his off fore-leg. In all probability the murderer had a florid face, and the finger-nails of his right hand were remarkably long. These are only a few indications, but they may assist you.'

Lestrade and Gregson glanced at each other with an incredulous smile.

'If this man was murdered, how was it done?' asked the former.

'Poison,' said Sherlock Holmes curtly, and strode off. 'One other thing, Lestrade,' he added, turning round at the door: ' "Rache" is the German for "revenge"; so don't lose your time by looking for Miss Rachel.'

With which Parthian shot* he walked away, leaving the two rivals open-mouthed behind him.

· CHAPTER 4 ·

What John Rance Had to Tell

IT was one o'clock when we left No. 3, Lauriston Gardens. Sherlock Holmes led me to the nearest telegraph office, whence he dispatched a long telegram. He then hailed a cab, and ordered the driver to take us to the address given us by Lestrade.

'There is nothing like first-hand evidence,' he remarked; 'as a matter of fact, my mind is entirely made up upon the case, but still we may as well learn all that is to be learned.'

'You amaze me, Holmes,' said I. 'Surely you are not as sure as you pretend to be of all those particulars which you gave.'

'There's no room for mistake,' he answered. 'The very first thing which I observed on arriving there was that a cab had made two ruts with its wheels close to the kerb. Now, up to last night, we have had no rain for a week, so that those wheels which left such a deep impression must have been there during the night. There were the marks of the horse's hoofs, too, the outline of one of which was far more clearly cut than that of the other three, showing that that was a new shoe. Since the cab was there after the rain began, and was not there at any time during the morning—I have Gregson's word for that—it follows that it must have been there during the night, and, therefore, that it brought those two individuals to the house.'

'That seems simple enough,' said I; 'but how about the other man's height?'

'Why, the height of a man, in nine cases out of ten, can be told from the length of his stride. It is a simple calculation enough, though there is no use my boring you with figures. I had this fellow's stride both on the clay outside and on the dust within. Then I had a way of checking my calculation. When a man writes on a wall, his instinct leads him to write about the level of his own eyes. Now that writing was just over six feet from the ground. It was child's play.'

'And his age?' I asked.

'Well, if a man can stride four and a half feet without the smallest effort, he can't be quite in the sere and yellow.* That was the breadth of a puddle on the garden walk which he had evidently walked across. Patent-leather boots had gone round, and Square-toes had hopped over. There is no mystery about it at all. I am simply applying to ordinary life a few of those precepts of observation and deduction which I advocated in that article. Is there anything else that puzzles you?'

'The finger-nails and the Trichinopoly,' I suggested.

'The writing on the wall was done with a man's fore-finger dipped in blood. My glass allowed me to observe that the plaster was slightly scratched in doing it, which would not have been the case if the man's nail had been trimmed. I gathered up some scattered ash from the floor. It was dark in colour and flakey—such an ash as is only made by a Trichinopoly. I have made a special study of cigar ashes—in fact, I have written a monograph upon the subject.* I flatter myself that I can distinguish at a glance the ash of any known brand either of cigar or of tobacco. It is just in such details that the skilled detective differs from the Gregson and Lestrade type.'

'And the florid face?' I asked.

'Ah, that was a more daring shot, though I have no doubt that I was right. You must not ask me that at the present state of the affair.'

I passed my hand over my brow. 'My head is in a whirl,' I remarked; 'the more one thinks of it the more mysterious it grows. How came these two men—if there were two men—into an empty house? What has become of the cabman who drove them?* How could one man compel another to take poison? Where did the blood come from? What was the object of the murderer, since robbery had no part in it? How came the woman's ring there? Above all, why should the second man write up the German word RACHE before decamping? I confess that I cannot see any possible way of reconciling all these facts.'

My companion smiled approvingly.

'You sum up the difficulties of the situation succinctly and well,' he said. 'There is much that is still obscure, though I have quite made up my mind on the main facts. As to poor Lestrade's discovery, it was simply a blind intended to put the police upon a wrong track, by suggesting Socialism and secret societies.* It was not done by a German. The A, if you noticed, was printed somewhat after the German fashion.* Now, a real German invariably prints in the Latin character,* so that we may safely say that this was not written by one, but by a clumsy imitator who overdid his part. It was simply a ruse to divert inquiry into a wrong channel. I'm not going to tell you much more of the case, Doctor. You know a conjurer gets no credit once he has explained his trick; and if I show you too much of my method of working, you will come to the conclusion that I am a very ordinary individual after all.'

'I shall never do that,' I answered; 'you have brought detection as near an exact science as it ever will be brought in this world.'*

My companion flushed up with pleasure at my words, and the earnest way in which I uttered them. I had already observed that he was as sensitive to flattery on the score of his art as any girl could be of her beauty.*

'I'll tell you one other thing,' he said. 'Patent-leathers and Square-toes came in the same cab, and they walked down the pathway together as friendly as possible—arm-in-arm,* in all probability. When they got inside, they walked up and down the room—or rather, Patent-leathers stood still while Square-toes walked up and down. I could read all that in the dust; and I could read that as he walked he grew more and more excited. That is shown by the increased length of his strides. He was talking all the while, and working himself up, no doubt, into a fury.* Then the tragedy occurred. I've told you all I know myself now, for the rest is mere surmise and conjecture. We have a good working basis, however, on which to start. We must hurry up, for I want to go to Hallé's concert to hear Norman-Neruda* this afternoon.'

This conversation had occurred while our cab had been threading its way through a long succession of dingy streets and dreary byways. In the dingiest and dreariest of them our driver suddenly came to a stand. 'That's Audley Court in there,' he said, pointing to a narrow slit in the line of dead-coloured brick. 'You'll find me here when you come back.'

Audley Court was not an attractive locality. The narrow passage led us into a quadrangle paved with flags and lined by sordid dwellings. We picked our way among groups of dirty children, and through lines of discoloured linen, until we came to Number 46, the door of which was decorated with a small slip of brass on which the name Rance was engraved. On inquiry we found that the constable was in bed, and we were shown into a little front parlour to await his coming.

He appeared presently, looking a little irritable at being disturbed in his slumbers. 'I made my report at the office,' he said.

Holmes took a half-sovereign* from his pocket and played with it pensively. 'We thought that we should like to hear it all from your own lips,' he said.

'I shall be most happy to tell you anything I can,' the constable answered, with his eyes upon the little golden disc.

'Just let us hear it all in your own way as it occurred.'

Rance sat down on the horsehair sofa, and knitted his brows, as though determined not to omit anything in his narrative.

'I'll tell it ye from the beginning,' he said. 'My time is from ten at night to six in the morning. At eleven there was a fight at the *White Hart*;* but bar that all was quiet enough on the beat. At one o'clock it began to rain, and I met Harry Murcher—him who has the Holland Grove beat—and we stood together at the corner of Henrietta Street a-talkin'. Presently—maybe about two or a little after—I thought I would take a look round and see that all was right down the Brixton Road. It was precious dirty and lonely. Not a soul did I meet all the way down, though a cab or two went past me. I was a-strollin' down, thinkin' between ourselves how uncommon handy a four of gin hot* would be, when suddenly the glint of a light caught my eye in the window of that same house. Now, I knew that them two houses in Lauriston Gardens was empty on account of him that owns them who won't have the drains seed to, though the very last tenant what lived in one of them died o' typhoid fever.* I was knocked all in a heap, therefore, at seeing a light in the window, and I suspected as something was wrong. When I got to the door—'

'You stopped, and then walked back to the garden gate,'* my companion interrupted. 'What did you do that for?'

Rance gave a violent jump, and stared at Sherlock Holmes with the utmost amazement upon his features.

'Why, that's true, sir,' he said; 'though how you come to know it, Heaven only knows. Ye see when I got up to the door, it was so still and lonesome, that I thought I'd be none the worse for some one with me. I ain't afeard of anything on this side o' the grave; but I thought that maybe it was him that died o' the typhoid inspecting the drains what killed him.* The thought gave me a kind o' turn, and I walked back to the gate to see if I could see Murcher's lantern, but there wasn't no sign of him nor of anyone else.'

'There was no one in the street?'

'Not a livin' soul, sir, nor as much as a dog. Then I pulled myself together and went back and pushed the door open. All was quiet inside, so I went into the room where the light was a-burnin'. There was a candle flickerin' on the mantel-piece—a red wax one—and by its light I saw—'

'Yes, I know all that you saw. You walked round the room several times, and you knelt down by the body, and then you walked through and tried the kitchen door, and then—'

John Rance sprang to his feet with a frightened face and suspicion in his eyes. 'Where was you hid to see all that?' he cried. 'It seems to me that you knows a deal more than you should.'

Holmes laughed and threw his card across the table to the constable. 'Don't get arresting me for the murder,' he said. 'I am one of the hounds and not the wolf; Mr Gregson or Mr Lestrade will answer for that. Go on, though. What did you do next?'

Rance resumed his seat, without, however, losing his mystified expression. 'I went back to the gate and sounded my whistle. That brought Murcher and two more to the spot.'

'Was the street empty then?'

'Well, it was,* as far as anybody that could be of any good goes.'

'What do you mean?'

The constable's features broadened into a grin. 'I've seen many a drunk chap in my time,' he said, 'but never anyone so cryin' drunk as that cove. He was at the gate when I came out, a-leanin' up ag'in the railings, and a-singin' at the pitch o' his lungs about Columbine's New-fangled Banner,* or some such stuff. He couldn't stand, far less help.'

'What sort of a man was he?' asked Sherlock Holmes.

John Rance appeared to be somewhat irritated at this digression. 'He was an uncommon drunk sort o' man,' he said. 'He'd ha' found hisself in the station if we hadn't been so took up.'

'His face—his dress—didn't you notice them?' Holmes broke in impatiently.

'I should think I did notice them, seeing that I had to prop him up—me and Murcher between us. He was a long chap, with a red face, the lower part muffled round—'

'That will do,' cried Holmes. 'What became of him?'

'We'd enough to do without lookin' after him,' the policeman said, in an aggrieved voice. 'I'll wager he found his way home all right.'

'How was he dressed?'

'A brown overcoat.'

'Had he a whip in his hand?'

'A whip—no.'

'He must have left it behind,' muttered my companion. 'You didn't happen to see or hear a cab after that?'

'No.'

'There's a half-sovereign for you,' my companion said, standing up and taking his hat. 'I am afraid, Rance, that you will never rise in the force. That head of yours should be for use as well as ornament. You might have gained your sergeant's stripes last night. The man whom you held in your hands is the man who holds the clue of this mystery, and whom we are seeking. There is no use of arguing about it now; I tell you that it is so. Come along, Doctor.'

We started off for the cab together, leaving our informant incredulous, but obviously uncomfortable.

'The blundering fool!' Holmes said, bitterly, as we drove back to our lodgings. 'Just to think of his having such an incomparable bit of good luck, and not taking advantage of it.'

'I am rather in the dark still. It is true that the description of this man tallies with your idea of the second party in this mystery. But why should he come back to the house after leaving it? That is not the way of criminals.'

'The ring, man, the ring: that was what he came back for. If we have no other way of catching him, we can always bait our line with the ring. I shall have him, Doctor—I'll lay you two to one that I have him. I must thank you for it all. I might not have gone but for you, and so have missed the finest study I ever came across: a study in scarlet, eh? Why shouldn't we use a little art jargon?* There's the scarlet thread* of murder running through the colourless skein* of life, and our duty is to unravel it, and isolate it, and expose every inch of it. And now for lunch, and then for Norman-Neruda. Her attack and her bowing are splendid.* What's that little thing of Chopin's* she plays so magnificently: Tra-la-la-lira-lira-lay.'

Leaning back in the cab, this amateur bloodhound carolled away like a lark* while I meditated upon the many-sidedness of the human mind.

· CHAPTER 5 ·

Our Advertisement Brings a Visitor

OUR morning's exertions had been too much for my weak health, and I was tired out in the afternoon. After Holmes's departure for the concert, I lay down upon the sofa and endeavoured to get a couple of hours' sleep. It was a useless attempt. My mind had been too much excited by all that had occurred, and the strangest fancies and surmises crowded into it. Every time that I closed my eyes I saw before me the distorted, baboon-like countenance of the murdered man. So sinister was the impression which that face had produced upon me that I found it difficult to feel anything but gratitude for him who had removed its owner from the world. If ever human features bespoke vice of the most malignant type,* they were certainly those of Enoch J. Drebber, of Cleveland. Still, I recognized that justice must be done, and that the depravity of the victim was no condonement in the eyes of the law.*

The more I thought of it the more extraordinary did my companion's hypothesis, that the man had been poisoned, appear. I remembered how he had sniffed his lips, and had no doubt that he had detected something which had given rise to the idea. Then, again, if not poison, what had caused the man's death, since there was neither wound nor marks of strangulation? But, on the other hand, whose blood was that which lay so thickly upon the floor? There were no signs of a struggle, nor had the victim any weapon with which he might have wounded an antagonist. As long as all these questions were unsolved, I felt that sleep would be no easy matter, either for Holmes or myself. His quiet, self-confident manner convinced me that he had already formed a theory which explained all the facts, though what it was I could not for an instant conjecture.

He was very late in returning—so late that I knew that the concert could not have detained him all the time. Dinner was on the table before he appeared.

'It was magnificent,' he said, as he took his seat. 'Do you remember what Darwin says about music?* He claims that the power of producing and appreciating it existed among the human race long before the power of speech was arrived at. Perhaps that is why we are so subtly influenced by it. There are vague memories in our souls of those misty centuries when the world was in its childhood.'

'That's rather a broad idea,' I remarked.

'One's ideas must be as broad as Nature if they are to interpret Nature,' he answered. 'What's the matter? You're not looking quite yourself. This Brixton Road affair has upset you.'

'To tell the truth, it has,' I said. 'I ought to be more case-hardened* after my Afghan experiences. I saw my own comrades hacked to pieces at Maiwand without losing my nerve.'

'I can understand. There is a mystery about this which stimulates the imagination; where there is no imagination there is no horror. Have you seen the evening paper?'

'No.'

'It gives a fairly good account of the affair. It does not mention the fact that when the man was raised up a woman's wedding-ring fell upon the floor. It is just as well it does not.'

'Why?'

'Look at this advertisement,' he answered. 'I had one sent to every paper this morning immediately after the affair.'

He threw the paper across to me and I glanced at the place indicated. It was the first announcement in the 'Found' column. 'In Brixton Road, this morning,' it ran, 'a plain gold wedding-ring, found in the roadway between the White Hart Tavern and Holland Grove. Apply Dr Watson, 221B, Baker Street, between eight and nine this evening.'

'Excuse me using your name,' he said. 'If I used my own, some of these dunderheads would recognize it and want to meddle in the affair.'

'That is all right,' I answered. 'But supposing anyone applies, I have no ring.'

'Oh, yes, you have,' said he, handing me one. 'This will do very well. It is almost a facsimile.'

'And who do you expect will answer this advertisement?'

'Why, the man in the brown coat—our florid friend with the square toes. If he does not come himself, he will send an accomplice.'

'Would he not consider it as too dangerous?'

'Not at all. If my view of the case is correct, and I have every reason to believe that it is, this man would rather risk anything than lose the ring.* According to my notion he dropped it while stooping over Drebber's body, and did not miss it at the time. After leaving the house he discovered his loss and hurried back, but found the police already in possession, owing to his own folly in leaving the candle burning. He had to pretend to be drunk in order to allay the suspicions which might have been aroused by his appearance at the gate. Now put yourself in that man's place. On thinking the matter over, it must have occurred to him that it was possible that he had lost the ring in the road after leaving the house. What would he do then? He would eagerly look out for the evening papers in the hope of seeing it among the articles found. His eye, of course, would alight upon this. He would be overjoyed. Why should he fear a trap? There would be no reason in his eyes why the finding of the ring should be connected with the murder. He would come. He will come. You shall see him within an hour.'

'And then?' I asked.

'Oh, you can leave me to deal with him then. Have you any arms?'

'I have my old service revolver and a few cartridges.'

'You had better clean it and load it. He will be a desperate man; and though I shall take him unawares, it is as well to be ready for anything.'

I went to my bed-room and followed his advice. When I returned with the pistol, the table had been cleared, and

Holmes was engaged in his favourite occupation of scraping upon his violin.

'The plot thickens,' he said, as I entered; 'I have just had an answer to my American telegram. My view of the case is the correct one.'

'And that is?' I asked eagerly.

'My fiddle would be the better for new strings,' he remarked. 'Put your pistol in your pocket. When the fellow comes, speak to him in an ordinary way. Leave the rest to me. Don't frighten him by looking at him too hard.'

'It is eight o'clock now,' I said, glancing at my watch.

'Yes. He will probably be here in a few minutes. Open the door slightly. That will do. Now put the key on the inside. Thank you! This is a queer old book I picked up at a stall yesterday—*De Jure inter Gentes**—published in Latin at Liège in the Lowlands,* in 1642. Charles's head* was still firm on his shoulders when this little brown-backed volume was struck off.'*

'Who is the printer?'

'Philippe de Croy,* whoever he may have been. On the flyleaf, in very faded ink, is written "Ex libris Gulielmi Whyte." I wonder who William Whyte* was. Some pragmatical seventeenth-century lawyer, I suppose. His writing has a legal twist about it. Here comes our man, I think.'*

As he spoke there was a sharp ring at the bell. Sherlock Holmes rose softly and moved his chair in the direction of the door. We heard the servant* pass along the hall, and the sharp click of the latch as she opened it.

'Does Dr Watson live here?' asked a clear but rather harsh voice. We could not hear the servant's reply, but the door closed, and someone began to ascend the stairs. The footfall was an uncertain and shuffling one. A look of surprise passed over the face of my companion as he listened to it. It came slowly along the passage, and there was a feeble tap at the door.

'Come in,' I cried.

At my summons, instead of the man of violence whom we expected, a very old and wrinkled woman hobbled into the apartment. She appeared to be dazzled by the sudden blaze of light, and after dropping a curtsey, she stood blinking at us with her bleared eyes and fumbling in her pocket with nervous shaky fingers. I glanced at my companion, and his face had assumed such a disconsolate expression that it was all I could do to keep my countenance.

The old crone drew out an evening paper, and pointed at our advertisement. 'It's this as has brought me, good gentlemen,' she said, dropping another curtsey; 'a gold wedding-ring in the Brixton Road. It belongs to my girl Sally, as was married only this time twelve-month, which her husband is steward aboard a Union boat,* and what he'd say if he come 'ome and found her without her ring is more than I can think, he being short enough at the best o' times, but more especially when he has the drink.* If it please you, she went to the circus last night along with—'

'Is that her ring?' I asked.

'The Lord be thanked!' cried the old woman; 'Sally will be a glad woman this night. That's the ring.'

'And what may your address be?' I inquired, taking up a pencil.

'13, Duncan Street, Houndsditch.* A weary way from here.'

'The Brixton Road does not lie between any circus and Houndsditch,' said Sherlock Holmes sharply.

The old woman faced round and looked keenly at him from her little red-rimmed eyes. 'The gentleman asked me for *my* address,' she said. 'Sally lives in lodgings at 3, May-field Place, Peckham.'*

'And your name is—?'

'My name is Sawyer—hers is Dennis,* which Tom Dennis married her—and a smart, clean lad, too, as long as he's at sea, and no steward in the company more thought of; but when on shore, what with the women and what with liquor shops—'

'Here is your ring, Mrs Sawyer,' I interrupted, in obedience to a sign from my companion; 'it clearly belongs to your daughter, and I am glad to be able to restore it to the rightful owner.'

With many mumbled blessings and protestations of gratitude the old crone packed it away in her pocket, and shuffled off down the stairs. Sherlock Holmes sprang to his feet the moment that she was gone and rushed into his room. He returned in a few seconds enveloped in an ulster and a cravat.* 'I'll follow her,' he said, hurriedly; 'she must be an accomplice, and will lead me to him. Wait up for me.' The hall door had hardly slammed behind our visitor before Holmes had descended the stair. Looking through the window I could see her walking feebly along the other side, while her pursuer dogged her some little distance behind. 'Either his whole theory is incorrect,' I thought to myself, 'or else he will be led now to the heart of the mystery.' There was no need for him to ask me to wait up for him, for I felt that sleep was impossible until I heard the result of his adventure.

It was close upon nine when he set out. I had no idea how long he might be, but I sat stolidly puffing at my pipe and skipping over the pages of Henri Murger's *Vie de Bohème.** Ten o'clock passed, and I heard the footsteps of the maid as they pattered off to bed. Eleven, and the more stately tread of the landlady passed my door, bound for the same destination. It was close upon twelve before I heard the sharp sound of his latch-key. The instant he entered I saw by his face that he had not been successful. Amusement and chagrin seemed to be struggling for the mastery, until the former suddenly carried the day, and he burst into a hearty laugh.*

'I wouldn't have the Scotland Yarders know it for the world,' he cried, dropping into his chair; 'I have chaffed them so much that they would never have let me hear the end of it. I can afford to laugh, because I know that I will be even with them in the long run.'

'What is it then?' I asked.

'Oh, I don't mind telling a story against myself. That creature had gone a little way when she began to limp and show every sign of being footsore. Presently she came to a halt, and hailed a four-wheeler which was passing. I managed to be close to her so as to hear the address, but I need not have been so anxious, for she sang it out loud enough to be heard at the other side of the street: "Drive to 13, Duncan Street, Houndsditch," she cried. This begins to look genuine, I thought, and having seen her safely inside, I perched myself behind. That's an art which every detective should be an expert at.* Well, away we rattled, and never drew rein* until we reached the street in question. I hopped off before we came to the door, and strolled down the street in an easy lounging way. I saw the cab pull up. The driver jumped down, and I saw him open the door and stand expectantly. Nothing came out though. When I reached him, he was groping about frantically in the empty cab, and giving vent to the finest assorted collection of oaths that ever I listened to. There was no sign or trace of his passenger, and I fear it will be some time before he gets his fare. On inquiring at Number 13 we found that the house belonged to a respectable paperhanger,* named Keswick, and that no one of the name either of Sawyer or Dennis had ever been heard of there.'

'You don't mean to say,' I cried, in amazement, 'that that tottering, feeble old woman was able to get out of the cab while it was in motion, without either you or the driver seeing her?'

'Old woman be damned!'* said Sherlock Holmes, sharply. 'We were the old women to be so taken in. It must have been a young man, and an active one, too, besides being an incomparable actor.* The get-up was inimitable. He saw that he was followed, no doubt, and used this means of giving me the slip. It shows that the man we are after is not as lonely as I imagined he was, but has friends who are ready to risk something for him. Now, Doctor, you are looking done-up. Take my advice and turn in.'

I was certainly feeling very weary, so I obeyed his injunction. I left Holmes seated in front of the smouldering fire, and long into the watches of the night I heard the low, melancholy wailings of his violin, and knew that he was still pondering over the strange problem which he had set himself to unravel.

47

· CHAPTER 6 ·

Tobias Gregson Shows What He Can Do

THE papers next day were full of the 'Brixton Mystery', as they termed it. Each had a long account of the affair, and some had leaders* upon it in addition. There was some information in them which was new to me. I still retain in my scrap-book numerous clippings and extracts bearing upon the case. Here is a condensation of a few of them:—

The *Daily Telegraph** remarked that in the history of crime there had seldom been a tragedy which presented stranger features. The German name of the victim,* the absence of all other motive, and the sinister inscription on the wall, all pointed to its perpetration by political refugees and revolutionists.* The Socialists* had many branches in America, and the deceased had, no doubt, infringed their unwritten laws, and been tracked down by them. After alluding airily to the Vehmgericht,* aqua tofana,* Carbonari,* the Marchioness de Brinvilliers,* the Darwinian theory, the principles of Malthus,* and the Ratcliff Highway murders,* the article concluded by admonishing the Government and advocating a closer watch over foreigners in England.

The *Standard** commented upon the fact that lawless outrages of the sort usually occurred under a Liberal Administration.* They arose from the unsettling of the minds of the masses, and the consequent weakening of all authority. The deceased was an American gentleman who had been residing for some weeks in the Metropolis. He had stayed at the boarding-house of Madame Charpentier,* in Torquay Terrace, Camberwell.* He was accompanied in his travels by his private secretary, Mr Joseph Stangerson. The two bade adieu to their landlady upon Tuesday, the 4th inst.,* and departed to Euston Station with the avowed intention of catching the Liverpool express. They were afterwards seen together upon the platform. Nothing more is known of them until Mr Drebber's body was, as recorded, discovered in an empty house in the Brixton Road, many miles from Euston.* How he came there, or how he met his fate, are questions which are still involved in mystery. Nothing is known of the whereabouts of Stangerson. We are glad to learn that Mr Lestrade and Mr Gregson, of Scotland Yard, are both engaged upon the case, and it is confidently anticipated that these well-known officers will speedily throw light upon the matter.

The *Daily News** observed that there was no doubt as to the crime being a political one. The despotism and hatred of Liberalism which animated the Continental Governments* had had the effect of driving to our shores a number of men who might have made excellent citizens were they not soured by the recollection of all that they had undergone. Among these men there was a stringent code of honour, any infringement of which was punished by death. Every effort should be made to find the secretary, Stangerson, and to ascertain some particulars of the habits of the deceased. A great step had been gained by the discovery of the address of the house at which he had boarded—a result which was entirely due to the acuteness and energy of Mr Gregson of Scotland Yard.

Sherlock Holmes and I read these notices over together at breakfast, and they appeared to afford him considerable amusement.

'I told you that, whatever happened, Lestrade and Gregson would be sure to score.'

'That depends on how it turns out.'

'Oh, bless you, it doesn't matter in the least. If the man is caught, it will be *on account* of their exertions; if he escapes, it will be *in spite* of their exertions. It's heads I win and tails you lose. Whatever they do, they will have followers. "Un sot trouve toujours un plus sot qui l'admire." '*

'What on earth is that?' I cried, for at this moment there came the pattering of many steps in the hall and on the stairs, accompanied by audible expressions of disgust upon the part of our landlady.

'It's the Baker Street division of the detective police force,'* said my companion gravely; and as he spoke there rushed into the room half a dozen of the dirtiest and most ragged street Arabs* that ever I clapped eyes on.

' 'Tention!' cried Holmes, in a sharp tone, and the six dirty little scoundrels stood in a line like so many disreputable statuettes.* 'In future you shall send up Wiggins alone to report, and the rest of you must wait in the street. Have you found it, Wiggins?'

'No, sir, we hain't,' said one of the youths.

'I hardly expected you would. You must keep on until you do. Here are your wages.' He handed each of them a shilling. 'Now, off you go, and come back with a better report next time.'

He waved his hand, and they scampered away downstairs like so many rats, and we heard their shrill voices next moment in the street.

'There's more work to be got out of one of those little beggars than out of a dozen of the force,' Holmes remarked. 'The mere sight of an official-looking person seals men's lips. These youngsters, however, go everywhere, and hear everything. They are as sharp as needles, too; all they want is organization.'

'Is it on this Brixton case that you are employing them?' I asked.

'Yes; there is a point which I wish to ascertain. It is merely a matter of time. Hullo! we are going to hear some news now with a vengeance! Here is Gregson coming down the road with beatitude written upon every feature of his face. Bound for us, I know. Yes, he is stopping. There he is!'

There was a violent peal at the bell, and in a few seconds the fair-haired detective came up the stairs, three steps at a time, and burst into our sitting-room.

'My dear fellow,' he cried, wringing Holmes's unresponsive hand, 'congratulate me! I have made the whole thing as clear as day.'

A shade of anxiety seemed to me to cross my companion's expressive face.

'Do you mean that you are on the right track?' he asked.

'The right track! Why, sir, we have the man under lock and key.'

'And his name is?'

'Arthur Charpentier, sub-lieutenant in Her Majesty's Navy,' cried Gregson pompously, rubbing his fat hands* and inflating his chest.

Sherlock Holmes gave a sigh of relief and relaxed into a smile.

'Take a seat, and try one of these cigars,' he said. 'We are anxious to know how you managed it. Will you have some whiskey and water?'

'I don't mind if I do,'* the detective answered. 'The tremendous exertions which I have gone through during the last day or two have worn me out. Not so much bodily exertion, you understand, as the strain upon the mind. You will appreciate that, Mr Sherlock Holmes, for we are both brain-workers.'

'You do me too much honour,' said Holmes gravely. 'Let us hear how you arrived at this most gratifying result.'

The detective seated himself in the arm-chair, and puffed complacently at his cigar. Then suddenly he slapped his thigh in a paroxysm of amusement.

'The fun of it is,' he cried, 'that that fool Lestrade, who thinks himself so smart, has gone off upon the wrong track altogether. He is after the secretary Stangerson, who had no more to do with the crime than the babe unborn. I have no doubt that he has caught him by this time.'

The idea tickled Gregson so much that he laughed until he choked.

'And how did you get your clue?'

'Ah, I'll tell you all about it. Of course, Doctor Watson, this is strictly between ourselves. The first difficulty which we had to contend with was the finding of this American's antecedents. Some people would have waited until their advertisements were answered, or until parties came forward and volunteered information. That is not Tobias Gregson's way of going to work. You remember the hat beside the dead man?'

'Yes,' said Holmes; 'by John Underwood and Sons, 129, Camberwell Road.'

Gregson looked quite crestfallen.

'I had no idea that you noticed that,' he said. 'Have you been there?'

'No.'

'Ha!' cried Gregson, in a relieved voice; 'you should never neglect a chance, however small it may seem.'*

'To a great mind, nothing is little,'* remarked Holmes, sententiously.

'Well, I went to Underwood, and asked him if he had sold a hat of that size and description. He looked over his books, and came on it at once. He had sent the hat to a Mr Drebber, residing at Charpentier's Boarding Establishment, Torquay Terrace. Thus I got his address.'

'Smart—very smart!' murmured Sherlock Holmes.

'I next called upon Madame Charpentier,' continued the detective. 'I found her very pale and distressed. Her daughter was in the room, too—an uncommonly fine girl she is, too; she was looking red about the eyes and her lips trembled as I spoke to her. That didn't escape my notice. I began to smell a rat. You know that feeling, Mr Sherlock Holmes, when you come upon the right scent—a kind of thrill in your nerves. "Have you heard of the mysterious death of your late boarder Mr Enoch J. Drebber, of Cleveland?" I asked.

'The mother nodded. She didn't seem able to get out a word. The daughter burst into tears. I felt more than ever that these people knew something of the matter.

' "At what o'clock did Mr Drebber leave your house for the train?" I asked.

' "At eight o'clock," she said, gulping in her throat to keep down her agitation. "His secretary, Mr Stangerson, said that there were two trains—one at 9.15 and one at 11. He was to catch the first."

' "And was that the last which you saw of him?"

'A terrible change came over the woman's face as I asked the question. Her features turned perfectly livid. It was some seconds before she could get out the single word "Yes"—and when it did come it was in a husky, unnatural tone.

'There was a silence for a moment, and then the daughter spoke in a calm, clear voice.

' "No good can ever come of falsehood, mother," she said. "Let us be frank with this gentleman. We *did* see Mr Drebber again."

' "God forgive you!" cried Madame Charpentier, throwing up her hands, and sinking back in her chair. "You have murdered your brother."

' "Arthur* would rather that we spoke the truth," the girl answered firmly.

' "You had best tell me all about it now," I said. "Half-confidences are worse than none. Besides, you do not know how much we know of it."

' "On your head be it, Alice!" cried her mother; and then, turning to me: "I will tell you all, sir. Do not imagine that my agitation on behalf of my son arises from any fear lest he should have had a hand in this terrible affair. He is utterly innocent of it. My dread is, however, that in your eyes and in the eyes of others he may appear to be compromised. That, however, is surely impossible. His high character, his profession, his antecedents would all forbid it."

' "Your best way is to make a clean breast of the facts," I answered. "Depend upon it, if your son is innocent he will be none the worse."

' "Perhaps, Alice, you had better leave us together," she said, and her daughter withdrew. "Now, sir," she continued, "I had no intention of telling you all this, but since my poor daughter has disclosed it I have no alternative. Having once decided to speak, I will tell you all without omitting any particular."

' "It is your wisest course," said I.

' "Mr Drebber has been with us nearly three weeks. He and his secretary, Mr Stangerson, had been travelling on the

Continent. I noticed a 'Copenhagen' label upon each of their trunks, showing that that had been their last stopping place. Stangerson was a quiet, reserved man, but his employer, I am sorry to say, was far otherwise. He was coarse in his habits and brutish in his ways. The very night of his arrival he became very much the worse for drink, and, indeed, after twelve o'clock in the day he could hardly ever be said to be sober. His manners towards the maid-servants were disgustingly free and familiar. Worst of all, he speedily assumed the same attitude towards my daughter Alice, and spoke to her more than once in a way which, fortunately, she is too innocent to understand. On one occasion he actually seized her in his arms and embraced her—an outrage which caused his own secretary to reproach him for his unmanly conduct."

' "But why did you stand all this?" I asked. "I suppose that you can get rid of your boarders when you wish."

'Madame Charpentier blushed at my pertinent question. "Would to God that I had given him notice on the very day that he came," she said. "But it was a sore temptation. They were paying a pound a day* each—fourteen pounds a week, and this is the slack season. I am a widow, and my boy in the Navy has cost me much. I grudged to lose the money. I acted for the best. This last was too much, however, and I gave him notice to leave on account of it. That was the reason of his going."

' "Well?"

' "My heart grew light when I saw him drive away. My son is on leave just now, but I did not tell him anything of all this, for his temper is violent, and he is passionately fond of his sister. When I closed the door behind them a load seemed to be lifted from my mind. Alas, in less than an hour there was a ring at the bell, and I learned that Mr Drebber had returned. He was much excited, and evidently the worse for drink. He forced his way into the room, where I was sitting with my daughter, and made some incoherent remark about having missed the train. He then turned to Alice, and before my very face proposed to her that she should fly with

him. 'You are of age,' he said, 'and there is no law to stop
you. I have money enough and to spare. Never mind the old
girl here, but come along with me now straight away. You
shall live like a princess.' Poor Alice was so frightened that
she shrunk away from him, but he caught her by the wrist
and endeavoured to draw her towards the door. I screamed,
and at that moment my son Arthur came into the room.
What happened then I do not know. I heard oaths and the
confused sounds of a scuffle. I was too terrified to raise my
head. When I did look up I saw Arthur standing in the
doorway laughing, with a stick in his hand. 'I don't think
that fine fellow will trouble us again,' he said. 'I will just go
after him and see what he does with himself.' With those
words he took his hat and started off down the street. The
next morning we heard of Mr Drebber's mysterious death.'

'This statement came from Madame Charpentier's lips
with many gasps and pauses. At times she spoke so low that
I could hardly catch the words. I made shorthand notes of
all that she said, however, so that there should be no
possibility of a mistake.'

'It's quite exciting,' said Sherlock Holmes, with a yawn.
'What happened next?'

'When Madame Charpentier paused,' the detective continued, 'I saw that the whole case hung upon one point.
Fixing her with my eye in a way which I always found
effective with women, I asked her at what hour her son
returned.

' "I do not know," she answered.

' "Not know?"

' "No; he has a latch-key, and he let himself in."

' "After you went to bed?"

' "Yes."

' "When did you go to bed?"

' "About eleven."

' "So your son was gone at least two hours?"

' "Yes."

' "Possibly four or five?"

' "Yes."

' "What was he doing during that time?"'

' "I do not know," she answered, turning white to her very lips.

'Of course after that there was nothing more to be done. I found out where Lieutenant Charpentier was, took two officers with me, and arrested him. When I touched him on the shoulder and warned him to come quietly with us, he answered us as bold as brass: "I suppose you are arresting me for being concerned in the death of that scoundrel Drebber," he said. We had said nothing to him about it, so that his alluding to it had a most suspicious aspect.'

'Very,' said Holmes.

'He still carried the heavy stick which the mother described him as having with him when he followed Drebber. It was a stout oak cudgel.'

'What is your theory, then?'

'Well, my theory is that he followed Drebber as far as the Brixton Road. When there, a fresh altercation arose between them, in the course of which Drebber received a blow from the stick, in the pit of the stomach perhaps, which killed him without leaving any mark. The night was so wet that no one was about, so Charpentier dragged the body of his victim into the empty house. As to the candle, and the blood, and the writing on the wall, and the ring, they may all be so many tricks to throw the police on to the wrong scent.'

'Well done!' said Holmes in an encouraging voice. 'Really, Gregson, you are getting along. We shall make something of you yet.'

'I flatter myself that I have managed it rather neatly,' the detective answered proudly. 'The young man volunteered a statement, in which he said that after following Drebber some time, the latter perceived him, and took a cab in order to get away from him. On his way home he met an old shipmate, and took a long walk with him. On being asked where this old shipmate lived, he was unable to give any satisfactory reply. I think the whole case fits together uncommonly well. What amuses me is to think of Lestrade, who had started off upon the wrong scent. I am afraid he won't make much of it. Why, by Jove, here's the very man himself!'

It was indeed Lestrade, who had ascended the stairs while we were talking, and who now entered the room. The assurance and jauntiness which generally marked his demeanour and dress were, however, wanting. His face was disturbed and troubled, while his clothes were disarranged and untidy. He had evidently come with the intention of consulting with Sherlock Holmes, for on perceiving his colleague he appeared to be embarrassed and put out. He stood in the centre of the room, fumbling nervously with his hat and uncertain what to do. 'This is a most extraordinary case,' he said at last—'a most incomprehensible affair.'

'Ah, you find it so, Mr Lestrade!' cried Gregson, triumphantly. 'I thought you would come to that conclusion. Have you managed to find the secretary, Mr Joseph Stangerson?'

'The secretary, Mr Joseph Stangerson,' said Lestrade gravely, 'was murdered at Halliday's Private Hotel about six o'clock this morning.'

· CHAPTER 7 ·

Light in the Darkness

THE intelligence with which Lestrade greeted us was so momentous and so unexpected that we were all three fairly dumbfounded. Gregson sprang out of his chair and upset the remainder of his whiskey and water. I stared in silence at Sherlock Holmes, whose lips were compressed and his brows drawn down over his eyes.

'Stangerson too!' he muttered. 'The plot thickens.'

'It was quite thick enough before,' grumbled Lestrade, taking a chair. 'I seem to have dropped into a sort of council of war.'

'Are you—are you sure of this piece of intelligence?' stammered Gregson.

'I have just come from his room,' said Lestrade. 'I was the first to discover what had occurred.'

'We have been hearing Gregson's view of the matter,' Holmes observed. 'Would you mind letting us know what you have seen and done?'

'I have no objection,' Lestrade answered, seating himself. 'I freely confess that I was of the opinion that Stangerson was concerned in the death of Drebber. This fresh development has shown me that I was completely mistaken. Full of the one idea, I set myself to find out what had become of the secretary. They had been seen together at Euston Station about half-past eight on the evening of the third. At two in the morning Drebber had been found in the Brixton Road. The question which confronted me was to find out how Stangerson had been employed between 8.30 and the time of the crime, and what had become of him afterwards. I telegraphed to Liverpool, giving a description of the man, and warning them to keep a watch upon the American boats. I then set to work calling upon all the hotels and lodging-houses in the vicinity of Euston. You see, I argued that if Drebber and his companion had become separated, the natural course for the latter would be to put up somewhere in the vicinity for the night, and then to hang about the station again next morning.'

'They would be likely to agree on some meeting-place beforehand,' remarked Holmes.

'So it proved. I spent the whole of yesterday evening in making inquiries entirely without avail. This morning I began very early, and at eight o'clock I reached Halliday's Private Hotel, in Little George Street.* On my inquiry as to whether a Mr Stangerson was living there, they at once answered me in the affirmative.

' "No doubt you are the gentleman whom he was expecting," they said. "He has been waiting for a gentleman for two days."

' "Where is he now?" I asked.

58

' "He is upstairs in bed. He wished to be called at nine."
' "I will go up and see him at once," I said.

'It seemed to me that my sudden appearance might shake his nerves and lead him to say something unguarded. The Boots* volunteered to show me the room: it was on the second floor, and there was a small corridor leading up to it. The Boots pointed out the door to me, and was about to go downstairs again when I saw something that made me feel sickish, in spite of my twenty years' experience.* From under the door there curled a little red ribbon of blood, which had meandered across the passage and formed a little pool along the skirting at the other side. I gave a cry, which brought the Boots back. He nearly fainted when he saw it. The door was locked on the inside, but we put our shoulders to it, and knocked it in. The window of the room was open, and beside the window all huddled up, lay the body of a man in his nightdress. He was quite dead, and had been for some time, for his limbs were rigid and cold. When we turned him over, the Boots recognized him at once as being the same gentleman who had engaged the room under the name of Joseph Stangerson. The cause of death was a deep stab in the left side, which must have penetrated the heart. And now comes the strangest part of the affair. What do you suppose was above the murdered man?'

I felt a creeping of the flesh, and a presentiment of coming horror, even before Sherlock Holmes answered.

'The word RACHE, written in letters of blood,' he said.

'That was it,' said Lestrade, in an awe-struck voice; and we were all silent for a while.

There was something so methodical and so incomprehensible about the deeds of this unknown assassin, that it imparted a fresh ghastliness to his crimes. My nerves, which were steady enough on the field of battle, tingled as I thought of it.

'The man was seen,' continued Lestrade. 'A milk boy, passing on his way to the dairy, happened to walk down the lane which leads from the mews* at the back of the hotel. He noticed that a ladder, which usually lay there, was raised against one of the windows of the second floor, which was wide open. After passing, he looked back and saw a man descend the ladder. He came down so quietly and openly that the boy imagined him to be some carpenter or joiner at work in the hotel. He took no particular notice of him, beyond thinking in his own mind that it was early for him to be at work. He has an impression that the man was tall, had a reddish face, and was dressed in a long, brownish coat. He must have stayed in the room some little time after the murder, for we found blood-stained water in the basin, where he had washed his hands, and marks on the sheets where he had deliberately wiped his knife.'

I glanced at Holmes on hearing the description of the murderer which tallied so exactly with his own. There was, however, no trace of exultation or satisfaction upon his face.

'Did you find nothing in the room which could furnish a clue to the murderer?' he asked.

'Nothing. Stangerson had Drebber's purse in his pocket, but it seems that this was usual, as he did all the paying. There was eighty-odd pounds in it, but nothing had been taken. Whatever the motives of these extraordinary crimes, robbery is certainly not one of them. There were no papers or memoranda in the murdered man's pocket, except a single telegram, dated from Cleveland about a month ago, and containing the words, "J. H. is in Europe." There was no name appended to this message.'

'And there was nothing else?' Holmes asked.

'Nothing of any importance. The man's novel, with which he had read himself to sleep, was lying upon the bed, and his pipe was on a chair beside him. There was a glass of water on the table, and on the window-sill a small chip ointment box* containing a couple of pills.'

Sherlock Holmes sprang from his chair with an exclamation of delight.

'The last link,' he cried, exultantly. 'My case is complete.'

The two detectives stared at him in amazement.

'I have now in my hands,' my companion said, confidently, 'all the threads which have formed such a tangle.

There are, of course, details to be filled in, but I am as certain of all the main facts, from the time that Drebber parted from Stangerson at the station, up to the discovery of the body of the latter, as if I had seen them with my own eyes. I will give you a proof of my knowledge. Could you lay your hand upon those pills?'

'I have them,' said Lestrade, producing a small white box; 'I took them and the purse and the telegram, intending to have them put in a place of safety at the Police Station. It was the merest chance my taking these pills, for I am bound to say I do not attach any importance to them.'

'Give them here,' said Holmes. 'Now, Doctor,' turning to me, 'are those ordinary pills?'

They certainly were not. They were of a pearly grey colour, small, round, and almost transparent against the light. 'From their lightness and transparency, I should imagine that they are soluble in water,' I remarked.

'Precisely so,' answered Holmes. 'Now would you mind going down and fetching that poor little devil of a terrier which has been bad so long, and which the landlady wanted you to put out of its pain yesterday.'

I went downstairs and carried the dog upstairs in my arms. Its laboured breathing and glazing eye showed that it was not far from its end.* Indeed, its snow-white muzzle proclaimed that it had already exceeded the usual term of canine existence. I placed it upon a cushion on the rug.

'I will now cut one of these pills in two,' said Holmes, and drawing his penknife he suited the action to the word. 'One half we return into the box for future purposes. The other half I will place in this wine-glass, in which is a teaspoonful of water. You perceive that our friend, the Doctor,* is right, and that it readily dissolves.'

'This may be very interesting,' said Lestrade, in the injured tone of one who suspects that he is being laughed at; 'I cannot see, however, what it has to do with the death of Mr Joseph Stangerson.'

'Patience, my friend, patience! You will find in time that it has everything to do with it. I shall now add a little milk to make the mixture palatable, and on presenting it to the dog we find that he laps it up readily enough.'

As he spoke he turned the contents of the wine-glass into a saucer and placed it in front of the terrier, who speedily licked it dry. Sherlock Holmes's earnest demeanour had so far convinced us that we all sat in silence, watching the animal intently, and expecting some startling effect. None such appeared, however. The dog continued to lie stretched upon the cushion, breathing in a laboured way but apparently neither the better nor the worse for its draught.

Holmes had taken out his watch, and as minute followed minute without result, an expression of the utmost chagrin and disappointment appeared upon his features. He gnawed his lip, drummed his fingers upon the table, and showed every other symptom of acute impatience. So great was his emotion that I felt sincerely sorry for him, while the two detectives smiled derisively, by no means displeased at this check which he had met.

'It can't be a coincidence,' he cried, at last springing from his chair and pacing wildly up and down the room; 'it is impossible that it should be a mere coincidence. The very pills which I suspected in the case of Drebber are actually found after the death of Stangerson. And yet they are inert. What can it mean? Surely my whole chain of reasoning cannot have been false. It is impossible! And yet this wretched dog is none the worse. Ah, I have it! I have it!' With a perfect shriek of delight he rushed to the box, cut the other pill in two, dissolved it, added milk, and presented it to the terrier. The unfortunate creature's tongue seemed hardly to have been moistened in it before it gave a convulsive shiver in every limb, and lay as rigid and lifeless as if it had been struck by lightning.

Sherlock Holmes drew a long breath, and wiped the perspiration from his forehead. 'I should have more faith,' he said; 'I ought to know by this time that when a fact appears to be opposed to a long train of deductions, it invariably proves to be capable of bearing some other interpretation.* Of the two pills in the box, one was of the most deadly poison, and the other was entirely harmless. I ought to have known that before ever I saw the box at all.'

This last statement appeared to me to be so startling that I could hardly believe that he was in his sober senses. There was the dead dog, however, to prove that his conjecture had been correct. It seemed to me that the mists in my own mind were gradually clearing away, and I began to have a dim, vague perception of the truth.

'All this seems strange to you,' continued Holmes, 'because you failed at the beginning of the inquiry to grasp the importance of the single real clue which was presented to you. I had the good fortune to seize upon that, and everything which has occurred since then has served to confirm my original supposition, and, indeed, was the logical sequence of it. Hence things which have perplexed you and made the case more obscure have served to enlighten me and to strengthen my conclusions. It is a mistake to confound strangeness with mystery. The most commonplace crime is often the most mysterious, because it presents no new or special features from which deductions may be drawn. This murder would have been infinitely more difficult to unravel had the body of the victim been simply found lying in the roadway without any of those *outré*** and sensational accompaniments which have rendered it remarkable. These strange details, far from making the case more difficult, have really had the effect of making it less so.'

Mr Gregson, who had listened to this address with considerable impatience, could contain himself no longer. 'Look here, Mr Sherlock Holmes,' he said, 'we are all ready to acknowledge that you are a smart man, and that you have your own methods of working. We want something more than mere theory and preaching now, though. It is a case of taking the man.* I have made my case out, and it seems I was wrong. Young Charpentier could not have been engaged in this second affair. Lestrade went after his man, Stangerson, and it appears that he was wrong too. You have thrown out hints here, and hints there, and seem to know more than we do, but the time has come when we feel that we have a right to ask you straight how much you do know of the business. Can you name the man who did it?'

'I cannot help feeling that Gregson is right, sir,' remarked Lestrade. 'We have both tried, and we have both failed. You have remarked more than once since I have been in the room that you had all the evidence which you require. Surely you will not withhold it any longer.'

'Any delay in arresting the assassin,' I observed, 'might give him time to perpetrate some fresh atrocity.'

Thus pressed by us all, Holmes showed signs of irresolution. He continued to walk up and down the room with his head sunk on his chest and his brows drawn down, as was his habit when lost in thought.

'There will be no more murders,' he said at last, stopping abruptly and facing us. 'You can put that consideration out of the question. You have asked me if I know the name of the assassin. I do. The mere knowing of his name is a small thing, however, compared with the power of laying our hands upon him. This I expect very shortly to do. I have good hopes of managing it through my own arrangements; but it is a thing which needs delicate handling, for we have a shrewd and desperate man to deal with, who is supported, as I have had occasion to prove, by another who is as clever as himself. As long as this man has no idea that anyone can have a clue there is some chance of securing him; but if he had the slightest suspicion, he would change his name, and vanish in an instant among the four million inhabitants* of this great city.* Without meaning to hurt either of your feelings, I am bound to say that I consider these men to be more than a match for the official force, and that is why I have not asked your assistance. If I fail, I shall, of course, incur all the blame due to this omission; but that I am prepared for. At present I am ready to promise that the instant that I can communicate with you without endangering my own combinations, I shall do so.'

Gregson and Lestrade seemed to be far from satisfied by this assurance, or by the depreciating allusion to the detective police. The former had flushed up to the roots of his flaxen hair, while the other's beady eyes glistened with curiosity and resentment. Neither of them had time to speak, however, before there was a tap at the door, and the spokesman of the street Arabs, young Wiggins, introduced his insignificant and unsavoury person.

'Please, sir,' he said, touching his forelock, 'I have the cab downstairs.'

'Good boy,' said Holmes, blandly. 'Why don't you introduce this pattern at Scotland Yard?' he continued, taking a pair of steel handcuffs from a drawer. 'See how beautifully the spring works. They fasten in an instant.'*

'The old pattern is good enough,' remarked Lestrade, 'if we can only find the man to put them on.'

'Very good, very good,' said Holmes, smiling. 'The cabman may as well help me with my boxes. Just ask him to step up, Wiggins.'

I was surprised to find my companion speaking as though he were about to set out on a journey, since he had not said anything to me about it. There was a small portmanteau in the room, and this he pulled out and began to strap. He was busily engaged at it when the cabman entered the room.

'Just give me a help with this buckle, cabman,' he said, kneeling over his task, and never turning his head.

The fellow came forward with a somewhat sullen, defiant air and put down his hands to assist. At that instant there was a sharp click, the jangling of metal, and Sherlock Holmes sprang to his feet again.

'Gentlemen,' he cried, with flashing eyes, 'let me introduce you to Mr Jefferson Hope, the murderer of Enoch Drebber and of Joseph Stangerson.'

The whole thing occurred in a moment—so quickly that I had no time to realize it. I have a vivid recollection of that instant, of Holmes's triumphant expression and the ring of his voice, of the cabman's dazed, savage face, as he glared at the glittering handcuffs, which had appeared as if by magic upon his wrists. For a second or two we might have been a group of statues. Then with an inarticulate roar of fury, the prisoner wrenched himself free from Holmes's grasp, and hurled himself through the window. Woodwork and glass gave way before him; but before he got quite through, Gregson, Lestrade, and Holmes sprang upon him like so many staghounds. He was dragged back into the room, and then commenced a terrific conflict. So powerful and so fierce was he that the four of us were shaken off again and again. He appeared to have the convulsive strength of a man in an epileptic fit.* His face and hands were terribly mangled by his passage through the glass, but loss of blood had no effect in diminishing his resistance. It was not until Lestrade succeeded in getting his hand inside his neckcloth and half-strangling him that we made him realize that his struggles were of no avail; and even then we felt no security until we had pinioned his feet as well as his hands. That done, we rose to our feet breathless and panting.

'We have his cab,' said Sherlock Holmes. 'It will serve to take him to Scotland Yard. And now, gentlemen,' he continued, with a pleasant smile, 'we have reached the end of our little mystery. You are very welcome to put any questions that you like to me now, and there is no danger that I will refuse to answer them.'

PART 2

The Country of the Saints *

· CHAPTER 1 ·

On the Great Alkali Plain

IN the central portion of the great North American
Continent there lies an arid and repulsive desert,* which
for many a long year served as a barrier against the advance
of civilization. From the Sierra Nevada to Nebraska, and
from the Yellow-stone River in the north to the Colorado
upon the south, is a region of desolation and silence. Nor is
Nature always in one mood throughout this grim district. It
comprises snow-capped and lofty mountains, and dark and
gloomy valleys. There are swift-flowing rivers which dash
through jagged cañons; and there are enormous plains, which
in winter are white with snow, and in summer are grey with
the saline* alkali dust. They all preserve, however, the common characteristics of barrenness, inhospitality, and misery.

There are no inhabitants of this land of despair. A band
of Pawnees or of Blackfeet may occasionally traverse it in
order to reach other hunting-grounds, but the hardiest of
the braves are glad to lose sight of those awesome plains,
and to find themselves once more upon their prairies. The
coyote skulks among the scrub, the buzzard flaps heavily
through the air, and the clumsy grizzly bear lumbers
through the dark ravines, and picks up such sustenance as it
can amongst the rocks. These are the sole dwellers in the
wilderness.

In the whole world there can be no more dreary view
than that from the northern slope of the Sierra Blanco.* As
far as the eye can reach stretches the great flat plain-land,
all dusted over with patches of alkali, and intersected by
clumps of the dwarfish chapparal bushes. On the extreme
verge of the horizon lies a long chain of mountain peaks,
with their rugged summits flecked with snow. In this great
stretch of country there is no sign of life, nor of anything

appertaining to life. There is no bird in the steel-blue heaven, no movement upon the dull, grey earth—above all, there is absolute silence. Listen as one may, there is no shadow of a sound in all that mighty wilderness; nothing but silence—complete and heart-subduing silence.

It has been said there is nothing appertaining to life upon the broad plain. That is hardly true. Looking down from the Sierra Blanco, one sees a pathway traced out across the desert, which winds away and is lost in the extreme distance. It is rutted with wheels and trodden down by the feet of many adventurers. Here and there are scattered white objects which glisten in the sun, and stand out against the dull deposit of alkali. Approach, and examine them! They are bones: some large and coarse, others smaller and more delicate. The former have belonged to oxen, and the latter to men. For fifteen hundred miles one may trace this ghastly caravan route by these scattered remains of those who had fallen by the wayside.

Looking down on this very scene, there stood upon the fourth of May, eighteen hundred and forty-seven,* a solitary traveller. His appearance was such that he might have been the very genius or demon of the region. An observer would have found it difficult to say whether he was nearer to forty or to sixty.* His face was lean and haggard, and the brown parchment-like skin was drawn tightly over the projecting bones; his long, brown hair and beard were all flecked and dashed with white; his eyes were sunken in his head, and burned with an unnatural lustre; while the hand which grasped his rifle was hardly more fleshy than that of a skeleton. As he stood, he leaned upon his weapon for support, and yet his tall figure and the massive framework of his bones suggested a wiry and vigorous constitution. His gaunt face, however, and his clothes, which hung so baggily over his shrivelled limbs, proclaimed what it was that gave him that senile and decrepit appearance. The man was dying—dying from hunger and from thirst.

He had toiled painfully down the ravine, and on to this little elevation, in the vain hope of seeing some signs of water. Now the great salt plain stretched before his eyes, and the distant belt of savage mountains, without a sign anywhere of plant or tree, which might indicate the presence of moisture. In all that broad landscape there was no gleam of hope. North, and east, and west he looked with wild, questioning eyes, and then he realized that his wanderings had come to an end, and that there, on that barren crag, he was about to die. 'Why not here, as well as in a feather bed, twenty years hence,' he muttered, as he seated himself in the shelter of a boulder.

Before sitting down, he had deposited upon the ground his useless rifle, and also a large bundle tied up in a grey shawl, which he had carried slung over his right shoulder. It appeared to be somewhat too heavy for his strength, for in lowering it, it came down on the ground with some little violence. Instantly there broke from the grey parcel a little moaning cry, and from it there protruded a small, scared face, with very bright brown eyes, and two little speckled dimpled fists.

'You've hurt me!'* said a childish voice, reproachfully.

'Have I though, the man answered penitently; 'I didn't go for to do it.' As he spoke he unwrapped the grey shawl and extricated a pretty little girl of about five years of age, whose dainty shoes and smart pink frock with its little linen apron all bespoke a mother's care. The child was pale and wan, but her healthy arms and legs showed that she had suffered less than her companion.

'How is it now?' he answered anxiously, for she was still rubbing the towsy golden curls which covered the back of her head.

'Kiss it and make it well,' she said, with perfect gravity, showing the injured part to him. 'That's what mother used to do. Where's mother?'

'Mother's gone. I guess you'll see her before long.'

'Gone, eh!' said the little girl. 'Funny, she didn't say goodbye; she 'most always did if she was just goin' over to auntie's for tea, and now she's been away three days. Say, it's awful dry, ain't it? Ain't there no water nor nothing to eat?'

71

'No, there ain't nothing, dearie. You'll just need to be patient awhile, and then you'll be all right. Put your head up agin' me like that, and then you'll feel bullier.* It ain't easy to talk when your lips is like leather, but I guess I'd best let you know how the cards lie. What's that you've got?'

'Pretty things! fine things!' cried the little girl enthusiastic-ally, holding up two glittering fragments of mica.* 'When we goes back to home I'll give them to brother Bob.'*

'You'll see prettier things than them soon,' said the man confidently. 'You just wait a bit. I was going to tell you though—you remember when we left the river?'

'Oh, yes.'

'Well, we reckoned we'd strike another river soon, d'ye see. But there was somethin' wrong; compasses, or map, or somethin', and it didn't turn up. Water ran out. Just except a little drop for the likes of you and—and—'

'And you couldn't wash yourself,' interrupted his compan-ion gravely, staring up at his grimy visage.

'No, nor drink. And Mr Bender,* he was the fust to go, and then Indian Pete,* and then Mrs McGregor, and then Johnny Hones, and then dearie, your mother.'

'Then mother's a deader too,' cried the little girl, drop-ping her face in her pinafore and sobbing bitterly.

'Yes, they all went except you and me. Then I thought there was some chance of water in this direction, so I heaved you over my shoulder and we tramped it together. It don't seem as though we've improved matters. There's an al-mighty small chance for us now!'

'Do you mean that we are going to die too?' asked the child, checking her sobs, and raising her tear-stained face.

'I guess that's about the size of it.'

'Why didn't you say so before?' she said, laughing glee-fully. 'You gave me such a fright. Why, of course, now as long as we die we'll be with mother again.'

'Yes, you will, dearie.'

'And you too. I'll tell her how awful good you've been. I'll bet she meets us at the door of heaven with a big pitcher of water, and a lot of buckwheat cakes, hot, and toasted on both sides, like Bob and me was fond of. How long will it be first?'

'I don't know—not very long.' The man's eyes were fixed upon the northern horizon. In the blue vault of the heaven there had appeared three little specks which increased in size every moment, so rapidly did they approach. They speedily resolved themselves into three large birds, which circled over the heads of the two wanderers, and then settled upon some rocks which overlooked them. They were buzzards, the vultures of the west, whose coming is the forerunner of death.

'Cocks and hens,' cried the little girl gleefully, pointing at their ill-omened forms, and clapping her hands to make them rise. 'Say, did God make this country?'

'In* course He did,' said her companion, rather startled by this unexpected question.

'He made the country down in Illinois, and He made the Missouri,'* the little girl continued. 'I guess somebody else made the country in these parts. It's not nearly so well done. They forgot the water and the trees.'

'What would ye think of offering up prayer?' the man asked diffidently.

'It ain't night yet,' she answered.

'It don't matter. It ain't quite regular, but He won't mind that, you bet. You say over them ones that you used to say every night in the waggon* when we was on the Plains.'

'Why don't you say some yourself?' the child asked, with wondering eyes.

'I disremember them,'* he answered. 'I hain't said none since I was half the height o'that gun. I guess it's never too late. You say them out, and I'll stand by and come in on the choruses.'

'Then you'll need to kneel down, and me too,' she said, laying the shawl out for that purpose. 'You've got to put your hands up like this. It makes you feel kind of good.'

It was a strange sight, had there been anything but the buzzards to see it. Side by side on the narrow shawl knelt the two wanderers, the little prattling child and the reckless, hardened adventurer. Her chubby face and his haggard, angular visage were both turned up to the cloudless heaven in heartfelt entreaty to that dread Being with whom they were face to face, while the two voices—the one thin and clear, the other deep and harsh—united in the entreaty for mercy and forgiveness. The prayer finished, they resumed their seat in the shadow of the boulder until the child fell asleep, nestling upon the broad breast of her protector. He watched over her slumber for some time, but Nature proved to be too strong for him. For three days and three nights he had allowed himself neither rest nor repose. Slowly the eyelids drooped over the tired eyes, and the head sunk lower and lower upon the breast, until the man's grizzled beard was mixed with the gold tresses of his companion, and both slept the same deep and dreamless slumber.

Had the wanderer remained awake for another half-hour a strange sight would have met his eyes. Far away on the extreme verge of the alkali plain there rose up a little spray of dust, very slight at first, and hardly to be distinguished from the mists of the distance, but gradually growing higher and broader until it formed a solid, well-defined cloud. This cloud continued to increase in size until it became evident that it could only be raised by a great multitude of moving creatures. In more fertile spots the observer would have come to the conclusion that one of those great herds of bisons which graze upon the prairie land was approaching him. This was obviously impossible in these arid wilds. As the whirl of dust drew nearer to the solitary bluff upon which the two castaways were reposing, the canvas-covered tilts of waggons and the figures of armed horsemen began to show up through the haze, and the apparition revealed itself as being a great caravan upon its journey for the West. But what a caravan! When the head of it had reached the base of the mountains, the rear was not yet visible on the horizon. Right across the enormous plain stretched the straggling array, waggons and carts, men on horseback, and men on foot. Innumerable women who staggered along under burdens, and children who toddled beside the waggons or peeped out from under the white coverings. This was evidently no ordinary party of immigrants, but rather some nomad people who had been compelled from stress of circumstances to seek themselves a new country. There rose through the clear air a confused clattering and rumbling from this great mass of humanity, with the creaking of wheels and the neighing of horses. Loud as it was, it was not sufficient to rouse the two tired wayfarers above them.

At the head of the column there rode a score or more of grave, iron-faced men, clad in sombre homespun garments and armed with rifles. On reaching the base of the bluff they halted, and held a short council among themselves.

'The wells are to the right, my brothers,' said one, a hard-lipped, clean-shaven man with grizzly hair.

'To the right of the Sierra Blanco—so we shall reach the Rio Grande,'* said another.

'Fear not for water,' cried a third. 'He who could draw it from the rocks* will not now abandon His chosen people.'

'Amen! amen!' responded the whole party.

They were about to resume their journey when one of the youngest and keenest-eyed uttered an exclamation and pointed up at the rugged crag above them. From its summit there fluttered a little wisp of pink, showing up hard and bright against the grey rocks behind. At the sight there was a general reining up of horses and unslinging of guns, while fresh horsemen came galloping up to reinforce the vanguard. The word 'Redskins' was on every lip.

'There can't be any number of Injuns* here,' said the elderly man who appeared to be in command. 'We have passed the Pawnees, and there are no other tribes until we cross the great mountains.'

'Shall I go forward and see, Brother Stangerson,' asked one of the band.

'And I,' 'And I,' cried a dozen voices.

'Leave your horses below and we will await you here,' the Elder answered. In a moment the young fellows had dismounted, fastened their horses, and were ascending the precipitous slope which led up to the object which had excited their curiosity. They advanced rapidly and noiselessly, with the confidence and dexterity of practised scouts. The watchers from the plain below could see them flit from rock to rock until their figures stood out against the skyline. The young man who had first given the alarm was leading them. Suddenly his followers saw him throw up his hands, as though overcome with astonishment, and on joining him they were affected in the same way by the sight which met their eyes.

On the little plateau which crowned the barren hill there stood a single giant boulder, and against this boulder there lay a tall man, long-bearded and hard-featured, but of an excessive thinness. His placid face and regular breathing showed that he was fast asleep. Beside him lay a little child, with her round white arms encircling his brown sinewy neck, and her golden-haired head resting upon the breast of his velveteen tunic. Her rosy lips were parted, showing the regular line of snow-white teeth within, and a playful smile played over her infantile features. Her plump little white legs, terminating in white socks and neat shoes with shining buckles, offered a strange contrast to the long shrivelled members of her companion. On the ledge of rock above this strange couple there stood three solemn buzzards, who, at the sight of the new comers, uttered raucous screams of disappointment and flapped sullenly away.

The cries of the foul birds awoke the two sleepers, who stared about them in bewilderment. The man staggered to his feet and looked down upon the plain which had been so desolate when sleep had overtaken him, and which was now traversed by this enormous body of men and of beasts. His face assumed an expression of incredulity as he gazed, and he passed his bony hand over his eyes. 'This is what they call delirium, I guess,' he muttered. The child stood beside him, holding on to the skirt of his coat, and said nothing, but looked all around her with the wondering, questioning gaze of childhood.

The rescuing party were speedily able to convince the two castaways that their appearance was no delusion. One of them seized the little girl and hoisted her upon his shoulder, while two others supported her gaunt companion, and assisted him towards the wagons.

'My name is John Ferrier,'* the wanderer explained; 'me and that little un are all that's left o' twenty-one people. The rest is all dead o' thirst and hunger away down in the south.'

'Is she your child?' asked someone.

'I guess she is now,' the other cried, defiantly; 'she's mine 'cause I saved her. No man will take her from me. She's Lucy Ferrier* from this day on. Who are you though?' he continued, glancing with curiosity at his stalwart, sunburned rescuers; 'there seems to be a powerful lot of ye.'

'Nigh upon ten thousand,'* said one of the young men; 'we are the persecuted children of God—the chosen of the Angel Merona.'*

'I never heard tell on him,' said the wanderer. 'He appears to have chosen a fair crowd of ye.'

'Do not jest at that which is sacred,' said the other sternly. 'We are of those who believe in those sacred writings, drawn in Egyptian letters on plates of beaten gold, which were handed unto the holy Joseph Smith at Palmyra.* We have come from Nauvoo,* in the State of Illinois, where we had founded our temple. We have come to seek a refuge from the violent man and from the godless, even though it be the heart of the desert.'

The name of Nauvoo evidently recalled recollections to John Ferrier. 'I see,' he said, 'you are the Mormons.'*

'We are the Mormons,' answered his companions with one voice.

'And where are you going?'

'We do not know. The hand of God is leading us under the person of our Prophet.* You must come before him. He shall say what is to be done with you.'

They had reached the base of the hill by this time, and were surrounded by crowds of the pilgrims—pale-faced, meek-looking women; strong, laughing children; and anxious earnest-eyed men. Many were the cries of astonishment and of commiseration which arose from them when they perceived the youth of one of the strangers and the destitution of the other. Their escort did not halt, however, but pushed on, followed by a great crowd of Mormons, until they reached a waggon, which was conspicuous for its great size and for the gaudiness and smartness of its appearance. Six horses were yoked to it, whereas the others were furnished with two, or, at most, four a-piece. Beside the driver there sat a man who could not have been more than thirty years of age,* but whose massive head and resolute expression marked him as leader. He was reading a brown-backed volume, but as the crowd approached he laid it aside, and listened attentively to an account of the episode. Then he turned to the two castaways.

'If we take you with us,' he said, in solemn words, 'it can only be as believers in our own creed. We shall have no wolves in our fold. Better far that your bones should bleach in this wilderness than that you should prove to be that little speck of decay which in time corrupts the whole fruit. Will you come with us on these terms?'

'Guess I'll come with you on any terms,'* said Ferrier, with such emphasis that the grave Elders could not restrain a smile. The leader alone retained his stern, impressive expression.

'Take him, Brother Stangerson,' he said, 'give him food and drink, and the child likewise. Let it be your task also to teach him our holy creed. We have delayed long enough! Forward! On, on to Zion!'*

'On, on to Zion!' cried the crowd of Mormons, and the words rippled down the long caravan, passing from mouth to mouth until they died away in a dull murmur in the far distance. With a cracking of whips and a creaking of wheels the great waggons got into motion and soon the whole caravan was winding along once more. The Elder to whose care the two waifs had been committed led them to his waggon, where a meal was already awaiting them.

'You shall remain here,' he said. 'In a few days you will have recovered from your fatigues. In the meantime, remember that now and for ever you are of our religion. Brigham Young has said it, and he has spoken with the voice of Joseph Smith, which is the voice of God.'

· CHAPTER 2 ·

The Flower of Utah

THIS is not the place to commemorate the trials and privations endured by the immigrant Mormons before they came to their final haven. From the shores of the Mississippi to the western slopes of the Rocky Mountains* they had struggled on with a constancy almost unparalleled in history. The savage man, and the savage beast, hunger, thirst, fatigue, and disease—every impediment which Nature could place in the way—had all been overcome with Anglo-Saxon tenacity.* Yet the long journey and the accumulated terrors had shaken the hearts of the stoutest among them. There was not one who did not sink upon his knees in heartfelt prayer when they saw the broad valley of Utah* bathed in the sunlight beneath them, and learned from the lips of their leader that this was the promised land, and that these virgin acres* were to be theirs for evermore.

Young speedily proved himself to be a skilful administrator as well as a resolute chief. Maps were drawn and charts prepared, in which the future city was sketched out. All around farms were apportioned and allotted in proportion to the standing of each individual. The tradesman was put to his trade and the artisan to his calling. In the town streets and squares sprang up as if by magic. In the country there was draining and hedging, planting and clearing, until the next summer saw the whole country golden with the wheat crop. Everything prospered in the strange settlement. Above all, the great temple which they had erected in the centre of the city grew ever taller and larger. From the first blush of dawn until the closing of the twilight, the clatter of the hammer and the rasp of the saw were never absent from the monument which the immigrants erected to Him who had led them safe through many dangers.

79

The two castaways, John Ferrier and the little girl, who had shared his fortunes and had been adopted as his daughter, accompanied the Mormons to the end of their great pilgrimage. Little Lucy Ferrier was borne along pleasantly enough in Elder Stangerson's waggon, a retreat which she shared with the Mormon's three wives and with his son, a headstrong, forward boy of twelve. Having rallied, with the elasticity of childhood, from the shock caused by her mother's death, she soon became a pet with the women, and reconciled herself to this new life in her moving canvas-covered home. In the meantime Ferrier having recovered from his privations, distinguished himself as a useful guide and an indefatigable hunter. So rapidly did he gain the esteem of his new companions, that when they reached the end of their wanderings, it was unanimously agreed that he should be provided with as large and as fertile a tract of land* as any of the settlers, with the exception of Young himself, and of Stangerson, Kemball, Johnston, and Drebber,* who were the four principal Elders.

On the farm thus acquired John Ferrier built himself a substantial log-house, which received so many additions in succeeding years that it grew into a roomy villa. He was a man of a practical turn of mind, keen in his dealings and skilful with his hands. His iron constitution enabled him to work morning and evening at improving and tilling his lands. Hence it came about that his farm and all that belonged to him prospered exceedingly. In three years he was better off than his neighbours, in six he was well-to-do, in nine he was rich, and in twelve there were not half a dozen men in the whole of Salt Lake City* who could compare with him. From the great inland sea* to the distant Wahsatch Mountains* there was no name better known than that of John Ferrier.

There was one way and only one in which he offended the susceptibilities of his co-religionists. No argument or persuasion could ever induce him to set up a female establishment after the manner of his companions. He never gave reasons for this persistent refusal, but contented himself by resolutely and inflexibly adhering to his determination. There were some who accused him of lukewarmness in his adopted religion, and others who put it down to greed of wealth and reluctance to incur expense. Others again spoke of some early love affair, and of a fair-haired girl who had pined away on the shores of the Atlantic. Whatever the reason, Ferrier remained strictly celibate.* In every other respect he conformed to the religion of the young settlement, and gained the name of being an orthodox and straight-walking man.

Lucy Ferrier grew up within the log-house, and assisted her adopted father in all his undertakings. The keen air of the mountains and the balsamic odour of the pine trees took the place of nurse and mother to the young girl. As year succeeded to year she grew taller and stronger, her cheek more ruddy and her step more elastic. Many a wayfarer upon the high road which ran by Ferrier's farm felt long-forgotten thoughts revive in their minds as they watched her lithe, girlish figure tripping through the wheatfields, or met her mounted upon her father's mustang,* and managing it with all the ease and grace of a true child of the West. So the bud blossomed into a flower, and the year which saw her father the richest of the farmers left her as fair a specimen of American girlhood as could be found in the whole Pacific slope.*

It was not the father, however, who first discovered that the child had developed into the woman. It seldom is in such cases. That mysterious change is too subtle and too gradual to be measured by dates. Least of all does the maiden herself know it until the tone of a voice or the touch of a hand sets her heart thrilling within her, and she learns, with a mixture of pride and of fear, that a new and a larger nature has awoke within her. There are few who cannot recall that day and remember the one little incident which heralded the dawn of a new life. In the case of Lucy Ferrier the occasion was serious enough in itself, apart from its future influence on her destiny and that of many besides.

It was a warm June morning, and the Latter Day Saints* were as busy as the bees whose hive they have chosen for their emblem. In the fields and in the streets rose the same hum of human industry. Down the dusty high roads defiled long streams of heavily-laden mules, all heading to the west, for the gold fever* had broken out in California, and the overland route lay through the city of the Elect.* There, too, were droves of sheep and bullocks coming in from the outlying pasture lands, and trains of tired immigrants, men and horses equally weary of their interminable journey. Through all this motley assemblage, threading her way with the skill of an accomplished rider, there galloped Lucy Ferrier, her fair face flushed with the exercise and her long chestnut hair floating out behind her. She had a commission from her father in the city, and was dashing in as she had done many a time before, with all the fearlessness of youth, thinking only of her task and how it was to be performed. The travel-stained adventurers gazed after her in astonishment, and even the unemotional Indians, journeying in with their pelties,* relaxed their accustomed stoicism as they marvelled at the beauty of the pale-faced maiden.

She had reached the outskirts of the city when she found the road blocked by a great drove of cattle, driven by a half-dozen wild-looking herdsmen from the plains.* In her impatience she endeavoured to pass this obstacle by pushing her horse into what appeared to be a gap. Scarcely had she got fairly into it, however, before the beasts closed in behind her, and she found herself completely imbedded in the moving stream of fierce-eyed, long-horned bullocks. Accustomed as she was to deal with cattle, she was not alarmed at her situation, but took advantage of every opportunity to urge her horse on, in the hopes of pushing her way through the cavalcade. Unfortunately the horns of one of the creatures, either by accident or design, came in violent contact with the flank of the mustang, and excited it to madness. In an instant it reared up upon its hind legs with a snort of rage, and pranced and tossed in a way that would have unseated any but a skilful rider. The situation was full of peril. Every plunge of the excited horse brought it against the horns again, and goaded it to fresh madness. It was all that the girl could do to keep herself in the saddle, yet a slip would mean a terrible death under the hoofs of the unwieldy and terrified animals. Unaccustomed to sudden emergencies, her head began to swim, and her grip upon the bridle to relax. Choked by the rising cloud of dust and by the steam from the struggling creatures, she might have abandoned her efforts in despair, but for a kindly voice at her elbow which assured her of assistance. At the same moment a sinewy brown hand caught the frightened horse by the curb, and forcing a way through the drove, soon brought her to the outskirts.

'You're not hurt, I hope, miss,' said her preserver, respectfully.

She looked up at his dark, fierce face, and laughed saucily.* 'I'm awful frightened,' she said, naïvely; 'whoever would have thought that Pancho* would have been so scared by a lot of cows?'

'Thank God you kept your seat,' the other said earnestly. He was a tall, savage-looking young fellow, mounted on a powerful roan horse, and clad in the rough dress of a hunter, with a long rifle slung over his shoulders. 'I guess you are the daughter of John Ferrier,' he remarked; 'I saw you ride down from his house. When you see him, ask him if he remembers the Jefferson Hopes* of St Louis.* If he's the same Ferrier, my father and he were pretty thick.'

'Hadn't you better come and ask yourself?' she asked, demurely.

The young fellow seemed pleased at the suggestion, and his dark eyes sparkled with pleasure. 'I'll do so,' he said; 'we've been in the mountains for two months, and are not over and above in visiting condition. He must take us as he finds us.'

'He has a good deal to thank you for, and so have I,' she answered, 'he's awful fond of me. If those cows had jumped on me he'd have never got over it.'

'Neither would I,' said her companion.

'You! Well, I don't see that it would make much matter to you, anyhow. You ain't even a friend of ours.'*

The young hunter's dark face grew so gloomy over this remark that Lucy Ferrier laughed aloud.

'There, I didn't mean that,' she said; 'of course, you are a friend now. You must come and see us. Now I must push along, or father won't trust me with his business any more. Good-bye!'

'Good-bye,' he answered, raising his broad sombrero, and bending over her little hand. She wheeled her mustang round, gave it a cut with her riding-whip, and darted away down the broad road in a rolling cloud of dust.

Young Jefferson Hope rode on with his companions, gloomy and taciturn. He and they had been among the Nevada Mountains* prospecting for silver, and were returning to Salt Lake City in the hope of raising capital enough to work some lodes* which they had discovered. He had been as keen as any of them upon the business until this sudden incident had drawn his thoughts into another channel. The sight of the fair young girl, as frank and wholesome as the Sierra breezes, had stirred his volcanic, untamed heart to its depths. When she had vanished from his sight, he realized that a crisis had come in his life, and that neither silver speculations nor any other questions could ever be of such importance to him as this new and all-absorbing one. The love which had sprung up in his heart was not the sudden, changeable fancy of a boy, but rather that wild, fierce passion of a man of strong will and imperious temper. He had been accustomed to succeed in all that he undertook. He swore in his heart that he would not fail in this if human effort and human perseverance could render him successful.

He called on John Ferrier that night, and many times again, until his face was a familiar one at the farmhouse. John, cooped up in the valley, and absorbed in his work, had had little chance of learning the news of the outside world during the last twelve years. All this Jefferson Hope was able to tell him, and in a style which interested Lucy as well as her father. He had been a pioneer in California, and could narrate many a strange tale of fortunes made and fortunes lost in those wild, halcyon days. He had been a scout, too, and a trapper, a silver explorer, and a ranchman. Wherever stirring adventures were to be had, Jefferson Hope had been there in search of them. He soon became a favourite with the old farmer, who spoke eloquently of his virtues. On such occasions, Lucy was silent, but her blushing cheek and her bright, happy eyes showed only too clearly that her young heart was no longer her own. Her honest father may not have observed these symptoms, but they were assuredly not thrown away upon the man who had won her affections.

One summer evening he came galloping down the road and pulled up at the gate. She was at the doorway, and came down to meet him. He threw the bridle over the fence and strode up the pathway.

'I am off, Lucy,' he said, taking her two hands in his, and gazing tenderly down into her face; 'I won't ask you to come with me now, but will you be ready to come when I am here again?'

'And when will that be?' she asked, blushing and laughing.

'A couple of months at the outside. I will come and claim you then, my darling. There's no one who can stand between us.'

'And how about father?' she asked.

'He has given his consent, provided we get these mines working all right. I have no fear on that head.'

'Oh, well; of course, if you and father have arranged it all, there's no more to be said,' she whispered, with her cheek against his broad breast.

'Thank God!' he said, hoarsely, stooping and kissing her. 'It is settled, then. The longer I stay, the harder it will be to go. They are waiting for me at the cañon. Good-bye, my own darling—good-bye. In two months you shall see me.'

He tore himself from her as he spoke, and, flinging himself upon his horse, galloped furiously away, never even looking round, as though afraid that his resolution might fail him if he took one glance at what he was leaving. She stood at the gate, gazing after him until he vanished from her sight. Then she walked back into the house, the happiest girl in all Utah.

· CHAPTER 3 ·

John Ferrier Talks with the Prophet

THREE weeks had passed since Jefferson Hope and his comrades had departed from Salt Lake City. John Ferrier's heart was sore within him when he thought of the young man's return, and of the impending loss of his adopted child. Yet her bright and happy face reconciled him to the arrangement more than any argument could have done. He had always determined, deep down in his resolute heart, that nothing would ever induce him to allow his daughter to wed a Mormon. Such a marriage he regarded as no marriage at all, but as a shame and a disgrace. Whatever he might think of the Mormon doctrines, upon that one point he was inflexible. He had to seal his mouth on the subject, however, for to express an unorthodox opinion was a dangerous matter in those days in the Land of the Saints.

Yes, a dangerous matter—so dangerous that even the most saintly dared only whisper their religious opinions with bated breath, lest something which fell from their lips might be misconstrued, and bring down a swift retribution upon them. The victims of persecution had now turned persecutors* on their own account and persecutors of the most terrible description. Not the Inquisition of Seville, nor the German Vehmgericht, nor the Secret Societies of Italy, were ever able to put a more formidable machinery in motion than that which cast a cloud over the State of Utah.

Its invisibility, and the mystery which was attached to it, made this organization doubly terrible. It appeared to be omniscient and omnipotent, and yet was neither seen nor heard. The man who held out against the Church vanished away, and none knew whither he had gone or what had befallen him. His wife and his children awaited him at home, but no father ever returned* to tell them how he had fared at the hands of his secret judges. A rash word or a hasty act was followed by annihilation, and yet none knew what the nature might be of this terrible power which was suspended over them. No wonder that men went about in fear and trembling, and that even in the heart of the wilderness they dared not whisper the doubts which oppressed them.

At first this vague and terrible power was exercised only upon the recalcitrants who, having embraced the Mormon faith, wished afterwards to pervert or to abandon it. Soon, however, it took a wider range. The supply of adult women was running short, and polygamy without a female population on which to draw was a barren doctrine indeed. Strange rumours began to be bandied about—rumours of murdered immigrants* and rifled camps in regions where Indians had never been seen. Fresh women appeared in the harems of the Elders—women who pined and wept, and bore upon their faces the traces of an unextinguishable horror.* Belated wanderers upon the mountains spoke of gangs of armed men, masked, stealthy, and noiseless, who flitted by them in the darkness. These tales and rumours took substance and shape, and were corroborated and recorroborated, until they resolved themselves into a definite name. To this day, in the lonely ranches of the West, the name of the Danite Band, or the Avenging Angels, is a sinister and an ill-omened one.*

Fuller knowledge of the organization which produced such terrible results served to increase rather than to lessen the horror which it inspired in the minds of men. None knew who belonged to this ruthless society. The names of the participators in the deeds of blood and violence done

87

under the name of religion were kept profoundly secret. The very friend to whom you communicated your misgivings as to the Prophet and his mission might be one of those who would come forth at night with fire and sword to exact a terrible reparation. Hence every man feared his neighbour, and none spoke of the things which were nearest his heart.

One fine morning John Ferrier was about to set out to his wheatfields, when he heard the click of the latch, and, looking through the window, saw a stout, sandy-haired middle-aged man coming up the pathway. His heart leapt to his mouth, for this was none other than the great Brigham Young himself. Full of trepidation—for he knew that such a visit boded him little good—Ferrier ran to the door to greet the Mormon chief. The latter, however, received his salutations coldly, and followed him with a stern face into the sitting-room.

'Brother Ferrier,' he said, taking a seat, and eyeing the farmer keenly from under his light-coloured eyelashes, 'the true believers have been good friends to you. We picked you up when you were starving in the desert, we shared our food with you, led you safe to the Chosen Valley, gave you a goodly share of land, and allowed you to wax rich under our protection. Is not this so?'

'It is so,' answered John Ferrier.

'In return for all this we asked but one condition: that was, that you should embrace the true faith, and conform in every way to its usages. This you promised to do, and this, if common report says truly, you have neglected.'

'And how have I neglected it?' asked Ferrier, throwing out his hands in expostulation. 'Have I not given to the common fund? Have I not attended at the Temple? Have I not—?'

'Where are your wives?' asked Young, looking round him. 'Call them in, that I may greet them.'

'It is true that I have not married,' Ferrier answered. 'But women were few, and there were many who had better claims than I. I was not a lonely man: I had my daughter to attend to my wants.'

'It is of that daughter that I would speak to you,' said the leader of the Mormons. 'She has grown to be the flower of Utah, and has found favour in the eyes of many who are high in the land.'

John Ferrier groaned inwardly.

'There are stories of her which I would fain disbelieve— stories that she is sealed to some Gentile.* This must be the gossip of idle tongues.

'What is the thirteenth rule in the code of the sainted Joseph Smith?* "Let every maiden of the true faith marry one of the Elect; for if she wed a Gentile, she commits a grievous sin."* This being so, it is impossible that you, who profess the holy creed, should suffer your daughter to violate it.'

John Ferrier made no answer, but he played nervously with his riding-whip.

'Upon this one point your whole faith shall be tested—so it has been decided in the Sacred Council of Four.* The girl is young, and we would not have her wed grey hairs, neither would we deprive her of all choice. We Elders have many heifers,*¹ but our children must also be provided. Stangerson has a son, and Drebber has a son, and either of them would gladly welcome your daughter to their house. Let her choose between them. They are young and rich, and of the true faith. What say you to that?'

Ferrier remained silent for some little time with his brows knitted.

'You will give us time,' he said at last. 'My daughter is very young—she is scarce of an age to marry.'

'She shall have a month to choose,' said Young, rising from his seat. 'At the end of that time she shall give her answer.'

He was passing through the door, when he turned, with flushed face and flashing eyes. 'It were better for you, John Ferrier,' he thundered, 'that you and she were now lying

¹ Heber C. Kemball, in one of his sermons, alludes to his hundred wives* under this endearing epithet. [ACD note]

blanched skeletons upon the Sierra Blanco, than that you should put your weak wills against the orders of the Holy Four!'

With a threatening gesture of his hand, he turned from the door, and Ferrier heard his heavy steps scrunching along the shingly path.

He was still sitting with his elbow upon his knee considering how he should broach the matter to his daughter, when a soft hand was laid upon his, and looking up, he saw her standing beside him. One glance at her pale, frightened face showed him that she had heard what had passed.

'I could not help it,' she said, in answer to his look. 'His voice rang through the house. Oh, father, father, what shall we do?'

'Don't you scare yourself,' he answered, drawing her to him, and passing his broad, rough hand caressingly over her chestnut hair. 'We'll fix it up somehow or another. You don't find your fancy kind o' lessening for this chap, do you?'

A sob and a squeeze of his hand was her only answer.

'No; of course not. I shouldn't care to hear you say you did. He's a likely lad, and he's a Christian, which is more than these folk here, in spite o' all their praying and preaching. There's a party starting for Nevada tomorrow, and I'll manage to send him a message letting him know the hole we are in. If I know anything o' that young man, he'll be back here with a speed that would whip electro-telegraphs.'*

Lucy laughed through her tears at her father's description.

'When he comes, he will advise us for the best. But it is for you that I am frightened, dear. One hears—one hears such dreadful stories about those who oppose the Prophet: something terrible always happens to them.'

'But we haven't opposed him yet,' her father answered. 'It will be time to look out for squalls when we do. We have a clear month before us; at the end of that, I guess we had best shin out of Utah.'

'Leave Utah!'

'That's about the size of it.'

'But the farm?'

'We will raise as much as we can in money, and let the rest go. To tell the truth, Lucy, it isn't the first time I have thought of doing it. I don't care about knuckling under to any man, as these folk do to their darned Prophet. I'm a free-born American, and it's all new to me.* Guess I'm too old to learn. If he comes browsing about this farm, he might chance to run up against a charge of buck-shot travelling in the opposite direction.'

'But they won't let us leave,' his daughter objected.

'Wait till Jefferson comes, and we'll soon manage that. In the meantime, don't you fret yourself, my dearie,* and don't get your eyes swelled up, else he'll be walking into me* when he sees you. There's nothing to be afeard about, and there's no danger at all.'

John Ferrier uttered these consoling remarks in a very confident tone, but she could not help observing that he paid unusual care to the fastening of the doors that night, and that he carefully cleaned and loaded the rusty old shot-gun which hung upon the wall of his bedroom.

· CHAPTER 4 ·

A Flight for Life

ON the morning which followed his interview with the Mormon Prophet, John Ferrier went in to Salt Lake City, and having found his acquaintance, who was bound for the Nevada Mountains, he entrusted him with his message to Jefferson Hope. In it he told the young man of the imminent danger which threatened them, and how necessary it was that he should return. Having done thus he felt easier in his mind, and returned home with a lighter heart.

As he approached his farm, he was surprised to see a horse hitched to each of the posts of the gate. Still more surprised was he on entering to find two young men in possession of his sitting-room. One, with a long pale face, was leaning back in the rocking-chair, with his feet cocked up upon the stove. The other, a bull-necked youth with coarse, bloated features, was standing in front of the window with his hands in his pockets whistling a popular hymn. Both of them nodded to Ferrier as he entered, and the one in the rocking-chair commenced the conversation.

'Maybe you don't know us,' he said. 'This here is the son of Elder Drebber, and I'm Joseph Stangerson, who travelled with you in the desert when the Lord stretched out His hand and gathered you into the true fold.'*

'As He will all the nations in His own good time,' said the other in a nasal voice; 'He grindeth slowly but exceeding small.'*

John Ferrier bowed coldly. He had guessed who his visitors were.

'We have come,' continued Stangerson, 'at the advice of our fathers to solicit the hand of your daughter for whichever of us may seem good to you and to her. As I have but four wives and Brother Drebber here has seven, it appears to me that my claim is the stronger one.'

'Nay, nay, Brother Stangerson,' cried the other; 'the question is not how many wives we have, but how many we can keep. My father has now given over his mills to me, and I am the richer man.'

'But my prospects are better,' said the other, warmly. 'When the Lord removes my father,* I shall have his tanning yard and his leather factory. Then I am your elder, and am higher in the Church.'

'It will be for the maiden to decide,' rejoined young Drebber, smirking at his own reflection in the glass. 'We will leave it all to her decision.'

During this dialogue John Ferrier had stood fuming in the doorway, hardly able to keep his riding-whip from the backs of his two visitors.

'Look here,' he said at last, striding up to them, 'when my daughter summons you, you can come, but until then I don't want to see your faces again.'

The two young Mormons stared at him in amazement. In their eyes this competition between them for the maiden's hand was the highest of honours both to her and her father.

'There are two ways out of the room,' cried Ferrier; 'there is the door, and there is the window. Which do you care to use?'

His brown face looked so savage, and his gaunt hands so threatening, that his visitors sprang to their feet and beat a hurried retreat. The old farmer followed them to the door.

'Let me know when you have settled which it is to be,' he said, sardonically.

'You shall smart for this!'* Stangerson cried, white with rage. 'You have defied the Prophet and the Council of Four. You shall rue it to the end of your days.'*

'The hand of the Lord shall be heavy upon you,'* cried young Drebber; 'He will arise and smite you!'

'Then I'll start the smiting,' exclaimed Ferrier, furiously, and would have rushed upstairs for his gun had not Lucy seized him by the arm and restrained him. Before he could escape from her, the clatter of horses' hoofs told him that they were beyond his reach.

'The young canting* rascals!' he exclaimed, wiping the perspiration from his forehead; 'I would sooner see you in your grave, my girl, than the wife of either of them.'*

'And so should I, father,' she answered, with spirit; 'but Jefferson will soon be here.'*

'Yes. It will not be long before he comes. The sooner the better, for we do not know what their next move may be.'

It was, indeed, high time that someone capable of giving advice and help should come to the aid of the sturdy old farmer and his adopted daughter. In the whole history of the settlement there had never been such a case of rank disobedience to the authority of the Elders. If minor errors were punished so sternly, what would be the fate of this arch rebel? Ferrier knew that his wealth and position would be of no avail to him. Others as well known and as rich as himself had been spirited away before now, and their goods given over to the Church. He was a brave man, but he trembled at the vague, shadowy terrors which hung over him. Any known danger he could face with a firm lip, but this suspense was unnerving. He concealed his fears from his daughter, however, and affected to make light of the whole matter, though she, with the keen eye of love, saw plainly that he was ill at ease.

He expected that he would receive some message or remonstrance from Young as to his conduct, and he was not mistaken, though it came in an unlooked-for manner. Upon rising next morning he found, to his surprise, a small square of paper pinned on to the coverlet of his bed just over his chest. On it was printed, in bold, straggling letters:

'Twenty-nine days are given you for amendment, and then—'

The dash was more fear-inspiring than any threat could have been. How this warning came into his room puzzled John Ferrier sorely,* for his servants slept in an outhouse, and the doors and windows had all been secured. He crumpled the paper up and said nothing to his daughter, but the incident struck a chill into his heart. The twenty-nine days were evidently the balance of the month which Young had promised. What strength or courage could avail against an enemy armed with such mysterious powers? The hand which fastened that pin might have struck him to the heart, and he could never have known who had slain him.

Still more shaken was he next morning. They had sat down to their breakfast, when Lucy with a cry of surprise pointed upwards. In the centre of the ceiling was scrawled, with a burned stick apparently, the number 28. To his daughter it was unintelligible, and he did not enlighten her. That night he sat up with his gun and kept watch and ward.* He saw and he heard nothing, and yet in the morning a great 27 had been painted upon the outside of his door.

Thus day followed day; and as sure as morning came he found that his unseen enemies had kept their register, and had marked up in some conspicuous position how many days were still left to him out of the month of grace. Sometimes the fatal numbers appeared upon the walls, sometimes upon the floors, occasionally they were on small placards stuck upon the garden gate or the railings. With all his vigilance John Ferrier could not discover whence these daily warnings proceeded. A horror which was almost superstitious came upon him at the sight of them. He became haggard and restless, and his eyes had the troubled look of some hunted creature. He had but one hope in life now, and that was for the arrival of the young hunter from Nevada.

Twenty had changed to fifteen, and fifteen to ten, but there was no news of the absentee. One by one the numbers dwindled down, and still there came no sign of him. Whenever a horseman clattered down the road, or a driver shouted at his team, the old farmer hurried to the gate, thinking that help had arrived at last. At last, when he saw five give way to four and that again to three, he lost heart, and abandoned all hope of escape. Single-handed, and with his limited knowledge of the mountains which surrounded the settlement, he knew that he was powerless. The more frequented roads were strictly watched and guarded, and none could pass along them without an order from the Council. Turn which way he would, there appeared to be no avoiding the blow which hung over him. Yet the old man never wavered in his resolution to part with life itself before he consented to what he regarded as his daughter's dishonour.*

He was sitting alone one evening pondering deeply over his troubles, and searching vainly for some way out of them. That morning had shown the figure 2 upon the wall of his house, and the next day would be the last of the allotted time. What was to happen then? All manner of vague and terrible fancies filled his imagination. And his daughter—what was to become of her after he was gone? Was there no escape from the invisible network which was drawn all round them? He sank his head upon the table and sobbed at the thought of his own impotence.

What was that? In the silence he heard a gentle scratching sound—low, but very distinct in the quiet of the night. It came from the door of the house. Ferrier crept into the hall and listened intently. There was a pause for a few moments, and then the low, insidious sound was repeated. Someone was evidently tapping very gently upon one of the panels of the door. Was it some midnight assassin who had come to carry out the murderous orders of the secret tribunal? Or was it some agent who was marking up that the last day of grace had arrived? John Ferrier felt that instant death would be better than the suspense which shook his nerves and chilled his heart. Springing forward, he drew the bolt and threw the door open.

Outside all was calm and quiet. The night was fine, and the stars were twinkling brightly overhead. The little front garden lay before the farmer's eyes bounded by the fence and gate, but neither there nor on the road was any human being to be seen. With a sigh of relief, Ferrier looked to right and to left, until, happening to glance straight down at his own feet, he saw to his astonishment a man lying flat upon his face upon the ground, with arms and legs all asprawl.

So unnerved was he at the sight that he leaned up against the wall with his hand to his throat to stifle his inclination to call out. His first thought was that the prostrate figure was that of some wounded or dying man, but as he watched it he saw it writhe along the ground and into the hall with the rapidity and noiselessness of a serpent. Once within the house the man sprang to his feet, closed the door, and revealed to the astonished farmer the fierce face and resolute expression of Jefferson Hope.

'Good God!' gasped John Ferrier. 'How you scared me. Whatever made you come in like that?'

'Give me food,' the other said hoarsely. 'I have had no time for bite or sup for eight-and-forty hours.' He flung himself upon the cold meat and bread which were still lying upon the table from his host's supper, and devoured it voraciously. 'Does Lucy bear up well?' he asked, when he had satisfied his hunger.

'Yes. She does not know the danger,' her father answered.

'That is well. The house is watched on every side. That is why I crawled my way up to it. They may be darned sharp, but they're not quite sharp enough to catch a Washoe* hunter.'

John Ferrier felt a different man now that he realized that he had a devoted ally. He seized the young man's leathery hand and wrung it cordially. 'You're a man to be proud of,' he said. 'There are not many who would come to share our danger and our troubles.'

'You've hit it there, pard,' the young hunter answered. 'I have a respect for you, but if you were alone in this business I'd think twice before I put my head into such a hornets' nest.* It's Lucy that brings me here, and before harm comes on her I guess there will be one less o' the Hope family in Utah.'

'What are we to do?'

'To-morrow is your last day, and unless you act tonight you are lost. I have a mule and two horses waiting in the Eagle Ravine. How much money have you?'

'Two thousand dollars in gold and five in notes.'*

'That will do. I have as much more to add to it. We must push for Carson City* through the mountains. You had best wake Lucy. It is as well that the servants* do not sleep in the house.'

While Ferrier was absent, preparing his daughter for the approaching journey, Jefferson Hope packed all the eatables that he could find into a small parcel, and filled a stoneware jar with water, for he knew by experience that the mountain wells were few and far between. He had hardly completed his arrangements before the farmer returned with his daughter all dressed and ready for a start. The greeting between the lovers was warm, but brief, for minutes were precious, and there was much to be done.

'We must make our start at once,' said Jefferson Hope, speaking in a low but resolute voice, like one who realizes the greatness of the peril, but has steeled his heart to meet it. 'The front and back entrances are watched, but with caution we may get away through the side window and across the fields. Once on the road we are only two miles from the Ravine where the horses are waiting. By daybreak we should be half-way through the mountains.'

'What if we are stopped?' asked Ferrier.

Hope slapped the revolver butt which protruded from the front of his tunic. 'If they are too many for us, we shall take two or three of them with us,' he said with a sinister smile.

The lights inside the house had all been extinguished, and from the darkened window Ferrier peered over the fields which had been his own, and which he was now about to abandon for ever. He had long nerved himself to the sacrifice, however, and the thought of the honour and happiness of his daughter outweighed any regret at his ruined fortunes. All looked so peaceful and happy, the rustling trees and the broad silent stretch of grainland, that it was difficult to realize that the spirit of murder lurked through it all.* Yet the white face and set expression of the young hunter showed that in his approach to the house he had seen enough to satisfy him upon that head.

Ferrier carried the bag of gold and notes, Jefferson Hope had the scanty provisions and water, while Lucy had a small bundle containing a few of her more valued possessions. Opening the window very slowly and carefully, they waited until a dark cloud had somewhat obscured the night, and then one by one passed through into the little garden. With bated breath and crouching figures they stumbled across it, and gained the shelter of the hedge, which they skirted until they came to the gap which opened into the cornfield. They had just reached this point when the young man seized his two companions and dragged them down into the shadow, where they lay silent and trembling.

It was as well that his prairie training had given Jefferson Hope the ears of a lynx.* He and his friends had hardly crouched down before the melancholy hooting of a mountain owl was heard within a few yards of them, which was immediately answered by another hoot at a small distance. At the same moment a vague, shadowy figure emerged from the gap for which they had been making, and uttered the plaintive signal cry again, on which a second man appeared out of the obscurity.

'To-morrow at midnight,' said the first, who appeared to be in authority. 'When the Whip-poor-Will* calls three times.'

'It is well,' returned the other. 'Shall I tell Brother Drebber?'

'Pass it on to him, and from him to the others. Nine to seven!'

'Seven to five!' repeated the other; and the two figures flitted away in different directions. Their concluding words had evidently been some form of sign and countersign. The instant that their footsteps had died away in the distance, Jefferson Hope sprang to his feet, and helping his companions through the gap, led the way across the fields at the top of his speed, supporting and half-carrying the girl when her strength appeared to fail her.

'Hurry on! hurry on!' he gasped from time to time. 'We are through the line of sentinels. Everything depends on speed. Hurry on!'

Once on the high road, they made rapid progress. Only once did they meet anyone, and then they managed to slip into a field, and so avoid recognition. Before reaching the town the hunter branched away into a rugged and narrow footpath which led to the mountains. Two dark, jagged peaks loomed above them through the darkness, and the defile which led between them was the Eagle Cañon in which the horses were awaiting them. With unerring instinct Jefferson Hope picked his way among the great boulders and along the bed of a dried-up water-course, until he came to the retired corner screened with rocks, where the faithful animals had been picketed. The girl was placed upon the mule, and old Ferrier upon one of the horses, with his money-bag, while Jefferson Hope led the other along the precipitous and dangerous path.

It was a bewildering route for anyone who was not accustomed to face Nature in her wildest moods. On the one side a great crag towered up a thousand feet or more, black, stern, and menacing, with long basaltic columns* upon its rugged surface like the ribs of some petrified monster. On the other hand a wild chaos of boulders and *débris* made all advance impossible. Between the two ran the irregular track, so narrow in places that they had to travel in Indian file, and so rough that only practised riders could have traversed it at all. Yet, in spite of all dangers and difficulties, the hearts of the fugitives were light within them, for every step increased the distance between them and the terrible despotism from which they were flying.

They soon had a proof, however, that they were still within the jurisdiction of the Saints. They had reached the very wildest and most desolate portion of the pass when the girl gave a startled cry, and pointed upwards. On a rock which overlooked the track, showing out dark and plain against the sky, there stood a solitary sentinel. He saw them as soon as they perceived him, and his military challenge of 'Who goes there?' rang through the silent ravine.

'Travellers for Nevada,' said Jefferson Hope, with his hand upon the rifle which hung by his saddle.

They could see the lonely watcher fingering his gun, and peering down at them as if dissatisfied at their reply.

'By whose permission?' he asked.

'The Holy Four,'* answered Ferrier. His Mormon experiences had taught him that that was the highest authority to which he could refer.

'Nine to seven,' cried the sentinel.

'Seven to five,' returned Jefferson Hope promptly, remembering the countersign which he had heard in the garden.

'Pass, and the Lord go with you,' said the voice from above. Beyond his post the path broadened out, and the horses were able to break into a trot. Looking back, they could see the solitary watcher leaning upon his gun, and knew that they had passed the outlying post of the chosen people, and that freedom lay before them.

· CHAPTER 5 ·

The Avenging Angels

ALL night their course lay through intricate defiles and over irregular and rock-strewn paths. More than once they lost their way, but Hope's intimate knowledge of the mountains enabled them to regain the track once more. When morning broke, a scene of marvellous though savage beauty lay before them. In every direction the great snow-capped peaks hemmed them in, peeping over each other's shoulders to the far horizon. So steep were the rocky banks on either side of them that the larch and the pine seemed to be suspended over their heads, and to need only a gust of wind to come hurtling down upon them. Nor was the fear entirely an illusion, for the barren valley was thickly strewn with trees and boulders which had fallen in a similar manner. Even as they passed, a great rock came thundering down with a hoarse rattle which woke the echoes in the silent gorges, and startled the weary horses into a gallop.

As the sun rose slowly above the eastern horizon, the caps of the great mountains lit up one after the other, like lamps at a festival, until they were all ruddy and glowing. The magnificent spectacle cheered the hearts of the three fugitives and gave them fresh energy. At a wild torrent which swept out of a ravine they called a halt and watered their horses, while they partook of a hasty breakfast. Lucy and her father would fain have rested longer, but Jefferson Hope was inexorable. 'They will be upon our track by this time,' he said. 'Everything depends upon our speed. Once safe in Carson, we may rest for the remainder of our lives.'

During the whole of that day they struggled on through the defiles, and by evening they calculated that they were more than thirty miles from their enemies. At night-time they chose the base of a beetling crag, where the rocks offered some protection from the chill wind, and there, huddled together for warmth, they enjoyed a few hours' sleep. Before daybreak, however, they were up and on their way once more. They had seen no signs of any pursuers, and Jefferson Hope began to think that they were fairly out of the reach of the terrible organization whose enmity they had incurred. He little knew how far that iron grasp could reach, or how soon it was to close upon them and crush them.

About the middle of the second day of their flight their scanty store of provisions began to run out. This gave the hunter little uneasiness, however, for there was game to be had among the mountains, and he had frequently before had to depend upon his rifle for the needs of life. Choosing a sheltered nook, he piled together a few dried branches and made a blazing fire, at which his companions might warm themselves, for they were now nearly five thousand feet above the sea level, and the air was bitter and keen. Having tethered the horses, and bade Lucy adieu, he threw his gun over his shoulder, and set out in search of whatever chance might throw in his way. Looking back, he saw the old man and the young girl crouching over the blazing fire, while the three animals stood motionless in the background. Then the intervening rocks hid them from his view.

He walked for a couple of miles through one ravine after another without success, though, from the marks upon the bark of the trees, and other indications, he judged that there were numerous bears in the vicinity. At last, after two or three hours' fruitless search, he was thinking of turning back in despair, when casting his eyes upwards he saw a sight which sent a thrill of pleasure through his heart. On the edge of a jutting pinnacle, three or four hundred feet above him, there stood a creature somewhat resembling a sheep in appearance, but armed with a pair of gigantic horns. The big-horn*—for so it is called—was acting, probably, as a guardian over a flock which were invisible to the hunter; but fortunately it was heading in the opposite direction, and had not perceived him. Lying on his face, he rested his rifle upon a rock, and took a long and steady aim before drawing the trigger. The animal sprang into the air, tottered for a moment upon the edge of the precipice, and then came crashing down into the valley beneath.

The creature was too unwieldy to lift, so the hunter contented himself with cutting away one haunch and part of the flank. With this trophy over his shoulder, he hastened to retrace his steps, for the evening was already drawing in. He had hardly started, however, before he realized the difficulty which faced him. In his eagerness he had wandered far past the ravines which were known to him, and it was no easy matter to pick out the path which he had taken. The valley in which he found himself divided and sub-divided into many gorges, which were so like each other that it was impossible to distinguish one from the other. He followed one for a mile or more until he came to a mountain torrent which he was sure that he had never seen before. Convinced that he had taken the wrong turn, he tried another, but with the same result. Night was coming on rapidly, and it was almost dark before he at last found himself in a defile which was familiar to him. Even then it was no easy matter to keep to the right track, for the moon had not yet risen, and the high cliffs on either side made the obscurity more profound. Weighed down with his burden, and weary from his exertions, he stumbled along, keeping up his heart by the reflection that every step brought him nearer to Lucy, and that he carried with him enough to ensure them food for the remainder of their journey.

He had now come to the mouth of the very defile in which he had left them. Even in the darkness he could recognize the outline of the cliffs which bounded it. They must, he reflected, be awaiting him anxiously, for he had been absent nearly five hours. In the gladness of his heart he put his hands to his mouth and made the glen re-echo to a loud halloo as a signal that he was coming. He paused and listened for an answer. None came save his own cry,* which clattered up the dreary, silent ravines, and was borne back to his ears in countless repetitions. Again he shouted, even louder than before, and again no whisper came back from the friends whom he had left such a short time ago. A vague, nameless dread came over him, and he hurried onwards frantically, dropping the precious food in his agitation.

When he turned the corner, he came full in sight of the spot where the fire had been lit. There was still a glowing pile of wood ashes there, but it had evidently not been tended since his departure. The same dead silence still reigned all round. With his fears all changed to convictions, he hurried on. There was no living creature near the remains of the fire: animals, man, maiden, all were gone. It was only too clear that some sudden and terrible disaster had occurred during his absence—a disaster which had embraced them all, and yet had left no traces behind it.

Bewildered and stunned by this blow, Jefferson Hope felt his head spin round, and had to lean upon his rifle to save himself from falling. He was essentially a man of action, however, and speedily recovered from his temporary impotence. Seizing a half-consumed piece of wood from the smouldering fire, he blew it into a flame, and proceeded with its help to examine the little camp. The ground was all stamped down by the feet of horses, showing that a large party of mounted men had overtaken the fugitives, and the direction of their tracks proved that they had afterwards turned back to Salt Lake City. Had they carried back both of his companions with them? Jefferson Hope had almost persuaded himself that they must have done so, when his eye fell upon an object which made every nerve of his body tingle within him. A little way on one side of the camp was a low-lying heap of reddish soil, which had assuredly not been there before. There was no mistaking it for anything but a newly-dug grave. As the young hunter approached it, he perceived that a stick had been planted on it, with a sheet of paper stuck in the cleft fork of it. The inscription upon the paper was brief, but to the point:

JOHN FERRIER
Formerly of Salt Lake City
Died August 4th

The sturdy old man, whom he had left so short a time before, was gone, then, and this was all his epitaph. Jefferson Hope looked wildly round to see if there was a second grave, but there was no sign of one. Lucy had been carried back by their terrible pursuers to fulfil her original destiny, by becoming one of the harem of the Elder's son. As the young fellow realized the certainty of her fate,* and his own powerlessness to prevent it, he wished that he, too, was lying with the old farmer in his last silent resting-place.

Again, however, his active spirit shook off the lethargy which springs from despair. If there was nothing else left to him, he could at least devote his life to revenge. With indomitable patience and perseverance, Jefferson Hope possessed also a power of sustained vindictiveness, which he may have learned from the Indians amongst whom he had lived. As he stood by the desolate fire, he felt that the only one thing which could assuage his grief would be thorough and complete retribution, brought by his own hand upon his enemies. His strong will and untiring energy should, he determined, be devoted to that one end. With a grim, white face, he retraced his steps to where he had dropped the food, and having stirred up the smouldering fire, he cooked enough to last him for a few days. This he made up into a bundle, and, tired as he was, he set himself to walk back through the mountains upon the track of the avenging angels.

For five days he toiled footsore and weary through the defiles which he had already traversed on horseback. At night he flung himself down among the rocks, and snatched a few hours of sleep; but before daybreak he was always well on his way. On the sixth day, he reached the Eagle Cañon, from which they had commenced their ill-fated flight. Thence he could look down upon the home of the Saints. Worn and exhausted, he leaned upon his rifle and shook his gaunt hand fiercely at the silent widespread city beneath him. As he looked at it, he observed that there were flags in some of the principal streets, and other signs of festivity. He was still speculating as to what this might mean when he heard the clatter of horse's hoofs, and saw a mounted man riding towards him. As he approached, he recognized him as a Mormon named Cowper, to whom he had rendered services at different times. He therefore accosted him when he got up to him, with the object of finding out what Lucy Ferrier's fate had been.

'I am Jefferson Hope,' he said. 'You remember me.'

The Mormon looked at him with undisguised astonishment —indeed, it was difficult to recognize in this tattered, unkempt wanderer, with ghastly white face and fierce, wild eyes, the spruce young hunter of former days. Having, however, at last satisfied himself as to his identity, the man's surprise changed to consternation.

'You are mad to come here,' he cried. 'It is as much as my own life is worth to be seen talking with you. There is a warrant against you from the Holy Four for assisting the Ferriers away.'

'I don't fear them, or their warrant,' Hope said, earnestly. 'You must know something of this matter, Cowper. I conjure you by everything you hold dear to answer a few questions. We have always been friends. For God's sake, don't refuse to answer me.'

'What is it?' the Mormon asked uneasily. 'Be quick. The very rocks have ears and the trees eyes.'

'What has become of Lucy Ferrier?'

'She was married yesterday to young Drebber. Hold up, man, hold up; you have no life left in you.'

'Don't mind me,' said Hope faintly. He was white to the very lips, and had sunk down on the stone against which he had been leaning. 'Married you say?'

'Married yesterday—that's what those flags are for on the Endowment House.* There was some words* between young Drebber and young Stangerson as to which was to have her. They'd both been in the party that followed them, and Stangerson had shot her father, which seemed to give him the best claim; but when they argued it out in council, Drebber's party was the stronger, so the Prophet gave her over to him. No one won't have her very long though, for I saw death in her face yesterday. She is more like a ghost than a woman. Are you off, then?'

'Yes, I am off,' said Jefferson Hope, who had risen from his seat. His face might have been chiselled out of marble, so hard and set was its expression, while its eyes glowed with a baleful light.

'Where are you going?'

'Never mind,' he answered; and, slinging his weapon over his shoulder, strode off down the gorge and so away into the heart of the mountains to the haunts of the wild beasts. Amongst them all there was none so fierce and so dangerous as himself.

The prediction of the Mormon was only too well fulfilled. Whether it was the terrible death of her father or the effects of the hateful marriage* into which she had been forced, poor Lucy never held up her head again, but pined away and died within a month. Her sottish* husband, who had married her principally for the sake of John Ferrier's property, did not affect any great grief at his bereavement; but his other wives mourned over her, and sat up with her the night before the burial, as is the Mormon custom.* They were grouped round the bier in the early hours of the morning, when, to their inexpressible fear and astonishment, the door was flung open, and a savage-looking, weather-beaten man in tattered garments strode into the room. Without a glance or a word to the cowering women, he walked up to the white silent figure which had once con-tained the pure soul of Lucy Ferrier. Stooping over her, he pressed his lips reverently to her cold forehead, and then, snatching up her hand, he took the wedding-ring from her finger. 'She shall not be buried in that,' he cried with a fierce snarl, and before an alarm could be raised sprang down the stairs and was gone. So strange and so brief was the episode that the watchers might have found it hard to believe it themselves or persuade other people of it, had it not been for the undeniable fact that the circlet of gold which marked her as having been a bride had dis-appeared.

For some months Jefferson Hope lingered among the mountains, leading a strange wild life, and nursing in his heart the fierce desire for vengeance which possessed him. Tales were told in the city of the weird figure which was seen prowling about the suburbs, and which haunted the lonely mountain gorges. Once a bullet whistled through Stangerson's window and flattened itself upon the wall within a foot of him. On another occasion, as Drebber passed under a cliff a great boulder crashed down on him,* and he only escaped a terrible death by throwing himself upon his face. The two young Mormons were not long in discovering the reason of these attempts upon their lives and led repeated expeditions into the mountains in the hope of capturing or killing their enemy, but always without success. Then they adopted the precaution of never going out alone or after night-fall, and of having their houses guarded. After a time they were able to relax these measures, for nothing was either heard or seen of their opponent, and they hoped that time had cooled his vindictiveness.

Far from doing so, it had, if anything, augmented it. The hunter's mind was of a hard, unyielding nature, and the predominant idea of revenge had taken such complete possession of it that there was no room for any other emotion. He was, however, above all things, practical. He soon realized that even his iron constitution could not stand the incessant strain which he was putting upon it. Exposure and want of wholesome food were wearing him out. If he died like a dog among the mountains, what was to become of his revenge then? And yet such a death was sure to overtake him if he persisted. He felt that that was to play his enemy's game, so he reluctantly returned to the old Nevada mines, there to recruit his health and to amass money enough to allow him to pursue his object without privation.

His intention had been to be absent a year at the most, but a combination of unforeseen circumstances* prevented his leaving the mines for nearly five. At the end of that time, however, his memory of his wrongs and his craving for revenge were quite as keen as on that memorable night when he had stood by John Ferrier's grave. Disguised, and under an assumed name, he returned to Salt Lake City, careless what became of his own life, as long as he obtained what he knew to be justice. There he found evil tidings awaiting him. There had been a schism among the Chosen People* a few months before, some of the younger members of the Church having rebelled against the authority of the Elders, and the result had been the secession of a certain number of the malcontents, who had left Utah and become Gentiles. Among these had been Drebber and Stangerson; and no one knew whither they had gone. Rumour reported that Drebber had managed to convert a large part of his property into money, and that he had departed a wealthy man, while his companion, Stangerson, was comparatively poor. There was no clue at all, however, as to their whereabouts.

Many a man, however vindictive, would have abandoned all thought of revenge in the face of such a difficulty, but Jefferson Hope never faltered for a moment. With the small competence he possessed, eked out by such employment as he could pick up, he travelled from town to town through the United States in quest of his enemies. Year passed into year, his black hair turned grizzled, but still he wandered on, a human bloodhound, with his mind wholly set upon the one object to which he had devoted his life. At last his perseverance was rewarded. It was but a glance of a face in a window, but that one glance told him that Cleveland in Ohio possessed the men whom he was in pursuit of. He returned to his miserable lodgings with his plan of vengeance all arranged. It chanced, however, that Drebber, looking from his window, had recognized the vagrant* in the street, and had read murder in his eyes. He hurried before a justice of the peace, accompanied by Stangerson,* who had become his private secretary, and represented to him that they were in danger of their lives from the jealousy and hatred of an old rival. That evening Jefferson Hope was taken into custody, and not being able to find sureties, was detained for some weeks. When at last he was liberated it was only to find that Drebber's house was deserted, and that he and his secretary had departed for Europe.

Again the avenger had been foiled, and again his concentrated hatred urged him to continue the pursuit. Funds were wanting, however, and for some time he had to return to work, saving every dollar for his approaching journey. At last, having collected enough to keep life in him, he departed for Europe, and tracked his enemies from city to city, working his way in any menial capacity, but never overtaking the fugitives. When he reached St Petersburg, they had departed for Paris; and when he followed them there, he learned that they had just set off for Copenhagen. At the Danish capital he was again a few days late, for they had journeyed on to London, where he at last succeeded in running them to earth. As to what occurred there, we cannot do better than quote the old hunter's own account, as duly recorded in Dr Watson's Journal,* to which we are already under such obligations.

· CHAPTER 6 ·

A Continuation of the Reminiscences of John Watson MD

OUR prisoner's furious resistance did not apparently indicate any ferocity in his disposition towards ourselves, for on finding himself powerless, he smiled in an affable manner, and expressed his hopes that he had not hurt any of us in the scuffle. 'I guess you're going to take me to the police-station,' he remarked to Sherlock Holmes. 'My cab's at the door. If you'll loose my legs I'll walk down to it. I'm not so light to lift as I used to be.'

Gregson and Lestrade exchanged glances, as if they thought this proposition rather a bold one; but Holmes at once took the prisoner at his word, and loosed the towel which he had bound round his ankles. He rose and stretched his legs, as though to assure himself that they were free once more. I remember that I thought to myself, as I eyed him, that I had seldom seen a more powerfully-built man; and his dark, sun-burned face bore an expression of determination and energy which was as formidable as his personal strength.

'If there's a vacant place for a chief of the police, I reckon you are the man for it,' he said, gazing with undisguised admiration at my fellow-lodger. 'The way you kept on my trail was a caution.'

'You had better come with me,' said Holmes to the two detectives.

'I can drive you,' said Lestrade.

'Good, and Gregson can come inside with me. You, too, Doctor. You have taken an interest in the case, and may as well stick to us.'

I assented gladly, and we all descended together. Our prisoner made no attempt at escape, but stepped calmly into the cab which had been his, and we followed him. Lestrade mounted the box, whipped up the horse, and brought us in a very short time to our destination. We were ushered into a small chamber, where a police inspector noted down our prisoner's name and the names of the men with whose murder he had been charged. The official was a white-faced, unemotional man, who went through his duties in a dull, mechanical way. 'The prisoner will be put before the magistrates in the course of the week,' he said; 'in the meantime, Mr Jefferson Hope, have you anything that you wish to say? I must warn you that your words will be taken down, and may be used against you.'*

'I've got a good deal to say,' our prisoner said slowly. 'I want to tell you gentlemen all about it.'

'Hadn't you better reserve that for your trial?' asked the inspector.

'I may never be tried,' he answered. 'You needn't look startled. It isn't suicide I am thinking of. Are you a doctor?' He turned his fierce dark eyes upon me as he asked this last question.

'Yes, I am,' I answered.

'Then put your hand here,' he said, with a smile, motioning with his manacled wrists towards his chest.

I did so; and became at once conscious of an extraordinary throbbing and commotion which was going on inside. The walls of his chest seemed to thrill and quiver as a frail building would do inside which some powerful engine was at work. In the silence of the room I could hear a dull humming and buzzing noise which proceeded from the same source.

'Why,' I cried, 'you have an aortic aneurism!' *

'That's what they call it,' he said, placidly. 'I went to a doctor last week about it, and he told me that it is bound to burst before many days passed. It has been getting worse for years. I got it from over-exposure and under-feeding among the Salt Lake Mountains. I've done my work now, and I don't care how soon I go, but I should like to leave an account of the business behind me. I don't want to be remembered as a common cut-throat.'

The inspector and the two detectives had a hurried discussion as to the advisability of allowing him to tell his story.

'Do you consider, Doctor, that there is immediate danger?' the former asked.

'Most certainly there is,' I answered.

'In that case it is clearly our duty, in the interests of justice, to take his statement,' said the inspector. 'You are at liberty, sir, to give your account, which I again warn you will be taken down.'

'I'll sit down, with your leave,' the prisoner said, suiting the action to the word. 'This aneurism of mine makes me easily tired, and the tussle we had half an hour ago has not mended matters. I'm on the brink of the grave, and I am not likely to lie to you. Every word I say is the absolute truth, and how you use it is a matter of no consequence to me.'

With these words, Jefferson Hope leaned back in his chair and began the following remarkable statement. He spoke in a calm and methodical manner, as though the events which he narrated were commonplace enough. I can vouch for the accuracy of the subjoined account, for I have had access to Lestrade's note-book, in which the prisoner's words were taken down exactly as they were uttered.

'It don't much matter to you why I hated these men,' he said; 'it's enough that they were guilty of the death of two human beings—a father and a daughter—and that they had, therefore, forfeited their own lives. After the lapse of time that has passed since their crime, it was impossible for me to secure a conviction against them in any court. I knew of their guilt though, and I determined that I should be judge, jury and executioner all rolled into one. You'd have done the same, if you have any manhood in you, if you had been in my place.

'That girl that I spoke of was to have married me twenty years ago. She was forced into marrying* that same Drebber, and broke her heart over it. I took the marriage ring from her dead finger, and I vowed that his dying eyes should rest upon that very ring, and that his last thoughts should be of the crime for which he was punished. I have carried it about with me, and have followed him and his accomplice over two continents until I caught them. They thought to tire me out, but they could not do it. If I die tomorrow, as is likely enough, I die knowing that my work in this world is done, and well done. They have perished, and by my hand.* There is nothing left for me to hope for, or to desire.

'They were rich and I was poor, so that it was no easy matter for me to follow them. When I got to London my pocket was about empty, and I found that I must turn my hand to something for my living. Driving and riding are as natural to me as walking, so I applied at a cab-owner's office, and soon got employment. I was to bring a certain sum a week to the owner, and whatever was over that I might keep for myself. There was seldom much over,* but I managed to scrape along somehow. The hardest job was to learn my way about, for I reckon that of all the mazes that ever were contrived, this city is the most confusing. I had a map beside me though, and when once I had spotted the principal hotels and stations, I got on pretty well.

'It was some time before I found out where my two gentlemen were living; but I inquired and inquired until at last I dropped across them. They were at a boarding-house at Camberwell, over on the other side of the river. When once I found them out, I knew that I had them at my mercy. I had grown my beard, and there was no chance of their recognizing me. I would dog them and follow them until I saw my opportunity. I was determined that they should not escape me again.

'They were very near doing it for all that. Go where they would about London, I was always at their heels. Sometimes I followed them on my cab, and sometimes on foot, but the former was the best, for then they could not get away from me. It was only early in the morning or late at night that I could earn anything, so that I began to get behindhand with my employer. I did not mind that, however, as long as I could lay my hand upon the men I wanted.

'They were very cunning, though. They must have thought that there was some chance of their being followed, for they would never go out alone, and never after night-fall. During two weeks I drove behind them every day, and never once saw them separate. Drebber himself was drunk half the time, but Stangerson was not to be caught napping. I watched them late and early, but never saw the ghost of a chance; but I was not discouraged, for something told me that the hour had almost come. My only fear was that this thing in my chest might burst a little too soon and leave my work undone.

'At last, one evening I was driving up and down Torquay Terrace, as the street was called in which they boarded, when I saw a cab drive up to their door. Presently some luggage was brought out and after a time Drebber and

Stangerson followed it, and drove off. I whipped up my horse and kept within sight of them, feeling very ill at ease, for I feared that they were going to shift their quarters. At Euston Station they got out, and I left a boy to hold my horse and followed them on to the platform. I heard them ask for the Liverpool train, and the guard answer that one had just gone, and there would not be another for some hours. Stangerson seemed to be put out at that, but Drebber was rather pleased than otherwise. I got so close to them in the bustle that I could hear every word that passed between them. Drebber said that he had a little business of his own to do, and that if the other would wait for him he would soon rejoin him. His companion remonstrated with him, and reminded him that they had resolved to stick together. Drebber answered that the matter was a delicate one, and that he must go alone. I could not catch what Stangerson said to that, but the other burst out swearing, and reminded him that he was nothing more than his paid servant, and that he must not presume to dictate to him. On that the secretary gave it up as a bad job, and simply bargained with him that if he missed the last train he should rejoin him at Halliday's Private Hotel; to which Drebber answered that he would be back on the platform before eleven, and made his way out of the station.

'The moment for which I had waited so long had at last come. I had my enemies within my power. Together they could protect each other, but singly they were at my mercy. I did not act, however, with undue precipitation. My plans were already formed. There is no satisfaction in vengeance unless the offender has time to realize who it is that strikes him, and why retribution has come upon him. I had my plans arranged by which I should have the opportunity of making the man who had wronged me understand that his old sin had found him out. It chanced that some days before a gentleman who had been engaged in looking over some houses in the Brixton Road had dropped the key of one of them in my carriage. It was claimed that same evening, and returned; but in the interval I had taken a moulding of it, and had a duplicate constructed. By means of this I had access to at least one spot in this great city where I could rely upon being free from interruption. How to get Drebber to that house was the difficult problem which I had now to solve.

'He walked down the road and went into one or two liquor shops, staying for nearly half an hour in the last of them. When he came out, he staggered in his walk, and was evidently pretty well on. There was a hansom just in front of me, and he hailed it. I followed it so close that the nose of my horse was within a yard of his driver the whole way. We rattled across Waterloo Bridge and through miles of streets, until, to my astonishment, we found ourselves back in the terrace in which he had boarded. I could not imagine what his intention was in returning there; but I went on and pulled up my cab a hundred yards or so from the house. He entered it, and his hansom drove away. Give me a glass of water, if you please. My mouth gets dry with the talking.'

I handed him the glass, and he drank it down.

'That's better,' he said. 'Well, I waited for a quarter of an hour, or more, when suddenly there came a noise like people struggling inside the house. Next moment the door was flung open and two men appeared, one of whom was Drebber, and the other was a young man whom I had never seen before. This fellow had Drebber by the collar, and when they came to the head of the steps he gave him a shove and a kick which sent him half across the road. "You hound!" he cried, shaking his stick at him; "I'll teach you to insult an honest girl!" He was so hot that I think he would have thrashed Drebber with his cudgel, only that the cur staggered away down the road as fast as his legs would carry him. He ran as far as the corner, and then seeing my cab, he hailed me and jumped in. "Drive me to Halliday's Private Hotel," said he.

'When I had him fairly inside my cab, my heart jumped so with joy that I feared lest at this last moment my aneurism might go wrong. I drove along slowly, weighing in my own mind what it was best to do. I might take him right out into the country, and there in some deserted lane have my last interview with him. I had almost decided upon this, when he solved the problem for me. The craze for drink had seized him again, and he ordered me to pull up outside a gin palace. He went in, leaving word that I should wait for him. There he remained until closing time, and when he came out he was so far gone that I knew the game was in my own hands.

'Don't imagine that I intended to kill him in cold blood. It would only have been rigid justice if I had done so, but I could not bring myself to do it. I had long determined that he should have a show for his life if he chose to take advantage of it. Among the many billets which I have filled in America during my wandering life, I was once janitor and sweeper-out of the laboratory at York College.* One day the professor was lecturing on poisons, and he showed his students some alkaloid, as he called it, which he had extracted from some South American arrow poison,* and which was so powerful that the least grain meant instant death. I spotted the bottle in which this preparation was kept, and when they were all gone, I helped myself to a little of it. I was a fairly good dispenser, so I worked this alkaloid into small, soluble pills, and each pill I put in a box with a similar pill made without the poison. I determined at the time that when I had my chance my gentlemen should each have a draw out of one of these boxes, while I ate the pill that remained.* It would be quite as deadly and a good deal less noisy than firing across a handkerchief. From that day I had always my pill boxes about with me, and the time had now come when I was to use them.

'It was nearer one than twelve, and a wild, bleak night, blowing hard and raining in torrents. Dismal as it was outside, I was glad within—so glad that I could have shouted out from pure exultation. If any of you gentlemen have ever pined for a thing, and longed for it during twenty long years, and then suddenly found it within your reach you would understand my feelings. I lit a cigar, and puffed at it to steady my nerves, but my hands were trembling and my temples throbbing with excitement. As I drove, I could see old John Ferrier and sweet Lucy looking at me out of the darkness and smiling at me, just as plain as I see you all in this room. All the way they were ahead of me, one on each side of the horse, until I pulled up at the house in the Brixton Road.

'There was not a soul to be seen, nor a sound to be heard, except the dripping of the rain. When I looked in at the window, I found Drebber all huddled together in a drunken sleep. I shook him by the arm, "It's time to get out," I said.

' "All right, cabby," said he.

'I suppose he thought we had come to the hotel that he had mentioned, for he got out without another word, and followed me down the garden. I had to walk beside him to keep him steady, for he was still a little top-heavy. When we came to the door, I opened it, and led him into the front room. I give my word that all the way, the father and the daughter were walking in front of us.

' "It's infernally dark," said he, stamping about.

' "We'll soon have a light," I said, striking a match and putting it to a wax candle which I had brought with me. "Now, Enoch Drebber," I continued, turning to him, and holding the light to my own face, "who am I?"

'He gazed at me with bleared, drunken eyes for a moment, and then I saw a horror spring up in them, and convulse his whole features, which showed me that he knew me. He staggered back with a livid face, and I saw the perspiration break out upon his brow, while his teeth chattered in his head. At the sight I leaned my back against the door and laughed loud and long. I had always known that vengeance would be sweet, but I had never hoped for the contentment of soul which now possessed me.

' "You dog!" I said; "I have hunted you from Salt Lake City to St Petersburg, and you have always escaped me. Now, at last your wanderings have come to an end, for either you or I shall never see tomorrow's sun rise." He shrunk still farther away as I spoke, and I could see on his face that he thought I was mad. So I was for the time. The pulses in my temples beat like sledge-hammers, and I believe I would have had a fit of some sort if the blood had not gushed from my nose and relieved me.

' "What do you think of Lucy Ferrier now?" I cried, locking the door, and shaking the key in his face. "Punishment has been slow in coming, but it has overtaken you at last." I saw his coward lips tremble as I spoke. He would have begged for his life, but he knew well that it was useless.

' "Would you murder me?" he stammered.

' "There is no murder," I answered. "Who talks of murdering a mad dog? What mercy had you upon my poor darling, when you dragged her from her slaughtered father, and bore her away to your accursed and shameless harem."

' "It was not I who killed her father," he cried.

' "But it was you who broke her innocent heart,"* I shrieked, thrusting the box before him. "Let the high God judge between us. Choose and eat. There is death in one and life in the other. I shall take what you leave. Let us see if there is justice upon the earth, or if we are ruled by chance."

'He cowered away with wild cries and prayers for mercy, but I drew my knife and held it to his throat until he had obeyed me. Then I swallowed the other, and we stood facing one another in silence for a minute or more, waiting to see which was to live and which was to die. Shall I ever forget the look which came over his face when the first warning pangs told him that the poison was in his system? I laughed as I saw it, and held Lucy's marriage ring in front of his eyes. It was but for a moment, for the action of the alkaloid is rapid. A spasm of pain contorted his features; he threw his hands out in front of him, staggered, and then, with a hoarse cry, fell heavily upon the floor. I turned him over with my foot, and placed my hand upon his heart. There was no movement. He was dead!

'The blood had been streaming from my nose, but I had taken no notice of it. I don't know what it was that put it into my head to write upon the wall with it. Perhaps it was some mischievous idea of setting the police upon a wrong track, for I felt light-hearted and cheerful. I remembered a

German being found in New York with RACHE written up above him, and it was argued at the time in the newspapers that the secret societies must have done it. I guessed that what puzzled the New Yorkers would puzzle the Londoners, so I dipped my finger in my own blood and printed it on a convenient place on the wall. Then I walked down to my cab and found that there was nobody about, and that the night was still very wild. I had driven some distance, when I put my hand into the pocket in which I usually kept Lucy's ring, and found that it was not there. I was thunderstruck at this, for it was the only memento* that I had of her. Thinking that I might have dropped it when I stooped over Drebber's body, I drove back, and leaving my cab in a side street, I went boldly up to the house—for I was ready to dare anything rather than lose the ring. When I arrived there, I walked right into the arms of a police-officer who was coming out, and only managed to disarm his suspicions by pretending to be hopelessly drunk.

'That was how Enoch Drebber came to his end. All I had to do then was to do as much for Stangerson, and so pay off John Ferrier's debt. I knew that he was staying at Halliday's Private Hotel, and I hung about all day, but he never came out. I fancy that he suspected something when Drebber failed to put in an appearance. He was cunning, was Stangerson, and always on his guard. If he thought he could keep me off by staying indoors he was very much mistaken. I soon found out which was the window of his bed-room, and early next morning I took advantage of some ladders which were lying in the lane behind the hotel, and so made my way into his room in the grey of the dawn. I woke him up and told him that the hour had come when he was to answer for the life he had taken so long before. I described Drebber's death to him, and I gave him the same choice of the poisoned pills. Instead of grasping at the chance of safety which that offered him, he sprang from his bed and flew at my throat. In self-defence I stabbed him to the heart. It would have been the same in any case, for Providence would never have allowed his guilty hand to pick out anything but the poison.

'I have little more to say and it's as well, for I am about done up. I went on cabbing it for a day or so, intending to keep at it until I could save enough to take me back to America. I was standing in the yard when a ragged youngster asked if there was a cabby there called Jefferson Hope, and said that his cab was wanted by a gentleman at 221B, Baker Street. I went round suspecting no harm, and the next thing I knew, this young man here had the bracelets on my wrists, and as neatly shackled as ever I saw in my life. That's the whole of my story, gentlemen. You may consider me to be a murderer; but I hold that I am just as much an officer of justice as you are.'

So thrilling had the man's narrative been and his manner was so impressive that we had sat silent and absorbed. Even the professional detectives, *blasé* as they were in every detail of crime, appeared to be keenly interested in the man's story. When he finished, we sat for some minutes in a stillness which was only broken by the scratching of Lestrade's pencil as he gave the finishing touches to his shorthand account.

'There is only one point on which I should like a little more information,' Sherlock Holmes said at last. 'Who was your accomplice* who came for the ring which I advertised?'

The prisoner winked at my friend jocosely. 'I can tell my own secrets,' he said, 'but I don't get other people into trouble. I saw your advertisement, and I thought it might be a plant, or it might be the ring which I wanted. My friend volunteered to go and see. I think you'll own he did it smartly.'*

'Not a doubt of that,' said Holmes heartily.

'Now, gentlemen,' the inspector remarked, gravely, 'the forms of the law must be complied with. On Thursday the prisoner will be brought before the magistrates, and your attendance will be required. Until then I will be responsible for him.' He rang the bell as he spoke, and Jefferson Hope was led off by a couple of warders, while my friend and I made our way out of the station and took a cab back to Baker Street.

· CHAPTER 7 ·

The Conclusion

WE had all been warned to appear before the magistrates upon the Thursday; but when the Thursday came there was no occasion for our testimony. A higher Judge had taken the matter in hand, and Jefferson Hope had been summoned before a tribunal where strict justice would be meted out to him. On the very night after his capture the aneurism burst, and he was found in the morning stretched upon the floor of the cell, with a placid smile upon his face, as though he had been able in his dying moments to look back upon a useful life, and on work well done.

'Gregson and Lestrade will be wild about his death,' Holmes remarked, as we chatted it over next evening. 'Where will their grand advertisement be now?'

'I don't see that they had very much to do with his capture,' I answered.

'What you do in this world is a matter of no consequence,'* returned my companion, bitterly. 'The question is, what can you make people believe that you have done. Never mind,' he continued, more brightly, after a pause. 'I would not have missed the investigation for anything. There has been no better case within my recollection. Simple as it was, there were several most instructive points about it.'

'Simple!' I ejaculated.

'Well, really, it can hardly be described as otherwise,' said Sherlock Holmes, smiling at my surprise. 'The proof of its intrinsic simplicity is, that without any help save a few very ordinary deductions I was able to lay my hand upon the criminal within three days.'

'That is true,' said I.

'I have already explained to you that what is out of the common is usually a guide rather than a hindrance. In solving a problem of this sort, the grand thing is to be able to reason backwards. That is a very useful accomplishment, and a very easy one, but people do not practise it much. In the every-day affairs of life it is more useful to reason forwards, and so the other comes to be neglected. There are fifty who can reason synthetically for one who can reason analytically.'*

'I confess,' said I, 'that I do not quite follow you.'

'I hardly expected that you would. Let me see if I can make it clearer. Most people, if you describe a train of events to them, will tell you what the result would be. They can put those events together in their minds, and argue from them that something will come to pass. There are few people, however, who, if you told them a result, would be able to evolve from their own inner consciousness what the steps were which led up to that result. This power is what I mean when I talk of reasoning backwards, or analytically.'

'I understand,' said I.

'Now this was a case in which you were given the result and had to find everything else for yourself. Now let me endeavour to show you the different steps in my reasoning. To begin at the beginning. I approached the house, as you know, on foot, and with my mind entirely free from all impressions. I naturally began by examining the roadway, and there, as I have already explained to you, I saw clearly the marks of a cab, which, I ascertained by inquiry, must have been there during the night. I satisfied myself that it was a cab and not a private carriage by the narrow gauge of the wheels. The ordinary London growler* is considerably less wide than a gentleman's brougham.*

'This was the first point gained. I then walked slowly down the garden path, which happened to be composed of a clay soil, peculiarly suitable for taking impressions. No doubt it appeared to you to be a mere trampled line of slush, but to my trained eyes every mark upon its surface had a meaning. There is no branch of detective science which is so important and so much neglected as the art of tracing footsteps. Happily, I have always laid great stress upon it, and much practice has made it second nature to me. I saw the heavy footmarks of the constables, but I saw also the track of the two men who had first passed through the garden. It was easy to tell that they had been before the others, because in places their marks had been entirely obliterated by the others coming upon the top of them. In this way my second link was formed, which told me that the nocturnal visitors were two in number, one remarkable for his height (as I calculated from the length of his stride) and the other fashionably dressed, to judge from the small and elegant impression left by his boots.

'On entering the house this last inference was confirmed. My well-booted man lay before me. The tall one, then, had done the murder, if murder there was. There was no wound upon the dead man's person, but the agitated expression upon his face assured me that he had foreseen his fate before it came upon him. Men who die from heart disease, or any sudden natural cause, never by any chance exhibit agitation upon their features. Having sniffed the dead man's lips, I detected a slightly sour smell, and I came to the conclusion that he had had poison forced upon him. Again, I argued that it had been forced upon him from the hatred and fear expressed upon his face. By the method of exclusion, I had arrived at this result, for no other hypothesis would meet the facts. Do not imagine that it was a very unheard-of idea. The forcible administration of poison* is by no means a new thing in criminal annals. The cases of Dolsky in Odessa, and of Leturier in Montpellier, will occur at once to any toxicologist.

'And now came the great question as to the reason why. Robbery had not been the object of the murder, for nothing was taken. Was it politics, then, or was it a woman? That was the question which confronted me. I was inclined from the first to the latter supposition. Political assassins are only too glad to do their work and to fly. This murder had, on the contrary, been done most deliberately, and the perpetrator had left his tracks all over the room, showing that he had been there all the time. It must have been a private wrong, and not a political one, which called for such a methodical revenge. When the inscription was discovered upon the wall, I was more inclined than ever to my opinion. The thing was too evidently a blind.* When the ring was found, however, it settled the question. Clearly the murderer had used it to remind his victim of some dead or absent woman. It was at this point that I asked Gregson whether he had inquired in his telegram to Cleveland as to any particular point in Mr Drebber's former career. He answered, you remember, in the negative.

'I then proceeded to make a careful examination of the room, which confirmed me in my opinion as to the murderer's height, and furnished me with the additional details as to the Trichinopoly cigar and the length of his nails. I had already come to the conclusion, since there were no signs of a struggle, that the blood which covered the floor had burst from the murderer's nose in his excitement. I could perceive that the track of blood coincided with the track of his feet. It is seldom that any man, unless he is very full-blooded, breaks out in this way through emotion, so I hazarded the opinion that the criminal was probably a robust and ruddy-faced man. Events proved that I had judged correctly.

'Having left the house, I proceeded to do what Gregson had neglected. I telegraphed to the head of the police at Cleveland, limiting my inquiry to the circumstances connected with the marriage of Enoch Drebber. The answer was conclusive. It told me that Drebber had already applied for the protection of the law against an old rival in love, named Jefferson Hope, and that this same Hope was at present in Europe. I knew now that I held the clue to the mystery in my hand, and all that remained was to secure the murderer.

'I had already determined in my own mind that the man who had walked into the house with Drebber was none other than the man who had driven the cab. The marks in the road showed me that the horse had wandered on in a way which would have been impossible had there been anyone in charge of it. Where, then, could the driver be, unless he were inside the house? Again, it is absurd to suppose that any sane man would carry out a deliberate crime under the very eyes, as it were, of a third person, who was sure to betray him. Lastly, supposing one man wished to dog another through London, what better means could be adopt than to turn cab-driver. All these considerations led me to the irresistible conclusion that Jefferson Hope was to be found among the jarveys of the Metropolis.*

'If he had been one, there was no reason to believe that he had ceased to be. On the contrary, from his point of view, any sudden change would be likely to draw attention to himself. He would probably, for a time at least, continue to perform his duties. There was no reason to suppose that he was going under an assumed name. Why should he change his name in a country where no one knew his original one? I therefore organized my Street Arab detective corps, and sent them systematically to every cab proprietor in London until they ferreted out the man that I wanted. How well they succeeded, and how quickly I took advantage of it, are still fresh in your recollection. The murder of Stangerson was an incident which was entirely unexpected, but which could hardly in any case have been prevented. Through it, as you know, I came into possession of the pills, the existence of which I had already surmised. You see, the whole thing is a chain of logical sequences without a break or flaw.'

'It is wonderful!' I cried. 'Your merits should be publicly recognized. You should publish an account of the case. If you won't, I will for you.'

'You may do what you like, Doctor,'* he answered. 'See here!' he continued, handing a paper over to me, 'look at this!'

It was the *Echo** for the day, and the paragraph to which he pointed was devoted to the case in question.

'The public,' it said, 'have lost a sensational treat through the sudden death of the man Hope, who was suspected of the murder of Mr Enoch Drebber and of Mr Joseph Stangerson. The details of the case will probably be never known now, though we are informed upon good authority that the crime was the result of an old-standing and romantic feud, in which love and Mormonism bore a part. It seems that both the victims belonged, in their younger days, to the Latter Day Saints, and Hope, the deceased prisoner, hails also from Salt Lake City. If the case has had no other effect, it, at least, brings out in the most striking manner the efficiency of our detective police force, and will serve as a lesson to all foreigners that they will do wisely to settle their feuds at home, and not to carry them on to British soil. It is an open secret that the credit of this smart capture belongs entirely to the well-known Scotland Yard officials, Messrs Lestrade and Gregson. The man was apprehended, it appears, in the rooms of a certain Mr Sherlock Holmes, who has himself, as an amateur, shown some talent in the detective line, and who, with such instructors, may hope in time to attain to some degree of their skill. It is expected that a testimonial* of some sort will be presented to the two officers as a fitting recognition of their services.'

'Didn't I tell you so when we started?' cried Sherlock Holmes, with a laugh. 'That's the result of all our Study in Scarlet; to get them a testimonial!'

'Never mind,' I answered; 'I have all the facts in my journal, and the public shall know them. In the meantime you must make yourself contented by the consciousness of success, like the Roman miser:

' "Populus me sibilat, at mihi plaudo
Ipse domi simul ac nummos contemplor in arca." '*

APPENDIX

I knew that the book was as good as I could make it, and I had high hopes. When *Girdlestone* used to come circling back with the precision of a homing pigeon, I was grieved but not surprised, for I acquiesced in the decision. But when my little Holmes book began also to do the circular tour I was hurt, for I knew that it deserved a better fate. James Payn applauded but found it both too short and too long, which was true enough. Arrowsmith received it in May, 1886, and returned it unread in July. Two or three others sniffed and turned away. Finally, as Ward, Lock & Co. made a speciality of cheap and often sensational literature, I sent it to them.

(ACD, *Memories and Adventures*, 90)

Who 'discovered'—I do not like the word in such connexion, but it is in common use to-day—Sherlock Holmes? The reply is, as shall here, for the first time be narrated, that my wife did. She [Jeanie Gwynne Bettany, d. 1941] was then the wife of the late [George Thomas] Bettany [1850–91], MA, BSc, at one time a Cambridge 'Don', but, later, chief Editor to Messrs. Ward, Lock, & Co.

One day a MS entitled 'A Study in Scarlet', penned in a beautifully clear and small round hand, arrived at Ward Lock's, and came before Bettany. As he was a science man (bracketed Third in the Natural Science Tripos) he took it home with him to say to his wife: 'You have published a novel, and have contributed stories to *Temple Bar*, *The Argosy*, and *Belgravia*, and are likely to be a better judge of fiction than I. So I should be glad if you would look through this, and tell me whether I ought to read it.'

Mrs Bettany's first intention was to be a doctor, so she had, at one time, attended lectures, and closely studied medical science. That is, no doubt, why she said to her husband: 'This is, I feel sure, by a doctor—there is internal evidence to that effect. But in any case, the writer is a born novelist. I am enthusiastic about the book, and believe it will be a great success.'

([John] Coulson Kernahan (1858–1943), 'Personal Memories of Sherlock Holmes', *London Quarterly and Holborn Review* (Oct. 1934))

Dear Sir,

   We have read your story *A Study in Scarlet,* and are pleased with it. We could not publish it this year, as the market is flooded at present with cheap fiction, but if you do not object to its being held over till next year we will give you £25/-/- (Twenty-five Pounds) for the copyright.

   We are

      Dear Sir,

          Yours faithfully,

             Ward, Lock & Co.

(To ACD, 30 Oct. 1886)

It was not a very tempting offer, and even I, poor as I was, hesitated to accept it. It was not merely the small sum offered, but it was the long delay, for this book might open a road for me. I was heart-sick, however, at repeated disappointments, and I felt that perhaps it was true wisdom to make sure of publicity, however late.

(ACD, Memories and Adventures, 90–1)

Dear Sir,

   In reply to your letter of yesterday's date. We regret to say that we shall be unable to allow you to retain a percentage on the sale of your work as it might give rise to some confusion. The tale may have to be inserted together with some other, in one of our annuals, therefore we must adhere to our original offer of 25£ for the complete copyright.

   We are

      Dear Sir,

          Yours truly,

             For Ward, Lock & Co. &c.

(To ACD, 2 Nov. 1886; quoted in Uncollected Sherlock Holmes, 43)

November 20th 1886

IN CONSIDERATION of the sum of Twenty-Five Pounds paid by them to me I hereby assign to Messrs, Ward, Lock & Co., of Warwick House, Salisbury Square, E.C. Publishers the Copyright and all my interest in the book written by me entitled A STUDY IN SCARLET.

   A. Conan Doyle MD

Bush Villa, Southsea.

(Quoted by Gibson and Lancelyn Green,
Bibliography of A. Conan Doyle, 10)

This story will be found remarkable for the skilful presentation of a supremely ingenious detective, whose performances, while based on the most rational principles, outshine any hitherto depicted. In fact, every detective ought to read *A Study in Scarlet* as a most hopeful means to his own advancement. The surprises are most cleverly and yet most naturally managed, and at each stage the reader's attention is kept fascinated and eager for the next event. The sketches of the 'Wild West' in its former trackless and barren condition, and of the terrible position of the starving traveller with his pretty charge, are most vivid and artistic. Indeed, the entire section of the story which deals with early events in the Mormon settlement is most stirring, and intense pathos is brought out in some of the scenes. The publishers have great satisfaction in assuring the Trade that no Annual for some years has equalled the one which they now offer for *naturalness, truth, skill, and exciting interest*. It is certain to be read, not once, but twice by every reader, and the person who can take it up and lay it down again unfinished must be one of those rare people who are neither impressionable nor curious. *A Study in Scarlet* should be the talk of every Christmas gathering throughout the land.

> (Ward, Lock, & Co., announcement for *Beeton's Christmas Annual, Publisher's Circular*, 1 Nov. 1887, quoted by Lancelyn Green (ed.), *Sherlock Holmes Letters*, 4–5)

Beeton's Christmas Annual (London: Ward, Lock & Co.) is now an old institution, and as regularly looked for as the holly and mistletoe. This year its contents are full and varied. The *pièce de résistance* is a story by A. Conan Doyle entitled *A Study in Scarlet*. It is the story of a murder, and of the preternatural sagacity of a scientific detective, to whom Edgar Allan Poe's Dupin was a trifler, and Gaboriau's Lecoq a child. He is a wonderful man is Mr Sherlock Holmes, but one gets so wonderfully interested in his cleverness and in the mysterious murder which he unravels that one cannot lay down the narrative until the end is reached. What that end is wild horses shall not make us divulge. After the *Study in Scarlet* come two original little drawing-room plays. One is of the nature of a vaudeville, and is called 'Food for Powder'; it should be effective as it is amusing. The other is 'The Four-Leaved Shamrock', a drawing-room comedietta in three acts, also very good of its kind. The number is enriched with engravings by D. H. Friston, Matt Streetch, and R. André.

> (*Glasgow Herald*, 17 Dec. 1887)

The chief piece in 'Beeton's Christmas Annual' is a detective story by Mr A. Conan Doyle, *A Study in Scarlet*. This is as entrancing a tale of ingenuity in tracing out crime as has been written since the time of Edgar Allan Poe. The author shows genius. He has not trodden in the well-worn paths of literature, but has shown how the true detective should work by observation and deduction. His book is bound to have many readers.

(*Scotsman*, 19 Dec. 1887)

In the flood of new books two little ones and good may have escaped the notice of readers who will enjoy either, or both. For a railway story, to beguile the way, few things have been so good, of late, as Mr Conan Doyle's *Study in Scarlet*. It is a shilling story about a murder, unluckily, for the [Jack the Ripper] horrors of recent months do not dispose one to take pleasure in the romance of assassinations. However, granting the subject, this is an extremely clever narrative, rich in surprises, indeed I never was more surprised by any story than when it came to the cabman. To say more would be 'telling', but one may admit that the weak place in the tale, as in most of Gaboriau's, is the explanation, the part of the story which gives the 'reason why' of the mystery. However, with this deduction, Mr Conan Doyle comes nearer to the true Hugh Conway [pseudonym of Frederick John Fargus (1847–85)] than any writer since the regretted death of the author of *Called Back* . . .

(Andrew Lang, 'At the Sign of the Ship', *Longman's Magazine* (Jan. 1889) 335–6)

He also was outrageous, upon his supposition that my countrymen 'loved Scotland better than truth', saying, 'All of them,—nay not all,—but *droves* of them, would come up, and attest any thing for the honour of Scotland.'

(Boswell, *Life of Johnson*, 21 Mar. 1775)

In 1889 I became junior Editor to Ward, Lock, & Co., and Assistant Editor of *Lippincott's* Magazine, which they published on this side of the Atlantic. Looking through the firm's file copies [*c.* Jan. 1890], I came across the 1887 issue of *Beeton's Christmas Annual*, and took it to the Managing Director. 'Is there anything being done with this?' I asked.

He shook his head to reply: 'It served its purpose, and did respectably as the Annual, but the sales were not great [when it was issued as a book in July 1888, presumably, the *Annual* having sold out fast] and few reviewers had anything to say of it [in book publication].'

'No', I answered, 'so many books appear at Christmas that reviewers are not likely to write at length, or even to notice the contents of one of the many Christmas Annuals. But since then, Doyle has published *Micah Clarke*, and *The Captain of the Pole-Star*. The complete novel in the next [Feb. 1890] issue of *Lippincott's Magazine* is 'The Sign of [the] Four' in which Sherlock Holmes is the leading character. I am as sure, as one can humanly be, that there is a great future for stories in which Sherlock Holmes figures. As you have *A Study in Scarlet*, the very first story about Sherlock Holmes, I suggest that you reissue it as a book, by itself, attractively produced, and attractively illustrated. I believe it will have a huge sale, and go on selling for years.'

(Kernahan, 'Memories of Sherlock Holmes')

I never at any time received another penny for it.

(ACD, *Memories and Adventures*, 91)

EXPLANATORY NOTES

A Study in Scarlet was published in *Beeton's Christmas Annual* for 1887, going on sale in November. It was the main feature, the rest of the annual containing plays for private performance—'Food for Powder' by R. André, 'a vaudeville for the drawing-room', and 'The Four-Leaved Shamrock' by C. J. Hamilton, 'a drawing-room comedietta'. André, who worked mainly as an artist, and Miss Hamilton were regular contributors to *Beeton's*.

The first book edition was published by Ward, Lock & Co., 2–16 July 1888. It sold for a shilling (like other 'shilling shockers'), chiefly on railway-stalls, and carried the following 'Publishers' Preface' (ACD having indignantly refused to give them another line without further remuneration):

> This book contains a story of thrilling interest, in which the expectation of the reader, and his faculties for conjecture and deduction are kept in employment from first to last. The 'Study in Scarlet' and the unravelling of the apparently unfathomable mystery by the cool shrewdness of Mr Sherlock Holmes, yields nothing in point of sustained interest and grateful expectation to the best stories of the school that has produced 'Mr Barnes of New York' [by Archibald Clavering Gunter (1847–1907): it sold over a million copies], 'Shadowed by Time' [by 'Lawrence L. Lynch', i.e. Emma Murdoch Van Devanter] &c, &c, &c, and the description of the deadly Mormon association of tyranny and vengeance, is as true in its features as it is enthralling in its interest.
>
> The work has a valuable advantage in the shape of illustrations by the author's father, MR CHARLES DOYLE, a younger brother of the late MR RICHARD DOYLE, the eminent colleague of JOHN LEECH, in the pages of *Punch*, and son of the eminent caricaturist whose political sketches, signed 'H.B.', were a feature in London half-a-century ago.
>
> The original issue of this remarkable story having been exhausted, it is now presented to the public in a new form, with these additional attractions, in the full expectation that it will win a new and wide circle of readers.

A second impression appeared in Mar. 1889. A third book printing (the second English edition), with forty illustrations by

George Hutchinson and much larger print (248 pages to the earlier 184) was issued in Dec. 1891 as No. 1 of 'The Warwick House Library'; there was also a Colonial issue in Ward and Lock's Colonial Library, and an impression for Lever Brothers at Port Sunlight in 1893 as part of their Sunlight Library, whose volumes were given free in exchange for soap wrappers. Another issue, with illustrations by James Greig, was presented with the *Windsor Magazine* Christmas number (Dec. 1895), a Ward, Lock & Bowden publication. Ward, Lock also published their third book printing in New York, but they had been preceded in America by the J. B. Lippincott Company of Philadelphia, who at ACD's earnest urging had published it following their success with its sequel, *The Sign of the Four*: it was sold at 50 cents from 1 Mar. 1890, with a cloth edition from Sept. at 75 cents. When Ward, Lock published in New York with the Hutchinson illustrations they charged $1.50 (as against their English price of 3/6).

A Study in Scarlet was serialized in the Bristol *Observer* (Oct.–Nov. 1890), *Tit Bits* (Apr.–June 1893), and the *Glasgow Weekly Mail* (Jan.–Mar. 1894). In America it was reprinted in the *Illustrated Home Guest*, New York (Nov. 1892) and the *Pennsylvanian Grit Story Companion* (1905). Later Ward, Lock editions carried Joseph Bell's review of the *Adventures of Sherlock Holmes* (*Bookman*, Dec. 1892), slightly truncated to disguise its occasion (see Introduction to the *Adventures* in the present series). Bell's preface was ultimately dropped, but the title continued to appear from Ward, Lock as a single volume long after ACD's death, selling alongside the rest of the individual Holmes volumes issued by John Murray, who had taken over the earlier editions. Meanwhile it also sold as part of Murray's *Sherlock Holmes: Collected Long Stories* (1929) and had duly taken its place in the Author's Edition (1903) of the works he was prepared to see collected and was included in the Crowborough Edition (1930).

3 *late*: once, but no longer. Whether or not ACD at this point saw any future to Holmes and Watson beyond *A Study in Scarlet*, the designation is consistent with Watson's departure from the Army medical corps after his marriage, in order to take up civilian medical practice ('A Scandal in Bohemia', *Adventures*). If the Southsea Notebook's jottings on the First Afghan War (1838–42) indicate an initial thought of making that, and not the Second, the cause of Watson's invalid status, then, as originally designed, 'late' may also have borne its other meaning—'dead'.

5 *1878*: ACD's final decision for the date in the past in which the story is to commence. But when he wrote its sequel, with 3 ½ years separating the dates of composition, he put *The Sign of the Four* into a much more recent past. Yet the *Sign* assumes very little distance in time from the Watson-related portions of the *Study*.

Doctor of Medicine of the University of London: i.e. Watson wrote a dissertation breaking new medical ground, as ACD had done in 1885. That it won him a doctorate from the non-residential multi-collegiate metropolitan institution does not mean he did his undergraduate work in London, though it is clear that he was a resident at an affiliated hospital, St Bartholomew's, at least while writing the thesis. By 1878 London had become the leading medical centre in Britain, Edinburgh's loss of pre-eminence dating from its failure to prevent the departure to London in 1877 of its Professor of Clinical Surgery, Joseph Lister (1827–1912), the great pioneer in antiseptics. In the self-parody 'The Field Bazaar' (see *The Return of Sherlock Holmes* in the present series) 'Holmes' alleges that 'Watson' is, like most British general practitioners, only a bachelor of medicine and surgery and hence not really entitled to be called 'Dr Watson'. Since ACD was 26 when he graduated MD, we may infer he thought of Watson as having been born in 1852.

Netley: the Royal Victoria Military Hospital at Netley, 3 miles from Southampton. It was built in 1856 after the Crimean War for wounded soldiers as a result of the outcry over the ill-treatment of British military casualties by the authorities. It accommodated over a thousand patients, was the chief military hospital in Britain, and was a major training institution for male and female personnel.

Fifth Northumberland Fusiliers: soldiers armed with a fusil, or flintlock musket, may have appealed to ACD as a British equivalent of the French musketeers immortalized by Alexandre Dumas *père* (1802–70). He may have intended to imply that Watson was connected by birth or family with Northumberland.

second Afghan war: Russian–British rivalry in central Asia, increasing after Britain thwarted Russian designs against Turkey in 1878, resulted in the Emir Shere Ali repulsing

British diplomatic attempts to counter Russian overtures in Afghanistan, whereupon the British Viceroy of India, the poet Edward Robert Bulwer Lytton second Baron Lytton (1831–91), son of the novelist much parodied by Conan Doyle, began the war in Nov. 1878. The British seized Kandahar, Jalalabad, and key mountain passes. Shere Ali fled and died in Feb. 1879; his son Yakub Khan signed the treaty of Gandamak in May 1879, giving Britain control of Afghan foreign policy, outlying tracts of land, and a permanent envoy at Kabul, where the British envoy was massacred with his entourage in Sept. Sir Frederick Roberts (1832–1914) defeated the Afghans and entered Kabul in Oct. Yakub Khan fled to India, and Shere Ali's elder brother's son, Abdur Rahman, was recognized by Britain as emir in midsummer 1880, giving Britain control of Afghan foreign policy. In July 1880 Ayub Khan, Shere Ali's younger son, who had held Herat since Shere Ali's death, marched on Kandahar.

5 *Bombay*: allowing six months for the Netley course, this would bring Watson to India in about May 1879, at which point he would probably have had to re-embark for Karachi in what is now Pakistan, making his way to the province of Baluchistan.

corps: by his corps Watson means the Fifth Northumberlands, not the medical corps, which would have been stretched out among the regiments. No doubt the word is chosen as a foundation for his nearly leaving his corpse as well.

Candahar: the next generation of whites would call it Kandahar, a later generation still Qandahar. Sir Donald Stewart (1824–1900) had easily entered Kandahar from Baluchistan via the Bolan Pass at the beginning of the war, using it as his headquarters from where he marched to Kabul in Dec. 1879 to put down a general tribal uprising against the British forces of occupation there. After the acceptance of Abdur Rahman by the British, Kandahar was severed from his rule at Kabul and Shere Ali Khan put in by the British as 'independent' ruler.

many: for instance General Sir Donald Stewart was made KCB 1879, GCB and baronet 1880, Commander-in-Chief in India 1880–5, and was invested by Queen Victoria with the Grand Cross of the Star of India on 3 Jan. 1886 shortly before ACD began *A Study in Scarlet*. General Roberts was made KCB 1878, GCB, baronet, and commander-in-chief of the

Madras Army 1880, and succeeded Stewart as Indian C-i-C, again on the eve of this book.

Berkshires: otherwise Princess Charlotte of Wales's Royal Regiment. By her death in childbirth Princess Charlotte (1796–1817), the daughter of the future George IV, made possible the accession of Queen Victoria.

Maiwand: 27 July 1880. Ayub Khan caught up with a British force from Kandahar intended to oppose him, at 'a place called Khushk-i-nakhud, and after our troops had suffered severely from the enemy's artillery fire . . . an advance of cavalry and a wild charge of Ghazis broke up the Bombay Native Infantry (Jacob's Rifles), who fell back in disorder on the 66th Regiment. All regular formation being presently lost, and our cavalry but ineffectively handled, it was not long, although the 66th fought magnificently, before the disorder degenerated into defeat, and defeat into rout. The remains of the force succeeded in getting into Candahar the following afternoon, and Ayoub [*sic*], following them up as closely as his losses, which were also very serious, would allow, laid siege to General Primrose, who, on the first news of the battle, had withdrawn into the citadel. The return of killed and wounded, published in the *London Gazette*, showed the following list of casualties in this disastrous affair as:—Europeans killed—officers, 20; non-commissioned officers and men, 290. Wounded—officers, 8; non-commissioned officers and men, 6. Natives killed—officers, 11; non-commissioned officers and men, 643. Wounded—officers, 9; non-commissioned officers and men, 109. Followers—killed, 331; wounded, 7; 201 horses were killed and 68 wounded' (Joseph Irving, *The Annals of Our Time 1871–87* (1889), 1341).

Presumably ACD, on board the Greenland whaler *Hope* at the time of Maiwand and not even knowing of it for several weeks, did not realize what very little attrition was suffered by the 'European' (i.e. white) officers. Had Watson been a native NCO or 'man' he would have been much less conspicuous as a casualty. Still, it helps explain why he could be singled out for so much attention: ACD would have had these details from Indian Army officers resident at Southsea.

shoulder: in *The Sign of the Four* Watson speaks of 'my wounded leg. I had had a Jezail bullet through it some time before, and, though it did not prevent me from walking, it ached wearily at every change of the weather' (Ch. 1). ACD's oral evidence and notebook jottings relative to Afghanistan seem exclusively on the First Afghan war, and his note of Dr William Bryden (1811–73), who rode wounded and half-dead alone of his company into Jalalabad in the retreat from Kabul (1842), suggests he thought of Watson, like Bryden, as having been wounded in several places, the shoulder first seeming worse but the leg proving more long-lasting.

5 *a Jezail bullet*: a bullet fired from a long, heavy Afghan gun, liable to cause infection in the wounds it made since its ingredients would be old nails, broken silver, etc., assembled in archaic fashion.

subclavian artery: a large artery at the base of the neck. Watson is a characteristic product of Edinburgh medical school auto-experiment reportage, coldly scientific in his self-diagnosis. *Round the Red Lamp* includes 'The Surgeon Talks' and 'A Physiologist's Wife' in which doctors diagnose their own imminent deaths.

Ghazis: veteran Muslim warriors, slayers of infidels enjoying high repute.

Murray: presumably from (Sir) John Murray (1841–1914) of the *Challenger* (see later in this chapter, note on 'astonish his professors', p. 7).

orderly: Watson's batman, an ordinary soldier with some medical knowledge picked up from his superior.

pack-horse: association of ideas with Bryden (see above, note on 'shoulder', p. 5).

train: Roberts relieved Kandahar from Kabul by defeating Ayub Khan on 1 Sept. Watson would have spent a very unpleasant August. The British then resolved on the evacuation of Kandahar, whence Watson's journey of over 300 miles back to Kabul, in convoy, the train being composed of fit as well as wounded men from Roberts's and Stewart's forces.

Peshawur: Watson and the other wounded, with escort, carried on up the Khyber Pass to what is now Pakistan.

enteric fever: typhoid fever.

our Indian possessions: 'possession' symbolizes very neatly the imperial idea of holding objects of gain.

6 *Orontes*: Lebanese river flowing through Syria into Turkey, past Antioch and into the Mediterranean, largely unnavigable. The trooppship was a frequent caller to Portsmouth in ACD's time at Southsea, and his practice was occasionally increased by patients from it.

Portsmouth jetty: one character in search of an author.

irretrievably ruined: exaggeration, clearly, in the light of later developments, but this was the prognosis on P. H. Watson after his enteric fever in Scutari and return to Scotland.

nine months: this is evidently the time-frame within which ACD saw both *A Study in Scarlet* and *The Sign of the Four* as taking place (together with 'The Speckled Band' and certain other *Adventures*). Any longer stay while Watson is still a member of the Army Medical Department is impossible. On internal evidence the stories appear to be set in 1882 and 1888, respectively, but in relation to one another they are nine months apart.

eleven shillings and sixpence a day: i.e. 57 ½ new pence per day. Longman cites 'The Noble Bachelor' (*Adventures*) where an itemized bill runs to eight shillings (40p) for rooms, two shillings and sixpence (12 ½p) for breakfast and lunch each, cocktail one shilling (5p), glass of sherry eightpence (two-thirds of 5p) at 'one of the most expensive hotels'. So Watson had to live cheaply but, as Longman says, 'many people's entire weekly wages at this period were well below eleven shillings and sixpence'.

cesspool . . . Empire . . . drained: this is the view from Portsmouth (not to speak of Plymouth, Birmingham, Edinburgh, and the African west coast), and not unreasonably ascribed to Netley and Afghanistan. It is an interesting starting-point for the most successful celebration of London since Dickens.

comfortless, meaningless existence: the periphery deriding the metropolis is firmly in action here much as, thirty years later, William Butler Yeats (1865–1939) in 'Easter 1916' spoke of 'polite meaningless words'. It also reflects the ancient anti-urban tradition so vigorously asserted from the Bible to Jefferson and Wordsworth. It is for Holmes in 'The Copper Beeches' (*Adventures*) to demolish Watson's surviving rural myths, maintained in the absence which makes hearts grow fonder ('It is my belief, Watson, founded upon my experience, that the lowest and vilest alleys in London do not present a more dreadful record of sin than does the smiling and beautiful countryside').

6 *metropolis . . . rusticate*: 'rusticate' is applied to the disciplinary removal of a student from a university for a period; Watson uses the word in its original sense of returning to the country, thus capturing an identification of city with university (more true of Edinburgh than elsewhere, at least in ACD's time).

Criterion Bar: the Criterion Restaurant, including bedrooms, theatre, and American (i.e. long, saloon-like) bar, had been built in 1873, and hence was more of a landmark to a visitor than to a born Londoner. It was situated in Piccadilly Circus.

Stamford: perhaps from Stamford Bridge where Harold II of England defeated his brother Tostig and Harold Hardrada of Norway in 1066, immediately before going south to face William the Conqueror at Hastings.

a dresser: a medical student whose duty is to dress wounds. Stamford would have been 'under' Watson in the sense of being a member of a surgeon's team in which he was inferior to Watson, the 'houseman' (a graduate resident doctor but not the principal operator on the patients, save in emergencies).

Barts: St Bartholomew's Hospital, West Smithfield, in the City of London, founded in 1123 supposedly after a vision of the apostle Bartholomew appeared to Rahere (d. .1144), a jester and prebendary of St Paul's. Bartholomew is usually taken to be the Nathanael referred to in John 1: 'Jesus saw Nathanael coming to him, and saith of him, Behold an Israelite indeed, in whom is no guile! / Nathanael saith unto him, Whence knowest thou me? Jesus answered and said unto him, Before that Philip called thee, when thou wast under the fig tree, I saw thee' (47–8). He seems a fitting saint under whose auspices ACD made Holmes and Watson meet one another.

the Holborn: a fashionable restaurant in High Holborn, slightly south-east of the British Museum, famous for its mosaic, majolica, and Masonic Hall. Watson's loneliness is evident in so extravagant a gesture. That Stamford could afford the time for drinks at the 'Cri' and a heavy lunch at the Holborn, when presumably a houseman himself at Bart's, suggests a lifestyle of some pretension (as does his manner to Watson,

which is patronizing despite his junior status), and less conviction in medical ideals than Watson normally preferred.

hansom: named after Joseph Aloysius Hansom (1803–82); a
one-horsed, two-wheeler, driven from behind the open-
fronted seating compartment by a high-perched driver,
they probably moved through London faster than any other
vehicle. At their peak they numbered 8,000. The minimum
charge was a shilling (5p) for two miles, with sixpence (2½p)
a mile beyond that but with no obligation to go more than
six miles: further charges were added beyond the 'Four Mile
Radius' from Charing Cross. Benjamin Disraeli (1804–81)
called the hansoms 'the gondolas of London', and no doubt
the weather frequently proved him right.

7 *too much for his purse*: gentlemen sharing lodgings as a literary
theme are found in *Box and Cox* (1847), adapted from two
French farces by John Maddison Morton (1811–91), in which
the co-tenancy is involuntary, which inspired *Cox and Box*
(1867), libretto by (Sir) Francis Burnand (1836–1917) and
music by (Sir) Arthur Sullivan (1842–1900). In Israel Zang-
will's story 'Cheating the Gallows' (1893) one tenant is hanged
for murdering the other, though they are finally revealed to
be the same person. (The story's opening sentence echoes the
Holmes–Watson situation: 'They say that a union of opposites
makes the happiest marriage, and perhaps it is on the same
principle that men who chum together are always so oddly
assorted.') Edgar Allan Poe, 'The Murders in the Rue Morgue'
(1841), comes into a different category: 'as my worldly circumstances were somewhat less embarrassed than his own, I was
permitted to be at the expense of renting, and furnishing in
a style which suited the rather fantastic gloom of our common
temper, a time-eaten and grotesque mansion, long deserted
through superstitions into which we did not inquire, and
tottering to its fall in a retired and desolate part of the
Faubourg St Germain'.

Holmes's straitened circumstances do not feature again. He
contemplates the departure of Watson with financial, if not
psychological, equanimity at the end of *The Sign of the Four* and
makes no effort to replace him, but within a few months he
was pulling in commissions from the kings of the Netherlands, Scandinavia, and, of course, Bohemia. By 'The Dying
Detective' (*His Last Bow*) 'his payments were princely. I have

no doubt that the house might have been purchased at the price Holmes paid for his rooms during the years I was with him'—i.e. after the commencement of the *Return*.

7 *systematic medical classes*: i.e. he has not followed any prearranged course of studies, suiting his own needs rather than those the university decided he ought to have.

astonish his professors: the classic instance of this behaviour known to ACD was (Sir) John Murray (see note to p.5, on p. 137), born at Cobourg, Ontario, who took course upon course in science and medicine at Edinburgh. He always refused to complete degree requirements until 1872 when, happening to be in the company of a professor whose colleague Wyville Thomson (1830–82) asked for a nominee to fill a place suddenly vacated on his marine scientific expedition on the *Challenger*, Murray was thrown into bathymetrical, biological, and oceanographical investigations of the Atlantic from the Arctic to the Falklands, for which his incredible range of exact knowledge in so many fields was ideally suited. He became chief assistant in the compilation of the huge report and took it over on Thomson's death, bringing it out over fifteen years. ACD had studied under Wyville Thomson and heard the story of the desultory and eccentric student who became the swan of his university's greatest multi-disciplinary scientific venture: the *Challenger* returned just as ACD began his own medical studies. In strict point of place in the saga, he is the first of the progenitors of Sherlock Holmes.

8 *He is sure to be at the laboratory*: it is the last time that he is seen there. ACD gave himself a good base on which to start by having his initial meeting in the type of surroundings and professional activity so familiar to himself. No doubt his milieu was not untrue to London, but the environment is certainly bleak enough for Edinburgh's Old College or Royal Infirmary.

washing your hands of the matter: an appropriately hygienic proceeding on Stamford's part, but also reminiscent of Pontius Pilate before the crucifixion of Jesus. In the event, Holmes was to prove a more Christlike figure; but from time to time Watson certainly qualified for martyrdom on a more mundane level.

mealy-mouthed: over-squeamish rather than smooth-tongued in this case. Stamford's delicacy is in deliberate contrast to that of his exemplar the actor-bookseller Thomas Davies (1712–85) who deliberately fomented potential causes of antipathy in making the great introduction between Samuel Johnson and James Boswell that inspired that of Holmes and Watson. (See Boswell, *The Life of Samuel Johnson, LL.D.* (1791), 16 May 1763.)

latest vegetable alkaloid: the most recent discovery of substances in the group including strychnine and nicotine (see Part II, Ch. 6, note on 'South American arrow poison').

take it himself with the same readiness: auto-experiment was one of the most honoured Edinburgh medical traditions, a famous example being the Professor of Midwifery, Sir James Young Simpson (1811–70), when he introduced chloroform for easing pain in childbirth, having previously tested its effects both on himself and his friends (1847). Professor Sir Robert Christison (1797–1882), the foremost toxicologist of his day, nearly lost his life by chewing a sample of the Calabar bean to diagnose its properties, only saving himself by drinking his morning's shaving-water and getting a passer-by to call in his neighbour Simpson. The two most famous literary uses of auto-experiment by Edinburgh authors are Robert Louis Stevenson, *The Strange Case of Dr Jekyll and Mr Hyde* (1886) and ACD's 'The Devil's Foot' (*His Last Bow*). ACD himself used auto-experiment with nitrite of amyl for his doctoral research and in other medical investigations.

beating the subjects in the dissecting-rooms with a stick: this was actually a forensic medical experiment carried out by Christison in Nov.–Dec. 1828 to discover if the bruises on the sole corpse obtained by the police from Dr Robert Knox (1791–1862), of the many supplied by William Burke (1792–1829) and William Hare (fl. 1828), were consistent with Burke's story that the bruises were caused by accidents in packing the deceased. Christison lined up a number of corpses of animals and human beings and struck them at varied intervals, carefully timed. His conclusion was that post-mortem bruises were possible if unlikely and hence that, while Burke probably had murdered the corpse in his possession, it was not absolutely impossible that he was telling the truth. This meant that, in order to obtain a victim, the Lord Advocate offered immunity to Hare, who had murdered sixteen persons no less than Burke, and while Burke was convicted and hanged, Hare was got away to England, the Crown intervening to prevent private prosecution from the relatives of one of his victims. ACD made some use of Burke and Hare in his early story 'My Friend the Murderer' as well as in 'The Resident Patient' (*Memoirs*) and 'The Disappearance of Lady Frances Carfax' (*His Last Bow*), and called his two German spies in 'His Last Bow' Von Bork and Von Herling. Christison wrote up his experiments in 'Murder by Strangling [*sic*: a typographical error for 'Suffocation'], with some remarks on the Effects of External Violence on the Human Body soon after Death' (*Edinburgh Medical and Surgical Journal*, XXXI (1829), 229–50).

9 *retorts*: glass receptacles for heating liquids in laboratory experiments.

test-tubes: small glass containers for chemical and medical experiment or storage. ACD's early pastiche on a grocer originally named Silas Dodd being swindled when he seeks to obtain a family ghost in his newly-rich persona as Argentine D'Odd, 'Selecting a Ghost' (*Uncollected Stories*), concludes with a professional opinion signed T. E. Stube, MD. If he ever made a worse joke, it is fortunately unknown to science.

little Bunsen lamps: gas-burners for laboratory use invented by Robert Wilhelm Bunsen (1811–99). Time is agreeably wasted in Christianna Brand's detective story *Heads You Lose* (1942) while the investigators fail to realize that the butler, Bunsen, is actually Burner.

a re-agent which is precipitated by haemoglobin: 'hoemoglobin' in late Ward, Lock texts. This is the type of discovery by which George Turnavine Budd (1855–89), ACD's treacherous colleague in the ill-fated Plymouth partnership (1882), was always proposing to make his name; Holmes's manner at this point is very close to what is known of Budd's (as shown in 'Crabbe's Practice' (*Tales of Medical Life*), in Cullingworth of *The Stark Munro Letters*, and *Memories and Adventures*, Ch. 6). P. G. Wodehouse based his character 'Stanley Featherstonehaugh Ukridge' in part on ACD's literary and (probably) oral portraiture of Budd.

You have been in Afghanistan, I perceive: a classical establishment of the Holmes–Watson relationship in variation on that of Johnson and Boswell: Johnson pronounces on Boswell's coming from Scotland, Holmes on Watson's coming from Afghanistan. Each asserts his own necessities within a possible relationship by so doing: someone to dazzle, but also someone to induce into stimulating response.

Don't you see: Holmes never discusses it afterwards, but his deductions presumably included the assumption that the returned wounded doctor is looking for the missing billet in the Baker Street apartment, of which Holmes had been speaking to Stamford, whence his grasping for a strong relationship—and a dominant one—from the first.

10 *bodkin*: the early Holmes alternates between drift almost to the point of self-destruction, and action. Professor Jeffrey Richards's argument in his inaugural lecture at Lancaster University, 'Sir Henry Irving and Victorian Culture' (15 Jan. 1992) that Irving (1838–1905) was yet another origin of Holmes depends initially on ACD's enthusiastic response to Irving's performance of *Hamlet* from the time when he first saw it as a 15-year-old boy on a visit to London at Christmas 1874. The 'To be or not to be' speech (III.i.125) contemplates making one's quietus 'with a bare bodkin'.

pipette: a thin, cylindrical receptacle.

mahogany: the colour of polished reddish-brown furniture.

the old guaiacum test: if applied to a bloodstain, a solution with percentage of resin from the guaiacum tree turned blue.

microscopic examination for blood corpuscles: it may not be wholly coincidental that his very last case, 'Shoscombe Old Place' (*Case-Book*), begins with Holmes noting that as a result of his activities 'they' at Scotland Yard 'have begun to realize the importance of the microscope'.

the Sherlock Holmes test: 'It is strange that this test is never heard of again, either in Holmes's cases or in general use. It may be that further experiment showed it to be not so universally effective as Holmes first supposed (after all, it was rather rash to claim it was precipitated by haemoglobin *and nothing else*), and Holmes preferred to say nothing more of it' (Dakin, 12).

11 *Von Bischoff at Frankfort*: fictitious, but not baseless. The name means 'of bishop'; Bishop was a criminal who sought to introduce the methods of Burke and Hare to London. It resulted in the rapid passage of the Anatomy Act (1831).

11 *Mason of Bradford*: possibly prompted by Charles Mason (1730–87) of Bradley's astronomical school at Greenwich, twice an observer of the transit of Venus. ACD's medical patient at the time of writing, General A. W. Drayson, was an enthusiastic astronomer.

the notorious Muller, and Lefevre of Montpellier: Holmes is evidently shooting off these names at great speed with the obsessiveness of a devotee determined to bombard his audience with proofs of their own ignorance in a field he intends to evangelize. It is therefore impossible to determine whether Muller's notoriety extended to Lefevre, and whether Lefevre's Montpellier residence enfolded Muller. The accurate spelling of 'Montpellier' (with two ls), in contrast to its use in 'The Empty House' (*Return*) and 'Lady Frances Carfax' (*His Last Bow*), either means that ACD was inconsistent (which as a rule he was not, persisting all his life, for instance, in the absurd misspelling 'McQuire', despite his almost purely Irish ancestry); or that *Beeton's Christmas Annual* had copy-editors beyond compare (again most unlikely for so ephemeral a production), or (most likely) that the aberration originated in the *Strand*'s house policy. Dakin remarks that 'The Notorious Muller . . . cannot have been the Franz Müller who was the first railway murderer (1864), since he *was* convicted, and that not by bloodstains, but by his absentmindedly going off with his victim's hat!' (p. 12).

Samson of New Orleans: a little reminiscent of Septimius Goring of New Orleans in 'J. Habakuk Jephson's Statement' (1884), although he murdered so many people it would be difficult to determine why any one of his corpses should be singled out.

diggings: from Australian miners' parlance, then becoming standard theatre speech to denote lodgings, more especially while on tour. By 1890 it had become general, and in the mid-twentieth century its abbreviation, 'digs' was conventional British usage.

'ship's': strong tobacco of the kind favoured by sailors, capable of drawing well in a high wind. It would have been more fashionable among cricket-players in a small port town, where the story was written, than in London medical circles, one suspects. By 'The Crooked Man' (*Memoirs*), set shortly after Watson's marriage, Holmes deduces 'Hum! you still smoke

146

the Arcadia mixture of your bachelor days, then!' Baring-Gould (i, 151, n. 17), conjectures that ' "ship's" with Watson was evidently a passing fancy, picked up from the sailors aboard the *Orontes*', but his medical condition was against his picking up anything on board the *Orontes*. It would make sense for a man starting a new life among active men to show his adaptability by deliberately cultivating customs of the sailors on his voyage out, as ACD did when he went for his first voyage of any length, doctor at sea on board the whaler *Hope*.

I get in the dumps: this is not a euphemism for taking cocaine, though in the context of the full canon it has to be read as such. ACD was evidently contemplating making his detective a drug-addict, but did not implement the thought until *The Sign of the Four*. The private Holmes can only be drawn on Budd (who did have morose and misanthropic patches: he seems to have been a manic depressive) or Waller (who in older age at least was bad-tempered and avoided human contact). Poe's C. Auguste Dupin more or less lives in the dumps: 'the Chevalier . . . relapsed into his old habits of moody reverie. Prone, at all times, to abstraction, I readily fell in with his humour; and, continuing to occupy our chambers in the Faubourg Saint Germain, we gave the Future to the winds, and slumbered tranquilly in the Present, weaving the dull world around us into dreams' ('The Mystery of Marie Rogêt', 1842).

two fellows: one of the strengths of the Holmes–Watson relationship is that it encompasses all ages in its models and in its development. This schoolboy terminology reminds us that the origin of the pair, as a pair, is Artie Doyle of Edinburgh and Jim Ryan of Glasgow in the English upper-class milieu of Stonyhurst, and (apart from the ill-fated partnership with Budd (who was, in any case, married)), the second linkage of 'two fellows' with which ACD was intimately familiar was when his little brother Innes joined him at Southsea. Naturally, the elder brother used terms such as 'two fellows' for purposes of establishing a friendship within the brotherhood, although he had to act as a surrogate parent. Innes developed into a soldier (indeed a general) whose vocabulary was very much of the 'two fellows' variety.

12 *I keep a bull pup*: a bulldog was a short-barrelled revolver of large calibre. Scott uses the term. Watson evidently means a

smaller gun, which duly makes its first appearance in the canon in Ch. 5 below. Sherlockians have expended much ink in quest of a domestic pet impossible in Afghanistan, illegal on the *Orontes*, inappropriate for a private hotel, and invisible in Baker Street.

12 *ungodly hours*: godly hours would involve early rising for Matins, the morning prayer, and so on to Vespers and Compline at nightfall, and that is what Watson, the brain-child of a Jesuit boy, actually meant. He was not an early riser, at least not in his convalescence (he was, of course, early enough when in practice). The term in modern times is normally concerned with lateness, not earliness: a cab would charge extra for ungodly hours.

another set of vices: drink? No: ACD, whose father's drinking had destroyed his youth, would never ascribe drinking to a doctor intended to typify social norms. Watson is punctilious to a confessional point in noting his own very occasional indulgence. Women? Holmes jokes about it, but the joke really turns on Watson being, if anything, more shy with women than is Holmes: he reveres them from afar. The beauty of his courtship of Mary Morstan in *The Sign of the Four* is its innocence, all the more touching from a man who had known death among soldiers and patients and had personally come very close to it in both capacities himself. As a military doctor most of his dealings had been with male patients. Holmes was at least used to interviewing female clients, not to speak of personal acquaintance with ladies who divided their talents between a winning demeanour and an infanticidal economy (*The Sign of the Four*). Watson speaks of over-spending in horse-racing bets in 'Shoscombe Old Place' (*Case-Book*) but this seems to amount to no more than the usual plunge on the Derby, to judge by his evident fear that Holmes's investigations might disqualify Sir Robert Norberton's entry on which Watson was so suspiciously well-informed (Holmes is the racing authority and occasional gambler in 'Silver Blaze' (*Memoirs*)). The allusion is to Rugby football ('The Sussex Vampire', *Case-Book*), and possibly, given his creator's predilections, to cricket. ACD liked games, which meant that he made jokes about them.

violin playing: because of Holmes's anti-social nature, ACD could not credit him with Robert Christison's predilection for part-singing and patronage of choral societies, his last public performance being on his 83rd birthday. The solitary solace of the violin took its place.

how the deuce: lexicographically assumed to be allied to the devil, possibly from the deuce in cards being the card of lowest value. But it seems more likely that deuce is a corruption of *dieu*, God, given the prevalence of Norman-French in Britain, and means 'how in the name of God?' Either way, it lays a subtextual foundation for Holmes as magician or enchanter, however rational his explanations.

very piquant: very stimulating. Watson's interest in Holmes begins as mental therapy. 'Piquant' means 'stinging', hence life at Baker Street was a kind of psychological astringent.

'The proper study of mankind is man': 'Know then thyself, presume not God to scan; / The proper study of mankind is man' (Alexander Pope (1688–1744), *Essay on Man*, Epistle II, 1–2).

study: although Holmes will later use the term 'a study in scarlet', and although Holmes and ACD mean different things by it, we are to understand that Watson's study of Holmes will prove to be in scarlet, both from the vividness of the impression and from the nature of its preoccupation.

Good-bye: it really is good-bye for Stamford, who passes from the Holmes canon as completely as all the rest of the medical *mise en scène* needed to launch it.

13 *No. 221B Baker Street*: it is notorious that at the time of writing there was no such address, neither '221' nor '221B'. As with so much else in this imaginary London, created from maps and experience of other cities, ACD's youthful memories supply his wants. He did not want an identifiable address. He was thinking of the rooms in 23 George Square in which he first learned the business of medicine from the lessee in whose charity his family now lived, Bryan Charles Waller (1853–1932), their residence there being from 1877 to 1881. Upstairs, reached by an entrance giving on to the street, was 23B (now inhabited by the Dominican Sisters, while the house below is given over to the male members of the order and is the Roman Catholic Chaplaincy to the University of Edinburgh). ACD drew on 23, where he had lived, for some features of the Baker Street rooms, not on 23B where he did not (there are more than seventeen steps to it).

13 *a couple of comfortable bedrooms*: the rooms in the author's mind's eye were clearly not those in which he was writing, 1, Bush Villas, Southsea, a narrow building with three floors. 23 George Square, Edinburgh has two floors and the bedrooms would have been on the second of these (first floor in British usage, second floor in more rational American). What seems to be involved is something more like the large one-storey flats occupied by the Doyle family in Edinburgh on the highest floor of 3 Sciennes Hill Place in 1868–75 (too high and too much of a backwater for the rooms in Baker Street) or 2 Argyle Park Terrace (1875–7) which stretched out over differently-numbered ground-floor premises; or 15 Lonsdale Terrace (1881–2) on the same plan. A large reception-room would give a view of the street below (those in Argyle Park Terrace and Lonsdale Terrace had bow-windows—not present in Baker Street but mentioned in 'The Beryl Coronet' (*Adventures*)—overlooking the great public greensward of The Meadows from opposite sides). The bedrooms would open off the corridor, the maid having the smallest and least comfortable, the lodgers the best. In the process of creation ACD might sometimes have thought of a two- or even three-level Baker Street (Watson goes 'down' to the sitting-room from his bedroom in 'The Speckled Band', *Adventures*); but essentially in the beginning, and probably for the most part subsequently, everything and everyone are on the same floor (e.g. in Ch. 5 below, where the landlady's footsteps pass Watson's sitting-room door as she goes to bed, the maid having previously done so: there is nothing about their going upstairs, although there are steps from the street to the flat). The flat is self-contained since the landlady and maid live in it, and do not simply serve it while living below in 221. (23A George Square was a separate house divided from 23 by the staircase leading to 23B.)

two broad windows: it is amusing to work out whether the view in any given passage is more likely to be ground-floor (in which case the memory is of George Square) or the next floor (Argyle Park Terrace or Lonsdale Terrace): the Southsea house gave on to a backwater with no direct view, as far as may be judged. No doubt after ACD's removal to London in 1891 touches from later residences topped off the layers of memory; but the origins of 221B Baker Street were irredeemably located in Edinburgh.

divided between us: Watson does not seem to have such an arrangement (nor does Holmes require it) after the *Return* begins; but in fact his status at that point is that of a resident doctor in attendance on a patient whose health necessitates weaning him from drugs ('The Missing Three-Quarter', *Return*) or removing him on holiday to prevent a complete breakdown ('The Devil's Foot', *His Last Bow*). During the joint-payment period Watson only gives medical advice to Holmes at the very end (*The Sign of the Four*) and his first medical attendance is in fact at the demand of the landlady, not Holmes (although he has engineered the call), and the illness is fraudulent ('The Dying Detective', *His Last Bow*); but he is then called in because of genuine collapse ('The Reigate Squire', *Memoirs*). Watson ultimately returns to practice (*Case-Book*) when on the verge of a second marriage, which Holmes thinks selfish, a term he did not apply to the first when he had no comparable claim on Watson. No doubt ACD intended us to assume that Watson treated Holmes when he caught a cold—in good Dickensian fashion he supposedly favoured hot Punch ('the doctor has a prescription containing hot water and a lemon which is good medicine on a night like this'— Holmes to Stanley Hopkins, 'The Golden Pince-Nez', *Return*).

the lowest portions of the city: i.e. the poorest, least socially acceptable, most violent, worst housed, most disease-ridden. 'Low' was a characteristic Victorian epithet to express contempt. There was a good deal of class hatred in the term 'lower-class', its polite version being 'working-class'.

the use of some narcotic . . . such a notion: whether ACD was contemplating the remote possibility of a sequel in which Watson would discover that his remote suspicions had been correct, we cannot say. But *The Sign of the Four* may not initially have been ACD's idea, and the structure of *A Study in Scarlet* suggests that a sequel was not planned. In any case the passage reminds us that if Holmes is partly Poe, Watson is by nature anti-Poe, however much he liked reading him.

14   *the man of determination*: Jeffrey Richards sees Holmes's appearance—'tall and spare, with a hawklike nose, a narrow face, a large forehead, piercing eyes and a quick, high, "somewhat strident" voice' as that of the great actor Sir Henry Irving (1838–1905). I have little doubt that he is right. ACD's

autobiographical remarks appear to support the thesis, albeit silently: 'He had, as I imagined him, a thin razor-like face, with a great hawk's-bill of a nose, and two small eyes, set close together on either side of it. Such was my conception. It chanced, however, that poor Sidney Paget who, before his premature death, drew all the original pictures, had a younger brother whose name, I think, was Walter, who served him as a model. The handsome Walter took the place of the more powerful but uglier Sherlock, and perhaps from the point of view of my lady readers it was as well. The stage has followed the type set up by the pictures' (*Memories and Adventures*, 125–6).

14 *stained with chemicals*: little is subsequently heard of this, and its original is evidently scientific rather than medical. A doctor would not wish to exhibit discoloured flesh before a fee-paying patient.

delicacy of touch: 'He has the healing touch—that magnetic thing which defies explanation or analysis, but which is a very evident fact none the less' ('Behind the Times', *Round the Red Lamp*). It is one of the most vital, and one of the most indefinable, of medical attributes.

philosophical: philosophy means 'love of wisdom' and it lay at the heart of the traditional Scottish university curriculum. It is a very useful word in the context, since Holmes is an amateur detective, but more professional in his methods than the official police. The issue is muddied by English class-obsessiveness, with the amateur scorning money and the professional being made for it. But Holmes takes money, and the absurdity of the whole thing was satirically underlined by his brother-in-law Ernest William Hornung (1866–1921) creating a criminal in imitation of Holmes whose exploits he chronicled in *The Amateur Cracksman* (1899): A. J. Raffles seldom allows his amateur status to get in the way of his profit.

how objectless was my life: Murray's had been an objectless life; Waller's became one. Many members of the upper classes had entirely objectless lives, and never troubled themselves about it, but ACD speaks for an inheritance—Scots scientific, Irish historical, Catholic artistic—which abhorred such a vacuum.

genial: the weather was normally personified in common speech in these years as 'the weather-clerk'.

I had no friends: Watson's friendlessness seems strange for one so obviously companionable. But ACD habitually spoke of himself as friendless, despite evidence to the contrary.

15 *No man . . . very good reason for doing so*: something of this derives from ACD's childhood mentor, the historian John Hill Burton (1809–81), author of a major *History of Scotland* (1853) and of a splendidly idiosyncratic tome in praise of bibliophily and its byways, *The Book Hunter* (1860). At the moment he is surfacing in the models for Watson; he will shortly become one for Holmes. Innes Doyle was named after Burton's father-in-law and fellow historian, Cosmo Innes (1798–1874).

Thomas Carlyle . . . and what he had done: this is an attack on Philistine medical scientists, and possibly some Jesuits; but it is also ironic with Holmes the creature being ignorant of the uses and value of his creator. ACD probably had in mind the quotation with which James Anthony Froude (1818–94) concluded his biography *Thomas Carlyle: A History of his Life in London* (1884): 'For, giving his soul to the common cause, he has won for himself a wreath which will not fade and a tomb the most honourable, not where his dust is decaying, but where his glory lives in everlasting remembrance. For of illustrious men all the earth is the sepulchre, and it is not the inscribed column in their own land which is the record of their virtues, but the unwritten memory of them in the hearts and minds of all mankind.'

the Copernican Theory and of the composition of the Solar System: Nicholas Copernicus (1473–1543), a Pole, announced in 1543 that the earth revolved round the sun rather than *vice versa* (to the great indignation of fundamentalist interpreters of Joshua 10: 12–13, where the sun is commanded to stand still and does). Holmes's alignment with scriptural fundamentalists is intentional, ACD being familiar with Catholic and Protestant varieties.

A fool takes in all the lumber: this has an echo in the third chapter of *Three Men in a Boat (To Say Nothing of the Dog)* (1889) by ACD's future editor for his medical stories in the *Idler*, Jerome Klapka Jerome (1859–1927): 'with reference to our trip up the river of life, generally. How many people, on that voyage, load up the boat till it is ever in danger of swamping with a store of foolish things which they think essential to the pleasure and comfort of the trip, but which are really only useless lumber . . .'

15 *useless facts elbowing out the useful ones*: contrast Holmes in *The Valley of Fear* (Ch. 7): 'Breadth of view, my dear Mr Mac, is one of the essentials of our profession. The interplay of ideas and the oblique uses of knowledge are often of extraordinary interest. You will excuse these remarks from one who, though a mere conoisseur of crime, is still rather older and perhaps more experienced than yourself.' The older Holmes scores off the younger.

16 *a pennyworth of difference to me or to my work*: cf. Katherine in Shakespeare's *The Taming of the Shrew*:

> Forward, I pray, since we have come so far,
> And be it moon or sun or what you please,
> And if you please to call it a rush candle
> Henceforth I vow it shall be so for me.

> (IV. vi. 12–15)

belladonna: a poisonous derivative from Deadly Nightshade. Holmes used it to convey the impression of his own imminent death to Watson in 'The Dying Detective' (*His Last Bow*).

opium: presumably essential knowledge for all detectives since its use by William Wilkie Collins (1824–89) in *The Moonstone* (1868), already drawn on by ACD for his as yet unpublished *The Mystery of Cloomber* (1889).

every horror perpetuated in the century: the social implications of this achievement were worked out by P. G. Wodehouse in the case of the child Cecil in 'The Return of Battling Billson' (*Ukridge*):

'The Canning Town 'Orror', he would announce.

'Yes, dearie?' his mother cast a fond glance at him and a proud one at me. 'In this very 'ouse, was it?'

'In this very 'ouse', said Cecil, with the gloomy importance of a confirmed bore about to hold forth on his favourite subject. 'Jimes Potter 'is nime was. 'E was found at seven in the morning underneaf the kitchen sink wiv 'is froat cut from ear to ear. It was the landlady's brother done it. They 'anged 'im at Pentonville' (*Strand*, Sept. 1923).

It is entertaining to wonder if Cecil in his turn inspired the practical activities of Jacky in 'The Sussex Vampire' (*Case-Book*), published in the *Strand* in Jan. 1924.

singlestick: a sport in which two men fight with sticks of a special type. Holmes found it useful in keeping thugs at bay, not always with complete success (see 'The Illustrious Client', *Case-Book*).

17 *Mendelssohn's Lieder*: songs with or without words by Felix Mendelssohn-Bartholdy (1809–47), captivatingly romantic.

Mr Lestrade: ACD is still thinking primarily in medical terms, whence Lestrade, whatever his official title, is described as 'Mr', like a surgeon (just as ACD always addressed Joseph Bell as 'Mr Bell'). Not until 'The Norwood Builder' (*Return*) is Lestrade called an Inspector, hitherto being termed a Scotland Yard official or some comparable unclassified term. (His rival Gregson is 'Inspector Gregson' in 'The Greek Interpreter' (*Memoirs*), but no significance is to be attributed to that.) Lestrade appears on or offstage in thirteen Holmes cases, more than any other police official, but unlike most of his colleagues we never discover his first name, only its initial ('G', given in a note to Holmes in 'The Cardboard Box', *Memoirs*). His manner to Holmes goes through a crisis in 'The Norwood Builder', moving from extreme contempt to profound recantation, and in 'The Six Napoleons' (*Return*) he pays Holmes a tribute of generosity beyond all other official salutes. Perhaps the name Lestrade (= 'lesser Strad': see note on 'Cremona fiddles', p. 161) embodies a joke on its owner's always playing second fiddle to Holmes.

seedy visitor . . . Jew pedlar: literary convention tended to portray Jews as excitable. The stereotyping is unappetizing, but quite authentic for a late Victorian military man. Unlike many of his contemporaries, there is virtually nothing which could be called anti-Jewish in the writings of ACD.

velveteen: imitation velvet. Rather charmingly, it is Watson who becomes the friend of a railway porter when he returns to practice ('The Engineer's Thumb', *Adventures*). Possibly ACD had an appreciative railway porter patient.

sitting-room: Waller may have requested some such arrangement from the Doyles before he established his own museum and consulting-rooms nearby.

18 *The landlady*: unnamed here, Mrs Hudson henceforth, save for 'A Scandal in Bohemia' (*Adventures*) where the name is Mrs Turner. Oddly, the cycle uses both Hudson and Turner for

names of criminals, Hudson being a Klan murder organizer ('The Five Orange Pips', *Adventures*) and a blackmailer ('The *"Gloria Scott"* ', *Memoirs*), while Turner is a country squire whose fortune is founded on banditry and secured by murder ('The Boscombe Valley Mystery', *Adventures*).

18 *mankind*: as Longman very rightly points out, men and not women are intended in this context.

The Book of Life: 'And I saw the dead, small and great, stand before God; and the books were opened: and another book was opened, which is the book of life: and the dead were judged out of those things which were written in the books, according to their works' (Revelation 20: 12). ACD's attempt to make a cultural Philistine of Holmes had broken down within a few pages; or, to put it another way, Holmes quickly proved resistant to attempts at intellectual emasculation. The character was taking on its own identity as it moved beyond the initial ingredients. In one interpretation the title is a brazen piece of blasphemy since its author was likening his own powers to those of the Almighty on Judgement Day. This is hardly intended to inaugurate the Christlike Holmes who develops in 'The Final Problem' (*Memoirs*), 'The Empty House' (*Return*), and 'The Dying Detective' (*His Last Bow*), though it anticipates the idea instructively; but it is consistent with the ex-Christian advocacy of history as Man's self-emancipation from religion exemplified in Winwood Reade, *The Martyrdom of Man* (1872), recommended to Watson by Holmes in *The Sign of the Four*. Well might Watson ironically speak of a 'somewhat ambitious title'.

propositions of Euclid: the Alexandrian-based Greek (350–300 BC) whose *Elements* consisted of problems and theorems logically dependent on their own progress from initial axioms. Having rejected the Pope and his infallibility, ACD was irritated by the claims of scientists and others on the same lines.

a necromancer: commonly used to mean sorcerer, but in strict usage a person calling up the dead to obtain information for the future. The first sentence of the ensuing extract is a voluptuous reworking of the Edinburgh-trained popular naturalist Sir Richard Owen (1804–92), whom ACD cited (in 'The Love Affair of George Vincent Parker', Strange Studies from

Life: II, *Strand*, Apr. 1901) for his reconstruction of 'an entire animal out of a single bone'.

19 *fellow-mortal*: 'me, thy poor earth-born companion / And fellow-mortal' (Robert Burns, 'To a Mouse', an interesting first poetic citation for Holmes).

the trade or profession: 'Nearly every handicraft writes its sign manual on the hands. The scars of the miner differ from those of the quarryman. The carpenter's callosities are not those of the mason. The shoe-maker and the tailor are quite different. The soldier and the sailor differ in gait . . .' (Joseph Bell to Harry How, 16 June 1892; How, 'A Day with Conan Doyle', *Strand* (Aug. 1892), 188).

callosities: 'Well do I remember the gasping astonishment of an outpatient to whom he suddenly remarked, "Of course I know you are a beadle and ring the bells on Sundays at a church in Northumberland somewhere near the Tweed."

' "I'm all that", said the man, "but how do you know? I never told you."

' "Ah", said Bell, when the outpatient had left bewildered, "of course, gentlemen, you all know about that as well as I did. What! You didn't make that out! Did you not notice the Northumbrian burr in his speech, too soft for the south of Northumberland? One only finds it near the Tweed. And then his hands. Did you not notice the callosities on them caused by the ropes? Also, this is Saturday, and when I asked him if he could not come back on Monday, he said he must be getting home to-night. Then I knew he had to ring the bells to-morrow. Quite easy, gentlemen, if you will only observe and put two and two together." ' (Charles Watson MacGillivray, 'Some Memories of Old Harveians', *Edinburgh Medical Journal*, n.s., viii, 121).

What ineffable twaddle: i.e. indescribable, unutterable (often with a theological implication, as when Milton speaks of ineffable divine love). ACD's favourite book was the *Critical and Historical Essays* of Thomas Babington Macaulay (1800–59), whose castigation of the poet Robert Montgomery (1807–55) ACD deplored but evidently enjoyed. Macaulay speaks of Montgomery's Satan as 'something of a twaddle and far too liberal of his good advice'.

19 *paradoxes*: Bell and his own mentor James Syme (1799–1870) taught by paradox to hold their points in the memories of their pupils.

a third-class carriage on the Underground: the Underground, like the ordinary railways at this time, had three classes of carriage supposedly to accommodate the upper, middle, and lower classes of society.

chimerical: imaginary and impossible of existence, like the creature of Greek mythology with three heads resembling goat, lion, and snake.

a consulting detective: Bryan Charles Waller called himself 'a consulting pathologist', and prided himself on having cases referred to him when the pathologists on the university staff were embroiled in disputes among themselves or unable to decide on a problem.

20 *the history of crime*: Edinburgh medicine at this time laid great emphasis on the study of case-histories. But Holmes's methods are those of the historian quite apart from his extensive chronicles of crime.

a little enlightening: the phrase combines the Creative 'Let there be light' (Genesis 1: 3), the clerical missionary principle, and eighteenth-century Scottish scepticism, belief in progress, and zeal for extended knowledge. See also the Carlyle passage, Introduction, p. xxxv.

21 *Edgar Allan Poe's Dupin*: this is homage to the great pioneer, but it is also the puppet coming to life, being unable to admit himself of an imaginary family. ACD himself virtually denied that any progress in the detective story was possible beyond Poe (see Introduction, p. xvii, and Lancelyn Green, *Uncollected Sherlock Holmes*, 159–63, 269–71).

That trick of his: perpetrated by Holmes himself in 'The Cardboard Box' (*Memoirs*) and 'The Dancing Men' (*Return*).

Gaboriau's works: the joke here is that Holmes picks up Watson's question to reveal his reading of *Monsieur Lecoq* (1869), whence some of his own behaviour is drawn in 'The Boscombe Valley Mystery' (*Adventures*) and elsewhere; but in *A Study in Scarlet* Holmes is much more derivative of Père Tabaret in *L'Affaire Lerouge* (1866). Tabaret's superiority to Lecoq is a principle reworked by ACD in the creation of Mycroft Holmes; but

Mycroft's real use is mainly satiric, and unlike Tabaret, he actually worsens any problem in which he is involved.

two characters whom I had admired: ACD's view, and it is instructive that Watson, and not Holmes, is the custodian of his literary values at this point. Neither ever fully commands ACD's opinions. The bracketing of Lecoq with Dupin (and hence Gaboriau with Poe) is important; ACD paid few tributes to Gaboriau in the years to come, but Poe was available for reading while Gaboriau's works went out of print after the 1880s.

What is the use of having brains in our profession?: Watson is not in Holmes's profession, and Holmes has just stated that he is the only consulting detective in the world. The sentence requires a question-mark, but was apparently written without one. We may infer that it slipped very quickly from the author's pen, and thus that it came from memory rather than imagination. ACD was primarily turned towards medicine by the influence of his family's lodger-benefactor, Bryan Charles Waller, who was deeply frustrated in ACD's first year of study at Edinburgh when his own doctoral research was held back by the new vivisection Act, under which he became (in Jan. 1877) the first applicant to whom permission to vivisect was denied (and one of only seven refusals in its first three years). The sentence in these circumstances is more applicable to Waller than Holmes, and to ACD as its recipient than Watson. But once in the canon, as with so many other relics of the many other models, it became a fixed part of the Holmes stock, variants being found in *The Sign of the Four*, 'The Norwood Builder', 'The Missing Three-Quarter' (*Return*), and 'Wisteria Lodge' (*His Last Bow*).

22 *even a Scotland Yard official*: a representative of the criminal investigation department of the Metropolitan Police, housed at 4 Whitehall Place, supposedly the point where Kings of Scotland resided when coming from Scotland to do homage to Kings of England. The origins of Holmes's sentiments may have been Waller's railings against the staff of the University of Edinburgh Department of Pathology who consulted him privately but would not publicly confess his superiority (of which he himself had no doubt). ACD seems to have initially sympathized with him, but to have increasingly come to

dislike him. Waller complained in the *Lancet* (16 Apr. 1881) 'when the head of every tom-cat in the British Islands is held sacred as that of the bull Apis in ancient Egypt, it is to be feared that any and every thing pertaining to [interstitial nephritis] must remain unsettled in the absence of experimental corroboration.'

22 *Royal Marine Light Infantry*: armed forces for marine combat duties beyond the firing of projectiles. In the USA these are officially part of the Navy; in the United Kingdom they are part of the Army.

23 *wondrously*: an early, if faint and probably involuntary, association of Holmes with Christ: 'And Jesus increased in wisdom and stature, and in favour with God and Man' (Luke 2: 52).

It was easier to . . . explain why I know it: ' "It's not such an easy matter, you see, to explain it to another, even though I can define it to my own mind well enough" ' (Tom Hulton in ACD's 'The Haunted Grange of Goresthorpe', National Library of Scotland). See also Introduction, p. xx.

24 *Commonplace*: this is the origin of the immortal but unuttered 'Elementary, my dear Watson', although 'The Crooked Man' (*Memoirs*) has:

> 'Excellent', I cried.
> 'Elementary', said he.

The lowest class in the Jesuit junior school at Hodder, where ACD studied before entry to Stonyhurst, was called 'Elements'.

3, Lauriston Gardens: Lauriston Gardens runs from its right angle with Lonsdale Terrace (at No. 15) to Lauriston Place, where the Edinburgh Royal Infirmary is situated.

Enoch J. Drebber: 'And Enoch walked with God: and he was not; for God took him' (Genesis 5: 24).

The surname seems to come from the German *drehbar*, i.e. turning or changing, presumably alluding to Drebber's schism from the Mormons, and the inconstancy of purpose which finally led to his death. (ACD knew German from his time at Feldkirch more as a spoken than as a written language.)

in statu quo: in the condition in which [I found it]. Gregson has rather more social pretentions than Lestrade. But Latin had only recently ceased to be the language of instruction in

Edinburgh medicine, much material was still only available in Latin, and ACD as a Jesuit pupil and altar-server would have used it very naturally.

TOBIAS GREGSON: this turns out to be a Mormon murder, the victim having been what was called an Avenging Angel, and the story of Tobias and his angel was a favourite with the Jesuits (the Book of Tobias (aka Tobit) being in the Roman Catholic but not the Protestant Bible). Gregson is from *grex* (Latin), 'flock'—i.e. one of the herd. It also suggests the egregious. There may be an implication of the hireling shepherd who is not the true shepherd and is an inadequate protector against wolves. After ACD's immersion in Jesuit teaching for eight years these things fell naturally into place.

25 *the most incurably lazy devil*: there may have been a touch of this in Waller—certainly his life when he settled down in Masongill from 1882 after failing to get the Pathology Chair at Edinburgh seems to have been sedentary; but the exemplar here is Dupin. This seems the only time when Holmes contemplates waving a case away when not either overburdened with other work, retired, or officially dead. See also *The Sign of the Four*: ' "Strange" said I, "how terms of what in another man I should call laziness alternate with your fits of splendid energy and vigour." / "Yes", he answered, "there are in me the makings of a very fine loafer, and also of a pretty spry sort of fellow . . ." '

an unofficial personage: this was the penalty Waller paid for his consultancy in the Department of Pathology at Edinburgh, which mainly involved arbitrating amongst the interns competing for the Chair of Pathology. He could have the power of imposing his judgements but not the glory. Holmes made a virtue of it, and Watson took care to circumvent its effects (see the end of *A Study in Scarlet*).

Cremona fiddles . . . a Stradivarius and an Amati: the Amati of Cremona were founded by Andrea (*c.*1520–80) whose earliest known label dates from 1564 and who developed the standard violin. His work was continued by his brother Nicola (1530–1600), his sons Antonio (1550–1638), and Geronimo (1551–1635), and Geronimo's son Niccolo (1596–1684) whose pupil Antonio Stradivari (1644–1737) produced over 1000 instruments. ACD originally proposed to give Holmes an Amati but evidently decided a Stradivarius was more sensible ('The Cardboard Box'). See also note on Lestrade (p. 155).

25 *It is a capital mistake to theorize . . . biases the judgment*: variants of this admirable dogma may be found in 'The Cardboard Box', 'The Reigate Squire' (*Memoirs*), 'The Abbey Grange', 'The Second Stain' (*Return*), 'Wisteria Lodge' (*His Last Bow*), and 'The Sussex Vampire' (*Case-Book*).

26 *a cataract*: an ironic foretaste of the interest in ophthalmic specialization that would lead to ACD's departure from Southsea in Jan. 1891; his failure to win patients resulted instead in a permanent lease of life for Sherlock Holmes and Dr Watson through the medium of short-story series in the *Strand*. The medical simile is appropriate for the convalescing Watson.

eruption: another medical analogy, this time linked to dermatology.

knot of loafers: loafing was probably more common in American rather than English speech at this time. ACD would have picked the word up from Mark Twain's *Tom Sawyer* and *Huckleberry Finn*. The knot indicates their mutual dependence in inactivity.

27 *a greater mess*: the French criminologist Alphonse Bertillon (1853–1914) (cf. *The Hound of the Baskervilles*, Ch. 1) frequently quoted this sentence in admiration and admonition.

in a cab?: a nice clue, but how did they come? Presumably they went to the local police station by public conveyance, interviewed Rance, and then walked with their supporting constables to 3 Lauriston Gardens.

he strode on into the house: without looking at the lock, which would have told him that it had not been forced and would thus have invited inquiries at the house-agent's that would quickly have led to news of a lost key having been returned by a cabman, Jefferson Hope. We can all do it, when it has been done.

the kitchen and offices: scullery, pantry, bathroom, etc.

28 *great strips had become detached and hung down*: ' "Why, Jack", he said, "you're making a regular old woman of me; it's only the rain that has got in after all and is dropping on that bit of loose paper on the wall yonder" ' ('The Haunted Grange of Goresthorpe').

heavy broadcloth frock coat: fine black cloth coat, reaching down to the knees, of a kind associated with evangelical preachers. As ACD had read the works of Fanny (Mrs T. H.) Stenhouse, recording her life among the Mormons, he was probably familiar with her criticism of Brigham Young for his self-indulgence in wearing broadcloth, a luxury she deemed inimical to Mormon principles. 'My wives insist that I shall wear better clothes', explained the Prophet, on which Mrs Stenhouse later commented: 'This is the only instance wherein Brigham Young was ever known to be ruled by his wives' (*A Lady's Life Among the Mormons*, 1873).

a singularly simious and ape-like appearance: ACD's uncle Richard (1824–83), who designed the front cover of *Punch* (unchanged for over a century), resigned in protest against its anti-Catholicism in 1851. *Punch* became increasingly identified with physiognomical caricatures of Irish Catholics as simian.

ferret-like: Lestrade, however intellectually unpromising in other respects, is possessed of remarkable facial versatility: having been 'rat-faced' in Ch. 2, he becomes likened to a bulldog in the *Hound*.

'There is no clue!': ends on a question mark rather than an exclamation mark in our only text; but Gregson would not be asking a question that would apparently defer to Lestrade's knowledge. He addresses Holmes.

29 *Van Jansen, in Utrecht*: the Utrecht Jansenists, in doctrine and discipline strict Roman Catholics, were known by their countrymen as *Oude Roomsch* ('Old Roman'). Since the blood came from the murderer's nose, one might imagine the allusion being to the Jesuits giving the Jansenists a bloody nose, which excommunicated them from Rome. ACD had been deluged with Jesuit history at Stonyhurst.

There is nothing new under the sun: 'The thing that hath been, it is that which shall be; and that which is done is that which shall be done: and there is no new thing under the sun' (Ecclesiastes 1: 9). ACD took this view of Sherlock Holmes but posterity was not convinced.

30 *Barraud, of London*: a real firm in existence from the beginning of the nineteenth century, but by 1882 it had become Barraud & Lund at 41 Cornhill. It is characteristic of the self-indulgence

and profligacy of Drebber that he should buy himself a gold watch from a leading London firm on arrival.

30 *Albert chain*: again, money lashed out by Drebber on the most ostentatious form of English watch-chain, with heavy links, associated with Queen Victoria's consort Albert (1819–61).

masonic device: some Mormons were Masons at this time, Brigham Young being photographed wearing a Masonic device. (Michael W. Homer kindly corrected Mormon data in these notes.)

Pocket edition of Boccaccio's 'Decameron': Giovanni Boccaccio (1313–75) is famous for his ribald collection of stories written over many years but assembled in 1349–51. We are to deduce that while Stangerson's interest in it was primarily sensual, he still had the cultivation to know something of its cultural significance. Drebber simply wanted the dirty bits. ACD probably (if anachronistically) meant the selection published in 1884 by George Routledge & Sons with an introduction by Henry Morley (1822–94) in 'Morley's Universal Library'.

Joseph Stangerson: 'Joseph' was the Christian name of the Mormons' founder, Joseph Smith (1805–44). Most Mormons would have been at Kirtland, Ohio, when Stangerson was born, about five years after the sect began to mushroom. 'Stangerson' is son of 'Saint-Ange', holy angel, again returning to the idea of the murderous angels (ACD's unpublished play on the same theme as Part II being called 'Angels of Darkness'). Gaston Leroux (1868–1927) paid homage to ACD by introducing two characters named Stangerson into his famous 'locked room' novel, widely held to be the best of the genre, *Le Mystère de la Chambre Jaune* (1907).

American Exchange, Strand: a focus for most Americans in London, having a collection of American newspapers unrivalled in Europe and offering financial advice, poste restante facilities, etc.

the Guion Steamship Company: an interesting implication that Drebber, or at least Stangerson, maintained some associations with the Mormons, since the Guion Company was linked with the Mormons. It had London offices, but its run was Liverpool–New York.

31 *rubbing his hands*: a gesture one seldom sees nowadays, yet in this story Watson, Lestrade, Gregson all perform it, as do

Holmes and various other characters elsewhere (and as does Gaboriau's Lecoq).

in blood-red letters a single word: 'he held up the piece of paper which had been hanging from the mildewed wall. Great heaven! it was all freckled and spotted with gouts of still liquid blood. Even as we stood gazing at it, another drop fell upon the floor with a dull splash. Both our pale faces were turned upwards tracing the course of the horrible shower. We could discern a small crack in the cornice, and through this as through a wound in human flesh the blood seemed to well . . .' ('The Haunted Grange of Goresthorpe').

Rachel: 'In Rama was there a voice heard, lamentation, and weeping, and great mourning, Rachel weeping for her children, and would not be comforted, because they are not' (Matthew 2: 18). ACD would have been very familiar with this text, which is read in Roman Catholic churches every Christmastide, especially on the Feast of the Holy Innocents. It is critical to the later story that Lucy Ferrier is innocent, that her adoptive father recovers his innocence after virtually dying, and that she is then raped and he is murdered. Lestrade, in a way, was quite right.

32 *he trotted noiselessly about the room . . . through the covert*: cf. *L'Affaire Lerouge* (Ch. 2), where Gaboriau describes Père Tabaret:

> He darted rather than walked into the second chamber.
>   He remained there about half an hour; then came out running, then re-entered and came out again; again re-entered, and again reappeared almost immediately. Daburon could not help comparing him to a pointer on the scent; restless and active, he ran hither and thither, carrying his nose in the air, as if to discover some subtle odour left by the assassin. All the while he talked loudly and with much gesticulation, apostrophising himself, scolding himself, uttering little cries of triumph or self-encouragement. He did not allow Lecoq to have a moment's rest. He wanted this or that or the other thing. He demanded paper and a pencil. Then he wanted a spade; and finally he cried out for plaster of paris and a bottle of oil. With these he left the cottage.

infinite capacity for taking pains: the joke here is that Holmes is apparently quoting Carlyle and deriding him in so doing, the *littérateur malgré lui*: ' "Genius" (which means transcendent capacity for taking trouble, first of all)' (*Frederick the Great*, Bk. IV, Ch. 3) was widely rendered as 'Genius is an infinite capacity for taking pains'. Samuel Butler (1835–1902) wrote in his *Note Books* (1912), Ch. XI: 'Genius . . . has been defined as a supreme capacity for taking trouble . . . It might be more fitly described as a supreme capacity for getting its possessors into pains of all kinds, and keeping them therein so long as the genius remains.' Butler presumably knew Holmes's opinion.

33 *'What do you think of it, sir?'*: the class-distinction between Holmes and the official detectives is always noticeable and contrasts with French and American norms.

Audley Court: Mary E. Braddon (1835–1915) produced the most sensational novel of her time in *Lady Audley's Secret* (1862), famous for its bigamy plot.

Trichinopoly cigar: a dark cigar, of dark Indian tobacco grown in Tiruchirapalli, open at both ends.

34 *Parthian shot*: identified incorrectly with a parting shot. The Parthians of north Persia were famous for shooting while departing, but their shots were (a) unexpected, in that they were taken to be in full flight, and (b) on target.

35 *in the sere and yellow*: Shakespeare, *Macbeth*, V. iii. 22–3: 'I have lived long enough. My way of life/Is fall'n into the sere, the yellow leaf.' P. G. Wodehouse also uses quotation by adjectives minus nouns.

a monograph upon the subject: George Turnavine Budd (1855–89) considered publication vital to medical success and was unscrupulous about the grounds on which he justified the originality and value of the content of work which would merit it. See ACD's story 'Crabbe's Practice':

'Davidson down the road, he is only an L.S.A. Talked about epispastic paralysis at the Society the other night—confused it with liquor epispasticus, you know. Yet that fellow makes a pound to my shilling.'
'Get your name known and write', said I.
'But what on earth am I to write about?' asked Crabbe. 'If a man has no cases, how in the world is he to describe them? Help yourself and pass the bottle.'
'Couldn't you invent a case just to raise the wind?'

'Not a bad idea', said Crabbe thoughtfully. 'By the way, did you see my "Discopherous Bone in a Duck's Stomach"?

'Yes; it seemed rather good.'

'Good, I believe you! Why, man, it was a domino which the old duck had managed to gorge itself with. It was a perfect godsend. Then I wrote about embryology of fishes because I knew nothing about it and reasoned that ninety-nine men in a hundred would be in the same boat . . . ' (*Boy's Own Paper*, Christmas Number 1884, not reprinted until *Tales of Adventure and Medical Life* (1922)).

On the other hand, Conan Doyle's mentor Reginald Ratcliff Hoare wrote no professional papers save for an utter demolition of Budd on Gout, clearly to discredit him in ACD's eyes (Budd, 'Gout', *British Medical Journal*, 18 Dec. 1880; Hoare, 'Clinical Memoranda: Gout', *BMJ*, 25 Dec. 1880; Budd, 'Clinical Memorandum: Gout', *BMJ*, 1 Jan. 1880). The exchange, published when ACD was on the African coast, probably decided the paranoid Budd on ACD's destruction *before* summoning him to the ill-fated partnership in Plymouth (see Rodin and Key, *Medical Casebook*; also my own monograph).

ACD's own second publication and first work of non-fiction was 'Gelseminum as a Poison' (*BMJ*, 20 Sept. 1879), which described auto-experiment; his last medical treatise to appear in the professional medical press was 'The Remote Effects of Gout' (*Lancet*, 29 Nov. 1884), which contained a startlingly original line of direction. Curiously, he does not seem to have sought a return to the professional journals to establish himself as an opthalmic authority in 1891. Had his heart been in it would he not have been writing monographs on eye disease instead of 'A Scandal in Bohemia' and 'A Case of Identity'? Holmes did not write monographs: he prevented his creator doing so.

A monograph should actually be a piece of writing by one hand, which one might feel means a self-standing work in covers rather than a journal article. But an offprint would have monograph status, and this seems to be what Holmes is referring to as a rule. ACD would be envisaging the detailed essays in the *Edinburgh Medical Journal*, which Joseph Bell edited 1873–96. He may also have drawn directly on the bibliography of the subject's publications in *The Life of Sir*

Robert Christison, Bart., edited by his sons and published by Blackwood (2 vols., 1886). The variety and style of Christison's titles have apparent echoes in Holmes's list of his own works in *The Sign of the Four*.

36 *cabman who drove them?*: presumably, the question which led Holmes to curtail his exposition.

Socialism and secret societies: Longman's note has now a period flavour of its own, composed as it was in 1979: 'in the nineteenth century Socialism had not yet become respectable and was popularly associated with terrorism and anarchism'. ACD had written several stories satirizing fears of Socialism and anarchism, such as 'An Exciting Christmas Eve or, My Lecture on Dynamite' (1883) (*Uncollected Stories*) and 'That Little Square Box' (1881) (*The Captain of the Pole-Star*). 'A Night Among the Nihilists' (1881) (*Mysteries and Adventures*) may have been intended to be taken seriously, but its rollicking tone throughout made it self-satire if not satire direct, and its author hardly minded which.

after the German fashion: German was still printed in Gothic script at this time.

in the Latin character: by 'prints' Holmes means 'writes block capitals' or 'characters of print likeness'. The Latin character is what you are reading.

in this world: a supernatural flavour is hinted once more. Holmes, however logical, still prompts thoughts of magic. And in the next world, God will prove the great detective (ACD's catechism, to be learned by heart, would have included 'God knows all our secret thoughts and actions').

of her beauty: Waller's naked ambition, and his capacity for in-fighting as ruthless as that of the rivals among whom he arbitrated, are reflected in this unconscious reply to Holmes's 'They are as jealous as a pair of professional beauties' of Lestrade and Gregson. 'Beauty' was often used sarcastically, especially of an unappetizing male criminal.

arm-in-arm: up to the First World War, men habitually walked together arm-in-arm as a token of friendship, and we are the poorer for its loss. Paget, for instance, depicts Holmes and Watson strolling around London arm-in-arm at the beginning of 'The Resident Patient' (*Memoirs*). It could, of course, be a gesture of physical rather than psychological or moral support, which proves to be the case here.

37 *into a fury*: 'fury' is here being used with an economy of meaning we have lost since its promiscuous employment on innumerable sensationalist headlines. We are to think of the Furies who hunted down patricides and matricides, as notably exhibited in the *Eumenides* of Aeschylus (c.525–456 BC). Drebber has been responsible for the death of Hope's wife; Stangerson murdered her father.

Hallé's concert . . . Norman-Neruda: Karl (later Sir Charles) Hallé (1819–95), Westphalian-born pianist and conductor, migrated to Manchester in 1848, founded his Manchester orchestra in 1857, organized concerts at the St James's Hall in London, was knighted and married as his second wife the great violinist Wilma (*née* Wilhelmina) Norman-Neruda (1839–1911), and would become first Principal of the Royal Manchester College of Music in 1893. Moravian-born, she gave her first public recital at the age of seven, in Vienna, after which she went on to a triumphant career, working with Hallé for twenty years before their marriage. She, too, had a Stradivarius (from 1876) and always played it at her concerts. Her first husband, Ludwig Norman (d. 1885) was a Swedish musician. They were married in 1864.

a half-sovereign: ten shillings (now 50p). Presumably, this item would be classified as miscellaneous in the expense account Holmes would later have put in to Lestrade and Gregson: he could hardly declare the bribery of a policeman. His expectation of reimbursement by the police may not be as strange as it looks: the Home Office paid quite a large number of private persons (chiefly criminal informers). Holmes's financial situation and way of life as described above (Ch. 2) would not permit him to assist the police *gratis*, as he evidently does later in his career.

White Hart: traditional name for an English public-house; but ACD was probably thinking of what the Scots historian Hector Boece (?1465–1536) called 'the farest hart that evir was sene afore', supposedly hunted by St David I of Scotland (c.1080–1153) until it vanished at the point where he then founded the Abbey of Holyrood, whose palace was restored by Charles Altamont Doyle (among others) and is the haunted scene mirrored in ACD's 'The Silver Mirror' (1908). It was commemorated by the White Hart Inn in the Edinburgh Grassmarket, which dates back to 1740: that was probably also well known to Charles Altamont Doyle, and lay close at hand to his place of work.

38 *a four of gin hot*: a measure of heated gin, sold for fourpence.

died o' typhoid fever: the war between private property and public health was a nineteenth-century Edinburgh phenomenon. In Bristol Budd's father William (1811–80) pioneered the discovery of transmission of typhoid infection by excreta, demanding the control of sanitation in sewers to prevent the disease reaching epidemic proportions.

to the garden gate: Holmes follows Bell in the display of omniscience. Its value, as ACD tactfully hints in 'A False Start' (*Round the Red Lamp*), was limited in medicine and could be counter-productive in seeking to elicit information from a suspicious and superstitious informant. The element of exhibitionism in Bell and Holmes was pronounced. Holmes, of course, did not have the outlet of university teaching.

the drains what killed him: ACD's lifetime interest in spiritualism and his ultimate adhesion to it have aroused such bigotry, much of it hysterical, that it is desirable to remark his exceptional comic sense in ghostly matters.

39 *Well, it was . . .* : this is the point of which G. K. Chesterton (1874–1936) was later to make such an excellent story in 'The Invisible Man' (*The Innocence of Father Brown* (1911)). A drunk, or a postman, means nobody is in the road, in the way in which general observation denies the humanity of certain figures. As the son of an alcoholic, ACD was all too familiar with the common reaction eliminating such persons from human status.

Columbine's New-fangled Banner: a valuable clue, reinforcing Holmes's conviction that the murderer is an American. Hope, surprised by Rance, automatically sings American patriotic songs ('Hail, Columbia!' and 'The Star-spangled Banner') to dispel suspicion.

40 *a little art jargon*: here a proclamation of ACD's sense of Holmes's place in the aesthetic movement, reaching out to it before the famous meeting with Wilde on 30 Aug. 1889 when

Lippincott's commissioned what would become *The Picture of Dorian Gray* and *The Sign of the Four*. The odd part is that while 'A Study in . . .' became a popular term after publication of the present work, it was not so widely used before (Whistler's Mother, for instance, was termed 'Arrangement in Grey and Black' by her filial offspring). But Wilde picked up the usage by sub-titling his study of the forger-murderer Thomas Griffiths Wainewright (1794–1847), published in the *Fortnightly* in Jan. 1889, 'Pen, Pencil and Poison: a Study in Green'. Had he read *A Study in Scarlet*, then selling on railway bookstalls? Did he indeed contribute any remarks on a Sherlock Holmes sequel during the Lippincott's dinner? Certainly Wilde's influence is evident in the *Sign of the Four* and the *Adventures*.

scarlet thread: 'thy lips are like a thread of scarlet, and thy speech is comely' (Song of Solomon 4: 3).

skein: the discarded title of the story was 'A Tangled Skein'.

Her attack and her bowing are splendid: from her infancy the strength of Neruda's bowing was universally admired.

that little thing of Chopin's: Frederic Chopin (1810–49) composed almost all his work for piano, but there was nothing to stop Hallé arranging a solo piano piece for violin performance by Neruda. It would lend particular charm were it known to be unique to her.

carolled away like a lark: cf. Christison's singing prowess, which was a perpetual amazement to those who knew him as an austere toxicologist.

41 *If ever human features bespoke vice . . . malignant type*: an allusion to Cesare Lombroso (1836–1909) whose *L'uomo delinquente* (1875) postulated the existence of a criminal human type distinguishable from the normal. ACD brought Holmes out against the thesis in *The Sign of the Four* (Ch. 2): . . . ' "I assure you that the most winning woman I ever knew was hanged for poisoning three little children for their insurance-money, and the most repellent man of my acquaintance is a philanthropist who has spent nearly a quarter of a million upon the London poor." ' But Watson retains some commitment to it, e.g. in 'The Illustrious Client' (*Case-Book*): 'If ever I saw a murderer's mouth it was there—a cruel, hard gash in the face, compressed, inexorable, and terrible. He was ill-advised to train

his moustache away from it, for it was Nature's danger-signal, set as a warning to his victims.'

41 *no condonement in the eyes of the law*: an interesting foretaste of the occasions when Holmes condones certain criminal actions in the light of their circumstances and lets their perpetrators, even murderers, walk free.

42 *what Darwin says about music*: Charles Darwin (1809–82) fled from Edinburgh medical school in horror at his first operation, and thus became a naturalist. The reference is to Darwin's *The Descent of Man, and Selection in Relation to Sex* (ACD probably used the second, revised, edition of 1885), 572: 'As we have every reason to suppose that articulate speech is one of the latest, as it is certainly the highest, of the arts acquired by man, and as the instinctive power of producing musical notes and rhythms is developed low down in the animal series, it would be altogether opposed to the principle of evolution, if we were to admit that man's musical capacity has been developed from the tones used in impassioned speech. We must suppose that the rhythms and cadences of oratory are derived from previously developed musical powers. We can thus understand how it is that music, dancing, song, and poetry are such very ancient arts. We may go even further than this, and . . . believe that musical sounds afforded one of the bases for the development of language.' Holmes and Watson make their first real alliance through music, understanding and liking each other in musical communication long before they do so through speech.

case-hardened: Watson is speaking of the cases to which he is accustomed, medical cases, but glides into the reference so easily that the medical–criminal boundary in case-work is elided, which is the basis of the creative process of this book.

43 *anything than lose the ring*: this was a long shot on Holmes's part. The ring might have been thrown on the body after it had been flourished before Drebber's eyes.

44 *De Jure inter Gentes*: Of the Law between Peoples; a treatise with this title, written by Richard Zouche, or Zouch (1590–1661) was published at Leyden in 1651.

Liège in the Lowlands: now in Belgium, then the Spanish Netherlands, or, in the speech of a Scot, Spanish Lowlands, a (Thirty Years) War theatre in 1642.

Charles's head: Charles I (1600–49).

struck off: printed. There is a hint of republicanism in the Holmes of this period with this rather cynical pun. ACD was limbering up for *Micah Clarke* with its respect for the old Ironsides, the Puritan troops serving under Oliver Cromwell (1599–1658).

Philippe de Croy: de Croy was a 'lowland' name, being the family name of the dukes of Aerschot, and of Solre, each of whom had a Philippe among their dukes, but naturally they were not printers. Croy is also a town in the western Scottish lowlands and there may be a private joke about a student or other acquaintance from there named Philip: the attached 'whoever he may have been' suggests as much.

William Whyte: there was a late seventeenth-century Scottish man of letters of this name who wrote epitaphs. This entire episode, presenting an image of Holmes as a book-hunter (like John Hill Burton) somewhat at variance with his specialist creed, is based on a youthful book-find by ACD: 'this old brown volume . . . is one of those which I bought for three-pence out of the remnant box in Edinburgh . . . See how swarthy it is, how squat, with how bullet-proof a cover of scaling leather. Now open the fly-leaf "*Ex libris* [from the library of] Guliemli Whyte 1672" in faded yellow ink. I wonder who William Whyte may have been, and what he did upon earth in the reign of the merry monarch [Charles II (1630–85)]? A pragmatical seventeenth-century lawyer, I should judge, by that hard, angular writing. The date of issue is 1642, so that it was printed just about the time when the Pilgrim Fathers were settling down in their new American home, and the first Charles's head was still firm upon his shoulders, though a little puzzled, no doubt, at what was going on around it. The book is in Latin—though Cicero might not have admitted it— and it treats of the laws of warfare' (*Through the Magic Door*).

Here comes our man, I think: this kind of intellectual chit-chat while waiting for the crisis is based on Joseph Bell and other Edinburgh surgeons making light conversation with their clerks and senior students while waiting for the anaesthetic to take effect on the patient before an operation. Compare:

'Narrow squeak for the Government', he said.
'Oh, ten is enough.'

'They won't have ten long. They'd do better to resign before they are driven to it.'

'Oh, I should fight it out.'

'What's the use. They can't get past the committee, even if they get a vote in the House. I was talking to—'

'Patient's ready, sir', said the dresser.

'Talking to McDonald—but I'll tell you about it presently.' He walked back to the patient, who was breathing in long, heavy gasps. 'I propose', said he, passing his hand over the tumour in an almost caressing fashion, 'to make a free incision over the posterior border and to take another forward at right angles to the lower end of it. Might I trouble you for a medium knife, Mr Johnson?' ('His First Operation', *Round the Red Lamp*)

44 *the servant*: other than here, a Baker Street maidservant is mentioned only in 'The Five Orange Pips' (*Adventures*) and 'The Bruce-Partington Plans' (*His Last Bow*), the domestic staff under allusion being chiefly the landlady, the page, and (once) the cook. When ACD started out in Southsea his only domestic staff was his brother Innes as page. The Irish-born Margaret Stafford was maidservant in the household of Charles Altamont Doyle, his wife Mary, her sister Kate, and their mother Catherine Foley when the Census was taken in 1861 (two years after ACD's birth) at 11 Picardy Place. Ten years later there was no maid, at 3 Sciennes Hill Place. Ten years after that, in 1881, at 15 Lonsdale Terrace, there was a maid once more. Nothing is known about them, but if Margaret Stafford remained with her employers after their move to Portobello and beyond, she would have been an important influence in the life of baby Arthur.

45 *a Union boat*: a vessel of the Union Line carrying passengers to South Africa.

when he has the drink: this invented story was later made the background of the horrific 'The Cardboard Box' (*Memoirs*).

13, Duncan Street, Houndsditch: Houndsditch derives its name from the depository for dead dogs which once encircled this part of the City of London proper. But the name was chosen as a joke at the expense of Edinburgh's bijou-residential suburb of Newington, whose Baptist church in Duncan Street was next door to No. 13. When ACD was champion of a street gang of poor boys their richer opponents were led by the offspring of the Baptist minister.

3 Mayfield Place, Peckham: Peckham was part of the borough of Camberwell. But Mayfield Place is, once again, a fashionable address in Newington.

Sawyer . . . Dennis: Samuel Langhorne Clemens ('Mark Twain') (1835–1910) was drawn on for Part II of *A Study in Scarlet*; here there is a link with *The Adventures of Tom Sawyer* (1876) and its sequel *Adventures of Huckleberry Finn* (1885). Whether with his mind running so much on childhood at this point ACD was inspired to produce the name 'Dennis' from Major-General Sir Denis Pack (?1772–1823), a much-vaunted maternal kinsman, must remain conjectural: at this period he was mildly derisive of his mother's ancestral obsessions. Another source could have been the Burgundian Denys in his favourite novel *The Cloister and the Hearth* (1861) by Charles Reade (1814–84). 'Tom' seems to relate again to Tom Sawyer.

46 *an ulster and a cravat*: the 'Ulster' overcoat, a long, loose garment of frieze or rough cloth, was introduced by John G. McGee & Co., of Belfast, in 1867, and the term was in common use from 1879. A cravat, from the Irish *carabhat*, was an ornate neck-cloth.

Henri Murger's Vie de Bohème: Murger (1822–61) described his life of privation and adventures in his *Scènes de la vie de Bohème* (1848), adapted for opera twice in 1896. The heroine may have had some influence on the writing of 'A Scandal in Bohemia' (*Adventures*) and the book certainly moulded its title.

a hearty laugh: one of the few points in which Holmes's manifold antecedents throw his constant image into disarray is his laughter. 'I have not heard him laugh often, and it has always boded ill for somebody' (*Hound*, Ch. 13); 'the dry chuckle which was his nearest approach to a laugh' ('The Sussex Vampire', *Case-Book*); 'Holmes seldom laughed' ('The Mazarin Stone', *Case-Book*). But he has 'a merry laugh' here (Ch. 1), bursts with Watson 'into an uncontrollable fit of laughter' (*The Sign of the Four*, Ch. 7), is rendered physically helpless with laughter ('A Scandal in Bohemia'), and nearly loses a client by tactless laughter ('The Red-Headed League').

47   *an art . . . an expert at*: and one which every juvenile street-gang leader was an expert at in the days of horse-transport.

drew rein: paused, as in the old Irish rhyme 'Draw a rein, draw a breath, / Cast a cold eye on life, on death'. Yeats adapted it for his epitaph.

paperhanger: a wall-paperer. Possibly an allusion to Robert Southey (1774–1843), who lived at Keswick for one-third of a century where 'He had written much blank verse, and blanker prose, / And more of both than any body knows' (Byron, *A Vision of Judgment*, stanza 98).

Old woman be damned!: notoriously the only time when Holmes's expletive made the printed page. The *Strand* outlawed expressions of the kind, but *Lippincott's* may also have observed Puritan standards. We cannot say how many damns were blue-pencilled.

an incomparable actor: henceforth the impersonations are largely limited to Holmes (with the exceptions of Irene Adler in boy's clothes ('A Scandal in Bohemia'), James Windibank ('A Case of Identity'), Neville St Clair ('The Man with the Twisted Lip') (*Adventures*), Silver Blaze ('Silver Blaze'), 'Arthur / Harry Pinner' ('The Stockbroker's Clerk') (*Memoirs*), Robert Carruthers ('The Solitary Cyclist', *Return*), and 'Jack Stapleton' (*Hound*), none of whom imposes on Holmes apart from Irene Adler and Stapleton. The quick-change of identity again reflects the influence of Irving, 'of whose genius I had been a fervent admirer ever since those Edinburgh days when I had paid my sixpence for the gallery night after night to see him in "Hamlet" and "The Lyons Mail"' (*Memories and Adventures*, 141). *The Lyons Mail* (1877)—which in addition to quick changes had a carriage-driver—was an adaptation of *The Courier of Lyons* (1854) by Charles Reade.

48   *leaders*: editorials with the opinion of the editor or proprietor expressed as 'we', intended to be leaders of public opinion and seldom of influence (save for provincial, ideological, ethnic, or religious journals).

Daily Telegraph: founded 1855. In politics it was friendly to Gladstone until (1876) they broke on the Bulgarian issue; but the *Telegraph* was primarily noteworthy as a 'news' paper and went to great and somewhat sensational lengths to obtain it. The parody here satirizes the *Telegraph* columns of George

Augustus Sala (1828–96), who had recently covered the assassination of Tsar Alexander II (1818–81) and the coronation of his successor Alexander III (1845–94) and whose florid style had been baptized 'telegraphese'.

German name of the victim: this may show Doyle's irritation at being termed a Fenian or Irish incendiary on account of his name ('That Little Square Box' lampoons the practice).

political refugees and revolutionists: repressive action against German Socialists had been conspicuous since 1878 when the anti-Socialist law of 18 Oct. prohibited Socialist public meetings, publications, and collections.

Socialists: there had been a demonstration of the unemployed in Trafalgar Square on 8 Feb. 1886, the dispersal of which had been followed by window-breaking of opulent private residences and shops, resulting in an estimated £50,000 in losses. The Socialist leaders of the demonstration were conspicuously British, and Irish.

Vehmgericht: the Vehmgerichte were medieval Westphalian tribunals with power over life and death, their jurisdiction administered by a secret society to which all freemen were eligible. Their privileges were curtailed by the Holy Roman Emperor Maximilian I (1459–1519) and they were formally abolished in 1811.

aqua tofana: *aqua* (Latin) = water. Tofana has been described as a Sicilian woman but is probably mythical. The Medicis of medieval Florence are supposed to have employed this preparation which 'would poison by penetrating the pores of the skin' ('The Silver Hatchet', *Mysteries and Adventures*).

Carbonari: a real Italian secret-society calling itself after the poor charcoal-burners among whom its members operated. It had some libertarian and social revolutionary principles in the earlier nineteenth century but became a self-perpetuating protection racket later and as such one of its branches forms the eponymous subject of 'The Red Circle' (*His Last Bow*).

the Marchioness de Brinvilliers: Marie Madeleine d'Aubray (c.1630–76) poisoned her father, brother, and sisters, and was tortured and executed. 'The Leather Funnel' (*Round the Fire Stories*) concerns her.

48 *the principles of Malthus*: the Revd Thomas Robert Malthus
(1766–1834) argued in his *Essay on Population* (1798) that population increases in geometrical progression while subsistence
increases only in arithmetical progression and population
must therefore be limited if we are not all to starve. In ACD's
'A Night Among the Nihilists' a rather fatuous young clerk is
talking to a Nihilist whom he takes to be a steward of his firm's
Russian client: 'we conversed on social life in England—a
subject in which he displayed considerable knowledge and
acuteness. His remarks, too, on Malthus and the laws of
population were wonderfully good, though savouring somewhat of Radicalism.'

the Ratcliff Highway murders: a London dockland street, re-
named St George St, where in Dec. 1811 John Williams was said
to have murdered a lace-merchant, Marr, his wife and baby,
and subsequently a publican, Williamson, his wife, and their
maid. Williams committed suicide while under arrest. The case
is discussed with rather revolting relish by Thomas de Quincey
(1785–1859) in his 'Murder Considered as one of the Fine Arts'.

The Standard: launched in 1827 as an afternoon paper, it
became a morning paper in 1857 and acquired its *Evening
Standard* in 1859; William Mudford (1839–1916), from its own
parliamentary staff, became editor in 1874 and manager in
1878. By the mid-1880s it was selling half a million copies
(including the *Evening Standard*). It was Conservative, but
fiercely contemptuous of party attempts to dictate to it (unlike
The Times, which became a party accomplice in the same
decade). Mudford retired in 1899. The *Standard* was closed
down in 1916. The *Evening Standard* survives. Gladstone once
observed 'When I read a bad leader in *The Standard* I say to
myself, Mr Mudford must be taking a holiday.'

a Liberal Administration: William Ewart Gladstone (1809–98)
formed his second Administration in Apr. 1880; it fell in June
1885. His third Administration (Feb.–Aug. 1886) was in power
while ACD was writing *A Study in Scarlet*. ACD would seem to
have broadly supported the former, and to have opposed the
latter, but his main ground of opposition, its proposal of Irish
Home Rule, was not announced until its introduction as a Bill
on 8 Apr. 1886, by which time the book may well have been
finished and in the hands of James Payn.

Charpentier: G. Charpentier *et Cie* were French publishers some of whose publications were read by ACD, e.g. *Lettres de Gustave Flaubert à George Sand* (1884), quoted at the end of 'The Red-Headed League' (*Adventures*).

Torquay Terrace, Camberwell: again, chosen for the absurdity of the juxtaposition. Torquay is a Devon seaside resort of towering respectability, probably well known as such to ACD from his Plymouth experience; according to Agatha Christie, it was said that 'everyone [i.e. who was anyone] has an aunt in Torquay' (*The Labours of Hercules* (1946), Ch. 8). Camberwell was a social point of no return. See Hilaire Belloc (1870–1953):

> Lord Lucky, by a curious fluke,
> Became a most important duke.
> From living in a vile Hotel
> A long way east of Camberwell . . .
>
> (*More Peers*, 1911)

the 4th inst.: the 4th instant, i.e. of the present month, as opposed to the 4th ultimo, i.e. of the past month, and the 4th proximo, i.e. of the future month. The attempted Latinization of English commerce was a depressing capitulation to the snobbery by which aristocracy protected its own fecklessness.

49 *Euston*: Euston Station, the oldest London terminus, lying between Camden Town and Bloomsbury and linking London and Liverpool, at that time by the London and North-Western Railway.

The Daily News: founded in 1845 by Charles Dickens (1812–70), it was Liberal to the day of its demise (1930) when it was amalgamated into the *News Chronicle* (which survived until 1960). Frank Hill (1830–1910) was then the editor (1869–86), although he was dismissed in Jan. before the completion of *A Study in Scarlet*. The Liberals, especially the vigorous Radicals, thought Hill hopelessly incapable of supplying the needful inspiration. He was replaced by (Sir) Henry Lucy (1843–1924), more famous as the *Punch* parliamentary diarist, but he was quickly eased out and the manager (Sir) John Robinson (1828–1901) took over the editorship, ostensibly from June 1887. Robinson's nephew Bertram Fletcher Robinson (1871–1907) gave ACD the original idea for *The Hound of the Baskervilles*.

49 *Continental Governments*: a perceptive appreciation of the complacency of Little-England Liberalism within the more generous libertarianism.

'*Un sot trouve toujours un plus sot qui l'admire*': (A fool always finds a greater fool who admires him) from 'L'Art Poétique' (1674), poem by Nicolas Boileau Despréaux (1636–1711).

50 *Baker Street division of the detective police force*: since this might be taken as implying these were actual junior recruits of the official police, it was changed in *The Sign of the Four* to 'the Baker Street irregulars', stressing their unofficial and guerrilla character. They also seem to come from further afield there, since they require reimbursement for transport. The distinction is that in *A Study in Scarlet* ACD was thinking of himself and his own childhood gang: 'We lived for some time in a *cul de sac* street with a very vivid life of its own and a fierce feud between the small boys who dwelt on either side of it . . . the poorer boys who lived in flats and . . . the richer boys who lived in the opposite villas' (*Memories and Adventures*, 16).

street Arabs: apparently homeless boys of nomadic disposition and indifference to authority.

so many disreputable statuettes: two early artists tried this, both disastrously. Charles Altamont Doyle, having drawn himself for Holmes, now gave Watson his beard and left Holmes clean-shaven and apparently bewigged; the boys salute with the wrong arm and are ragged but have an oddly bourgeois presence (which given their autobiographical Edinburgh antecedents is understandable). George W. C. Hutchinson, unlike Charles Doyle, made them really ragged, but also differed from him in making at least the foremost urchin a figure of classical, if cynical, beauty of feature.

51 *rubbing his fat hands*: 'fat' at this juncture makes Gregson, like the book, acquire more body than was at first apparent.

I don't mind if I do: stage-English phrase to indicate the speaker's control of his alcohol intake. It is perhaps a little below the social level of his earlier Latinisms.

52 *never neglect a chance, however small it may seem*: Gregson may be quoting from Pittacus, according to Diogenes Laertius (*c*.200).

To a great mind, nothing is little: 'nothing is little to him that feels it with great sensibility' (Samuel Johnson to Giuseppi Baretti (1719–89), 20 July 1762, quoted by Boswell, *Johnson*).

53 *Arthur*: ACD from time to time used his own first name for a figure of wrongfully-accused chivalry, e.g. Arthur Holder ('The Beryl Coronet', *Adventures*), or Arthur Cadogan West ('The Bruce-Partington Plans', *His Last Bow*). The protection of sisters is a theme in 'The Speckled Band', 'The Copper Beeches' (*Adventures*), and 'The Solitary Cyclist' (*Return*).

54 *a pound a day each*: this is almost twice Watson's income. Drebber and Stangerson were evidently paying both for obscurity (to protect themselves against Hope) and for tolerance (to offset reprisals against Drebber).

58 *Little George Street*: there is a Little George Street, off Euston Square, very near Euston Station. It had no private hotels in it. Halliday is a Scottish name.

59 *Boots*: usually a boy, though sometimes a man, whose duty it was to polish the guests' shoes (cf. the Boots in the Northumberland Hotel in the *Hound*).

twenty years' experience: Lestrade's length of service without promotion has been the cause of unkind jocosity. But the Edinburgh interns in Pathology who called in Waller kept the Department going for quite some time and won no promotion. It is a reflection of the source, not a reflection on Lestrade.

mews: in the nineteenth century, cobblestoned areas where carriages would be housed or left in waiting.

60 *chip ointment box*: a 'chip' was a basket of very thin wood, usually carrying light fruit such as strawberries. Hence here a very light round box, easily carried, with no appreciable weight.

61 *not far from its end*: on 15 Apr. 1886, shortly after writing, ACD spoke at a Southsea meeting on kindness to animals, championing vivisection if it alleviated human suffering.

our friend, the Doctor: in autobiographical writings at this time ACD would often introduce himself as 'the Doctor' and use someone else, possibly imaginary, as narrator (see particularly *Essays in Photography*).

62 *some other interpretation*: Baring-Gould, i. 194, lists variations: 'One should always look for a possible alternative and provide against it. It is the first rule of criminal investigation' ('Black Peter', *Return*); 'When you follow two separate trains of thought, you will find some point of intersection which should approximate to the truth' ('The Disappearance of Lady Frances Carfax', *His Last Bow*); 'One drawback of an active mind is that one can always conceive alternative explanations, which would make our scent a false one' ('Thor Bridge', *Case-Book*).

63 *outré*: a word Holmes makes his own, adding to its customary sense of exaggerated, excessive, unusual, shocking, extraordinary, or (most revealingly of all in German) *übermodern*, a sense of the grotesque, not merely of the outrageous but the outraged, an event distorted beyond nature. Dupin of course uses it, but with a redundant emphatic as though finding its properties insufficient ('you will admit that there was something *excessively outré*', 'The Murders in the Rue Morgue'), and the effect is in any case rather weakened as it seems practically his only word of French.

taking the man: the Latin *capio*, I take, easily elided 'I take captive' into 'I take' as though avoiding tautology.

64 *four million inhabitants*: Holmes was well abreast of the latest census findings, which had put London far above any other centre of population on the globe with 3,834,194 inhabitants, having increased by a quarter million in the previous three years.

65 *They fasten in an instant*: this advocacy of automatically locking handcuffs is an instance of ACD's occasional pioneering achievements in the Holmes saga. They were not introduced by the police until 1896.

66 *epileptic fit*: a very revealing touch. Charles Altamont Doyle was certified as epileptic, and it seems extremely likely that it followed at least one violent seizure in which ACD had to restrain his father with Waller's assistance. Once Jefferson Hope is quiet he proves himself a deeply sympathetic figure, who had taken his actions for what he thought to be the best motives. There is a strong element of ACD trying to understand and sympathize with the fate of his father, although his alcoholism is also represented in the story in the person of

Drebber. How far either of these sentiments were conscious we cannot say, but evidently they were sublimated sufficiently for ACD to get his father the artist's commission. Charles Altamont Doyle, on the other hand, may have read himself into the figures of Drebber and Hope—he was, as his incessant self-portraits in the drawings indicates, a self-obsessed man. Such a reading might account for his obvious want of sympathy with the book, although that alone cannot account for his decline as an artist.

67 *The Country of the Saints*: evidently a seminal influence on 'The Country of the Blind' by H. G. Wells (1866–1946), where the role of Lucy Ferrier becomes that of the hero-narrator, obliged to sacrifice sight at the demand of the Utopian community where Lucy had to lose her right to monogamy (which in any case meant less to Wells than to ACD). F. Scott Fitzgerald (1896–1940), whose work from the initial 'Mystery of the Raymond Mortgage' to *The Great Gatsby* directly reflects the impact of *A Study in Scarlet* in particular and the Holmes saga in general, indicates a debt to 'The Country of the Blind' in 'The Diamond as Big as the Ritz' (see my monograph in A. Robert Lee, *Scott Fitzgerald: The Promises of Life* (1986)).

69 *an arid and repulsive desert*: a very widespread myth in the literature of the period, which conflated actual deserts, from the Wahsatch Mountains in central Utah to the Sierra Nevada in California stretching down to Arizona and New Mexico, with the flat, dry, and treeless Great Plains east of the Rocky Mountains, resistant to immigration until the introduction of Russian winter wheat. The most eminent British traveller of the period in that region, (Sir) Richard Burton (1821–90), speaks in his *The City of the Saints* (1861), reasonably enough for the time, of 'the great uncultivatable belt of plain and mountain', but this in due course becomes 'the great American Sahara'. Sahara or not, it claimed many victims, and was doubtless desert enough to them.

saline: containing salts. A device, conscious or otherwise, to cast the shadow of Salt Lake City before.

the Sierra Blanco: this whole passage is greatly, and deliberately, idealized. As a medical man, ACD knew exactly what the condition of John Ferrier and Lucy would have been in the final throes of starvation, and his readers would not have wanted to know about it. They would probably have been blind. Cannibalism took over in the case of some stranded pioneers at this time. The Sierra Blanca (ACD failed to allow for gender agreement in Spanish) is 600 miles south of the Mormon Trail, in what is now New Mexico and was then, like Salt Lake City, still Mexico and at war with the United States. It has been argued that ACD meant the Blanca Peak, 4364 feet and just inside Colorado, not too far (but quite far enough) from the Rio Grande, and 300 miles north of the Sierra Blanca. The Mormons would still have been in what is now Wyoming. But the story only requires that the Mormons should save them from death, and if the author described the wrong landscape, he did it effectively.

70 *the fourth of May, eighteen hundred and forty-seven*: the Mormon pioneer party was crossing the Platte, entering the Sand Hills, and thankfully had found its first buffalo, on 1 May. In the Mexican War, American troops had by now fought their way to within 100 miles of Mexico City. Meanwhile, as ACD was highly conscious, the Irish famine was at its height.

to forty or to sixty: Ferrier's origins are literary, the most obvious being the famous creation of James Fenimore Cooper (1789–1851), Leatherstocking alias Hawkeye alias Natty Bumppo, who is pictured at very different ages in *The Pioneers* (1823), *The Last of the Mohicans* (1826), *The Prairie* (1827), *The Pathfinder* (1840), and *The Deerslayer* (1841). In the last two of these he is much younger and there would have more effect on the youthful Jefferson Hope. Cooper's romanticism, idealization of the young girl, and his tremendous landscapes, would have been powerful influences on ACD.

71 *'You've hurt me!'*: ACD's two youngest sisters, Jane Adelaide Rose ('Ida'), born 1875, and Bryan Mary Julia Josephine ('Dodo'), born 1877, seem the most probable alternative origins of this line, and its sequel, with himself as the recipient (he was big and conscious of being clumsy). Dodo was under five when he left home for good. Francis Bret Harte (1836–1902) is reflected here in the love of the miner 'Kentuck' for the baby Tommy, the eponymous 'Luck of Roaring Camp' (1868), who is born in 1850 and dies with Kentuck in 1851. ACD described Harte as 'one of those great short story tellers who proved himself incapable of a longer flight. He was

always like one of his own gold-miners who struck a rich pocket, but found no continous reef. The pocket was, alas, a very limited one, but the gold was of the best. "The Luck of Roaring Camp" and "Tennessee's Partner" are both, I think, worthy of a place among the immortals' (*Through the Magic Door*, 110). Harte seems to have returned the obligation with interest in his *A Waif of the Plains* (1890), in which an 11-year-old boy and an unrelated 7-year-old girl are accidentally marooned on the Great Plains in 1852.

72 *bullier*: better. Not then absolutely *de rigueur* in allegedly authentic frontier talk until noisily adopted by Theodore Roosevelt (1858–1919).

mica: glass-like mineral of silicon content.

brother Bob: a hint that the child is from a broken home, as ACD's now was, since brother Bob is not among the pioneers later mentioned by Ferrier.

Mr Bender: the Benders were cannibals, possibly human, possibly not, preying on Great Plains pioneers.

Indian Pete: another uncomfortable frontier allusion, this time to Injun Joe in Twain's *Tom Sawyer*, the half-breed murderer whose threatened vengeance terrorizes Tom and almost overtakes him when Tom and Becky are lost in the cave.

73 *In course*: *Beeton's* and Author's edn. 'of course' in later texts. Frontier dialect is intended.

Missouri: the Missouri joins the Mississippi near St Louis, but was by now far to the north in what is now Montana.

waggon: *Beeton's* and Author's edn.; 'wagon' in later texts.

disremember them: again supposedly authentic frontier talk, but in fact a careful usage implying deliberation in the act of ceasing to remember.

75 *the Rio Grande*: ultimately forming the present Texas–Mexico frontier, it rises near the Blanca Peak though nowhere near the Sierra Blanca.

He who could draw it from the rocks: this again is ACD limbering up for *Micah Clarke*. The Mormon pioneers talked in much less elevated terms, and presumably would have cited the Book of Mormon as readily as Exodus 17: 6: 'Behold, I will stand before thee there upon the rock in Horeb; and thou shalt smite the rock, and there shall come water out of it, that the people may drink. And Moses did so in the sight of the elders of Israel.'

75 *any number of Injuns*: in reality, and 300 miles northward, Brigham Young was in fact firing the Mormons' cannon at this point as a warning to any nearby Indians. There was argument as to whether William Empey saw, as he insisted, 400 Indians or 400 antelope.

77 *John Ferrier*: from the Roman Catholic legend of St Christopher, who carried a little child who proved to be Christ. *Fero* (Latin), I carry, infinitive *ferre*. Susan Ferrier (1782–1854) was a major Scottish novelist.

Lucy Ferrier: the heroine of the Stevensons' 'Story of the Destroying Angel' describes how her father first sees her mother in a famine-ridden Mormon party: 'I will call my mother Lucy. Her family name I am not at liberty to mention; it is one you would know well. By what series of undeserved calamities this innocent flower of maidenhood, lovely, refined by education, ennobled in the finest taste, was thus cast among the horrors of a Mormon caravan, I must not stay to tell you' (*More New Arabian Nights: The Dynamiter*).

Nigh upon ten thousand: Brigham Young (1801–77) in fact selected a gross—twelve times twelve—of his dwindling Mormon followers to make up the pioneer party. But around 10,000 immigrated to Utah within the first five years.

Angel Merona: the Angel was in fact called Moroni, whose Irishness ACD may have subconsciously rejected. He was the son of Mormon.

Joseph Smith at Palmyra: Smith (1805–44), like Young a Vermonter, had a series of visions at Palmyra, NY, informing him of God's choice of him to restore the Church of Christ. It was at Manchester, NY, in 1827 that he received the golden plates which contained the particulars of Christ's supposed people in America in Christ's lifetime; having translated these by miraculous means he published *The Book of Mormon* at Palmyra. 'Handed unto the holy Joseph Smith at Manchester' would have been unduly comic for a British audience. Smith was shot by a mob in Carthage, Illinois.

Nauvoo: the final Mormon headquarters east of the Mississippi was at Nauvoo. The pioneer party actually commenced their effective trek from Kanesville (now Council Bluffs, Iowa, at the Iowa–Nebraska state line).

you are the Mormons: dramatically, ACD was quite right. In fact they preferred to call themselves the Church of Jesus Christ of the Latter-Day Saints.

our Prophet: the religious name for the second President of the Mormon Church. Brigham Young, a Methodist from 22, was converted after two years' study following his reading of *The Book of Mormon* just after its publication. He was chosen third of the Quorum of the Twelve Apostles, 1835, and was first by 1838; he proved an outstanding missionary, including (1839–41) a successful apostleship in Britain, and became the leading Mormon fiscal officer. Smith announced for the US Presidency in 1844 and Young led his campaign, but on his death took over the church and decided on migration. A brilliant if despotic organizer of virtually no education, he was an inspiring master of sublimity and invective, with little interest in theory. Bernard De Voto, the American popular historian and critic (1897–1955), described Young as 'one of the foremost intelligences of our time' and, more reasonably, 'the first American who learned how to colonize the desert'.

78 *more than thirty years of age*: the Prophet was not quite as young as that, but the error is instructive as to his vigour.

Guess I'll come with you on any terms: this has elicited much recrimination. It is certain that the Mormons succoured others whom they encountered on their journey (black and white), but they may have put some pressure on waifs and strays of no personal conviction. In general they respected the convictions of Jews and Roman Catholics but fought with Protestants: the former were accepted as intransigent, the latter as brands to be saved from the burning (in which Mormons deeply believed). The antecedent of the Ferrier conversion, bearing in mind the hint of his rather checkered past, was the Mormon (Nathaniel) Thomas Brown, wanted by Sheriff William Bonney (*not* to be confused with the as yet unborn Billy the Kid) who wrote him up in the *The Banditti of the Prairies* (1850): Brown had knifed a German across the Mississippi from Nauvoo. Young kept him under firm control, but he eventually returned to the East and was killed in a brawl in Council Bluffs.

78 *On, on to Zion*: a Mormon cry but also a fascinating insight. The Mormons, like the later Zionists, were distinguished by their denial that the USA is the ideal final destination on earth. They had created the first purely American major religion, complete with an insistence that Jesus Christ had travelled there after His crucifixion to found it in person; but their choice of Utah made it clear that they wanted to live outside American dominions. Naturally, when the USA enlarged its boundaries to the Pacific in 1848, the Mormons implied they were simply an advance party, but the rejection (reasonable enough after Smith's martyrdom) was quite explicit. Zion means the holy place, implicit in Young's cry on arrival at the future Salt Lake City 'This is the Right Place!' (usually rendered as 'This is the Place').

79 *From the shores of the Mississippi to the western slopes of the Rocky Mountains*:

> So he journeyed westward, westward . . .
> Crossed the rushing Esconaba,
> Crossed the mighty Mississippi,
> Passed the Mountains of the Prairie,
> Passed the lands of Crows and Foxes,
> Passed the dwellings of the Blackfeet,
> Came unto the Rocky Mountains,
> To the kingdom of the West-Wind,
> Where upon the gusty summits
> Sat the ancient Mudjekeewis,
> Ruler of the winds of heaven.
>
> (Henry Wadsworth Longfellow (1807–82), *The Song of Hiawatha* (1855), 4)

The savage man . . . overcome with Anglo-Saxon tenacity: an ironic adoption of Mormon hagiographical literature (as a descendant of savage men overcome with Anglo-Saxon tenacity in the counties of Wexford and Waterford, ACD could see the bitter humour of this self-congratulation: he himself, when serious, employed the term 'Anglo-Celtic').

Utah: originally Deseret, established in March 1849, with Young as Governor, claiming land from Carson City to San Diego, Santa Fe, North Platte. It was organized as Utah

188

territory, limited roughly to what is now the states of Utah and Nevada, in 1850 but was not admitted to the Union until 1896. Nevada had been admitted in 1864.

virgin acres: this captures the almost sexual nature of American land hunger, on whose mythology see Henry Nash Smith, *Virgin Land: the American West as Symbol and Myth* (1950), but its symbolism is related here to the acquisition of human virgin acres.

80 *as fertile a tract of land*: ACD is here unduly influenced by the Stevensons' 'Destroying Angel' in which Lucy's husband is wealthy to the displeasure of Young. The initial settlement had to be communitarian to survive, and Ferrier would have been restricted, as were the rest, to the dictates of community and the primacy of family need. Ferrier would have been decently rewarded, but not so as to become an object of extortion from his own benefactors.

Stangerson, Kemball, Johnston, and Drebber: Heber Chase Kimball (1801–68), yet another Vermonter by birth, was Young's chief lieutenant and adviser. Luke S. Johnson (1807–61) played a part of some small significance in the pioneer party, proving himself courageous and industrious. But he seems to have been of no note thereafter (the Scots pronounce 'Johnston' or 'Johnstone' as 'Johnson', and frequently write 'Johnson' with an intrusive 't'). Drebber and Stangerson existed in ACD's mind alone.

Salt Lake City: Young arrived here on 24 July 1847, stating he had seen it in a vision and choosing the site for the Temple on 28 July; in August he gave it the name of City of the Great Salt Lake. Each city block was 10 acres divided into lots of 1¼ acres assigned to professional and business men. Five-acre lots were given to 'mechanics'; 10-acre and 20-acre parcels of land to farmers. All dwellers in the greater city benefited, the smaller but wealthier tracts being in the inner city, the larger at a greater distance. It was nearing 10,000 inhabitants by 1861 and had 45,000 by 1890.

the great inland sea: the Great Salt Lake, north-west of the city.

Wahsatch Mountains: i.e. the more remote of them, in the far south of Utah; those nearer at hand were Salt Lake City's southern neighbours.

81 *celibate*: again, there is a hint here of a more reprehensible earlier life, the possible survival of a deserted wife being for Ferrier a prohibition against further marriage.

mustang: not just local colour but necessary for the plot. A mustang was half, if not wholly, wild.

the whole Pacific slope: i.e. from San Diego to Vancouver and back to Salt Lake City. Similar sentiments are found in Irish folk-songs that would have been known to ACD, for example:

> From Bantry Bay
> Up to Derry Quay
>   And from Galway to Dub(e)lin town
> No maid I've seen
> Like the sweet colleen
>   That I met in the County Down.

82 *Latter-Day Saints*: what the Mormons called themselves. 'Deseret' means 'honey-bee' according to the *Book of Mormon* and the tabernacle architecture was like a hive.

gold fever: the famous 1849 gold rush. Young wisely told the Mormons not to take part in it, but to make their money by selling goods and fittings to the gold migrants. It proved extremely lucrative.

Elect: this looks a little like the recollections of a Catholic boy growing up in Calvinist Edinburgh. In the strictest sense the Mormons thought of themselves as predestined or Elect, and they were convinced that blacks, as the children of Cain, could not be saved or be admitted into the priesthood (they have been since 1978).

pelties: 'peltries' in some corrupt late readings. Pelts are animal skins. ACD's usage may be more Scots than American.

plains: presumably the plains east of Utah beyond the Rockies, by then being settled (Kansas became a state in 1861).

83 *saucily*: ACD was unfamiliar with London speech, which would have used the term as an indication that Lucy Ferrier was not as innocent as she might have been. He would have used it as a synonym for 'playfully'.

Pancho: 'Poncho' in all texts. ACD's 'o' and 'a' were occasionally not very distinguishable. But 'poncho' is a Latin-American cloak worn with the head through a hole; 'pancho' is a man's, and therefore a probable horse's name, especially if it had been bought from a Mexican trader.

the Jefferson Hopes: we have to assume a family settled in Missouri whose father, Jefferson Hope senior, was probably a Virginian or Kentuckian (where the name would have been popular, Thomas Jefferson (1742–1826) being a Virginian and associated with Kentucky, which was mostly populated by former Virginians). The example obviously to ACD's hand, the President of the Confederate States of America Jefferson Davis (1808–89), was born in Kentucky. The *Hope* was the name of the Greenland whaler on which ACD had served for seven months as doctor in 1880. There is a possibility that ACD had toyed with it for his detective: it was the family name of the earls of Hopetoun, who were Edinburgh locals.

St Louis: the chief city of Missouri (admitted to the Union as a state in 1821), its population in 1850 was 78,000. Its reputation in the 1850s was very tough, which the public would recall from the assassination of one of its best-known sons, Jesse Woodson James (1847–82) in his home in St Joseph (there are some Jesse James touches in Jefferson Hope). Mark Twain was another Missouri product whose less humourous aspects would contribute to the portrait.

84 *You ain't even a friend of ours*: this is very much in the style of Becky Thatcher talking to Tom Sawyer; both Lucy and Becky show signs of incipient womanhood (even though Becky is much younger than Lucy). There is a strong implication that boy-and-girl romances were not very probable in a poly-gamous society, hence Jefferson Hope is the first person to touch this chord in Lucy.

Nevada Mountains: the Sierra Nevada is chiefly in California, but the single spur of Washoe is in Nevada. Behind Hope is the growing anger in what is now western Nevada at being administered from Salt Lake City, with the new settlements at Carson City near the Californian border seeking affiliation with California. Jefferson Hope typifies the mining immi-grants whose experience of the Mormons was of being bullied and exploited.

lodes: here the allusion is to the Comstock lode, near Virginia City, Nevada, which would prove so profitable for gold and silver. Hope presumably is to be taken as having found some other lode, on which the Salt Lake City financiers would be likely to drive a hard bargain.

86 *the victims of persecution had now turned persecutors*: 'The persecutions which the Mormons suffered so long—and which they consider they still suffer in not being allowed to govern themselves—they have endeavoured and are still endeavouring to repay' (Mark Twain, *Roughing It* (1872), Appendix B: 'The Mountain Meadows Massacre'. ACD also drew on Appendix A: 'Brief Sketch of Mormon History', and on Chs. 12–17). This allegation has been bitterly contested, and is indeed far too general and sweeping in its terms. But it is true that in 1857–8 the Mormons were in a millenarian state of panic, with some ugly results. They had unwisely, and contrary to their advisers in Washington, DC, formally announced their doctrine of polygamy in 1852 (it had been practised among them long before). As a result, the newly-formed Republican party made the eradication of polygamy one of the main planks in its political platform. Brigham Young had not endeared himself to the Federal authorities by his words in July 1851 on the late president, Zachary Taylor, who had died in office: 'Zachary Taylor is dead, and in hell, and I am glad of it'. President James Buchanan (1791–1868: President 1857–61), desperately trying to divert attention from sectional conflict and restore some cohesion to the Democratic party, sent federal troops against Young, whom he ousted as Governor. Young answered with a proclamation forbidding US troops from entering Utah, calling on all troops to defend the territory, and proclaiming martial law. In Oct. 1857 Mormons burnt three federal supply-trains and later drove off 800 of the troops' oxen for their own use. At this point the Mormons seem to have believed that the reign of Jesus Christ on Earth was about to begin, and any interference with the work of His Prophet was intolerable and blasphemous. Moreover, the settlement was clearly in a security crisis. Hence it would not be surprising if measures were taken to deal with persons known to be hostile to Young's rule. Jedediah Morgan Grant (1817–56) revived Smith's doctrine of 'blood atonement' in which sinners could only remit their sins by the shedding of their blood. Young was quoted as saying that 'cutting people off from the earth ... is to save them, not to destroy them'. Ultimately, peace was patched up between Buchanan and Young in 1858.

87 *no father ever returned*: cf. the Stevensons' 'Story of the Destroying Angel', where Lucy's husband disappears in such a
fashion.

rumours of murdered immigrants: ACD's principal source here is
the confession of the Mormon elder John Doyle Lee (1812–
77), before he was executed, that he had perpetrated with
official authority the Mountain Meadows Massacre in south-
west Utah on 11 Sept. 1857 when a party of over a hundred
immigrants were murdered. ACD owned a copy of Mrs
Fanny Stenhouse's *An Englishwoman in Utah: the Story of a Life's
Experience in Mormonism* (1880), which, as well as a preface by
Harriet Beecher Stowe, included Lee's confession.

Fresh women . . . an inextinguishable horror: there seems no evidence for this sentence which savours of the old Roman legend
of the rape of the Sabine women. The Mormons hardly
needed fresh blood for the harems, given the level of breeding
in the community. Some children did survive the Mountain
Meadow Massacre, which may be the origin of this story.
ACD wanted to underline the ultimate rape of Lucy Ferrier,
which convention would not let him assert, and this was one
way of doing it.

the Danite Band, or the Avenging Angels . . . an ill-omened one: the
Danites were organized in 1838 to exact vengeance, their
name coming from the insistence of their founder that he was
of the tribe of Dan among the sons of Jacob in Genesis.
Joseph Smith apparently expelled the group and proscribed
the institution. Something of the kind seems to have been
revived in 1856–8, when similar bands of assassins and
vigilantes were rife in the Kansas conflict over the slavery
issue (which often simply boiled down to land-grabbing or
private feuding). Not all the killings were nocturnal; nor were
all the perpetrators unknown. The Pacific slope hummed
with stories of the kind, and they were reworked as various
revelations (e.g. from Brigham Young's twenty-seventh and
fugitive wife) which emerged in the 1870s; Joaquin Miller
(1839–1913) produced his play *The Danites in the Sierras*, and the
presses disgorged reams of soft pornography on the theme.
The Stevensons planted the idea firmly in ACD's mind: 'And
even if the talk should wax still bolder, full of ominous si-
lences and nods, and I should hear named in a whisper the

Destroying Angels, how was a child to understand these mysteries? I heard of a Destroying Angel as some more happy child might hear in England of a bishop or rural dean, with vague respect and without the wish for further information.'

89 *Gentile*: Mormon usage for a non-Mormon, as with old Jewish usage for a non-Jew.

thirteenth rule in the code of the sainted Joseph Smith: Young did not talk in this fashion, which in any case is getting close (possibly intentionally) to Catholic catechetics. An example of Young's doctrinal pronouncement (which any Catholic might accept) is: 'Let small men or large men, officers of state, emperors, kings, or beggars say or do what they please, it is all the same to the Almighty. The king upon his throne, the president in his chair, the judge upon the bench, and the beggar on the street are over-ruled in their actions by the Almighty God of Heaven and earth. Who can successfully fight against him?'

a grievous sin: Catholic catechetical vocabulary of the time.

the Sacred Council of Four: this did not exist, and ACD's source for it remains obscure.

heifers: 'I have not observed a sign in the streets, an advertisement in the journals, of the Mormon Metropolis, whereby a woman proposed to do anything whatever. No Mormon has ever cited to me his wife's or any woman's opinion on any subject; no Mormon woman has been introduced or has spoken to me as, although I have been asked to visit Mormons in their houses, no one has spoken of his wife (or wives) desiring to see me, or desiring me to make their acquaintance, or voluntarily indicated the existence of such a being or beings . . . "If I did not consider myself competent to transact a certain business without taking my wife's or any woman's council with regard to it, I think I ought to let that business alone" [stated Brigham Young] . . . Let any such system become established and prevalent, and women will soon be confined to the harem . . .' (Horace Greeley (1811–72), *New York Tribune*, 20 Aug. 1859).

his hundred wives: 'Heber C. Kimball, the next in office to Brigham, frequently mentions his [45] wives by the endearing appellation of his "cows".' (Edward P. Hingston, Introduction to the lecture *Artemus Ward among the Mormons* (1865). Ward

(Charles Farrar Browne (1834–67)) performed it in Edinburgh on the British tour ending with his death at Southampton.

90 *electro-telegraphs*: invented by Samuel Finley Breese Morse (1791–1872) and first operated on 24 May 1844 with Morse's own message, 'What hath God wrought?'

91 *it's all new to me*: Young's despotism was new to his fellow Americans. Whether the Mormons could have survived without it is another question.

my dearie: a Scotticism, and one probably used by ACD to his infant daughter Mary (born two years later).

walking into me: derives from male physical expressions of anger in the animal kingdom, human or otherwise.

92 *the Lord stretched out His hand . . . the true fold*: i.e. Stangerson's father saved Ferrier's life, and thus Ferrier owes a debt to him.

He grindeth slowly but exceeding small: i.e. I get what I want, an adaptation from Longfellow's 'Retribution (1845), translated from Friedrich von Logau (1604–55):

> Though the mills of God grind slowly yet they
>   grind exceeding small;
> Though with patience He stands waiting, with
>   exactness grinds He all.

When the Lord removes my father: a blasphemous adaptation of 'the Lord gave, and the Lord hath taken away; blessed be the name of the Lord' (Job 1: 21). Job was speaking of the deaths of his children and the loss of his property.

93 *You shall smart for this*: 'He that is surety for a stranger shall smart for it' (Proverbs 11: 15). An indication that Stangerson, the more intelligent, takes this as proof of a bond between Ferrier and Hope.

You shall rue it to the end of your days: again, ironic for the user since the original is the folk-song line 'I rued the day I sought her, oh'.

The hand of the Lord shall be heavy upon you: 'For day and night thy hand was heavy upon me' (Psalm 32: 4).

canting: used in two senses, that Stangerson and Drebber are hypocritically quoting Scripture when about the business of gratifying their lust and avarice, and that their use of it is rather like a thieves' code.

93 *I would sooner . . . the wife of either of them*: Macaulay's 'Virginia' (*Lays of Ancient Rome* (1842)) is an influence here, in its relevance to *his* dearly-loved sisters, in the heroine's ambiguity between girlhood and nubility, in the inability to withstand the lust of the powerful, and in the desirability of preventing it by death.

Jefferson will soon be here: Lucy's last reported words.

94 *puzzled John Ferrier sorely*: a variation on the Stevensons' Mormon Eye, symbolic and visible but apparently ineffectual, whereas here the Eye is invisible but extremely effectual.

watch and ward: from Macaulay's 'Ivry' (1824), supposedly sung after the Huguenot victory:

> Ho! gallant nobles of the League, look that your arms
>   be bright;
> Ho! burghers of Saint Genevieve, keep watch and ward
>   to-night.

95 *his daughter's dishonour*: again, by any means ACD can say it, forced marriage is rape.

97 *a Washoe*: Hope's prospecting area in the Sierra Nevada.

a hornets' nest: 'hornet's' in all printings, but the hornets are in the plural.

two thousand dollars in gold and five in notes: the Mormons struck gold pieces of their own up to $20 in value; there would also be gold tokens from California. The notes, if drawn on Utah banks, might be discounted elsewhere for less than their face value. It was nevertheless a considerable fortune.

Carson City: still theoretically within the limits of Utah territory, though about to be removed from it early in 1861 with the rest of what is now the state of Nevada. Jefferson Hope would have good reason to take it as a centre of anti-Mormon sentiment, but that did not prevent the Mormons from exercising the last months of their jurisdictions.

servants: a man like Hope would not have used a British genteelism like this: 'hands' or 'hired men' would have been more in keeping.

98 *the spirit of murder lurked through it all*: this sounds like another memory of Ireland in 1881.

the ears of a lynx: a momentary zoological solecism. A lynx is famous for vision. The only notable thing about its ears is that they are tufted.

99 *Whip-poor-Will*: an American night-jar, harsh voiced.

100 *long, basaltic columns*: Utah rock, volcanic in origin, has this extraordinary, almost unearthly, feature of cylindrical, or sometimes polygonal, appearance.

The Holy Four: the last reported words of John Ferrier.

102 *big-horn*: Rocky Mountain sheep, whence the famous battle of Little Big-Horn.

103 *None came save his own cry*: ACD would return to this moment in Watson's account of what he takes to be the death of Holmes ('The Final Problem', *Memoirs*): ' "I shouted; but only that same half-human cry of the fall was borne back to my ears." '

105 *the certainty of her fate*: once again ACD does all he can to indicate rape.

106 *Endowment House*: opened in 1855 for Mormon ceremonies.

words: rather too British a way of saying 'dispute'.

107 *the effects of the hateful marriage*: the medical consequences of rape.

sottish: a little premature. The Mormons forbade alcohol. Possibly Drebber had his own supply.

sat up with her . . . the Mormon custom: it is certainly the Irish Catholic one.

108 *under a cliff a great boulder crashed down on him*: another detail to be recalled in 'The Final Problem', this time with Holmes as the intended victim and Professor Moriarty as the instigator.

a combination of unforeseen circumstances: the American Civil War 1861–5.

109 *a schism among the Chosen People*: 'Chosen People' is now a bitter memory for the reader of Ferrier's weak joke when dying of starvation in Part II, Ch. 1. The schism is evidently the 'Morrisite' one of 1862 when various persons refused to submit to militia activity. Its leaders were killed, and the

197

resultant bitterness prompted the flight of Mormons who felt their own lives were in danger from vengeful Morrisites, orthodox Mormon vigilantes, or from the federal authorities.

109 *had recognized the vagrant*: we have to assume Jefferson Hope had become known to his rivals when he was courting Lucy, although they were careful not to come forward until he was gone. On the other hand, it was clearly they who asked Young to intervene. Fanny Stenhouse (*An Englishwoman in Utah*) speaks of Young undertaking the same function for his own son where her daughter was concerned. The marriage took place, giving young Young yet another wife.

accompanied by Stangerson: the inability of Drebber and Stangerson to separate themselves from one another despite their mutual hatred adds a purgatorial dimension to Hope's vengeance.

110 *Dr Watson's Journal*: there is no sign that the Watson material in the Holmes cycle is a journal, although extracts from his diary are given in one chapter of the *Hound*. (The more absorbing question, if we accept the statement in *The Sign of the Four* that all of *A Study in Scarlet* is Watson's—not an assumption here—is whence came the material in the foregoing five chapters? The only possible answer would seem to be from the only confidant Hope is known to have had: his young actor friend whose performance as Mrs Sawyer was so successful.)

may be used against you: correctly, 'may be used in evidence against you'. ACD uses a humorous variant in 'The Dancing Men' (*Return*):

'I guess the very best case I can make for myself is the absolute naked truth.'
    'It is my duty to warn you that it will be used against you', cried the inspector, with the magnificent fair-play of the British criminal law.

112 *an aortic aneurism*: a local ballooning-out of the aorta, the largest and longest artery in the body, caused by a weakening of the artery walls.

113 *forced into marrying*: rape reasserted.

They have perished, and by my hand: 'Of old hast thou laid the foundation of the earth: and the heavens are the work of thy hands. They shall perish, but thou shalt endure' (Psalm 102: 25, 26).

114 *There was seldom much over*: ACD's knowledge of cab-drivers can also be seen in 'The Cabman's Story' (1884; *Uncollected Stories*).

117 *York College*: usually assumed to be New York University, but there seems no reason why ACD should not endow York, Pennsylvania, with an imaginary college if he wished.

South American arrow poison: curare. Commentators have pointed out that it only poisons if taken by means of an injection or other skin-puncture.

while I ate the pill that remained: ACD later satirized this as a literary device in his skit on a film being made ('The Nightmare Room', *Tales of Terror and Mystery*).

119 *who broke her innocent heart*: the final euphemism.

120 *the only memento*: a reminder of how swiftly reunion, flight, and final parting had happened.

121 *Who was your accomplice?*: oddly uncelebrated; he remains the Great Unknown among Holmes's adversaries.

he did it smartly: our last word from Jefferson Hope, and it is good that after a lifetime of solitary hatred it should be one of appreciation and admiration of a friend.

122 *What you do . . . of no consequence*: 'What profit hath a man of all his labour which he taketh under the sun?' (Ecclesiastes 1:3). Holmes does not modernise the quotation in its spiritual sense, but that does harmonise with the earlier allusion to 'a higher Judge'.

123 *synthetically for one who can reason analytically*: a touch of self-mockery, since of course the author works synthetically, from causes to effects, where the rare master of the analytical goes from results to their origins.

growler: four-wheeled cab.

brougham: a one-horse closed carriage, two-wheeled or four-wheeled, named after the brilliant and unpopular Lord Chancellor (1830–4), Henry Lord Brougham (1778–1868).

124 *The forcible administration of poison*: it was, for instance, described in legend as being performed on Fair Rosamund de Clifford (d. ?1176), mistress to Henry II of England (1133–89), by his wife Eleanor of Aquitaine (?1122–1204).

125 *a blind*: except that it was also a correct statement of the motive for Drebber's death and was in the language of Drebber's ancestors.

126 *jarveys of the Metropolis*: more a name for an Irish jaunting-car driver than a cabby, but the Irish were traditionally London chairmen in the days of Sedan chairs and may have held a reasonable proportion of the carriage trade that replaced them.

Doctor: to the end of this case, Watson is addressed by Holmes in this fashion; Watson does not appear to call Holmes anything except 'you'.

Echo: a halfpenny evening paper (1868–1905), at this period owned by the Scots-born American steel magnate Andrew Carnegie (1835–1919) and the Liberal MP for Sunderland, Samuel Storey (1841–1925). This would make a really delicious irony of the *Echo* telling Americans to keep their feuds off British soil. But they did not purchase the paper from John Passmore Edwards (1823–1911), the Cornish Radical, until 1884 and had probably resold it to him when ACD was writing.

127 *a testimonial*: 'In my experience it is only an amiable man in this world who receives testimonials' (Sherlock Holmes, *The Hound of the Baskervilles*, Ch. 1).

Populus me sibilat ... contemplor in arca: Quintus Horatius Flaccus, *First Satire*, ll. 66–7: 'The public hiss at me, but I cheer myself when in my own house I contemplate the coins in my strong-box.' By 'the Roman miser' Watson was using shorthand for 'the miser created by the Roman author', the character in question being an Athenian. Watson's assumption that Holmes, whatever his limits, has no difficulties in translating Latin or placing a quotation from Horace is a return to the Latinate tradition of Edinburgh medicine. 'Contemplor' has hitherto been rendered 'contemplar' (see Note on the Text, p. xxxix).